I0682648

Thank you to all who have supported me during this project. Claudia for the first major edit, Katrina and Hazel for read throughs and all the friends who let me use their names. I hope you enjoy entering the world of my dreams. This book is dedicated to all who have a disability. Do not let your differences stop you from reaching your dreams.

The Darayca Diaries

(In the not to distance future)

A book was found deep in the heart of a rock face in the Pacific Ocean while some miners and scientists were digging to do research on types of soil in the underwater crevasse. While excavating they found a box with an odd lock and symbols were carved into the wooden surface, which no one had ever seen before in the history of mankind. After looking over the box the scientists decided to open it carefully and inside they found a book with what seemed to be a text made up of the same type of symbols which were on the outside of the box. The book was tested to be more than 20 million years old. After many years of studying the text scientist believe this is the best translation they could do without knowing the true language of the text. The scientists named the book, Darayca's Diary -the unknown text. They also do not know if the writing is fact or fiction. Many believe it to be fiction but who wrote it and how it found its way into the depths of the ocean. The world may never know.

Prologue: Reflection

The day is closing as I run through the green grass field. As I run, I can feel the warm blades of grass crush into the earth under my feet. As I pick up speed, I flex the muscles in my back and open my wings. With my powerful and long wings I take flight and soar up into the clouds. The wind weaves through my black soft fur and I relax my long, slender and powerful tail. My arms are kept to my side, while my claws retract into the tips of my fingers. Flying toward the cliff, which is my reflection spot, I start to reflect about my life. At the age of 18 I realize how young I am and at my young age I have already been on a long and tiring journey already full of battles, lost ones and loves. I have been alone for most of my journey and have just now started to find my place in the world.

As I approach the cliff I fly low to the Earth and begin to cross to the other side. Looking down I spy one of the many rivers, this ones' name is the Jagged River, I think because of all the bends and the jagged rocks which are scattered throughout the rivers winding path. I reach the other side; I flex my back muscles and bring my wings up to aid my landing. Once on the ground I walk to the nearby tree and sit to rest and reflect. As the sun sets the clouds change colors. The sky turns shades of pinks, reds and yellow. The scene relaxes me.

I now begin to think of my life before I found the place full of new ways of living and new friends and foes. I look out into the sky and find myself deep in thought about my child hood. My story is a strange one and is full of emotion. But before I tell you about my life I think I should introduce myself and tell you who I am.

My real name Zeaytera KatOynera which means 'wondrous one', but here I am known as Darayca which means dragon and I am a guardian. My species are called zatxs. We have many feline traits one could say. There are four kinds of zatx. One walks on all fours. A second kind walks on all fours but has wings and a third stands upright. The last kind stands upright and has wings. Of the zatx who has wings there are two types; some can fly while others can only glide. Common traits we all share are: we are covered in fur of all patterns and colors, long tails for balance, triangle shaped ears and we have sharp claws, which are retractable, and fangs. Zatx in general have somewhat slender necks, broad shoulders, long base feet. If the zatz stands upright then they have four fingers and a thumb on each hand. We have five toes but our feet are shaped differently from our hands. Overall we have great hearing, sense of smell and day vision is just as good as our night. Zatx are the top predator in the land. Zatos or males tend to be a little taller than females. When a female or zatz is with child she could give birth to any of the four kinds of our species.

One last important concept I wish to express before I move on to my life is what is a Guardian. All Guardians have wings, which can fly. The most important thing a Guardian has which, set him or her apart is a computer. I was born with a computer with artificial intelligence. Each computer has a sex and a rank. Most of the time the sex matches the zatx. The ranks are shown by color, from strongest to weakest is black, blue, green, red, yellow, and last is bronze. The more advance the life long friend the more tools there are to work with. For example, my computer has tracking systems and communication devices along with a list to long to get into but it is a very powerful tool. Each computer rests where the wrist ends and the arms begin. The great tool looks like a long bracelet.

But enough about the zatx let me continue with the story of my life. Here I am sitting under a tree watching the sun set as dusk turns into night, I smell the sweet flowers and the scents on the warm summer breeze as it generally flows past me. Also, on the wind I can smell the smoke of the fire in the clans across the meadow. The stars are now out to play and shine in the dark blue sky. And the moon lets its beams down for me so I may see the trees and the fields around me. As I stand to stretch, I look down to see the river still flowing now playing with the light of the moon while the sun rested for the next day to come. The crickets sing in the summer night, which helps me reflect. As I close my eyes, I picture my family, my mother, father and older brother. I also picture my village and what it was like before I came to be.

Part I: The Beginning

The Coming

"Domatu (bear), Domatu. Where are you? Domatu, Domatu we need you!" "I am coming. I am coming." Running from his hut Domatu with spear in hand and pack on his back he headed for the cries of help. As he ran his black fur shined in the sunlight and one could only see his blacker spots at cretin angles. His large golden eyes searched his running path as he made his way to the crowd. Once reaching the edge of the village Domatu could see the two youngest twins of the village were sinking in quicksand. He quickly opened his pack and snatched his rope. He ran to the nearby tree, tying one end of the rope to himself and the other to the tree. He dove into the death trap. Grabbing the twins he pulled himself out of the sand. As the onlookers cheered, the mother came running from her peers to reclaim her frightened children. As Domatu was gathering his rope Hutto (sparrow) came running up to him. "How are you sir?"

"I am fine Hutto, all in a days work. How is the village this morning?"

"Good, Sir, nothing has happened except for the twins. When you get the chance Yaottyro (bright star) would like to see you."

"Thank you, Hutto go on your rounds. After you have checked in with everyone come give me the night report."

"Yes, Sir."

As Hutto headed to the West end of the village, Domatu headed to the hut of Yaottyro. As he walked over to the river, which ran through camp he pondered what the leader of the village would want to see him about. Reaching the river Domatu dove into the cool water to wash off the sand and to swim a few laps. After he swam for ten minutes he came out of the cool water. He walked to his hut where he dried off and changed. Soon after, Sunyro (sunray) came into the hut with the first meal of the day. Domatu embraced his wife with loving arms and kissed her lightly. "How are you, my wife?"

"I am fine, I slept well and I heard you have already had a morning full of excitement."

"Yes, the twins were in trouble again. I am glad you slept well, as did I with you by my side. How is our little one?"

"The little one is kicking a little but doing fine. I talked to the doctor and she said the little one will come any day now. I cannot wait till I can hold this one. I hope it is as strong as Gyro (talon)"

"Where is our son?"

"He went on the hunt which left this morning. He wants to be a hunter or a protector even though he is not a true guardian. He wants to be like his father, chief of the guardians and the name of the village guardian."

"I am very proud of our son, but at 18 he is still so young. He has a long way to go to reach my title."

"He has a great shadow to fill."

"Thank you for this meal, Yaottyro wishes to see me so I must be off but I will come see you later."

"Kata (sweet water) is coming over to help me with the hut and the meals for you and Gyro for when he returns he will be hungry. I will await you my love."

"Till then my love"

After a hug and kiss goodbye Domatu started for the center of the village where Yaottyro's hut was located. Each fellow villager said "hi", bowed or showed some sign of respect. He was addressed and those who need help knew without fear could come up to him and talk about their problem. He always answered back and helped whenever he could. Upon reaching Yaottyro's hut Domatu called out Yaottyro's name and declared his name. Once Yaottyro came out Domatu went down on one knee. Seeing this Yaottyro nodded his head and asked Domatu to rise while he advanced his arm out for Domatu to shake. As the two shook arms they greeted each other. "Good work this morning"

"Thank you, Yaottyro, how are you?"

"I am fine thank you for asking Domatu. How is your son Gyro?"

"He grows stronger and braver each day. Right now he is on the hunt. I believe his mind is set on being a hunter or protector."

"Well, if he is anything like this father nothing but good thing will happen in this village. Right now everyone is happy and our village is thriving and how about your wife, Sunyro?"

"As you know she is with child and is due any time now but is in great health."

"I am happy to hear all is well in your family. My daughter is doing well and might be looking at Gyro as more than a friend. We will have to see if their relationship grows. My wife is also doing well she told me she was going to your hut to help Sunyro with some of her chores. But onto why I have called you here today. The other night a gang of an unknown species appeared. The village on the other side of Diptha (big rock) Forest was attacked. They called them Rootuas (dark ones). I would like you to go over there with a few of your best zatx and spend a day there get information and helping them rebuild the damages which the Rootuas have done to the village. I know your wife is with child but you are my best guardian. You are to leave tomorrow morning. Send me who is to take your place while you are gone and I will ask Kata to stay with Sunyro while you are away. Also when the hunt returns check with them if they have seen any sign of the Rootuas heading this way. Last, have our watchers doubled both night and day to watch out for these Rootuas."

"Thank you for watching over Sunyro while I am gone and giving me the rest of the day. I will leave at dawn. Is there anything else I may do for you?"

"No, thank you Domatu"

"Bye Yaottyro."

"Bye my guardian"

Waiting for Domatu outside was Hutto. He reported all the night watchers had no problems but they could smell more smoke in the air than normal. All the watchers now were at their posts and we all well rested. Everything was as it should be. Domatu asked Hutto to double all the watchers for both day and night. Hutto and Domatu shook arms and then both went off on their various paths for the day.

As morning turned into mid-day Domatu made his rounds and talked to his fellow guardians making sure everyone was over all happy. He went to his hut to rest and hope for the hunt to return soon. Kata came in to his room with the second meal of the day. "Your wife is resting," she said softy. "Thanks Kata you are a great help if there is anything I can do for you."

"You already do enough. Now eat and rest."

Then she left Domatu to rest and get ready for the remainder of the day. After eating and resting for an hour Domatu stood and walked into the room where Sunyro was. Looking at her with a smile he could see her soft golden fur and long slender back she had some black marking and a long black stripe starting from the top of her head down her back and onto her tail. She was sleeping securely in her son's bed. Placing one hand on his wife's stomach and the other by her head he gently kissed her brow and was off for the rest of the day.

First he went to the trees by the river and began to consider who to bring with him when he is off to the village across Diptha Forest. Knowing the Rootuas were out there he did not want to take all of his best protectors. He did not want to take his second because he wanted him to stay with the village. Soon he decided he would take Duma (kitty), Gratei (meadow), Outght (owlhawk), Naughi (shadow), Mujua (July), Vencea (stared one), Tatti (rain) and Synyye (swift). Domatu went to Hutto and told him about the matter of the Rootuas, his mission and how he would take Domatu's place while he was gone. Hutto was overjoyed and honored to take Domatu's place even for a day.

Domatu asked Hutto to round up the protectors he wished to take with him to the village in need. With a nod Hutto was off to find his peers and Domatu remained by the riverbed sitting by the trees. Soon after Hutto left, the members of the mission started to appear in front of Domatu. After all the members were present he told them of the village in need with Hutto over his shoulder. All were happy to help and honored to be chosen by Domatu to go with him. After all the questions were answered and everyone was clear on the matter they were free for the rest of the day. They were to be ready to go at dawn. Afterward Domatu went over all the things he want Hutto to do for him while he was on the mission. After Hutto felt he knew everything he must do for the next day and night Domatu went to his hut to be with his wife.

As Sunyro and Domatu were sitting in each others company and talking of the little one to be born a large roar came from the East side of the village. Domatu got up at once and was off toward the large cheer. The hunting party had returned. The whole village was overjoyed to see all returned with no harm done. Leading them in was Heato (fame) he came to Domatu with arms open and a smile. Quickly Domatu told him to gather everyone who went on the hunt and meet in the xera (meeting) hut now. Once everyone who was on the hunt was inside, Domatu took the floor.

He talked of the Rootuas and of the village across the way. No one had seen any sign of the Rootuas but now they knew why they could smell the stronger scent of smoke in the air the other night. They were all allowed to leave and as they left the Hutto gave them their new times to watch over the village. After everyone was out of the xera hut Domatu put out the flames which lit the room and headed home.

To his surprise Gyro was waiting for him outside of the hut. With a smile they shook arms followed by a hug. As they walked home Gyro talked of the hunt. Domatu looked at his son. Seeing his well built body covered in golden coat with a white underside and the black line down his back with his coat splashed with spots. His coat looked a lot like his mother just a little lighter and he had the white underside also he had more spots. As for Domatu he had a black coat with darker spots, which were hard to see. All of his loved ones had yellowish-green eyes. Domatu was happy to hear of his son's great success at the hunt. Once they were home Sunyro extended her arms in which Gyro came into them. Gyro was happy to hear that any time now he would have a younger sibling. At the last meal of the day Domatu told his family about the mission and told Gyro to stay home and help him mother. Gyro disappointed because he could not go with father but happy to know he might be the first to hold the little one. After the meal they were all off to bed.

Before the sun was up to brighten the day Domatu was up and packing for the mission. In front of the village he waited for the rest of his peers to join him. Right when the light of the sun started to kiss the land the group was off to the village in need. As they gathered by Domatu he went over the mission and told everyone to stay on their toes and made sure everyone spoke up if they had a problem or fear of what was to come. Domatu would make sure everyone took turns taking the point and the rear of the troop. As they entered the forest Domatu took the point. Ears always perked listening for any change in the calling birds, chirping insects and other clamor of yelping animals.

As the sun rose its beams gave little light for the small band of peers. Most of the time the black leader walked in front of the group always on guard and ready for action. For about an hour he would fall back and then let another take it for a half hour then he would be back in front. Soon they stopped for a break at the Jina (green) River. They ate and drank while resting their feet. Domatu never seemed to fully rest; he was always looking around or moving to different sides of the group. After everyone got a drink they were on their way. Through the vines, river, mud and around trees they walked.

After a short time they reached a strange clearing in the forest. The trees were cut and the bushes cut. They discontinued walking and looked around for any signs of what made the clearing but deep down they all knew the Rootuas probably made it. There were burn marks on the trees no one could recognize. Finding nothing Domatu decided to move on to the village he wanted to reach there before dark and it was already about mid-day. As they got closer to the village they could smell smoke in the air. They quickened their pace from a walk to a run.

Happy to be out of the forest the group entered a meadow, which would lead them to the village. They would have no problem finding the village because of the large smoke clouds in the distance rising from the golden ground. Once they were in yelling distance of the broken camp they stopped and called out to anyone who might be there. There was no answer. The peers walked into the village slowly and cautiously. The ones who had computers used them to scan for life. Most the huts were burnt or caved into the ground. Everyone one on the mission was silent they did not know what to say or feel only knowing they wanted to find someone. In the center on the village there was one hut, which was fenced. Domatu scanned the hut and could see there was some sign of life. After a group effort the tired warriors were able to get into the center hut. Upon entering they found a large group of the villagers all zatzs and little ones. When the zatzs saw the group they jumped to their feet with tears of joy in their eyes. Domatu asked who was in charge of the small group and a strong, tiger zatz stood out from the group. Domatu talked with the tiger zatz and the others in his group checked on the frightened zatzs and little ones.

Domatu had to calm the tiger zatz down they were all jumpy. The tiger's name was Reay (ruby) she was a protector and the last one still at the camp. She told Domatu the Rootuas came at night and would take anyone they could and drag them off into the drakness. They think they took them north. Also the attackers took all the dead zatx who were protecting the rest of the zatz and little ones. Because of the Rootuas numbers the protectors did not have a chance against their attackers. With the sun almost setting the same clan quickly set sound traps and trapped the villagers back in their center hut. They planed to hide in the nearby huts and fight the Rootuas. They hoped to surprise the Rootuas when they came for the rest of the camps life. If they could they would follow the Rootuas to find where they were taking the others. Soon they were ready saying a quick prayer and wishing each other luck they checked their weapons and prepared for the fight to come. Turning on their scanners to full power they hoped to be able to tell if the Rootuas were coming. Sure enough an hour later the computers were picking up a strange signal. There were 20 of them coming form the North. All of the clan would wait for Domatu's signal and then they would all strike the Rootuas.

As the 20 outsiders entered the camp they came with out pausing and fear. They headed straight for the center hut. They all circled the hut and they each pulled out a gray, small, odd shaped object, which had some sort of tiger because when the leader pulled back his finger a red beam came out of the end of the object, which began to burn into the wood protecting the hut. All the clan had to fight with were staffs with sharpen rock and metal at the end. Others had bow and arrows, sling shots, swords, axes and etc. None of them had the power to burn with a red beam. The orders from Domatu were to kill but try to keep one alive. The clan could not tell male from female but the leader was wearing red while the others were wearing blue. They were green with skin that looked like scales. They had black beady eyes. They were about twelve feet tall and had claws, an armored chest and belly. They had no tail, sharp teeth and they walked on two feet, which looked great for running. They had two slits on their muzzles which were their noses and they had little pointed ears.

When all the Rootuas started to fire their red beams Domatu jumped out of his hut and took down one of them. The others joined in and the fight was finally started. Quickly the clan found out the red beams would burn them and if they hit the beam with the metal on the end of their staffs they could reflect the red beams. With a lot of effort the clan could spear the Rootuas but the bow and arrows did not work. Naughi was the first to be hit. Domatu and Duma hid her in a near by hut. The fight continued into the night. Domatu and the clan watched each other's backs and when one got hurt the others would help hide the hurt one into a near by hut. The Rootuas' skin was tough and hard to break and the plates on their belly and chest were very hard to cut. Soon Domatu told his remaining band to use their sling-shots to hit the Rootuas' eyes. They were small but once hit the Rootuas were easier to take down and kill. Vencea was very good with a sling-shot and in no time the only one left standing was the leader, the rest of his band was dead.

Domatu and Duma jumped on him and pinned him down while Tatti tied the leader up with rope and then Tatti knocked him out cold. Domatu checked on all of the members of his clan. Outght and Synyye were both not conscious and not doing very well they were losing a lot of blood. The zatzs who were hiding in the center hut came out to help Domatu and his fallen friends. Domatu, Vencea and Tatti worked on a cage to transport the Rootua, Naughi and Gratei checked on the others then started to look and bury the dead Rootuas and Duma watched the leader making sure when he woke up he would not escape. Within three hours everyone's task was done. Because Gratei and Duma could fly he ordered them to fly Outght and Synyye home and once there to tell Yaottyro of the missions status. The black leader also told them to return as soon as they could.

They would start to move into the woods for protection because Domatu was worried more Rootuas would come looking for their fallen comrades. The remaining clan members moved the leader into his cage and then told the villagers to pack what they needed. While Mujua went into the woods to find a good and safe place to camp the rest got ready to move. The first signs of day were just appearing in the sky. Vencea, Tatti, Naughi and Domatu carried the cage holding the Rootua, and the villagers followed them. Waiting outside the woods was Mujua who led them to the new campsite, which was about an hour of walking. There was a small clearing with a pool of water and a hollow tree on the ground. The clan started at once to set up perimeter traps and alarms while the villagers drank and set up camp.

A day later Duma return with 50 others who could all fly they were to fly home at once. Domatu was the last to leave the ground and once in the air took the point and kept his eye on the cage with the Rootua. Once on the ground over 100 villagers were there to help the clan member and newcomers. With out hesitation Domatu went to the hospital to check on Outght and Synyye. After talking with the doctors Domatu found out both had died over the night from blood loss and other complication. The doctors said there was nothing Domatu could have done to save them they were hit with the red beams, which hit the liver and other body parts, which killed them. Looking over the bodies Domatu said a prayer and thanked Outght and Synyye for all they did for the village and for him. As a tear run down his check he felt a hand on his back. Yaottyro gave him a hug and told him to go home and come see him later the next day not in the morning because Domatu needed the rest. Before Domatu went to his hut he walked to the hut of Outght where he wished the family well and expressed he do anything he could to help them. The family thanked him. They talk for a few minutes and then Domatu was off to Synyye's family once there he again wished the family well and conveyed his willingness to help. There again they talked for a few minutes and then finally Domatu headed home to his hut to see his family and lay down for some much needed rest.

Entering his hut he was greeted by his son and Kata who then went home. Domatu told his son he would talk of the mission in the morning but now wanted some rest and asked where his mother was. Gyro told his father his mother was in the bedroom resting. He joined his wife in the grass bed and fell into a deep sleep.

In the late morning Domatu awoke well rested and a meal put together by Sunyro. He ate the meal happily while he looked at his wife. She held his hand as he looked down while they talked of the loss of his two friends. Gyro sat next to his father waiting to hear of the mission. Domatu talked about the village and the fight. His son hung on his every word. After he was finished Domatu kissed his wife and told his son to watch over his mother. Gyro was a little disappointed but did as his father said. With the sun already high in the sky Domatu walked towards the center of the village to talk to Yaottyro and check on the Rootua.

"Good day Yaottyro. How are you this fine day?"

"I am well, Domatu and yourself?"

"I am rested and happy to see my family. How is the Rootua?"

"He is not talking. He ate when he woke up this morning. And Kata who gave him his food said he said

"Thank you". We think his name is Jabo (flame)"

"May I see him?"

"Go ahead; I will be in the center hut if you need me"

"Thank you"

Domatu went to the hut where the Jabo was. He asked to be left alone with him and the others left. Once alone Domatu shut the door of the hut grab a stool and sat down in front of the cage where the chained one sat. "Let me begin by saying sorry for your loss of friends and comrades in the last battle I too know what it is like to lead and lose friends. I was told your name is Jabo if I am wrong I am sorry and well be more than happy to correct myself. I did not want to fight and I do not want a war, more killed and a chance for anther village to be destroyed. I do not know why your kind attacked the other village and where you took the ones who lived there. I cannot make you speak or tell me what your kind wants or needs but I am sure if you are willing we can come to some kind of agreement".

There was a long pause than Jabo shifted in his chair, cleared his throat and started to speak.

"We want your land and you will be our slaves and that is all I will say but there are more of us then of you and soon when my kind comes your kind will bow to us and you will be my personal slave".

Domatu looked at Jabo for a while then got up and left. He walked to Yaottyro's hut. Once there he told Yaottyro what Jabo said. "Do you think he is telling the truth?" Yaottyro asked. "I am not sure but why would he lie he has nothing to lose I do not think we should take any chances. He said they want our land. They are coming from the north. What type of land is up there?"

"I think there is some grass land but I know for a fact there are mountains and the land and air is cooler up there".

"Do you want me to try to talk to Jabo again"?

"Yes, see if you can get any more information about why they want our land or anything just something. I am going to call a village meeting in three rounds. The first one will be in three hours I want you to be there."

"I will be there. I will see you there"

"Till then"

Domatu then walked back to the hut where Jabo was and again asked to be alone. Domatu sat on a stool and faced Jabo who was staring at him with his black, cold beady eyes.

"Why make us slaves, why not just kill us and why come here now, where do you come from? As you can tell I have many questions Jabo. Are you going to talk or just sit there"?

"Why should I tell you anything soon my kind will be here and all your questions will be answered"?

"Making me a slave and killing my friends will not answer my questions."

"You are an inferior species you do not need to know the answers."

"How do you know we are the inferior species?"

"We are smarter and after doing test on your species from the village we are better."

"Why come down here? Why come and attack us?"

"We like your land better we can benefit from your land. In our homeland the weather is getting colder and colder each year and we do not like the cold. So since we cannot go over the mountains we are going to come here. Why make your kind move when your kind can make great slaves."

"We will fight many will die why not just come and talk to us?"

"There is nothing you can say or do. You will be a slave and many may die but in the end the benefit will out weigh the cost. Many are ready to die to save the millions to come. I will do everything in my power to save you from death so you can be my slave"

"Out of everyone why do you want me as a slave?"

"I not sure, I like you. I think you would be a good slave."

"My kind would rather die then be slaves to your kind"

"Just so you know my kind is called Qothos (cobras) I am done talking to you. I will talk to you again once you are my slave."

"Till we meet again Jabo"

Domatu left the hut with much on his mind. He now had to tell the village the species called the Qothos were coming from the north to enslave them. Entering the large hut he saw Yaottyro coming to him. Domatu told his leader what Jabo said. Yaottyro wanted to open the meeting and because the villagers trusted Domatu would tell them about the Qothos and how they would get ready for the invasion because he was the village protector. As the first set of the villagers came into the tent Yaottyro and

Domatu went over for one last time what they were going to say. The noise grew as the tent filled up with the zatxs.

Yaottyro walked into the center of the tent and by the time he reached his resting spot all one could hear was his footsteps. He looked around the group seeing all eyes were on him. He began with a greeting and then moved onto asking the first group not to tell the other groups about the information they would be receiving that night the other groups would know in time then everyone could talk. Next he told them if they had any question they were to come talk to him or Domatu after the meeting or later on in the evening or next day. Last Yaottyro asked Domatu to join him in the center. Domatu walked to join his friend in the middle of the tent as he walk the group whispered quickly amongst themselves. Domatu wiped his arm across his brow and it came back wet. With his opposite hand he shook arms with Yaottyro and they switched places.

As Yaottyro left the center Domatu began to speak of the other village how it was no more and of the Qotho they had in a cage across the village. Then he spoke of what the Qotho named Jabo said about the coming of his kind. Last Domatu spoke of how they would fight the Qothos when they came from the cold north. After he was done speaking one from the crowd yelled, "They will never take me alive" the crowd roared. Everyone said they would not be slaves and fight till the death.

As the first group left some came down and talk to Yaottyro and Domatu. One zatz was with child and did not want her child to grow up to be a slave and said she would rather die or even kill her child she said this with tears in her eyes. Yaottyro said we would fight and one part of the plan was to find a safe hiding for zatzs and little ones. The female's husband came over and helped carry her home after giving is leader and friend a sign of respect. Yaottyro and Domatu looked at each other and watched as the second group came into the tent the two speaker did their talks two more times and then finally they were done. The whole village knew of the Qothos. After everyone left the tent in the last meeting Yaottyro and Domatu went into Yaottyro's work hut and began to work.

They would send 20 protectors out to the West to look for a safe hiding place you zatz who could not fight and little ones. They would send two groups of 50 to set up traps and alarms around the camp. Also a group of 50 would go and collect food in case they were trap in the village. A group of 100 would build a wall around the village and a group of 20 would build new weapons and shield. The rest of the camp would be learning how to fight or making food for the workers. The next day the one by one each member in the village would line up in front of their leader who would place them in a working group. Then they shook arms and they went home to their huts to sleep.

The next morning as the village awoke one by one they came to Yaottyro and Domatu who were in the center tent. By the end of the day everyone had their group and the next day they would begin to prepare for the coming of the Qothos. Again Yaottyro and Domatu stayed up late going over the groups one more time. They would double lookouts and have at least five guardians in the sky looking out for everyone at all times. As night came Yaottyro and Domatu wrapped up their business and then headed home. When Domatu got to his home Sunyro and Gyro who both were happy to see him greeted him. They all sat down for the last meal of the day. Domatu asked his wife how she was feeling and how the little one was doing. Sunyro said she was tired and ready for the little one to come. She said Kata and Gyro were taking very good care of her while he was gone. She also talked of the doctor coming over and checking on her and she said everything was great and the little one should come anytime now. This information pleased Domatu they talked of what group Sunyro and Gyro were in for the next few days. Sunyro was in the food group that way she could stay near her hut and would not have hard work to do while Gyro was in the perimeter group because he was young, strong and knew the area well. After the meal was done and they were done talking they went off to bed they all needed the rest for the events to come in the following days.

The next few days the village was at work. Yaottyro had meetings with his advisers and other top zatxs of the village to talk about the best way to attack and defend themselves against the Qothos. If Domatu was not in a meeting he was always moving checking on the different groups making sure all was well. Everyone was working hard and by the end of the fourth day the wall was already half way done and the perimeter groups were nearly complete with their goal. All the protector groups were switching on time and everyone was getting breaks and the food was always ready for anyone on break. The village was at work around the clock. If the food group was not sleeping or cooking they were watching the children of the village.

During the sixth day Domatu sat by the river on his break and looking at the newly completed wall. Now the wall group was spilt between the weapons and perimeter group. He just got out of a meeting with Yaottyro; they were talking about killing the Qothos and the red beams. Later in the evening the perimeter group finished their work and joined the weapons and watch groups. Once all the construction was done the villagers were resting, practice fighting, watching or making weapons. The food group stayed the same. Soon Domatu felt the village was ready the only problem was the search group had not found a hiding place yet this worried Domatu knowing he had a little one on the way. As he closed his eyes he released the breath from his lungs and cleared his mind of all the compilations and ideas of what was to come.

The Arrival

Right as the moon came into the sky Sunyro went into labor. The midwife and the doctor came to the small hut as soon as they could. As Domatu stayed at his wife's side Gyro waited outside the hut pacing back and forth waiting to hear a cry or any news from anyone. Some of his friends joined him waiting with him to hear of Domatu's little one.

As the night pressed on all they could do was make Sunyro as conformable as possible. Just as the sun kissed the land Domatu's little one was born. Sunyro relaxed with joy and relief and Domatu held his little one for the first time then he passed on his little female child to his loving wife who kissed the little daughter and welcomed her to the world.

The little one was a guardian but something was different her computer was black at the bottom then turned into a dark green and last into a dark blue. She had little slits at the base of her ears and had deep green eyes. She had a pure black coat no spots like her father. As the doctor looked at the little girl the midwife went outside to tell the crowd that Domatu's little one was a little girl. Gyro jump with joy he had a little sister.

Domatu and Sunyro decide the little girl's name would be Zeaytera KatOynera. Domatu held his daughter high and was happy to finally have his little one in his arms. Gyro came in and held Zeaytera KatOynera. A few minutes later the doctor took the new baby and her parents into a different room. There he would talk about their daughter different physical feathers. When the doctor pushed on the baby's back she changed from a two feet guardian to a four-foot guardian no one in all of history could do that. Both Domatu and Sunyro looked at each other. Because she could do this the muscles in her back allowed her to tuck her wings into her body. Whatever form she was in it was possible for her to look like she had no wings.

The doctor did some test to make sure the he had made no mistakes. The slits behind the ears almost looked like gills on a fish but he was still not sure and she had five extra eyelids, a white, red, green, black and blue. The doctor's best guess for the extra eyelids was they were there for protection when she was fighting and most probably changed her vision. The blue one looked like it was to use while she was under water the doctors did not know what to make of them.

In the history of the zatx no one had ever been born with a pure black coat like Zeaytera KatOynera's. She did not have darker spots like her father. Other than her differences she is very strong and healthy. They should be very happy everything went well and now they have a little girl named Zeaytera KatOynera. Domatu call her Kat or Zea for short. As the word spread of the birth of Zeaytera KatOynera the whole village was happy to hear of a success for birth of Domatu's little girl. As soon as Yaottyro heard he headed over with Kata. As they came in Yaottyro and Domatu shook arms and Kata went straight for Sunyro who was holding Kat. The rest of the day the father and mother watched and held the baby while Gyro worked for a while then would check in then go back to work.

The next few days Domatu only left the hut unless someone needed him or if there was a meeting with Yaottyro he had to attend. The village was ready for any attack and sadly no one had found a hiding place yet. The group had gone in all the directions but north for at least a day and could not find a good place, which could hide and support a group of the villagers for a long time.

As the days went by and there was no sign of the Qothos the villagers began to question if there was going to be an invasion. Each time Domatu went into the hut where Jabo was Jabo only called him slave. And Jabo would be cockier with each meeting. Domatu thought Jabo was telling the truth about his kind coming. He thought the Qothos would be smart to wait a while before attacking. The longer the village went without a sighting the more they questioned what Jabo said about his kind.

Kat was doing great. She was a true guardian like her father but the difference in the color of her computer. She was a quick learner and was always ready to play. She loved to play games with Gyro and cuddle with her mother. Her deep green eyes were always full of wonder and joy.

Yaottyro and Kata came over a lot to see Kat and how she was doing. The doctor came over too to check on the little girl and to test and see if she could find and explain the child differences.

One night as dusk was moving into night Jabo was full of excitement. This worried Domatu. When the night reached its peak the warning bell went off the watchers had spotted a large mass of what they thought to be Qothos heading towards the village. Everyone took their places in the village or on the wall. As the time went on they could hear the premature alarms go off and the screams of the Qothos as they fell into the traps which were set for them but there were so many Qothos once a trap was set the other went past it and it looked like the ground was moving.

Domatu ran to his hut where his family was preparing for the attack. He held Kat up into the air and looked at with loving eyes and gave her a hug. Kat's eyes were alive with joy and love. Domatu ordered his daughter's computer to open the compartment with the family chips. He put in his, Sunyro and Gyro's chips in Kat's so if she lives her computer can teach her the history of not only her family but her kind. This way she would grow to be strong and a true guardian. Domatu hugged his family and told his wife to be safe protect the little one. He gave her a kiss and ran off to the gate with Gyro next to him. Once they got to the gate they could here the sound of soldiers march. The hitting of mettle and wood hit the ground. Domatu turned to his son, placed his hand on this shoulder and said: "You are my son. I am so pound of you. Whatever happens today I want you to know you are strong and never alone. If you make it, do everything you can to watch after your sister and mother. Remember the code. You will make a great guardian; fight well, never, give in or up, never show weakness to your enemy and I love you my son." Gyro hugged his father and said he loved him too and promised he would do as his father said. Then they both got their bows and arrows ready as they both faced the Qothos coming.

"Fire. Fire. Fire," Domatu yelled and the arrows were off into the air. As the battle began Domatu could hear Jabo laughing from his cage in the hut. The red beams started to burn into the wood of the wall. The red beams burned the villagers but they kept fighting they would not give up to the attackers. As more of the Qothos reached the wall they started to climb the wall or try to knock the massive barrier down to the ground. The villagers poured hot water and other liquids onto the aggressors below them. Domatu had some of best guardian attack from the back they flew up and into the cloud and over the mass of Qothos. Domatu gave the sign and the guardian started to attack the back to the army, which did some good but they were out numbered.

As time passed on the Qothos's red beams burned a hole into great wall. Domatu picked up his son and flew to the ground to be able to fight. Domatu was untouchable he was a master fighter. He helped others around him but was upset to look around and not see his son. As he looked he saw Jabo come out of the hut and talk to his supervisor then point to him. The hairs on the back of neck pricked up into the air and he then began to fight again as two Qothos tried to take him down to the ground. The Qothos spoke a different language then the zatxs. The battle continued into the night. Domatu and his villagers had better senses for the night but they were getting tired and they were still out numbered by many.

In the morning when the sun awoke there were still some guardians fighting but almost all of the villagers were in a cage or dead. Domatu was very dehydrated and drops of sweat fell from his body as each challenger came and fought him. Domatu then heard someone clap and a familiar laugh. He knew who was clapping as soon as he heard the laugh. "You fight well my slave. I am happy to see you were not killed during the night. Are you ready to begin your new life with me? As soon I take you down I will find what is left of your family and they well be mine too" Jabo said with a smile as he walked calmly to where Domatu was standing. Jabo and his comrades circled Domatu and after many attempts managed to place ropes on him. A rope was placed on each arm and two around his neck. Within minutes the mighty warrior hit the Earth. The zatx who were watching looked down and became silent. A part of them was broken and they were all sad to see their symbol of strength fall and not get back up to fight once more.

Choices

Domatu awoke to crying. His body aced and his head was pounding. He was chained to the wall. Two steel bands with chains were on each of his arms. The chains were attached to the wall by a hoop and the rest of the chains rope went up into a system of ropes and pulleys, which could be used to raise or low Domatu's body. There was a smaller chain rope connecting his legs and a third one round his neck, which was attached to wall and could be unlatched.

Looking around he saw his peers of all ages in cages. On the ceiling were heat lamps, which made the room very warm with the fur coats. Domatu backed up so his wings hit the stone wall. This action made some slack in the chain for his massive arms to move somewhat freely. With the loud clicks from the chain hitting Domatu wiped his arm across his bow and took in a deep breath of the air full of tears, sweat, dust and cries.

Domatu seeing the caged ones look at him he raised his head high and started to site the guardian's oath. Then he told the others around him he would stay strong and never give into the Qothos. He would rather die then make them happy and soon he would escape and free all of them. Some were filled with hope while others looked down they were lost in a world where there dreams and hope were now gone. - Domatu, Domatu - "yes computer," Domatu said while looking down at his arm. Now seeing why his computer called him. The Qothos had put some kind of computer brace around his arm. The brace allowed him to talk to his computer, mentally or out loud, but the computer was useless to help Domatu but to be a talking friend. Both Domatu and his A.I. companion were sad but both would not give in or let the Qothos see them in their melancholy state.

Some time later Domatu's ears pricked up as he heard footsteps coming down the corridor. In walked Jabo with a smile on his scaly face. His sharp and crooked teeth gleamed in the firelight. His forked tough moving up and down while he cackled at the fallen hero.

"Well it seems the tables have turned. Now you are in the cage while I walk free. I have bought you now and you are mine. My next step is to find your family. I have my ways and I know I will have no problem finding them," Jabo stated while pacing in front of the chained one. "I will never serve you. I will only kill your kind," Domatu declared while raising his head once more. "We will see how your attitude changes once I have your little one and you get use to being a slave. The job will grow on you and you will find I am a good slave owner compared to others you are lucky to have me as a master. By the way Master is the name you will call me now that I have you," Jabo announced to Domatu. "Never!" Domatu uttered while he spit at Jabo. "You try my patience," the master hissed. Then turned his back and started to walk out of the stuffy room. "Bring him," Jabo ordered the others who came with him. With those words the other Qothos grabbed the chains and pulled the still fighting warrior out of the dark room. "There is no use fighting," Jabo stated calmly.

The bright light of day hurt Domatu's eyes as they went outside of the underground prison. As he paused to adjust his eyes the ones pulling him yanked the chains causing him to fall. He could hear the sound of many Qothos laughing. Clinching his teeth he grabbed one of the chains and pulled as hard as he could making two of the Qothos drop to the earth.

Then the Qothos around him jumped onto him pinning him to the dirt floor. Hitting him with metal poles until Jabo ordered them to stop; Domatu just held his head and waited for the beating to stop. Once the attackers subdued Domatu raised to his feet and waited for directions on where to go next. As he looked around he realized he was in a new camp.

The Qothos must have moved the captured zatx once they were, caged, chain or out cold. This must have been the reason the Qothos took so long to attack the village. Jabo looked at him with eyes of little respect and walked on towards a large hole, which led underground. Immediately after they reached the opening at the bottom of the passageway Domatu could see many holes leading different ways. They had a built a large underground maze which would be almost impossible to escape. After taking different passage ways Domatu could smell the scent of blood, sweat and tears as they made there way deeper into the maze.

They stopped in an opening with different young zatos chained to the walls. As Domatu eyed each one he recognized each of the young fighters. Some he had helped train and raise. He made a fist as he looked at all of the beaten bodies chained to the wall. None of them cried or showed their pain, this made Domatu happy to see them holding their own. Like a father of all, he worried about their health as he saw the open wounds in the dirt floors. Again there were heat lamps above them, which made the room more unbearable. To the left of him was a zato with broken bones who was bleeding form the head and chest. He looked tired but ready to fight if needed. His fur a reddish-brown with all the mud and blood mixed into the once soft fur. This one was in the worst shape and as the young one looked up at his father hope filled his heart. Both son and father were happy to see the other alive and somewhat well but did not want to give a clue to their relationship. "Which one is your son?" Jabo asked suddenly.

"They are all my sons I raised and trained all in the village. The village is my family," Domatu stated peacefully.

"Do not play games with me slave! Which one is of your blood?"

"I gave you my answer."

"Very well, I will cut each zato till you tell me or he comes forward and reveals who your real son is. I do not care if one of these pitiful creatures dies. If I kill the one I am looking for then that is one less mouths to feed for everyone. I will kill them all slave if no one comes forward. If someone just tells me the truth there will be less pain for everyone. Resisting is pointless."

Jabo glared at Domatu who just stared at the wall then took at deep breath while closing his eyes. "Very well," Jabo said. With an up and down motion of his fingers two Qothos raised the chains and all the zatos were brought to their feet. All were in a lot of pain but none showed it. All were strong.

One of the Qothos walked over to the zato who was first on the right and slowly pulled a jagged blade from his belt. With a smile again slowly pointed the blade to the leg then to the arm next to the chest showing his choices of places to strike. When the blade pointed to the leg for the third time Jabo nodded and with that motion the Qothos struck the young ones leg. The youth made a fist in both hands and clinched his teeth but made no real sound. His eyes watered and in his eyes you could see all the pain he was feeling. Gyro looked at his friend and with all his strength came forward and said "I am Domatu's true son." Then the warrior to his left did the same. All the young zatos in the room even the newly wounded one stated the same as Gyro did.

"We are getting no where. I will give you one more chance slave who is your blood son? If you do not answer me the next in line well be cut," Jabo hissed to the chained ones. The Qothos with the blade took a step and start to choose where to strike on his next victim. Domatu looked at each warrior who each closed his eyes and nodded his head, which was the signal to Domatu. This told the leader everyone was in agreement for Domatu to show to Jabo his true son Gyro. "My true son is Gyro who is standing to my left," Domatu announced while he pointed to Gyro. "Now that was not so hard," Jabo said walking to Gyro. He grabbed Gyro's chin and moved it from left to right looking over his torn face.

Next he looked at the boys tattered body and spat at his feet and stated to the room, "he is not much to look at slave" looking at Domatu. Gyro tried to spring forward but the chain held him back. Jabo laughed while saying, "He is full of sprit like his father, and how did I not pick him out once I came into this shit hole". He said something in his native tongue to one of the Qothos and walked to the exit. The Qothos holding Domatu's chains once again began to pull Domatu out of the small den like room.

Once again outside Domatu squinted his eyes under the sun. He was happy to be under the sun's glow and not the heat of the lamps, which spotted the underground mazes.

Next Domatu was hauled in to a metal box looking building. Much to his surprise the inside the room was cooler than outside in the sun. The room was three stories tall each floor had three catwalks. Between the catwalks were box cages. The pens were stacked one on top of the other and each side by side there were about 81 cells in the mettle box.

In each cage the bottom, top right and left sides were steel sheets and the front and back walls were bared. In each cage was a mother and baby zatx. The babies were too young to be away from the mother. Like him, all the guardians had the braces even the babies had them.

"Based on our records this should be your female," Jabo said while stopping in front of a cage in the middle of the first floor. Domatu looked into the cage. He saw Sunyro with Kat. Sunyro had some cuts on your body and looked like she had been beaten but his little one look fine like nothing had happen to her but she did have a brace like her father. Sunyro came up to her knees the pen was too small for her to stand. With one arm she reached out for her husband and Jabo hit her arm as soon as it came to a stop while exclaiming, "Stay in there you beast!"

Domatu bolted at Jabo but before he could hurt him all the Qothos in the area subdued him. Jabo got up from the cold floor, walked up to Domatu and struck him across the face. Directly after Domatu spit at Jabo's feet. Jabo without pausing kicked the chained warrior who then made a fist but made no sound of pain or discomfort. "When will you learn fighting is pointless, you will never win," Jabo yelled to the room. "I will never give into you. You will have to kill me or always watch your back for I am a guardian and I will never let you win," Domatu roared to Jabo! When he finished speaking every zatz in the room cheered "Shut Up all of you or I will not feed you for a week and we will see you long your young live with out food," Jabo hissed loudly at the room. Jabo then walked over to a Qothos at a desk said something in his native tongue and walk towards Domatu. Walking passed the chained guardian and out the back door Domatu was soon to follow against his will.

Next they walked to the center of the camp. By this time, Domatu would walk with the group of Qothos holding him but they always had to be ready for when the relaxed Domatu would try to yank the chain out of their hands. But he did try to run knowing it was pointless to do so he would do his best to make his aggressors mad.

As they entered the middle of camp Domatu fell to his knees. He looked down and fell into a prayer. In the middle of camp was his best friend, Yaottyro, his dead, broken and tattered body hanging from two poles. Domatu felt a single tear fall from his eye knowing how much pain his friend was in before his enemies killed him. He blocked out the Qothos yelling at him and hitting. After he said his prayer he calmly stood and again walked on bowing his head in respect for not only his beloved friend but his fallen leader. As Jabo walked by he laughed and spit at Yaottyro's body; this action made Domatu's blood boil with anger. Domatu started to call out the guardian's code and everyone within earshot joined him. No one could silence him as he faced Yaottyro and said the code once finished he bowed his head and moved on following Jabo.

Now that Yaottyro had passed on, Domatu was the leader of his zatxs. As he walked when anyone passed him he got the respect and motions his leader once got. Next Jabo led Domatu into the master hut in the very center of the camp once inside he broke into a small sweat again because of the heat lamps. In the back of the hut was a Qothos who had a black vest with a red circle on and a red belt. As he slowly looked up from his work as the small band entered Domatu could see this Qothos had a scar starting about two inches above the eye and ended two inches below the eye. Domatu could not tell if he was blind in the scarred eye but it was a grey not the normal black. Jabo and the others all got down on one knee. Jabo got up and with a metal pole hit Domatu as hard as he could in the back of the knee. This forced Domatu to his knees when he tried to stand up Jabo hit him again but this time on the shoulder. The other Qothos then stood up and Domatu joined them. "Well aren't we the fighter, just like your weak leader. If I understand what my council has told me you are next in line to be leader of your pitiful race. I am the leader of the Qothos. My name is Moojigo (scared one). Your leader did put up a fight but did not last long. Jabo has requested you as his slave but I wanted to own the leader. Your leader's family served as a great way to torture Yaottyro if that was his name. This does not matter he is dead and so is family. He cried, begged and suffered greatly after I slowly ate his family while he watched. Your kind tasted rather good. If there is ever a food storage I know what to do. As I cut his daughter and wife and drank their blood and they cried out in pain your leader fought but was not strong enough to save them, which makes me wonder if you are. I have heard you are the best and strongest fighter. I heard you little code outside and I heard others join you. In my eyes you are the leader. Do you accept the responsibly of be leader of your people?" Moojigo asked Domatu who just looked forward then down in thought.

"If my kind wishes for me to lead them I will serve my kind as they wish. They are my family," Domatu calmly stated to Moojigo. "I think I would enjoy having you are a slave I can see why Jabo wants you as his own (turning to Jabo). Do you think you can handle him?" Moojigo asked Jabo. "Without a doubt in my mind I will make him a good respectful slave," Jabo quickly answered back. Jabo looked at Moojigo with hope filled eyes at that point Domatu knew their relationship and he smiled. "What are you smiling about?" Jabo snapped at Domatu.

"I can tell it is all in your eyes Jabo."

"What is in my eyes slave?"

"The way you act and your eyes tell me Moojigo is your father. Once you have a son you will understand and see what I did today."

"Shut up slave, I do not to hear a sound out of you or see a stupid grin. Is that clear?"

Domatu just looked forward. Moojigo looked at the chain warrior with surprised and respectful eyes. "Very observant, warrior, you are the only one ever to pick up on our relationship. You have very good skills your reputation matches you," the leader said while walking back to his desk. "Very well Jabo, you may this slave and his family but I will check up on your work and if I feel you cannot handle this warrior and his family. I will take them for myself. I will give no warning. Is this clear?" "Yes my lord. I will do a great job, you will see. I will make you proud," Jabo stated to his father. The two shared some words in their native language. They shook hands and then Jabo walked out of the hut. As Domatu was walking out he heard Moojigo say, "Well done Domatu, we will see what surprises you have in store when our paths meet again."

Once outside again Domatu was happy to get a breath of fresh air. As Domatu walked through the camp he could see his friends in chains and was saddened. Everyone gave him the sign of respect and this reminded him of his friend whom he would never see again. He held his head high as he walked by other zatx who gave him the same sign of respect that he once gave to Yaottyro. The sight of seeing little ones with chains on and serving sickened the new leader. As he walked he kept his eye on the layout of the camp and told his computer mentally to make a map of what he said. This way he could try to plan an escape.

After walking a while the group came to rest in front of a large gated hut. The group walked into the small opening on the left side of the dwelling. Inside Domatu saw a main room with chairs, a table and a type of rug on the ground, and to the left there was small room, which looked like a kitchen. In front of him looked like another room, a good size bedroom and then the group walked to the right into the third room. In there were poles, chains, cages and in the middle a table with metal hoops to pin down a body. "This is your new home and or room what ever you want to call it, I hope you like it," Jabo said with a smile. In the room already in the right bottom corner was a small steel cage with Sunyro and Zeaytera KatOynera and on the left chain to steel pole was his son sitting and resting from capture. "Put him on the table," Jabo ordered. Once Domatu was pinned down and Jabo checked the locks he walked out of the room with the group of Qothos shutting and locking the door behind him.

Domatu did his best to turn his head towards the cage in the corner of the room. "Are you alright my wife? Is our little one in good health?" Domatu asked Sunyro softly. "I am ok, our little one is doing well, the Qothos took her but they returned her she looked fine. She is sleeping right now. I did my best to protect her but there were too many of them." "I know I am glad to hear you are doing well despite what has happened." Domatu shifted his body and faced Gyro. "I am very proud of you my son. Not only did you fight well but you also did very well when they were causing you great pain and you did not give in to them. You are a great warrior." "Thank you father. After I could not find you, I headed towards our home to help mom out and Zea. I did the best I could." "Now what do we do now?" Gyro said to room.

There was silence for a while then Sunyro told the males in the room they must look out for the little one. The Qothos have no compassion for any of them. Blackmail might come into play and she heard once the young ones were old enough they were taken from their family and put into some kind of school. She also talked about how Jabo might let the family stay together if we do as he says. The choices we make now well affect of future greatly. At the end of her speech she said whatever plan they came up with she would follow and support. Again the room was quite for a while.

Then a Qotho dressed in white came in and said to the room, "I am a doctor. Your master has asked me to look at your wounds. I will do no harm to you and will do my best to tell you what I am doing as I try to dress your wounds. My name is Toghti (night)." Toghti went around the room first checked Zeaytera KatOynera then Sunyro. Next she went to Domatu and last went to Gyro who was in the worst condition of the family. The chained ones all thanked Toghti after she looked at them. "I am going to tell Jabo how dehydrated you are and how to take care of your wounds. And just for your information Jabo is a good master and is fair if you mind him well. I hope not to see you for a while," Toghti said softy as she left the room and once again silence took over the room. "I feel better now," Gyro voice quietly. "I will do anything to keep you all from harm even be a slave to Jabo. I will still try to plan an escape while doing what Jabo asks me to do unless one of you does not like my plan," Domatu stated to the room. After some time Sunyro told Domatu she would do what ever she could do to help. "How come you let Jabo win?! Why would you let you and your family become slaves? You will let your kind down and not be a true guardian," Gyro spat at his father.

"My son, fighting is not always the answer. If I always fight then I might break up the family and cause not only the death of my family but also others of our kind. Have you been taught the lesson of keeping your friends close and your enemies closer? If we learn the Qothos weakness we can learn the best way to attack and win. If we work together we can make a layout of the camp and find the best way to escape. I cannot find this out by always being chained in this room or wounded by Jabo. And if I am confined to this room I will not be able communicate with other members of the village. If you know a better way of doing this then by a means share your plan."

"You are right my father, I am sorry I questioned you. I still have much to learn."

"Life is a learning process, Gyro; one's quest for knowledge is never done."

They all agreed on the strategy and would do their best to spread the word on Domatu's plan.

When night came to the camp Jabo came into the small room with some water. He held a glass in front of Sunyro and asked, "What is my name?" Sunyro replied, "Master Jabo." Jabo then gave her the large glass of water. Next he walked over to Domatu and asked the same question.

Domatu answered, "Jabo." He turned to Gyro and asked the same question for a third time. Gyro said the same as his father. Jabo poured a large glass of water over each of the guy's heads. We well try this again later and he walked out with a smile on his face. Sunyro drank the half of the glass and offered it to the warriors who said they did not want any. She finished the drink and got ready to nurse Zeaytera KatOynera. A few hours went by and Jabo once again entered and with water. Like he did the first he went up to Sunyro who gave him the same answer and she again got water. This time when he asked Domatu and Gyro the father replied back, "If you do not call me slave I will call you Master Jabo." Jabo stopped and thought for a moment and finally said to Domatu, "What should I call you?"

"By my name, Domatu,"

"I cannot call you by your name this will reflect poorly on me"

"I will make life easier for you and be more productive if you call me by my name and not slave, my working for you shows I am below you, the chains show this too. There is no need to put my name down."

"I shall think about your request."

Then Jabo poured half the water out and gave the rest to the two warriors then proceed out of the small dark room. "Father, are you going to call Jabo, 'Master Jabo'", Gyro asked? "I am going to talk with him next time he comes in and if we can come to agreement then yes, to make him happy I will call him 'Master Jabo,'" Domatu answered his questioning son. "If I make a deal with him you will go along with it to ensure harmony. Is this clear?" Domatu stated to Gyro "Yes father," Gyro said with disappointment. The next time Jabo walked into the room Domatu told him he wished to speak to him in private and gave his word he would not fight and would let him chain him up again when they were done. Domatu then swore on Zeaytera KatOynera's life. Jabo pondered the idea and then accepted the deal. He untied Domatu and they walked into the main room.

Domatu and Jabo sat in chairs facing each outer. Domatu rubbed his arms where there the chains were once bounding him. He cleared his throat and than spoke to Jabo, "First, thank you for listening to me. I would like to offer you a deal. My family and I will call you, 'Master Jabo' and we will do your every wish without thinking or talking back if you do us one small favor. All we ask is we stay together. I have heard of families being split and the little ones being put into some kind of school. We just want to be together. I will go into chains when you ask. I will not fight you. And Gyro well also do whatever you ask. This well make your life very easy and save you time of trying to train us. Last I would like to be called by my name but I will be called slave if my family can stay together. I understand this might be a lot to ask but we can both benefit from this. One more thing, as true guardians, I took an oath never to kill another being unless there is no other way, so that might be the only command Gyro and I might have trouble following."

Domatu looked down at the floor while Jabo shifted in his chair and began to think about what the one in front of him was asking. "You are right you are asking a lot of me," Jabo began," the school you talk of is to teach your little ones about our history and to erase yours. They are to learn in the order of life they are lower than us so it is their places in the world to be are slaves. If I let your little one stay with you than, you must never try to teacher her your language or history. You must go along with the teaching I teacher her. Also tomorrow all of you but the little one will get collars. These collars have chips in them and if you try to take them off they will set off an electric blast, which will kill you. They will also detonate if you get too far from a different chip, which I will have on me at all times. I can kill you or any member of your family whenever I want.

As for your name, I will call you by your name in some places but in others I will can you slave, if you call me master. Do you agree so far with everything I have told you?" "I will do all you ask if our family can stay together," Domatu said softy. "Very well, Domatu your family will stay together but if I find your little one looking up to you before me, speaking your half-witted language or knowing your history I will break your family without thinking or showing any compassion for I am doing a large service by letting you stay together," Jabo told Domatu. "I fully understand, Master Jabo and I thank you," the warrior said. Jabo stood up and started to walk back to the small room full of chains. Domatu followed in silence. Once in the room Domatu let his master chain him to the wall opposite of his son. "See you in the morning," Jabo said while shutting the door.

The Domatu told his wife and son everything Jabo and he talked about while they were out of room. Gyro was not happy about being a slave but his father quickly reminded him they could stay together. Sunyro was unsettled about the idea of her daughter not knowing her language or her past. Again the father had to be comfort his loved one and remind his loving wife their daughter had a computer and could teach her everything she ever needed to know. This made Sunyro feel better. Domatu also told him family once Kat was old enough they would teach her and tell her not to tell anyone. Once the family had discussed everything they fell into a deep sleep.

In the morning the slaves woke up when Jabo and a few Qothos came into the room to put on the collars. They put a little bracelet on Zeaytera KatOynera. The slaves let the Qothos work when the collars were on everyone left but Jabo. He reminded the family how the collars worked. Once everyone understood Jabo put the Sunyro to work in the house while Domatu and Gyro went with him to work. Zeaytera KatOynera stayed with her mother during this time.

A year went by and everyone knew their places. Domatu did some hard labor outside and some service at meeting with Jabo and other high-ranking Qothos. Gyro did mostly labor, cleaning, building and odd jobs. Sunyro worked around the house, cleaning, cooking and gardening. Zeaytera KatOynera stayed with her mother during the day and once old enough helped with the housework and once a day got a lesson from Jabo. The child found out it was easier to run and do some of her chores with her wings tucked into her back. Most times her wings were tucked there unless she needed to stretch them. She was not allowed to fly so she never really used them. At home she tried to fly a little from one end of the hut to the other. At night the guys were chained at the feet, Sunyro was put in a large cage where she could stand and lie down and Zeaytera KatOynera always slipped through the bars of her mother's cage and slept with her father. Who took all his families chips and up dated them then put them back in his daughter's computer.

Domatu, Sunyro and Gyro learned basic words in the Qothos's language. They could only understand a few main phrases, which were mainly orders. Kat could speak both if she wanted. With Jabo teaching her his language by day and Domatu teaching her, her native tongue by night she always knew who was saying what. In front of Jabo and other Qothos she pretended she could not understand what her kind said and only spoke their language. And outside of the small room of chains she only spoke the Qothos's tongue unless she was doing chores with her mother and there was no one else within ear shot but inside with her family Kat could translate anything her family asked her too and could teach as well as be taught. In the hut no one really talked a lot. Jabo gave orders to his slaves and gave Kat her daily lesson. If Jabo really needed to talk to Domatu, Sunyro or Gyro he would speak to them in their native tongue.

As the second year of the enslavement came to an end Domatu and Gyro worked hard to keep an open line of communication between other zatxs. Soon a rumor was going around and Jabo as well as other high-ranking Qothos heard it. They did not like the sound of Domatu leading an escape during the winter. They decided they must put an end to the strong leader. Jabo had a great idea. He went to his father to ask if he would agree with his plan. Domatu noticed Jabo acting strangely. One night he told his family his life was in danger. He told Gyro to take care of Sunyro and Kat if anything happened to him. He told Gyro how proud he was of his strong son. How much he loved his wife.

That night as he held Kat he told her how much he loved her and continued to teach her their language and history. He made her promise never to tell anyone about their talks even if asked. Her father also asked her to hide her different features. She could share them with her family but never with anyone else even other zatxs. She always sealed her promise with a kiss. She loved and looked up to her father. Domatu learned how different his daughter really was compared to other zatxs and guardians. She was very quick at learning and understanding ideas. Also she could speak to Domatu only using her mind but she was not very good at it. Kat had great, dark, deep green eyes, and seemed to have great reflexes and sense for her age. He soon found her eyelids went along with her mood and how mad she was and they did give her different vision. She would make the perfect guardian if she had the right training. In the chips Domatu put into Kat's computer he made a training program to make her a great warrior. He could tell just by looking at her computer it could do things he could only imagine. A tear rolled down his cheek when he remembers he would never she his little one grown up and to know she might never be free. He closed his eyes in anger knowing she was going to grow up in this camp. He pulled a small piece of metal from his belt and carved a heart, which was flat and smooth on one side and round on the other. When he was finished he held his daughter close to his heart and fell asleep.

In the morning Jabo came in to unlock his slaves. Domatu hugged his wife good morning as he did this he handed the heart to her and said, "This is to be passed down through our family." Gyro came to his father and they shook arms. Kat was very happy this morning for today was the day of her birth and her father always did something special for her on this day. Unlike a normal day Jabo took the whole family out with him. As they walked Domatu whispered to his family how he could tell Jabo was up to something. He spoke in his native language and low so Jabo could not hear him. At the end Kat asked what her dad said to help make Jabo think she did not know her native tongue. This made Jabo smile. Domatu told his family to stay together, be strong and how much he loved them. The father turned to Gyro and told him never to forget the code and to teach it to Kat. The group entered into a large metal building. Sunyro and Gyro were forced to the left and Jabo, Domatu and Kat went to the right. Mother and son were chained to a wall in a sound proof room. Opposite to them was a window where they could see a large room.

Soon Jabo, father and daughter entered the large room. All the wife and warrior could do was watch. Sunyro began to shake in fear of what was going to happen. Gyro tried to comfort her he reached out his hand. She took his hand without pausing. In the large room Kat hugged her father and he hugged her back. The ones in the large room could not see the on lookers. Jabo walked Domatu over to one end of the room. "Stay here," Jabo ordered. Then Jabo walked over to the middle of the room and placed Kat on the ground. Last he walked to the opposite side as Domatu. "Zeaytera KatOynera, listen to me. I am going to ask you do to something for me. What ever you choose well impact you greatly. So follow my directions, do you understand?" Jabo told Kat. "I understand, Master Jabo I will do what you ask of me because it is my place in life to serve you and make you happy. Is that not what you have taught me?" Kat replied back. "Yes, very good Zeaytera KatOynera, I want you to go to the one you respect the most Domatu or me. Make your choice," Jabo stated strongly. Kat looked at Jabo and said, "As you wish Master Jabo." and turned and started to walk to her father.

Jabo was not happy with the young ones choice and hit Domatu's chip. Without a sound Domatu's caller went off and the strong guardian fell to the ground. Seeing her father fall she ran to him. Sunyro screamed and cried out into the room. Gyro full of rage did his best to help his mother. Kat on reaching her father gently pushed his great arm, "Daddy why are you sleeping this is not the right time. The sky is still light night has not come yet. Wake up. Wake up daddy," Kat told her father. Domatu was still breathing but he breaths were getting slower.

She ran to her father's massive head and again gently pushed and then tried to awake her forever-sleeping role model by tenderly biting and pulling on his ear. "You are being silly daddy," Kat said playfully. She then pushed herself under his failing body and laid down trying to sleep like her father next to her. As Domatu took his last breath a single tear ran from his eye, down his cheek and fell onto his loving daughter. When Kat realized she could not feel or hear her father's heart beat which always helped her fall asleep she started calling out to her fallen family. "Daddy, wake up. Please Daddy wake up. I need you, please," Kat yelled at her lost guardian.

Jabo walked over to the fallen hero to pick up the little one. "Come on Zeaytera KatOynera there is work to be done," Jabo ordered. As Kat got up she asked Jabo, "What about Domatu?"

"He is resting. Come."

Jabo brought Kat back to the hut and gave her some food. Then he told her to stay there. As he left he told her Sunyro would be home shortly.

Gyro did his best to hold Sunyro while they watched their leader fall and their little one try to awake him. Sometime after Jabo and Kat left the room some Qothos went into the large room picked up Domatu's body. They would display his body the same way Yaottyro's body was when they first came into the camp. All Gyro could think to do was say the guardian's code and the fallen warrior's prayer. These words calmed Sunyro and she joined in with her praying son.

As the two chained ones were ending the prayer for the second time Jabo walked into the room with a smile. "Quiet!" he yelled at them. "I did not even get to say goodbye," Sunyro wept. "Now where would be the fun if you knew what was going to happen. I find this experience more fun if I only know what is going to happen then I know where look for good expressions," Jabo said cheerfully. "Have you no compassion, you monster," Gyro yelled. "What!?!" Jabo asked sharply. "I am sorry Master Jabo, I forgot my place. Please forgive me. I am just caught up in all the emotion of the moment which, is no excuse. I again apologize again for my rude and unforgivable action. Forgive me Master Jabo," Gyro said in a low voice. Jabo looked at him with cold eyes, "you will only get water for the next five days," Jabo said loudly. "Yes, thank you, Master Jabo, you are full of compassion," Gyro again said soft and low. The master unchained his slaves and they started walking back to the house. When they walked by Domatu's dead body, Gyro stopped and started to state the guardian's code. Jabo quickly snapped at him, "You are trying my patience today, stop Gyro. NOW!" Gyro who looked at his mother who was about to cry again and then he stopped talking. The group walked back to the house where Sunyro was left to do the work and Gyro was off with his master for the day.

Sunyro walked into the house and fell to the floor. Her salt tears hit the dirt floor then she heard a noise. Startled she looked up and saw Kat running to her. "Mother, why are you crying?"

"We will talk about it later tonight. We have a lot of work to do. Let's get started little one."

"Yes, Mother. Let's get this day moving. I want night to come soon so father can give me my surprise for my day of birth." Sunyro looked down, let her last tears fall and then picked herself up off the ground. She did all her chores for the day. Thinking about how she would tell her daughter she would never see her father again. A few times during the day Kat saw her mother go into the back room and cry. The little one did not fully understand what was wrong but did not like seeing her mother cry.

As Sunyro started to put food onto the table as Jabo and Gyro walked into the hut. Jabo sat down to eat while the others stood to his left with their heads looking down at the Earth. When Jabo was done eating he told Sunyro he had better from her and was disappointed. She told him she was sorry. He then walked to his room but first took Kat with him for her daily lesson. Sunyro then sat down to eat. She ate a little but was not in the mood to eat. Gyro only had water. After the mother was done eating she started to do the dishes and clean the table. Gyro helped his mother. This made them both a little uneasy for this is what Domatu used to do every night. Soon after the two finished, Jabo and Kat joined them in the main room. "Is father home yet?" the little one asked the room. Jabo turned to the child and said in a strong voice, "Because of you, Zeaytera KatOynera, your father will never come home. Because of your choice you made this morning in the cold room; you will never be allowed to see your father again. Because of your choice your father is dead all because of you!" Tears came her face as she looked at her mother and bother who looked down at the ground. "I did what you told me to do what did I do wrong? I do not understand," Kat cried to Jabo. "Stop crying, you made the wrong choice so Domatu died. You must learn to mind me. Now go to bed," Jabo said coldly to Kat. Jabo walked the slaves into their small room and locked them. Then he went to bed.

The whole night Kat cried to her mom, saying how sorry she was. How she did not mean to hurt the family and take her father away. Sunyro tried to tell Kat this was not her fault and anyone would have made the same choice she did. Hearing his little sister in so much pain brought a tear to Gyro eye. He called for his little sister who slipped through the bars of her mother's cage and went to her older brother. He held her like Domatu use to hold her. She looked over at his empty spot and cried harder. Gyro held her and rocked her to sleep. His heartbeat like his father before him rocked the little one asleep.

A new leader

In the fallowing days Sunyro did not sleep well, dinner and nighttime was the hardest part of the day. She was proud of Gyro he was always doing his best to comfort the broken family. He was doing a great job stepping into Domatu's place. Every night Kat now slept with her older brother who taught her the history and native language of the zatxs. She never let Jabo know she had lessons from Gyro at night. One day Jabo came into the small room and unlocked the zatzs. The zatz stared laboring in the kitchen.

While Gyro slept Sunyro started to cut fresh fruit and Kat cleaned and set the table. Then the little one walked into the small kitchen with her mother and help make the first meal of the day. Jabo came into the room sat down at the table and Kat came in with his drinks of water and juice. Following her was Sunyro was a plate of meat, fruit, bread and eggs. As Jabo ate both Sunyro and Kat stood at his left and waited for him to finish his meal. Jabo told the two next to him the meal was good and then got up to wake up his worker. While the master left Sunyro and Kat cleaned the table and washed the dishes. Gyro came into the kitchen and gave his mother a hug and kissed Kat on the head as she gave his glass of water and a plate with a sandwich of egg, cheese, and meat. He ate his food quickly and thanked them for making him a great first meal. When Jabo came out of his room he called the young warrior and they both were gone for the day.

As Sunyro finished the dishes Kat cleaned the table one last time and then both of them walked into Jabo's room where they cleaned the room and last took the bedding for cleaning which they would do later. The mother prepared to leave the house. The two left the house and walked to the end of camp where the well was and picked up buckets of water. The mother carried two buckets and the child carried one small one. As they walked they waved and said, "Hi," to other zatzs who were working in other huts. Sunyro made sure Kat was next to her at all times.

When the two reached Jabo's hut Sunyro stayed outside with the water while Kat ran into the hut and found the soap to bring to her waiting mother. Next Kat grabbed the bedding and again brought it to her mother. The two washed the bedding and laid it out to dry in the warm sun. During their work Kat asked her mother question about life and nature. Sunyro did the best she could to answer the sometimes difficult questions. Soon Sunyro put Kat down for her nap. During this part of the day Sunyro time to herself. She reflected on life and did her best to think of ways to save her daughter from her fate. The tireless mother cleaned the house and got ready to go out one more time. This trip would be to obtain food for Jabo's last meal of the day. As the mid-day was coming to an end Kat woke up and gave her mother a hug.

The two made their way to pick up water, meat, and other things for the guys to eat when they returned from a hard days work. Once they got home mother and daughter worked on dinner. There was not much Kat could do for she was so young but help whenever she could. She made sure the table was perfect. When there was nothing left for Kat to do she played with the dirt on the floor making pictures.

When Jabo came home Sunyro told her daughter to clean up and get ready to serve their master who went directly to his room. Gyro came in next he slowly walked over to Sunyro and gave her a hug and walk to Kat who was just finishing with washing her hands. As he patted her on the head he whispered, "How are you little Zea?" "I am doing well. I had so much fun with mom today," she said with joy. Sunyro looking at her son saw he had large cuts going down his back. "What happen to you my son, what did they do to you?" the worried mother asked. "I fell behind today and so I was whipped. I will be fine. Do not worry about me. Make sure everything is ready for Master Jabo," Gyro said calmly. Kat ran over to her mother who gave her the drinks to put on the table. Just as Kat put the drinks down on the table Jabo entered the room. Gyro took his spot to the left of Jabo's seat. Once he sat down at the table Sunyro came to him and served him his supper and last took her place next to Gyro on the left. Kat who was next to Gyro played with her brother's tail. Still being young she loved to play. Gyro gave her a sign to stop and wait till later and this was not the time. She stood next to him with her arms crossed.

When Jabo was finished eating he got up and went to his room as he walked he called Kat to come with him. When Kat was gone Sunyro gave her son food. As the warrior ate his mother tended his wounds. "I love your cooking I do not think I could ever get enough. Thank you for cooking the last meal of day for me," Gyro said softly. "Anything for my strong warrior son," she answered back to him. Just as they finished Jabo and Kat joined them in the room. Jabo seemed to be in a better mood after Kat's lesson. He did not send the family to bed but they all sat in the main room. While Kat played on the floor Sunyro looked at her with loving eyes. She slowly turned to Jabo and said softy, "Thank you, Master Jabo, thank you for letting me see my little one grow. I cannot put into words what my heart feels." "I am happy you made the right choice by accepting your fate. You are strong workers. I have even noticed compared to other young ones your child is…unique. But to get back to my point I think Zeaytera KatOynera is the youngest one in the camp. All the others I think are dead. I am glad you followed my rules. She is worth a lot," Jabo said to Sunyro who looked at him with eyes filled with sadness and wonder. They talked for a little longer and then Jabo put the family to bed.

Most of the days were the same for Sunyro for the next two years she watched her children quickly grow. Kat started to have bad nightmares but always awoke in the arms in a loved one. So could fall back asleep. Kat was happy her day of birth was in one week. She would be turning four years of age. She was getting better at doing all the chores her mother could do but was still too young to carry the large buckets of water and cook full meals. During the night Sunyro, talked to Gyro, "Jabo is acting like he did before Domatu was taken from us. I think we should be ready for anything on little Kat's day of birth. What ever happens we have to take care of Kat." "I will do what ever takes to make sure Kat lives a good life. I love you and her with all my heart," Gyro said but had to stop he found his eyes watering thinking he might lose his mother, or his own life. Then he thought of his lost father. Sunyro did not sleep well that night and the next few days she spent as much time with Kat as she could, hugging her and keeping her close. At night Gyro did the same and made sure he continued giving her lesson just like Domatu would have been doing.

When the day came Sunyro and Gyro had not slept the night before and Sunyro made Kat sleep with her. As she held her sleeping daughter she pulled out the heart Domatu gave her and carved into the metal. She carved the round part of the heart so the flat part could be seen when looked from straight on. The now top heart was a little smaller than the flat heart it rested on top of and she added a hoop on top so some day someone could wear it as a necklace. The round heart looked like it had a small border. When see was done she hugged Kat and fell asleep.

At dawn Jabo came in and unlocked all of them. He then chained all of them and once again they walked to the place they were two years before that day. Kat was shaking and Sunyro and Gyro were holding hands the whole way there. As they walked Sunyro turned to her son and gave him the heart and said the same words Domatu said to her. Then she told him where she got it and he took the little shaped metal and hid it in his belt. Once they got to the time to split up and go the different ways. Jabo, Sunyro and Kat went to the right and Gyro once again was forced to the left. He was again chained to the wall and had the same view when he was there two years earlier. Deep down he knew whatever choice Kat made his mother would never hold him again. His eyes watered.

In the large room Jabo took Sunyro to one side of the room and then walked Kat to the middle of the room. He spoke to Kat in a strong loud voice, "Zeaytera KatOynera, listen to me. I am going to ask you to do something and you are to do it. It is a simple question. Do make the same mistake you did last time," then Jabo walked to the other side of the room, "Zeaytera KatOynera, who do you respect more ME or Sunyro? Walk to the one you respect. Make your choice" Kat looked at her mother then at Jabo. She looked at her mother one last time and then started to walk to Jabo. The master looked down in disappointment. Kat heard the sound of a body hit the floor.

Turning her head she could see her mother on the cold floor. Kat ran to her mother and tried to get her to stand up and move. But all her mother could do was look at her little one and just like her husband on her last breath a tear rolled from her eye and onto the crying child rubbing her face against her mother's. Gyro yelled in anger seeing his mother fall then he went into a mode of prayer just like he did when his father passed. Jabo calmly walked over to the sobbing little one and said in a cold voice, "I am very disappointed in you. You not only killed your father but now your mother. What is wrong with you? Did you love them? I do not know what you were thinking. You hesitated. There should be no question in your mind this shows me you are lying. Lets go." They walked out of the room where Gyro joined them. They walked back to the hut where Kat was left there. Jabo told her to stay there and not to leave. Gyro wanted to comfort the crying one and cry himself but he could not, he now had to go to work. He did not have a choice.

Today Jabo made Gyro go to his father's hut and fix the back wall. After he made the sticky mud he had to carefully put it onto the wall. The worker had to make sure everything was even before the hot sun dried the moist mud. Mud dried in his coat and some golden fur was ripped out while he moved but by now Gyro was used to pain. When he was finished with, the wall, he walked to the front of the house where Moojigo was standing talking to other Qothos. When the tried warrior saw him, he walked in front of the leader and then went down to one knee. Moojigo told him to stand.

Gyro informed the leader his house was fixed and asked if he would like to check to make sure the work was satisfactory. Moojigo told Gyro his work was finished, to wash off the mud and last to come back to his hut. Gyro walked down to well where he started to wash off the mud. As he did this zatz who were doing housework came to the water well. All of them looked at Gyro and saw his father. They asked if the attack was still on when winter came. Gyro said he still had some planning left but as of now yes. He asked them to try to count how many warriors would be able to fight. When the young leader was done washing he ran back up to the hut where he had spent the whole morning. Moojigo was waiting for him. Gyro saw Jabo was leaving. Looking back at the Qothos's leader he got down on one knee and waited for his next task from Moojigo. "Come in young slave," he said to the kneeling one. Gyro stood and walked into the hut. They sat at a table and Moojigo spoke, "Gyro, I see the other zatxs look up to you. I see them giving you signs of respect and I also know your late father was planning to attack a few winters ago. I am not sure if you fully realize as of right now you are the leader of your kind. This is not the best position to be in my eyes. Every leader before you have been killed for entertaining this roll. Now as the leader I know you can talk and if you wanted you could have everyone attack tonight. But I have some information for you. (Handing Gyro a piece of paper) Here are the numbers of your kind. As you can see, your little sister is the youngest and there are many your age and a decent number of older warriors. If you think about it, if the zatx as a whole attack they cannot possibly win. Even if a few escape over half would die. Ever since we captured your kind there have been no new births and only deaths. No female will carry a child knowing the little one will end with their same fate of enslavement and therefore, there have been suicides. Your race is dying. If you attack you only make your time on this planet much shorter. You may do what ever you want but talking leader to leader with the numbers in front of us even if my group was weak, in winter, there is no way you and your dying race could win. I am not trying to break your hope but save lives. This life might not seem like much but it could be a lot worst." "How do I know these numbers are right?" Gyro asked

"Do they look wrong? I assure you, I am not bluffing. When you walk around the camp you will notice the numbers should be right. There is no way you could win with the collars on how are you going to fight us. Reflect on all you have to accomplish, first you all have to get the callers off, then the ones with braces have to get those off and last you have to fight. That is a lot of work. And Masters might just start pushing the chips and ones who are not fighting might die. You have a lot to think about young leader. I will let you go home now. I am sure your little sister would like to be with you at this time. I have told Jabo to give you the rest of the day and night to relax. I will talk to you in a few days."

"Thank you, I would really like to comfort Zea."

"I thought her name was Kat?"

"I call her Zea it is a big brother thing."

"I will see you soon. Think about what I have told you."

"I will thank you again, Master Moojigo."

Once Gyro got back to the hut he was tired and just wanted to sit and rest but he had to find Zea. He walked into the dwelling and could not see his little sister. After looking in main places he just sat and listened for her. As he listened to the quiet room he could not hear her. Next he quietly called out to his sister. There was no answer. He tried again this time a little louder. Holding his head in his hands he could remember what Jabo had yelled at her after their mother passed. He was full of anger. Then he heard the sound of moving chains. Turning his head and looking in the room where he slept he could not see anything. Walking into the room he could not see her. Once again he called out her name softly. Looking around the room he finally saw Zea; she was hiding under a massive pile of Domatu's old chains. Gyro slowly and carefully picked up the chains till he could fully see the little fur ball shaking in fear and sadness. Once he could he picked up Zea and held her to his chest and walked to the wall where the two sat in each others company for a while. "Are you okay Zea, do you want to talk or sit some more?" Gyro whispered. Zea shifted so she could look at her brother. Gyro could see the dust on her face and two tear trails running down from her eyes to her chin. He smiled warmly at her and wiped her face. "Hi, little one, are you ok?"

"I am ok. I just feel bad; I am so sorry, Gyro. I did not mean to take mother and father from you. I hope you are not mad at me. I feel so bad" Zea began to cry again.

"Shhhhh, Shhhhh, there, there it is ok. I am not mad at you Zea; it is not your fault. You well see this when you are older. I am here for you, always. Do you want to know a secret?"

"Sure," she said while wiping her eyes. No matter what happens Domatu, Sunyro and I will always be with you."

"How?"

"We are in here, and no can take us from you," he stated while pointing to her heart.

"If you ever need to find a lost one, look up at the sky, they are looking down on you watching and trying to help you and if you talk to them they may not answer in words but they well always send you a sign in one way or anther," the brother told the little one in his arms. "Really, that is really true?" Zea asked with wonder in her eyes. "Yes, why would I lie to you," He answered back to her. The two sat and talked for a while and enjoyed each other's company for they were all they had left.

Later in the evening Jabo came back to his home with a guest. He had a female Qotho who held his hand. Gyro came up to his master and bent down to one knee to show thanks for letting him have the day off with his little sister. Zea who followed her brother also got down to her knees and waited for Jabo to tell her what to do.

Jabo looked at them and was pleased. He told them the females name was Uta (creek) and she was going to be saying with them. He told them Zea would be getting her lesson from her and would be taught everything from history to cooking. Gyro would continue to work for Jabo doing labor outside the hut. Uta took Zea into the kitchen where they began to cook. Gyro saw his little sister still fresh with emotion start to tear. He walked to the opening of the kitchen asking if he could help. But Jabo had other plans for him. "No, Gyro come sit with me we must talk," Jabo called from the other room. Bending down to his little sister Gyro told her to do her best and everything would be okay then proceed to the room where Jabo was sitting.

As he entered the main room Jabo gave him the signal to sit down across from him. Gyro did as Jabo asked but was not happy to sit in the same room as the murderer of his parents. "Gyro, you are a strong male and have lots of power over your kind and your little sister," Jabo began. "I do not want you putting any ideas in Zeaytera KatOynera's head. If anything changes so does this deal and I will sell you or her. Do not ever underestimate me or test my patience."

"I understand Master Jabo, thank you."

"Dinner is ready," Uta called out from the other room. Both males stood up, Jabo first, and then they walked to the table. Jabo took his place at the head of the table while Gyro and Zea took their places to his left. Uta sat next to Jabo on the right side of the table. Gyro could not understand everything the eating couple were saying where Zea could understand all it. He had picked some up the Qothos language up over the years. When the two finished eating Zea and Gyro started to clear the table and do the dishes as the two masters went to the main room. When the chores were done the two workers sat and ate what little supper was left and cleaned their plates. Jabo then took them and put them into the chains and cage.

Once the small family was alone Gyro started to give Zea her daily lesson and changed the chips in her computer. After her lesson the little one would show her brother her differences. She worked on her mental power and controlling her eyelids. She also worked on self-control over her wings keeping them tucked into her back and changing from a two-legged zatx to a four-legged zatx. The big brother taught the little one different exercise to do. So when she was in a small space or could not use her wings she could still keep her muscles strong. Gyro was amazed about his sister's abilities. He loved teaching her and helping her develop her skills. As the nights went on Zea became very good at controlling herself and knowing her history. She could now speak to Gyro only using her mind. She would have him think of an idea and she would read his mind. Next she would tell him what he was thinking. They made a game out of her mental abilities. Kat still had her nightmares from time to time but again awoke in the arms of her loving brother and was rocked back to sleep.

Soon Moojigo wanted to see Gyro. Jabo took his slave to see his father. There the two sat by themselves and talked of the future. "Have you thought about what we talked about last time we met?" The leader asked. "I have," Gyro answered. "I know you do not want an upraise because if most or all us died you would not have anymore slaves. And there would be a waste of life. If I order there not to be an up rise can you make me a promise?"

"I cannot make you any promises till I have heard your proposal. When you tell me your idea I will think about it and do my best to make it so both of us are happy by the end of our discussion. What promise would you like me to make, young one?"

"I have heard your kind have been doing experiments on us zatx. I wish you to stop these painful and useless tests. Taking a computer off a guardian will kill them no matter what and it is the most painful death you could give to a warrior. I wish you to stop trying to make my kind reproduce. The zatz will only kill themselves or the young ones. They well not let a child grow up in this environment and it is a waste of life. Let my kind live the rest their lives in less pain. We are already in enough agony."

"I understand. I will do this. I will make you this promise. You keep your kind from uprising and I will stop the testing and trying to force your race to reproduce."

The two shook hands show agreement both showed their signs of respect from one leader to another and moved on their different paths. Once Gyro was done working for the day he loved to come home and see Zea. She was growing so fast in his eyes. Everyday she was doing more and more of the chores. Also she was growing strong from doing all the housework. Carrying the buckets of water from the well to the hut made her arms very strong. He loved to play games with her and seeing smile made him feel happy. He felt like he was her father and would do anything for her. Like his father he found his eyes watering thinking about his little one growing up in this horrible camp and never knowing the freedom, which was taken from her. At night he held her close and did his best always to be happy around her.

The years went by fast and soon Zea's birthday was coming. This time she would be six years of age. Both brother and sister would fear this day. This made Gyro very upset. He felt no one should fear their own birthday. When the night came both Gyro and Zea did not sleep they talked all night and enjoyed each other's company. This time Gyro came up with a plan. When morning came Jabo came to unlock the two just like he had done two years prior. They walked to the same room. Both of them walked to the large room. Then Jabo put Gyro and the little sister end of the room and then he walk to the opposite. He asked Zea the same Question he asked her every two years. This time after Jabo asked Zea who she respected the most she went running to Jabo. Kissing his feet and showing him every sign of respect she knew. Jabo smiled and looked over at Gyro who hung his head. Gyro looked like he was going to cry. Jabo's smile grew and patted Zea on the head telling her she made the right choice and he was proud of her.

They all walked back to the hut together. Zea walked by Jabo's side and not her brother's. Gyro looked at the ground as he walked back to the hut. Gyro went to work with Jabo as Zea stayed at the hut to labor on with her chores. When the master looked at his slave he could see that a part of his soul was gone this made him cheerful and again grin grew on his scaly lips. Gyro worked very hard that day and was tired from not sleeping the previous night.

When he got home Zea did not going running up to him but came up to Jabo where she asked him about his day and once they were done talking ran off the finish making the last meal of the day. When dinner was served she stood at the right on Jabo not the left with her brother. This pleased the master. When all the dishes were clean Jabo locked up his slaves for the night. Once their owner was gone Zea started to laugh. Jumping trough the bars and into her brother open arms, "It worked your plan worked. I am so happy you are so smart, my brother, you told what to do when I read your mind that way I was doing what you told me too but we made Master Jabo happy. I did not kissing his feet but you are alive so it was worth it. I would do anything for you."

"I am happy our plan worked too, you did a great job acting and doing what I told you too. I am pleased we can talk only using our minds. You see being different is not too bad."

"I guess you are right. You did a good job acting too, did you see Jabo smile! He was so happy to see you sad. He is an odd one."

"Yes, I know Zea," he said while giving her a hug. The two slept well that night. Zea woke up just before Jabo reached the door and she ran to her cage squeezed between the bars and closed her eyes. Jabo walking in smiled seeing his slaves not sleeping together and he woke Zea who pretended to wake up to start the day. The two walked out where Zea started to work on the first meal of the day.

As the weeks and months went by life went on the same for the two slaves they would pretend not to know each other during the day and at night were inseparable. The two did their lessons, playing games and working on Zea's skills. Soon two years were up and Zea was getting ready to turn eight years of age. That night she slept well while Gyro was up all night he did know what to expect. He knew Jabo would have something planned. He worked on the heart his father made years ago. He cut into the back of the flat metal making a heart shaped hole in the back of the little charm. Next he carved little slits into the top heart to make the little one on top to the flat one stand out.

As soon as he finished he woke Zea up and told her again about how her family is always with her and repeated what he had told her after they had lost their mother. Last he gave the charm to her. He told her the piece of metal's history. There was a spot of a rope so she could wear the charm as a necklace but Gyro told her not to wear it when Jabo might see. The older brother told his sister the master would take it from her and destroy it. She promised to always keep her new gift hidden from the world until she was safe. They hugged and enjoyed each other's company.

When morning came and the sun kissed the ground, Jabo came in unlocked his slaves. This time they walked to a different building. Qothos did not like water unlike zatx they could not swim well. In this building there was a large pool. Zea was put at one end of the pool and Jabo walked Gyro over to the opposite side. Both Jabo and Gyro were tied up so if pushed in the water they would not be able to swim.

The hairs on Zea's neck stood on end. — What do I do? — Zea asked her brother with her mind. — No matter what you do I will never see the light of day again. If you save me Jabo well kill me and if you save Jabo I will die. It is a trap. There is nothing you can do. Remember all I have taught you. I will always be with you. I am so proud of how far you have come and I know you will do great things in your life. You must promise me. No matter how hard things get you will never give up and always respect the guardian's code — Zea read the thoughts in Gyro's mind. — I promise. My brother, I love you. I will never forget all the lessons you have taught me. Someday I will the strongest guardian that ever lived, please always be there for me. Please give mom and dad a hug for me and not only watch over me but please help guide me though life. —

— I will always be with you. Be strong Zea, never forget where you came from and never let the Qothos win. Fight! Fight! And never forget how much you are loved. —

Jabo's voice echoed off the walls, "Zeaytera KatOynera, listen to me. You can only save one of us. Choose well. Save your brother or me. Make your choice!" As soon as he finished both males were pushed into the waters. Without thinking Zea jumped into the water and her blue eyelids moved in front of her eyes. She had perfect vision underwater. She could see everything just as if she was above water. Her gills also kicked in and started to work. This was a new feeling to breath underwater. She swam straight to her brother where she kissed him giving him air and then with her claws cut the ropes, which were holding Gyro down to the bottom of the pool. She helped her brother to the surface where once out of the water by the edge of the pool they hugged. "I am so proud of you, Zea," Gyro said softly. "In the code family comes first and nothing else matters," Zea said to her brother. Then she felt a fast wave go through her brother's body and he clasped onto the floor she continued to hug her brother until his last breath and tear came out of his now dead body. Zea went into prayer and for the first time in front of the Qothos she spoke her native tongue. She said the same prayer Gyro had said when her mother and father were taken from her. Once the other Qothos pulled Jabo out and of water and he caught his breath, he heard the language coming out of the little ones mouth. He was full of rage. He figured out somehow the two siblings had tricked him and he had let them stay together for an extra two years. Full of jealously and rage he walked up to the now crying child picked her up by the fur on the back of her neck and walked back to his hut.

Alone, with a new friend?

Once back at his hut Jabo walked into the room with all the restraints and chained the little one to the wall. So she faced the wall and her back was facing Jabo. He then walked to his room and came back with a whip in hand. "I will teach you to be obey me. You will never question me, talk back to me, disobey me," as the master went on he whipped the young one and gave her, her first scars. Tears fell from Zea's eyes but she did everything in her power not to cry out as the whip cut into her back.

When she tried to pull her wings in for protection Jabo yelled at her and then proceed to nail them to the wall. As her blood and sweat fell to the floor Jabo got all his rage out on the eight year old. Once he had enough he left her there to hang in her misery. Once she was alone she let go and cried. Her body shook because of the pain. About an hour later Uta came in from visiting her family and could smell blood. When she walked in on Zea she gasped seeing Zea's little back torn and her wings nailed to the stonewall. She quickly walked up to the little one and began to carefully take her down from her chains but a voice cut through the air, "LEAVE HER!" "But Jabo," Uta began to say. "She must learn her lesson. I said leave her. Now shut the door and come to me," Jabo ordered his wife. With disappointment she did what he asked.

Zea hung there all day and night without any nutriment. When morning came her muscles were stiff and she ached all over her body. Her eyes burned from crying, her stomach gowned because of her missed meals, her head pounded from dehydration and the emotional stress she went through. Her back and wings were on fire.

About mid morning Uta came into the small room and told Zea she was going to try to take her down with inflicting as little pain as possible. She also told the little one that Jabo had left for the day and had nothing to fear. First Uta pulled out the two nails, which were pinning Zea's wings to the wall. Next she carefully unchained the young ones hands. Once Zea was finally on the ground and was completely free from the wall her body clasped. Uta carried the small one to her cage where she had set up some blankets. Last Uta left the room and came back to Zea with some water and soup. "I know you do not feel like eating but I need you to take this soup and water," Uta spoke softly. Zea did as she was asked. Immediately after she finished Uta left Zea to sleep and the eight year old got some much needed rest.

Zea woke up when the sun was low in the sky. Uta was walking into her small room and had some water and white cloth. She opened the cage and dressed the young ones wounds. "I am sorry, Zeaytera KatOynera, but you need to get up and start on Jabo's meal. He will be home soon. I will do my best to help you but once Master comes home I will not be able to assist you," the Qotho said in a low voice.

Zea slowly stood up, her body began to ache once again with all her strength she walked into the small kitchen and began the last meal of the day. Uta did her best to help the slave. The female Qotho set the table and lifted the heavy pots. Once Jabo walked into the hut, Uta came to him with a hug and a small kiss. By the time the female left her mate Zea was kneeling in front of her master. Jabo looked at her with cold eyes. He walked past her and sat at his place on the table. Soon Zea stood and walked to the kitchen to finish her work. She served the two Qothos and stood at Jabo's side in silence. When they were done they walked into bedroom and left the slave to clean up their mess. Zea ate what she could but she did not feel well. She cleaned up the dishes and went to her room. There the little one made a small nest out of her passed father's chains and drifted into sleep.

Zea awoke to a sharp pain followed by hitting the near by wall. "You are to sleep in your cage. Nowhere else and you must ask me for your day to end. You do not get to decide," Jabo snapped after he kicked the sleeping one. Zea brought herself to her feet and asked for her master's forgiveness. She said she was sorry and apologized for not thinking and being selfish. Jabo grabbed his slave and chained her to the wall so she was hanging by her hands. "You like the chains so much; I will give them to you!" Jabo yelled as he stormed out of the room. Zea cried her self to sleep out of pain and the loss of her family.

In the morning Jabo came and unchained Zea who rubbed her hands as she followed Jabo out of the room. Zea went to the kitchen where once again she made Jabo his meal. When the meal was over and Jabo was gone Zea started on her chores. As she walked down to the well the other zatx saw the little ones new wounds and wanted to go help her but all they could do was watch and whisper to each other how young Zea was to have so many wounds on her body.

The days were long and painful for the little slave who now had nothing to look forward to at night. She had no one to hug, no one to help her, to love her, and comfort her. As her scars healed she was happy she did not have the pain in her back anymore. Jabo was now cold to his slave and would punish her if she made even a very small mistake. Uta wanted to help the little one but there was nothing she could do her loyalty was to her husband. At night Zea talked with her computer who continued to give her lessons and training exercises which her late brother used to give her. Her computer tried to comfort on the hard days and Zea was happy she had someone to talk too.

The little one did not sleep well her nightmares were more frequent but now she had no one to rock her to sleep. Her computer did the best it could to comfort the little one who woke up shaking and crying. She did not know what she would have done without her life long partner. Jabo loved to torture Zea he would wake her up by throwing ice-cold water on her. Zea soon became a very light sleeper and trained herself to wake up when she could here Jabo's footsteps coming into the room. Her master made her life hard and he enjoyed watching her struggle. Zea took the challenge and believed her computer when it told her, — What does not kill you makes you stronger. — Zea soon could see the Qothos did not like winter or water. She soon stopped talking to her master. She was whipped for her action but continued to be silent. She only spoke to her computer at night.

For Zea's tenth birthday she got a Collar and a beating. The whole night she said prayers up to her lost family and did her best to nurse her wounds. — Zeaytera KatOynera, what name do you want me to call you? — "I do not know computer, all my names have a different meaning, anything but my full name. It makes me think of Jabo. Kat reminds me of my mother and father and Zea reminds me of my brother"

— What ever you decide do not let Jabo make your name a bad thing, you should be pound of your name. —

"You are right computer; I think I would like you to call me Kat"

— Ok, Kat it is, never let Jabo win. You are getting older, we have to find a way of getting out of this camp. —

"We will find a way, I promised my family I would not let the Qothos win"

— We will think of a plan but right now you need sleep —

"Ok, good night computer"

— Good night Kat —

In the morning Zea woke up, Jabo came in and the slave started her chores for the day. As she looked out the small window in the kitchen she could tell winter was coming. She knew that would be the best time to escape but how. Jabo walked in and sat at the table. Seeing this Zea quickly finished his meal and served it to him. "Your cooking is better than your mothers," Jabo stated his first meal of the day. "Thank you Master Jabo for your kind words," Zea answered back to the Qotho. When Jabo was done Zea started on Uta's meal. When she was just setting the food on the table the other female walked into the room form where she was sleeping. "Good morning, Zeaytera KatOynera, did you sleep well," Uta asked. There was no reply from Zea who just looked at the floor while her second master ate. "You never talk anymore, Zeaytera KatOynera, what has happened to you? I know you are not in the happiest place but I have done my best to make Jabo go easy on you and I have tried to help you over the years, I am a friend," Uta expressed to her slave. There was still no answer and Uta looked down in disappointment. When she was done eating, Uta left her slave to do the chores of the house.

Today as Kat did her chores she did her best to speak to all the older zatxs she saw as she walked down to the well. Many of her kind could not talk. The little one tried to find out if any knew any more weakness the Qothos had during the winters that might aid her in the escape. She did not find out much. The only real information she obtained was the collars could be taken off by one of the red ray guns the Qothos owned. As the weeks went by she got an idea who was around her in the camp. She also found out she was the youngest zatx left alive and she was one of the last guardians still standing. Also as she socialized with her fellow zatx she met friends and was happy to have someone to talk to even if it was for a short time.

At night Kat always wondered what it was be like to use her computer freely with no brace. She knew she was again different because she had never heard of a guardian with a multi-color computer. — I wonder what it well be like to see you up and running for the first time and be able to see our full capability — Kat expressed to her computer. — I cannot wait to be free. I want to be able to scan the area or help you get out of this hellhole. We well do it some day soon. Do not worry. — The computer stated back to Kat. — I wish to do it this winter. I do not know if I can take another year of this enslavement —

— You are strong and still young. You can do so much. We will fight till we die —

— You are right computer. I guess I am going to sleep see you in the morning —

— Good night, sweet dreams. —

As winter came and the days grew shorter and shorter Kat had the same workload. She knew that most days Jabo woke up in a bad mood because he did not like the wintertime. If there was snow on the ground he was even more irritable. Kat did not want to add to the artwork of scars on her back and wing so she did her best to do everything perfect in the wintertime. As winter rolled on snow soon fell on the ground and Kat loved the snow. She enjoyed to play and the feel of the compacted snowflakes under her feet. She thought everything looked so beautiful covered in a sparkling white blanket.

One day while Kat was getting water out of the well her arm fell in to one of buckets she was trying to fill. The slave ran home with the water in hand and once inside she started to dry off her cold wet hand. As she continued with her chores she could hear water inside her brace move around from one end to the other. — Computer do you have any water inside you? — Kat asked. — No, I am still dry. Why do you ask little one —

— I think I might have an idea about finally getting out of this camp. I will run it by you tonight —

— That is fine by me —

Uta walked into the room with a smile. "Did you have a good day little one?" adult female asked. "Yes, I did. Thank you master, Uta" Kat answered. Uta stopped in her tracks and looked at the slave. "You talked to me. That is a change what makes today different from the days before?" Uta voiced. "I am in a good mood, I like the winter and I guess I was being rude to you before. After reflecting I realize you have always tried to make my life better," Kat told her master. "Oh. Well, I am glad you are in a good mood," Uta stated and walked out of the room. Kat finished her house chores and moved on to making Jabo and Uta's last meal of the day. When Jabo walked into his home it was obvious he was not happy. Kat stopped smiling knowing this action would make him upset. He sat down and his slave started to serve him without hesitation. Uta walked up to him to show him her affection and he shook her away. She bowed her head and took her place at the table. Kat made sure to do everything perfect that night. Once Jabo locked her up for the evening. Kat told her plan to her computer who was delighted and told her that it would most probably work. Kat was excited and could not wait to try out her plan. Her computer told her the dangers and how to prevent them. Her computer also told her how smart it was to come up with such a great plan. Kat thanked her friend and they went to sleep.

It snowed all night and when the sun tried to kiss the white land the clouds blocked the warm rays. Jabo was not happy about this and awoke in a bad mood. He went to wake up his slave but once he opened the door she was already awake. The little slave was pacing her small cage trying to keep warm. He opened her pen and Kat went quickly into the kitchen where she began to make the first meal of the day. Jabo wolfed down his meal and chugged his warm drink. Once finished he slammed his cup on the wood and Kat instantly cleared the table and asked her master if there was anything she could do for him. He looked at her coldly and told her not to talk unless asked too. She bowed her head in silence. She went to the kitchen where she washed the dishes and out of the corner of her eye spotted Uta coming into the main room. By the time she sat down Kat already had her meal on the table. She stood waiting for Uta to finish her food. As Uta ate Jabo looked at her with out blinking. His black, cold, and beady eyes never moved just looked off into the distance. Uta was being very quite too. This made Kat extremely nervous. Soon with out waning Jabo stood up and knock over the table. The chairs, plates and food fell to floor. With out thinking Kat garb a cloth and began to clean the mess her master made. Keeping her eye on her master and making sure her back was never to him she bent down and began to clean but before she could really get started Uta's voice cut through the air, "Kat leave us, go to the back yard and sit there till one of us calls you, do not talk just sit there."

"No, clean," Jabo yelled. Kat knew to mind Jabo she did not want to get whipped again. "I said leave! Now!" Uta shouted out into the air. Kat looked at Jabo who nodded his head slightly and did not look content. Kat ran to the kitchen where she dumped what little food she had in a bucket of water. She dunked her arm into the water. Whiling running out of the hut she gapped a towel. Once outside Kat rapidly and carefully wrapped her hand in the towel and placed her arm deep into the snow.

After a while her arm became very cold and she could feel her limb start to tingle. — Are you ok? — her computer asked softly. — I am ok. I can do this — Kat answered back strongly. — I am a guardian like my father, I have the strength of my mother and brother — while expressing this she raised her free hand griping the heart shaped charm. An hour went by and Kat soon could not feel her arm and she did not have a lot of clothes on her small and skinny frame. Wrapping her wings around her body she did her best to stay warm. Soon she began to shake and her arm went from no pain to intense aching. Time went on but the little one refused to move her arm. Right when Kat thought she was going to pass out of pain she heard little popping noise. With all her might she pulled out her arm. With a very large smile she looked at her arm and realized her plan had worked. When she put her arm in the bucket of water inside the hut to drop off the food the brace which was trapping her computer got water inside of it. When the water froze because of cold it expanded forcing the brace to move and brake. She ripped off the brace and for the first time her computer was free. Her senses were over whelmed. She now could get a lay out of the camp, see how many zatxs were in the camp and where, which one of the zatxs were guardians and where all the Qothos were. She almost fainted.

— Computer —

— Yes, Kat—

— Well you make a hologram of the brace so no knows it is off my arm—

— yes, I will but remember if any touches it they well find out very quickly it is a hologram. —

—Ok, thank computer how do you feel?—

— I feel so free. We have to talk tonight—

— Ok computer. I still have to get use to you. Now, that you are working. Wow. I need to sit down on the ground. —

With a smile Kat sat down on the towel that was once on her arm and waited for Jabo or Uta to tell her it was acceptable for her to come back inside the hut. She sat quite in the back yard letting her computer check all her systems for the first time in years.

As the sun was getting lower in the sky Kat started to pace in the back yard. She waited and waited. Soon the sun was setting. The slave soon jogged in a circle as the air became cooler and dusk turned into night. For the first time in her life she got a good look at the stars. She stopped moving and just stared at the awe-inspiring sight of the night sky. The beauty, wonder and memories of what her brother said brought tears to her eyes. Looking at the dark blue blanket sprinkled with sparkling dust she said a prayer to her lost family and asked them to watch over her and showed the sky her arm now free. She could not keep her eyes off the sky.

Hearing the sound of footsteps her ears turned toward the noise. Recognizing the footfalls she slowly took her eyes off the dazzling sky and looked at her master walking towards her. She fell to her knees and bowed her head when he reached her. "What were you looking at slave?" he asked. "I was looking at the sky, Master Jabo. I have never seen the stars until now," the little one told Jabo softy. The overlord looked at the one kneeling in front of him and then gazed up at the night sky. "Never?" Jabo asked. "In my room there are no windows and you told me to always stay in the house once you come home. You always come home at sunset," Kat told her master. As Kat observed at Jabo she could tell something was different, but she could not tell what it was. He was acting different. Jabo took in a deep breath and released it slowly in the air where he could see it. Then he realized how cold he was and his feet were beginning to hurt. "Come on, lets go back inside," Jabo said as he turned towards the house. Kat took one more at the sky and led the way into the hut. She opened her wings to stretch them as she walked and for the first time in a long spell Jabo saw the art her created on her back. The majority of the area was covered in scars. He did not like to look at them. Once inside the hut Uta had made them both some hot soup. "You were out there for a long time what were you doing?" Uta inquired as she set the table. "Looking at the stars," Jabo answered. After Kat was done eating Jabo took her cage to sleep.

Once Jabo was gone and asleep with his wife in his warm bed, Kat felt it was safe for her to talk to her computer. She slipped out of her cage and stood in an open space in the small room. — Kat, I have been doing some research after looking at the history of our kind and what I am capable of doing we are very different.— "How so computer?" Kat whispered. — Well, to start we know your physical differences. We have your gills, eyes, physique, wings, the way you can go from a two legged to a four legged guardian and now me. I am different from other guardian's computers. First I am more high tech. As you can see I am multi colored. In the history of our kind we are the only one born with a multi colored computer. Not only do I have better systems but I also have weapons. You know the red rays Jabo has?— "Yes, I have them?" Kat quietly asked. — Yes. Your weapons are, red rays, throw nets, darts, and a sound wave. The sound wave creates a sound, which hurts the foe's ears. I am not fully sure if it will work on the Qothos but we can play with the pitch and see what we can do. — Kat stood there for a few minutes thinking about what her computer just told her. "I wish to see," Kat finally spoke. — Which one would you like to see first? — "I can I see the ray first?" Kat asked softy. Kat raised her arm and felt her computer shift as the top open and out came a long slender circler shape. There was an opening pointing out and away from her. The ray gun was a bright gold and black color. — You can control the power of ray, which comes out of the gun. Just tell what power level you want. If you do not give me a number I will use my best judgment if we are short on time. Just like your sound wave you have ten levels. With your two major guns: power one, being just stinging or an annoyance to ten, being able to cut through bone or making one deaf. The tenth level is capable of killing. — Wow, computer. I will have to come up with a new plan of escaping. May I please see my net thrower now?-- Kat enquired her computer.

Kat once again felt her computer shift and she watched as the ray gun lowered back into her computer. Taking the ray guns place was large cylinder looking thing that was black and blue. — You can shoot up to twenty feet away or two feet away from where you stand. I have targeting gear, which well help you attack. — "Next may I see my darts and what I will use to shoot them?" Kat asked. A black and green small cylinder took the place of the large one and under the gun Kat could see a row of little darts with clear middles. She could see the different colored insides. — I can load them for you or you can do it. The different colors show how strong the drug is. You again have different levels. From sleep for five minutes to knockout for a few hours and last the ability to kill. I will go more into the power of to darts later. Because the metal tips you can shoot the Qothos. — "Last computer may I please see my sound wave?"

— Sure—

Kat again watched her weapons change with new eyes. This last weapon was black and same shape of all the weapons. Coming out of the medium sized cylinder was a cone looking shape. "Wow, I cannot believe all this I feel like I am in a dream," Kat spoke. — I have already told you about the power levels of this one now you need sleep time to go to bed.— "Alright," Kat said as she start to walk back to her cage. As she ambled and got into her cage her computer brought her weapon back inside her metal casing and told her about firing the weapons. — When you use your artilleries you use up energy. If you fire at power ten you well become weak once you stop firing. I will warn you about your energy level as it lowers. Also as I have been looking at your difference you heal faster than normal. I think it is because of our weapons system. But if you were wounded with focus you could heal faster. But again it depends on your energy level. If you healed a cut and then used almost all of your energy on your weapons then your cuts could come back and reopen. I am not sure if you can heal others but I will continue looking into my systems and learn what we are capable of doing. — The computer informed her friend. The two talked for a little while and then Kat fell fast asleep.

In the morning Kat woke up like she always did a few seconds before Jabo came into her small room. She went to the kitchen and started her same routine as always. After Uta and Jabo were gone Kat was so happy. She let her wings out and started to get ready to go down to the well. She wanted to tell everyone she was free and how to get rid of the braces. As she walked to the well she kept her eyes open for a guardian. On her way back she saw one who was also walking to the well. As she passed the guardian she faked to trip letting go of the two buckets of water she was carrying and had to head back to the well to refill them. As she reached into the dark tunnel with the other guardian to get more water Kat removed the hologram from her computer. The other guardian's eyes lit up and look at Kat who nodded. "How?" the guardian whispered. "I put water in the brace and let the water freeze. The water expanded and broke the brace," Kat whispered back. The guardian smiled and nodded her head. "I will spread the word little one," the guardian told Kat while she patted her on the head. Kat was overjoyed she had started the beginning of the end.

Escape

The word spread like wild fire that a guardian had escaped from the braces and how the guardian broke free. All the zatx were very quiet about it so the Qothos would not find out what was going happen in the next few days. The zatx as a whole were happy and rekindled with hope. The plan was each zatx would take down his or her master. Get their red ray gun and shoot off their collar. Kat could not wait.

As the night came close she wondered if she would be able to take down her master. She was only ten years of age and not very big yet and Jabo was a good size strong male. Kat and her computer talked about their own plan. Kat would first shoot off her own collar then shoot a net to pin down Uta. Next she would shoot Jabo so he would not die but not be able to fight her or recapture her. She did not want to kill anyone. She did not think it was right and it was part of the guardian code. Killing was only done if there was no way out of any situation. They both thought this was the best plan of action.

The next day as Kat went to the well everyone was smiling at her and showed her small signs of respect. This made her joyful. The same guardian she showed her arm to earlier that came to the well was ther once more. When they reached in to get water Kat could see her computer was free. The two computers shared information and as Kat walked back to the hut her computer told her they were planning the attack a half an hour after sundown. Kat's life long friend could tell when a computer came back online and would tell Kat each time one was freed. When Jabo came home that night he looked very happy. Uta was with him and she had something in her arms. A chill ran down Kat's spine as she saw what Uta had in her arms.

Wrapped in a white cloth was a baby Qotho. The little one was a male and looked like a strong and health infant. — Does this change our plan? — Kat asked her computer. — I am not sure. I guess it depends on where the young one sleeps. Hopefully with the mother you can net them both in one shot. I am worried most about Jabo. He will be more dangerous with a young one in the house, — the computer replied to Kat. Kat's eyes were big and full of fear as she looked at the new one. "His name is Darco, (venom)" Uta said softly and lowered her body so the slave could see. Jabo shifted his weight and look nervous. Kat stood on her tiptoes and looked into the white cloth. The young Qotho was sleeping and was a pale green. Darco was so small, helpless and innocent. Knowing the fight was going to happen that night made Kat very uneasy. Sensing Jabo was not relaxed Kat backed away from the new mother and into the kitchen to finish this last meal of the day.

When she came into the main room and walk to the table she gave Jabo his last meal of the day then Uta. After the main meal and drinks were severed, Kat gave Uta some warm milk and some clean towels. When the sun was just going down Kat was locked in her cage. Start a ten-minute timer Kat told her computer and also asked if her red ray gun could be activated. Once her gun was powered up Kat very carefully cut and collar and for the first time in her life, the slave was fully free of from the Qothos. All she had to do now was escape.

When ten minutes had passed Kat heard a large crash and yelling from outside the hut. Kat heard Jabo get up out of bed and start to come into the room. The young guardian stayed in the caged looking just as surprised to hear the fight noises coming from the camp. He locked the door and she could hear him tell Uta it would be ok as he ran out the door. Once Jabo was gone Kat slipped out of her cage and shot through the door. Uta was in the main room rocking Darco. Kat pointed her gun at Uta whose face turned pale. "Zeaytera KatOynera, what are you doing?" Uta questioned the little one. "I learned how to get the brace off my computer and taught all the guardians how to do the same. They pick a time to attack and this is it. I really do not want to kill or hurt you. I have a red ray and I will use it if I have to I am a little jumpy right now," as Kat stated this as she fired her gun at a spot on the wall to show her master she was not joking. "Now, All I ask is you go into the small room and let me chain you by the foot. I really just want to leave not hurt your family," Kat strongly voiced to the female and her young. Uta agreed and thanked Kat for being merciful. Uta led the way to the small room where the master let the slave chain her.

After Uta was in irons Kat went to the Kitchen where she got towels and some water. She gave the items to Uta who thanked her. Kat then walked out of the room and exited the house.

The now free slave ran from the hut and into chaos trying to help anyone who needed it while looking for a good way to get out of camp. As she ran she could see dead bodies of both races on the floor she saw some zatx who were not guardians fighting to get their collars off there necks. Kat went around and carefully removed the braces from her peer's necks who thanked her before joining in the fight.

As Kat was running through the camp, she looked behind her and ran right into one to the Qothos. Looking up she saw a large male Qotho wearing white and had a scar over his eye. The leader of the Qothos quickly picked up the little one by the neck until they were eye to eye. "Do I know you?" asked the Qotho. "I do not know?" Kat answered while struggling to get out of her captures hands. "Oh, yes, I remember you now. You are Domatu's little one. My, how you have grown, young slave. I have heard some crazy stories. You would not happen to know how this got started would you?" the Qotho inquired. "And if I tell you will you let me go?" Kat questioned back to the leader. "I suggest you just tell me, now," yelled Moojigo. "I started it," the little guardian roared. Moojigo's face turned into a puzzled looked as he asked Kat how she could start such a large battle. "LIKE THIS," Kat yelled as she raised her arm. Then in her native tongue she said red ray and her computer brought up her gun. "Power five," Kat continued. With that command the computer fired and the leader with a very surprised looked was knocked down to the ground. Kat was released.

Landing on her feet she aimed her gun at Moojigo. He slowly got up looking at the little one. "How is that possible how can you have a red gun?" he pondered. Kat said nothing only looked at him. — Kat behind you! — her computer warned her friend. Kat jumped into the air doing a backward flip as Jabo rushed to his father. Checking his father making sure he was not hurt to badly Jabo turned his full attention to the little guardian. Kat was shaking seeing the anger in her master's eyes. "First you attack my wife and child then you go after my father. What were you planning next my friends or me? Come back to the hut now and I will not give you as big as a whipping," Jabo shouted to Kat. "I will not be a slave again your rein over me is through," Kat exclaimed. Jabo jumped on Kat who was now pinned to the ground. "I am going to enjoy whipping you just like I enjoyed watching each one of your family members slow and painfully die," Jabo hissed with a smile.

For the first time Jabo saw Kat's eyelids fall into place. First her eyes turned white then red, next green and last black. "Sound gun, power ten," Kat yelled in her native tongue and without hesitation. Jabo fell backwards holding his ears. Kat stood and asked her computer for her red ray gun and to put it on power ten. She then proceed to slowly cut up Jabo from his toes to his head. He cried out in pain as she made the first cut, which was his toes and next were his feet. Hearing his son cry out Moojigo rose to his feet and ran at the attacker. Before he could get very far Kat turned to him and took off his head with her gun.

Jabo screamed in anger and pain watching his father fall. Kat heard footsteps behind her and without think she turned and fired. Now falling to the ground was Uta and the baby. Uta was cut in two and the young one now screaming in pain like his father. He hit the ground and rolled to his only remaining family member who with tears in his eyes picked up his now legless son. Kat continued to fight any Qotho who came near her she would kill without mercy. She lost all control, with her black eyelids her vision changed, which allowed her to see her enemies in a different light so she would only kill the Qothos and not her kind.. She also had an easier time judging distance and so much more.

After sometime passed she walked over to where Jabo was lying on the ground and he was crying. Now holding his dead son who died of blood loss and he was almost gone too. He looked at his slave with cold fading eyes and could not believe it was not a mighty warrior like Domatu to kill him but a child. Jabo now almost completely deaf yelled to Kat, "You are less compassionate than I ever was." Without thinking Kat cut Jabo again with her red ray causing him to cry out one last time. — Kat you need to find a place to hide your energy is almost gone. You need rest. — Kat computer stated. The young warrior did not listen; she was in her own world. She continued to kill Qothos until she finally clasped.

Kat woke up about mid-day. She was under a tree by a river. Her head pounded and she could not really remember what happen last night. As her eyes adjusted to the sunlight a shadow blocked the blinding light. She tried to get up but was sore and her body aced. "Are you all right, little one you have been sleeping for a long time?" the shadow asked. "I am ok. Where am I? What happen last night?" She questioned the voice. "You are by the Giko (water drop) forest which is runs into the Lolly (mystery) meadow which is cut buy the Yatuka (dark color) river. Last night we escaped from the Qothos," the voice answered.

"Are there any Qothos left?"

"Yes, but they are trying to regroup we have some time before they attack us. If they want to challenge us again let them come. Some one killed their leader last night."

"Did all of are kind escape from the Qothos?"

"Yes, we are all that is left the rest of our kind is dead. My you are so young and full or questions."

"I am sorry, my name Zeaytera KatOynera daughter of Domatu and Sunyro and sister to Gyro. I started the escape I was first to get the brace off my computer. Last night I lost control of myself. I cannot remember what I did but it is slowly coming back to me. I should remember everything in a few minutes."

"Wow, you have been very busy little one. Do you know who killed their leader Moojigo?"

"What did he look like and why?"

"You see little one, who ever killed him gets to lead what little group of us is left. Let's see, he always wore white and had a scar over his eye."

"Oh, I see, well I killed him. His son was my master and he was trying to protect his son, Jabo, when I killed him. But I cannot lead our group. I am too young and still have too much to learn. May I ask who you are I have been talking to you for a while now?"

"My name is Kazti (stalker). I am one of a few guardians still alive. You sit here and rest and when you feel ready you can come join us by the river. We have some food and water for you. See you soon."

Kazti walked away leaving Kat with her thoughts and computer. "What happened last night Computer?" Kat asked out loud. "You did not listen to me. That is what happened. You lost control. I am glad you are alright." the computer voiced. "Woe, I have never your voice outside of my head. I like it. Sorry, I lost control. Will you show me what I did last night?" Kat asked. "Sure," the computer replied. The computer made a screen in front of her friend like movie played what Kat did last night. As the little one watched her actions tears came to her eyes. She was saddened at the sight of seeing herself killing so many with no compassion. Kat was also troubled at the slight of innocent ones dying. Jabo's last words repeated in her mind as she said out loud, "What have I done?" "It is ok, Kat, You were not the only one killing last night and if you were captured again they would have killed you or made you a slave. You were fighting for your life."

"Thank you, computer but that dose not excuses what I did. I have broken the code and disgraced my family." As the computer closed the screen Kat tried to get up from her resting place. Slowly she stood and started to walk over to the water.

When She joined the group she realized she was the only female there. She was the youngest by at least ten years. The female guardian felt uneasy all of the males by the river who welcomed her and gave her some water and a type of soup. They were planning another attack while the Qothos were still weak. Kat asked to group if that was the guardian way. They just looked at her and told her to leave the planning to the men. This made Kat mad but could not do much so she went back to the tree where she was before and rested while talking to her computer.

When night came the group of warriors planned to attack the Qothos. Kat did not want to go back to the camp. She was happy to be free and never wanted to see, smell or hear a Qotho ever again. The leader of the small group of zatx name was Lye (light ray). He was a strong, about twenty-five years old and had a dark brown coat with yellow eyes. He was a true guardian. He told the small band they would attack at dusk because they had better night vision than the Qothos. He ordered Kat to stay behind and protect the campsite they set up the night of the escape. Kat was not happy about staying behind by herself but did it anyway because Lye was now her new leader. As the clan left with the setting sun Kat wished them luck and a safe return.

Kat began to clean up camp and went to the near by forest where she gathered some berries and caught ten birds for the group to eat when they came back to camp. She prepared and began to cook the food. She also made beds for her new friends. When the night was half way over the small group of fighters came home. They were happy they had food and a place to lie down and rest. They were in high sprits not only did they attack and win they also found the last living zatx who were still in captivity. They thanked Kat for the good food and nice beds. Kat also brought water to everyone who needed it.

When everyone was done Lye came in front of the fire and told them they were going to attack again at dawn because no one will expect it and that way there would be less Qothos in the world. Again Kat was not happy about this. To her killing was wrong and they should just leave. She was still a little guardian and had much to learn she was uneasy about her actions the night of the escape. Her computer continued to try to help and calm the little female but she would not let the fact that she killed so many innocent ones go away. When the Warriors left for a second time Kat again stayed behind and helped the ones who had wounds. As the sun kissed the land Kat looked at the world in a new light with new eyes. She was so happy to be free and could not believe the day had finally come. She was free no more cages, chains, whips, and chores. When morning was coming to an end the band came back from their fight to rest. As they ate and slept, Kat did the same. She was unrestricted and was blissful to feel the warm sun on her face.

Lye went around to everyone getting their name and rank. He wanted to know who was left and what they could do. When he came to sleeping female he gently rubbed her arm and she awoke. "How are you?" the leader asked. "I am doing well, it feels good not to sleep in a cage," answered the little one. "I need to know your name and rank," Lye stated to Kat. Who answered back, "My name is Zeaytera KatOynera. I am a true guardian and I am not sure what my rank is."

"Let's see your Computer," Lye expressed. Kat slowly raised her arm showing her multi-colored computer. The new leader looked puzzled at the little one's arm. "Why do you have a muti-colored computer?" Lye enquired. "I do not know I was born with it," Kat responded. Lye turned his head and called out, "Boomati (Black owl)!" The oldest of the group walked over to where the leader and the female were sitting. Boomati looked at Kat's computer and told the other two a few zatx were born with computers during the time of the enslavement but none were known to live. Kat must have been the only one to survive the Qothos. Boomati went on about he heard the multi-colored computers were very hi-tech and could not be compared to anything in the history of their kind. He had always thought they were silly myth. He added that he had always wanted to see one and felt honored to be able to see one. "May I look inside your computer?" Boomati asked Kat. — Computer is this all right with you? — Kat mentally inquired to her computer. — Yes, Kat but be careful— the computer responded. "Yes you may," Kat stated to Boomati as she opened her computer for him to see. His eyes grew at the sight of her computer. Out of the corner of her I, Kat could see Lye's mouth drop. After Boomati looked over the computer he said his goodbyes and walked back over to the main group by the river. That night Kat climbed a near by tree to sleep in she still needed her space from all the males.

In the morning Kat awoke to Lye calling her name. She quickly climbed down the tree and walked over to where the leader was standing. "Would you go out and collect so food for us again like you did yesterday?" Lye asked nicely. "Sure," Kat pronounced as she turned and started to walk into the woods. While in the woods she again caught a few birds and fish and while walking she picked different types of berries. As morning turned into mid-day Kat headed back for camp. When she was all most to her stopping point she could hear the zatos talking. She hid in the bushes so she could hear what they were saying.

"We need to take out the rest of the Qothos but once we have done this we need to think of how we as a race are going to continue to live."

"This is true, Boomati but as you can see we are all male."

"You are forgetting about Zeaytera KatOynera, Lye."

"She is only ten; she could not carry so many little one, Boomati."

"The genes could only go so far."

"There are many of us males and if we plan it right we can make it work, but we need to plan it very carefully."

"She will be back at any time now so we will finish this later."

The group broke up and Kat sat there and tried to think of what the males were talking about. She did not fully understand what was meant about her carrying a lot of little ones. She asked her computer who told her she was not old enough or ready for that lesson in life. Disappointed, Kat backtracked and walked back into camp. Once there everyone looked at her funny. She felt out of place with all the males.

Over the next few weeks Kat got use to living with all the zatos. She met and knew almost them all by name. She went from a village of over 500 to a group of 32 zatos. She felt like part of the group and the zatos taught her different skills about living off the land that she did not learn while in captivity with the Qothos. At night they shared stories about the time before the Qothos and during. Kat always felt different when the others would talk about her father. She remembered how she took him away from her family. Many nights after the stories Kat would cry herself to sleep thinking if she had made the right choice she would still have a family and not just a piece of metal. She never took the heart off her neck. She cleaned it and made a strong metal chain with the elements and her red ray. One day while she was by the Tika (sand) river she drew pictures in the sand. Playing around she shot the sand with her red ray and looking at what she made her eyes grew. The end product was smooth and clean, "what is this computer?" Kat asked. "I am sure it might be gape (glass). This is made when sand melts together. Gape was first found when some zatx built a fire over wet sand. I think that is what you just made," the computer told the young one. "Oh, thank you computer," Kat stated. She played with the gape then headed back to camp. The others around her were also starting to see her difference. Kat did not like being different. She wished she was like the others.

One Day as she was again walking back to camp she heard the others again talking about her and little ones. She also did not like being left out because she was young or a zatz. One clear night Kat looked up at the sky. Seeing the diamonds sprinkled over the navy blue blanket and she realized there was no moon that night. Walking to a field the little guardian laid down on her back looking up at the never ending sky. "Hi, father, can you hear me? Mother, Gyro? I miss you guys so much. I hope you saw me escape but I hope you are not mad at me for what I did. I am sorry. I never meant for any of this to happen. I do now know what is going in camp but, I know you are watching over me, right? I am so sorry for splitting the family up but now you guys are together. I will make you proud of me again I promise," Kat voice to the night air as she began to cry. "I will be a strong fighter and a true guardian. You will see. I will not let our kind die. We will win," Kat stated in a clear and strong voice to the night sky as she held the heart in her hand. Kat wiped the tears from her eyes while saying a prayer to her lost loved ones and the warm wind kissed her cheek. Kat got back to her tree where she climbed and went to bed.

In the morning everything went as normal. Everyone seemed to be in good sprits. There were not many Qothos left and the small group attacked their enemies less. The season was changing and spring was on the way. Kat could not wait to be able to run through the fields free. One night as see was lying in the field she heard footsteps. She crouched down in the long grass waiting to attack any threat when she heard a soft low voice, "Zeaytera KatOynera, are you there?" "I am here in the long grass. Who is there?" Kat whispered. "Hi, I need you to do me a favor. We are playing a night game and I am going to help you. Do you have anything back at camp that you care about?" the voice asked. "No, everything I need is with me right now, what is the name of this game?" Kat enquired. "The name of the game is KurooPatti (night tag/run)," the voice answered. "Take my hand. The game has already started," the voice continued. "I love games!" Kat joyful told the voice as they ran off into the night.

Part II: The Journey

The Crusade

Kat and the zato ran all night and at the edge of the forest they met up with another zatx. He continued with them running during until dawn was turning into morning. They ran in silence till finally Kat asked them a question. "We have been running all night; if we are going to get back to camp should we not start heading back? And is the game over because the sun is now rising?" Kat questioned the zatos. The one who seemed to be leading them stopped running and turned to Kat. He got down on one knee and placed his hand on her shoulder. As he looked into the little one's deep green eyes he softly said, "Zeaytera KatOynera, we are not going back to the camp. You will never see those zatos again." The small one looked up in disbelief and asked, "Why?"

"I knew your father before he passed and I promised him I would watch over his family if anything ever happen to him and you are his family. The other zatos did not have your health in their mind. When you are older then I will explain to you why."

"No, why? I am sick of not knowing what you guys are talking about. What did Lye and Boomati mean when they said I would have to carry little ones?"

The zato eyes widen as he spoke, "How did you now about that?" "I have good ears and I like to hide in bushes, and my computer will not tell me what you guys were talking about because I am too young," Kat told him as she looked at the earth. "Well, you are a female and the rest of the group was male. They wanted to make little ones so our kind could continue living."

"So I am our spices only hope?"

"Yes, but you could not do what they were going to ask of you. You would die."

"But would I be able to save our kind?"

"Yes, but I could not let you become unhappy and unhealthy when your action would not truly save our kind. You see our gene pool would still be very weak."

"But our kind will die if I do not go back, we have to go back. Right now. I promised my father I would not let the Qothos win. I cannot let our kind die."

"Little one, you must understand once the Qothos took us in captivity our kind was dead. Once all of our little ones died we lost, but you of course, we skipped to many generations. To beat the Qothos we had to escape and live a happy life without chains. You have already fulfilled that promise and now it is my turn to fulfill agreement to your father."

"I do not even know who you are!"

"I am sorry; I should have told you a long ago. My name is Hutto and this is my good friend Zutiyro (brave one)."

"Hi, I am pleased to meet you." (Zutiyro)

"This does not feel right. I think we should go back. I do want to let my father down and fail him. I have already dishonored him once. I will not do it again. We have to go back to camp right now."

"Kat, listen to me. You were not safe there in the camp, I am doing what your father asked me to which is to protect you. You will not fail your father by leaving the camp. Our kind is dead. There is still hope for you. You are young and still have a lot of fight in you. If we travel over the mountains there is a small chance there is life over there. Then we can live a full life and not slowly die here in this valley of death. Please believe me when I tell you if you go back you will die but if we go on you have a chance to live and that is what your father wants you to do. Live a full happy life."

"Hutto, may I think for a minute?"

"Sure little one."

— Computer did Hutto really work with my father? —

— According to my files Hutto was your fathers second in command and a very trusted friend. —

— Thank you computer. —

— Anytime Kat —

"Ok, I will go with you two guys. I will trust you."

"Thank little one, shall we go on," Hutto said as he start the walk in the direction of the mountains. The three walked in silence for a long time. Then Kat asked Hutto to tell her some of the stories of her father. Hutto acquired a large smile on his face and he began to share his favorite memories of his lost friend. Every now and then Zutiyro would share a story as well. Kat loved to here about her family and the times before the Qothos came to the peaceful village. Kat asked her two new friends' questions and told them what she could remember growing up with the powerful warrior.

When Kat's legs were tired one of the zatos carried her. About half way through the day Hutto remember Kat had wings. He asked her why she did not fly and this would save the two guardians the trouble of carrying her. Kat told them no had ever taught her how to fully use her wings. "Well I will have to teach you," Zutiyro stated to the little one. Kat got a huge smile on her face. She could not wait to learn how to use her wings. "Tomorrow I will give you your first lesson," Zutiyro voiced to Kat. "Why not now?" Kat questioned. "The sun is going to set soon and we need to find a good place to spend the night," Zutiyro told Kat. The three walked for a few more minutes till Hutto found a suitable place to sleep. He told Kat because they were in a land they did not know to stay close and to be ready for anything. Kat went to go collect firewood as the two zatos made camp for the Nox (night). When Kat returned the camp was set up and the zatos were ready to cook dinner.

As Kat watched the two guardians cook their food she noticed Hutto reminded her of Gyro but older he looked like he would be the same age her father would have been if he was still with her. They had the same body shape. Hutto was a little bigger properly because he was older. His reddish fur and golden eyes were opposites of each other. Like Gyro Hutto also had a long and black stripe down his body starting from the top of his head to the tip the tail. Sprouting form the long solid stripe were small perpendicular stripes and he had some random spots, which were also black. Zutiyro was true guardian. He had a blue computer and was not as old as Hutto but close. He had thick, soft and white fur with big and small black dots, which covered his body. He also had black rings on his long tail. Zutiyro had dark brown eye with a tint of yellow.

"Little one, little one, where did you go?" Zutiyro asked. "What do you mean?" Kat inquired. "You were day dreaming and I was wondering where you were," the guardian answered. "Oh, I was thinking about what my brother looked like compared to you and Hutto," Kat replied. "I have a question," Hutto joined into the conversation. "What?" both Kat and Zutiyro voiced. "Little one, what should we call you. Your father called you Kat but your brother called you Zea and others called you Zeaytera KatOynera. I do not know what name you prefer," Hutto stated with a smile. Kat laughed. "You may call me what ever you wish. Many called my little one and others called me forms of my name. I do not really care," Kat said to the males. The two warriors looked at each other each with a smile. After talking for a while the two leaders came up with an answer as Kat laughed in the background. They decide to call the little one Z. K. or what ever they felt like at the time. Kat just laughed and agreed with her friends. After they had there fun they went to sleep and rested for the next days travel.

The next morning Kat awoke with the sun. She could not wait for the day to start because today she would really learn how to fly. After everyone was up and had some food. The small group packed up camp and left. As Hutto walked on the ground Zutiyro picked up Kat by the shoulder and flew up into the sky. He taught her how to fly. First she opened her wings so she could feel the wind. The older guardian lifted her high into the air and would release his grip. After some falling and instruction Kat flew for the first time without any help. When they stopped of the second meal of the day Kat thanked Zutiyro many times. He told her once she could fly on her own He would teach her take off and landing and last how to do aerial moves. Kat was so excited she could not wait. By the end of the day Kat could fly on her own and take off from a tree or a high point. She still had to build up her muscles. She did not tell her travel partners but she went to be very sore.

The three had lots of fun while they traveled. If one of the two zatos were not giving Kat a lesson on living off the land, history and or over the code of a guardian they were playing games or just talking about nothing. Kat soon looked at her companions as a father, Hutto, and an old brother, Zutiyro. Kat got in some trouble as the small band moved on their crusade for a new home. They found new animals and plants. The warriors had to fight the weather and nature obstacles in their way. Kat could not always keep up with the zatos who had to carry her every now then. The little one became stronger everyday was able to walk and fly a little farther. Hutto and Zutiyro were very proud of her and each other for teaching her. They met Kat's computer and over time Kat showed her differences to the two guardians. The males always looked at each other and both their eyes got very big when Kat showed them, on different occasions, her wings, eyelids, computer, and the way she could change forms.

The two males could not believe how different Kat was. Kat found she was able to walk father without getting as tiered if she was in her four legged form and so once her friends were use to her looking different she mainly walked in her four legged form and Zutiyro help her be able to fly in both forms and with lots of practice be able to change while in the air. Most of the time the female would take off while running on four legs because she could gain more speed. Then once in the air could quickly change into her other from. Zutiyro told her soon she would just need to jump and flex her wings to leave the ground. They would have to work together to develop her muscles.

The two zatos were astonished and felt a little strange when they found out the little one could read their minds. Kat promised she would never read anyone's mind without asking their permission. She told them it was wrong to invade ones mind without asking not only was it rude but it was also morally wrong. The two males believed their friend and would play some games with her so they could see what she was capable of doing. Kat found out she could still read Zutiyro mind even after he flew over a mile up and away from where she was walking with Hutto. Kat also found out she could put pictures in another's mind. And when Zutiyro was sleeping she made him have a dream she was thinking about. The dream was a good but Kat was afraid to tell her companions she was able to play with their subconscious. The two zatos noticed that Kat had bad dreams a few times a week. They knew she had a troubled past and did their best to comfort the little one. They asked if she wanted to talk about it but she always said no because she was afraid to tell them she had killed their hero and the rest of her family. She still felt that the loss of her family was her fault despite what everyone had expressed to her. The two males communicated they were always there for her.

Another night by the campfire Kat showed her travel buddies her different eyelids again. They both liked the white, green and red lids but the black one gave them the creeps because it looked like the little one had no eyes but they knew her eyes were open and looking at them. She tried to describe her different vision but was having a hard time. They tested her and she amazed them with her good memory and great vision. They wished they could see like the little guardian. "Maybe I can trick your mind. Using my metal abilities I could make you see the way I do," Kat told the two zatos. Who looked at each other. "I would be willing to try; I mean what is the worst thing that could happen? The vision would not work?" Hutto voiced. Kat and Hutto both climbed a near by tree where Kat could see a mountain and Hutto could just make it out in the dark night. The little one got behind Hutto and Put both her hands on Hutto's shoulders. As she closed her eyes she told her brave friend to look out at the mountain. He did as she asked and when a minute or two pasted Kat instructed the warrior to close his eyes and relax. Kat focused on Hutto's mind and mainly on his eyes. She slowly opened her eyes and stared into the distance. Then she spoke softly to Hutto, "slowly open your eyes and just relax, if this works your mind will not be use to what you will see. "Ok, Z.K. I am going to go nice and slow and I will tell you if I see again thing different," Hutto replied. He took a deep breath and slowly opened his eyes. He glazed out in the distance and focused his eyes. "Wow, I can see the mountain. Zea it is working. Oh, wow, this is amazing," Hutto gasped. "Hold on, I am going to try to switch my eyelids," Kat whispered.

Kat closed her eyes and reopen them in her first eyelid, which was her white. Hutto had a hard time refocusing but after a while got it and was stunned. When Kat went to the red and green lids she had Hutto close his eyes too and it worked a lot better and last Kat showed him her black lids. Hutto could not believe what he was seeing with Kat's "eyes" now he knew what she talking about and was happy to finally understand. "I have to stop now," Kat told Hutto softly. They both closed their eyes and climbed down the tree. Kat went straight to bed showing Hutto her vision made her very tried and used up a lot of her energy. The males stayed up talking during the night.

The next day Kat was tried but got up and packed up camp with the guys and they head off for the day. Soon they came to a lake, which seemed like a good place to break. Zutiyro wanted to go swimming. Spring was well on its way and the sun was very warm with his thick fur. Poking his tail into the lake Zutiyro tested how cold the water was. His toes touching surface making little ripples in the perfect reflection of the water. "The lake feels great. I am going for a dip. I will see you guys in a while. I have not been swimming in so long. I use to go all the time as a little one," the guardian yelled as her prepared to jump into the lake. Kat and Hutto stayed on the shore and talked and about nature and their travels.

As Kat looked out over the water she saw a fin in the water. Worrying about her friend she scanned the water for Zutiyro. The little one asked Hutto if he had seen their friend when he told her, "no," without hesitation she jumped into the lake. Opening her blue eyelids she quickly swam to the middle of the lake using her wings and legs. She scanned the water for her friend. She saw a large grey fish looking creature trying to get into a small hole on a underwater cliff. She saw little bubbles coming out of he hole. She swam at the large fish and dug her claws into its flesh. The large underwater predator started to swim violently and when it turned from the hole Kat let go and swan into the dark cave.

Once inside she saw Zutiyro almost out of air looking like he was about to inhale water. The little warrior swam up him and kissed him letting him breathe through her gills. Once he got a good breath she went to the opening where she saw the large fish swimming in circles. The little guardian went back her friend and pointed to her head then his. He nodded understanding she was going to speak with him mentally. — I am going to give you one more breath then I want you to swim to the surface. I am going to attack the fish. Once the sea creature is dazed I am going to come up from underneath you so you can fly out of the water, do you understand? — Kat asked. Zutiyro nodded again. Kat once again gave Zutiyro a breath of air and then she quickly swam out of the cave and at the fish. The young female attacked the monster's eyes and gills. The brave warrior fought the monster. Once Kat herd the sound of Zutiyro splashing on the surface she gave one last punch to the creature's gills and swam for the surface. Coming up under her swimming friend she told him mentally, — I am coming up. — Then she came out of the water with Zutiyro holding her back. Once they were high enough the guardian took flight.

On shore the two swimmers caught there breathe while Hutto asked many questions. After the two rested they told Hutto what happen. He was happy to see his two friends were safe and unharmed. Zutiyro talked about the weird experience to breath through Kat's lungs but it saved his life so he was grateful. Zutiyro thanked the little one for saving his life. Once the two rested for a few minutes the group walked onward.

Time went on and soon the three had barely any secret form each other and they were the best of friends. Kat soon was very good at flying. Kat and Zutiyro would play a game like Leoi (tag). She could do more aerial moves because her wings were larger and were able to move in different positions than the other guardian. Zutiyro was a great teacher and soon Kat could keep up with her mentor and fly at the age of ten. She could always be better but with a lesson almost everyday Kat was making great improvements, she still was not as strong as Zutiyro. Kat was finally delighted with her life for the first time in a long time.

The Pass

On Kat's eleventh year of birth she reached the mountain range. This is the most dangerous part of the journey. They had to cross many mountains and they could not fly because the wind was too strong. There was little food and it was very cold in the range. Both Hutto and Zutiyro thought Kat could make it over the range but they did not want her to go off by herself. They rested at the base because the journey would be harder now and they wanted a fresh start in the morning. They wanted to celebrate Kat's day of birth. Kat played and talked with her two friends for the rest of the evening. They all got a good nights rest under the moon's light, which kissed Kat's cheeks as she slept.

The three travelers awoke to a bright sunny morning and the birds chirping. Kat stretched and packed up her bedding. The group gathered food and ate the first meal of the day. When everyone was ready they started to climb the mountain. The mountain was steep at some points and a nice climb at others. The band still talked and played games. About half way through the day the trio stopped for a break. There Kat wanted to learn something new. Zutiyro decide to teach her how to really use her ears. She knew how to sleep lightly because she needed to wake up each day before Jabo came into the small room to wake her. Zutiyro told her everyone had a different way of walking and after practice she could be able to tell Hutto and him apart by hearing them walk. Also he would teach how to protect herself. Zutiyro opened a compartment in his computer and pulled of a ball shaped object. Kat's eyes grew with amazement and wonder. This is for you. I will teach you how to use it later for now put it in your computer. Kat did was she was asked, took a drink of water and began to walk again with her friends up the mountain.

By the end of the first night they were at the top of the first peak and all they could see was an endless sea of mountains each with snowy peaks and rocky valleys between them. Kat was astonished she had never seen so many mountains up close before now. The group camped for the night and all slept together because it was so cold on top of the snowy peak.

The trio continued their travels in rain, snow or shine they did not stop of any reason. Kat learn many lesson on to being a guardian. She found night was the hardest time for her. She always found herself thinking of her lost family because she could now see the stars almost every night. She was worried she let her family down by leaving the camp and her kind to slowly die. She missed your brother and parents loving touch and many nights cried herself to sleep. She did her best to hide this fact from the zatos who were with her. She did not want them to know she was sad. When the group walked in silence or when Kat flew alone she also thought about her family. While traveling she looked for a strong chain for her heart. One day Kat took some rock from the mountain and used her red gun and melted the rock. Then she made a simple but strong chain. Hutto help her put it on and she told them it would never be out of her keep. Hutto saw Kat as a daughter loved to teach her and see her eyes light up when learning something new.

One day when the group was resting on a flat summit of a mountain. Hutto took a nap as Kat and Zutiyro sat on the ground opposite of each other. "Do you still have the metal ball I gave you a while ago?" The guardian asked. "Yes, I do," she answered as she pulled it out of her computer. Zutiyro took the object and twisted the two halves and the ball started to float in the air. "Watch," the leader ordered. He then closed his eyes and said, "Yu-e cotamati sosoray." The little ball started to move around the zato. She could not hear the little object, but then without warning the little ball shot a pebble at Zutiyro who with his eyes closed caught it. "You can change the speed and the size of the pebble the ball shoots but soon you will be able to hear a weapon coming at you. Then you will be able to protect yourself. Kat tried to do as Zutiyro did but still had a lot to learn. The two males laughed watching the little one try to catch the pebbles. They remember when they had to learn this trick of the trade. "Time to continue," Hutto called. And again the group was on the move.

Even with the sun out the weather was very cold. The wind was extremely strong and Kat kept her wings tucked into back so the airstream would not push her back as much. Kat was really surprised when Zutiyro asked her for the first time how she escaped from Jabo. The two zatos knew Kat was the one who started the escape but they did not know how. Kat told them about Uta, fighting Jabo and how she stood outside with her arm in the snow for hours. They both agreed the little guardian was very smart to come up with a plan like that. Zutiyro said another guardian cut both his collar and brace off his body. The three talked a little about their captivity but no one really enjoyed discussing it. Both leaders did not like looking at Kat' back because of the artwork of scars on it. They could not believe what Jabo had done to her just for loving her family. One night when they were sitting by the campfire Hutto asked if he touch her back. Kat said, "Sure," as she turned her back to Hutto and opened her wings. The leader slowly reached out and carefully touched her back. His hands were cold on the little one's vertebral. As the Hutto was looking for firewood Kat and Zutiyro played more games, which were teaching the little one, skills she would need to be called a true guardian.

"You are doing well for your age. If you practice everyday then soon you will be a strong guardian," The leader said to the student. "I will, you are a good teacher. Thank you for helping me," the zatz stated. They smiled and enjoyed each others company and the lesson went on into the night. Hutto joined them sitting by the fire. "Let's test your ears," Zutiyro told the student while getting to his feet. "Close your eyes," he ordered was he walked to where Hutto was standing. "Now, one of us is going to walk and when the footsteps stops I want you to call out who moved. Do you have any questions?" Zutiyro asked. "I am ready when you are," the little one stated. Kat listened very carefully to the footsteps, which walked up and then pasted her. When the sound came to an end then Kat would call out, "Hutto." "Good. Again," Zutiyro stated. The Hutto walked back to where he started and then the game began all over again. Over all Kat did a good job she only got one answer wrong. Even when both walked at the same time she could point to where the two stopped walking. Zutiyro gave Kat a challenge by flying but Kat felt the wind and his landing and still pointed to him. When they were done playing the group went to sleep for the night.

In the morning right before the sun came out to play Kat rose and watched the sun raise and greet her for the day. She could now see where they would travel would lead them. The trio used the sun as a guide for their journey. One of the first things the warriors taught Kat was how to follow the stars and sky when they were traveling so she would always know how to walk in the direction they wish to go. Kat could see one more large grouping of mountains, which ended the range. A smile appeared on her face thinking that would be the last mountain she would have to climb. When the males were ready the group headed onward. Hutto said there goal was to reach the large and maybe last mountain, which was in the distance.

The leaders tested Kat on her knowledge of traveling, and the guardian code. She did well but still had a lot to learn. She made her computer make a checklist of all the things she needed to be able do in order to be a guardian. When the group was taking their break for the day Zutiyro asked Kat, "May my computer meet yours?" "I cannot see why not but let me asked to be sure." "Computer would you like to me Zutiyro's computer?" Kat inquired to her computer. "Sure I would love to meet his computer," the computer responded. Zutiyro smiled as he herd the good new. The two sat across from each other and they each open a compartment with an outlet and a wire. They switched wires and plugged them into their computers. As their computers shared data Zutiyro and Kat lied down, rested and talked. Hutto joined them and they relax for a while. Once it was time to move on the two true guardians let their computers continue talking as they walked.

The sun was bright and high in the sky. The trio continued their quest for a new home. Kat broke and silence, "How do you know when we have found a new home?" "I guess we will find another group to take us in or we find a nice place where it seems like home. We would camp out there for the rest of our time," Hutto answered. "Oh, I have never really seen what our home use to look like. I was in the Qotho camp my whole life," Kat stated. "You will know when we have found home because you will be with another group or the place you will make you happy and deep down you know it just feels right to be there," Zutiyro replied. The three proceeded to what they hoped to be the last mountain in the range.

When the group reached the top of large mountain they stopped to see if this was truly the last mountain. All of them grew smiles on their faces because all they could see was shades of green. They could see a valley of trees and rivers, which stretched for miles. The sun was setting and the two leaders had to decide if they should just get down the mountain or camp at the top, which was not a safe place to camp. The males determine they would chance the night and just head down the peak. Then they would rest the next day out of celebrating of being out of the mountain rage. The trio started to head down the pass as dusk was turning into dark. All of them knew that it was dangerous to travel on the mountain at night. Hutto lead the way with Kat coming in second and Zutiyro taking the rear. The white, sparkling and cold ice crushed under the traveler's feet as they climbed down the mountain. Kat loved to try to step in the zato's footprints in front of her. She had to jump because she still little to the ones she traveled with on her search for a new home.

The small band was half way down when Kat got a strange feeling. Kat could hear a different rumbling sound. "What is that noise?" Kat asked out loud. "What are you talking about Z.K.?" Hutto asked. "I hear a rumbling sound. What do you not hear it?" Kat replied. "I do not hear anything," Hutto said as he looked at Zutiyro then crouch down to feel the ground. He did not feeling anything different so he told the other two they were going to head onward. Kat did not like feeling she could hear sometime the males could not.

They continued down but Kat could still hear the odd rumbling. Hutto took a step and then stop walking. Kat who was jumping form footprint to footprint ran right into Hutto's leg. Now on the ground she looked up at the leader who was standing perfectly still and looking straight off into the distance. Seeing this Zutiyro joined Hutto in being absolutely still and listening. Kat copied her friends but was not sure what they were doing. "RUN!" Hutto told the little on and his friend. They all started running down the mountain. Then Kat realized how loud the rumbling was looking behind she saw a large cloud of white coming after them. She could feel the wind and flakes of snow form the avalanche trying to catch her. "Zutiyro there is no way we can out run this take Kat, you can help her fly away. You cannot carry me there is too little time and you will not be able to get high enough before the snow takes us. I am holding you back. Go, Go now. There is no time!" Hutto yelled at the top of his lungs. Zutiyro very quickly shook arms with the one he was running next too. "I will take over your promise. Come on Kat lets take flight," Zutiyro cry out to his friends. "But we cannot leave Hutto," Kat cried. "Now!" Zutiyro yelled as he grabbed Kat and threw her into the air then open his wings and followed her. The wind from the crashing snow allowed the Zutiyro to take flight with ease and He help the screaming one fly up and away from the danger. "Hutto, Hutto. NO. Hutto," Kat screamed into the night air. Once they were high enough the leader held on to the little one who cried and tried to fly down to save her friend who was now lost in a world of snow. After awhile the two flew down to the end of mountain.

Once they reach the ground they began to search for their lost friend. They used their computers and flew over the new laid snow. Soon the crying zatz got a faint sign on her computer. She landed and began to dig furiously. She soon could see Hutto's fur in the snow. The little one carefully dug around her friend and pulled him out of his resting place. By then Zutiyro was there to help. Hutto slowly opened his eyes and looked at his companions. "Hutto?" Kat cried. With all his strength he reached out his hand and placed it on Kat's head. She grabbed her fallen friend's free hand and came closer to him so she could hear him. "Z.K. I want you to know, there was nothing you could have done to stop this from happening. I am very proud of you and all that you have become. I want you to always listen to Zutiyro. Never forget and remember you are a strong guardian," Hutto whispered. "I promise Hutto, thank for your saving my life and teaching me," Kat told the protector. "Zutiyro remembered all that we have talked about. Be strong you are the leader now and watch after our little one," Hutto whispered while turning to his long time best friend. Taking his hand off Kat head he shook arms with Zutiyro. The fallen warrior then started to state the guardian's code. The others joined in and took over for Hutto failing voice. By the time the code was finished Hutto's hands relaxed in his two friend's hands. The two sat there for a while in silence they could not believe their leader and rock was now at rest. They hugged and cried as they watched the sun rise for the first time on their own.

Zutiyro carried his lost companion's body and walked to a tree, which was by a river. The two grieving friends berried Hutto and said a few prayers. They each said their goodbyes. Then the two proceed a little ways down stream and then rested for the rest of the day. Both very tired from climbing and walking all night and from the avalanche. Both talked for a while but were also emotionally tired as well and fell asleep in each other's arms.

The valley of darkness

The two slept for the rest of the day and night. They woke up the next morning very early and both were ravenous. They caught some fish and ate in silence. Both were still uneasy about losing their friend. Once the two were done eating Zutiyro asked, "Shall we head onward, little one?" "Sure," Kat answered quietly. They got up and began to enter the forest. After watching the sun rise they knew once they got in the forest it would be very hard to see the sun so they would follow the river and do their best never to go o far north or South, but to keep heading west.

Kat and Zutiyro walked for a while and soon the female broke the silence, "How did you meet Hutto?" Zutiyro smiled thinking of some of the good memories with his fallen hero. "I think I met him right before the Qothos came he was my new teach for guardian training. I remember being so mad because he was not a true guardian so I thought he would not be a good teacher. But he was a great teacher; he also had been trained by the best. I think you knew his name, Domatu," Zutiyro began. Kat smile and listened as her leader continued to talk. "When the Qotho attack all chaos broke loose. Out of all the confusion I woke up chain up next to him. I was happy to see him. Well by some chance of fate I was bought but a very old Qotho and a year later when my master passed away I was given to his son. He happen to be a very strong a rich Qotho, who own Hutto. We were very happy to be together again. He began to teach me and help me live under the Qothos's rule. We both escaped together thanks to you and found a little half dead, zatz, guardian lying on the ground in the mud. Picking her little body and realizing she was still alive we continued our escape with the little one. Later we found the group and rested. We quickly discovered the little guardian we save was the daughter of great and brave Domatu. Hearing what the group was planning to do to the little guardian we decide the clan was not a safe place to the little zatz to grow and trick her into running off with us into the night in order to save her life," Zutiyro finished while looking at Kat who was smiling. "Thank you, for everything. You are a great friend," Kat told the leader while giving him a hug. The duo continued on talking once again and enjoying each other's company.

The forest leaves blocked the sun's light from reaching the two travelers. This was Kat's first time in a real forest. Zutiyro had gone on many huts before the Qothos came so he was knew how to survive in the woodland. Kat had to get use to all knew sounds while they slept at night and walked during day. Zutiyro told the little one they might start traveling at night because it was safer. They had great night vision and it was cooler during the dark hours to travel. Then on the nights where there was no moon the duo would rest. Kat asked why the moon changed every night and her leader told her it was because of the planets shadow or something like that. The guardian decided that they would travel one more day then start continuing their journey by night.

Under the tree tops the two rested and did their best to stay up all night so they could sleep during the day. Once the sun's warmth was gone for the day Kat could hear the sound of the night. Each time she herd a new noise she was ask her friend what made it. "What is that strange singing call?" Kat asked. "I think that is a Katrina Detu (pink furred one)," Zutiyro replied. "I believe it is a small pink mammal with large ears, eyes and a trunk for a nose. They are very agile and can jump from branch to branch at night. They sing in the moon light to talk to each other and they eat fruit," He continued. "Wow, you know a lot. I wish I was as smart as you," the little one spoke in wonder. "Some day you will. I have been working on something for you. It is a game; I think you will like it. Once I teach it to you, you can make this game when ever you want," Zutiyro said as he grabbed his pack. He pulled out a board and a bag of pieces. The board was bi-colored; it was made up of little colored squares. He pulled out the pieces and began to explain each one. The game was called koumata (war game). There were two teams and each matched one of the colors of the board. There were Rowku (slaves), Robroger (king), Sarasyiboon (queen), Kyn (mystic), Kevjeff (soldier), and a Cluad (guard). Each piece moved differently and the goal was to kill the other team's Robroger. Kat loved the game was a quick leaner. The two would play every night there was no moon. Soon Kat was an even match for her teacher and as time went by surpassed him.

As they walked during the night they were always on their guard for anything. Zutiyro told her about more games he played as he was growing up and training to be a guardian. One of his favorites was Xvo (flags). In the game there would be a group that split into two teams and on a felid would try to find and take the opposite teams Xvo. Kat wished to someday to play all the games her friend was telling describing to her. Zutiyro was now Kat's full time protector, teacher, father and friend without Hutto there to help him he was alone. Kat asked many questions and wanted many things described to her. He now had to do his best to help her. When she had her nightmares he alone did his best to help her and make her feel better and go back to sleep.

Kat woke up a few times during the day because she was a light sleeper and was still not use to sleeping during the light hours. Zutiyro felt bad for the little one, she had so many nightmares, scars and such a light sleeper at such a young age. He always looked down when Kat opened her wings and he could she the artwork on her back. Jabo had left his mark in Kat's life. She never asked what it looked like. Now anyone who ever spotted her back would have to feel some kind of emotion. He sometimes asked Kat what she was thinking about when they walked in silence or when she was staring off into the distance. Most of the time Kat gave him a vague answer and would talk the about time she was with the Qothos or with her family. Every now and then Kat went into detail about life with Jabo or about her scars but she always cried so did not like to go into that part of her life. The guardian respected the little ones decision and would wait till she was ready to share.

At night the two traveled farther because they did not get tired from the hot sun. One night while the two were walking Kat could smell something very good. She started to walk towards the smell; losing track of what was behind her. She soon came to a small clearing where there was a blue pool with green stream coming off the top of the water. The little guardian got down and her knees and cupped her hands. She began to lower them into the water.

Once her hands touched it she felt a large shape pain. Quickly the little one tried to pull her hands out of the water but something was holding them down in the liquid. The smell was gone and she woke out of her trace. The water now started to drain and vines were now visible. One of the blue and purple vines had Kat's hands and was trying to pull her into the pit of the plant. Looking up Kat could see a large blue, pink, green and purple flower pedals beginning to close trapping her. A different type of vine started coming out of the pit. It had little yellow and back flowers. When the flowered vines came to a stop they shot black quills at the one fighting to escape. "Computer, red gun power ten," she screamed at the top of her lungs. The gun moved into place and fired. The flower cried out in pain and began to cave in on its self. Kat continued to fire till the death trap released her. Next Kat pulled the black quills out of her neck. Once she was out of danger she focused on her wounds and felt the little holes heal. She then started too called out to her friend only using her mind but passed out soon after because she was exhausted.

When Kat came too she saw Zutiyro looking over her. "Are you alright? You disappeared, and I tired to find you. When I heard you I came running and found you here on the ground passed out cold," Zutiyro said quickly in one big breath. Kat slowly sat up and held her head. She then whispered, "I do not remember everything but I could smell something. I followed the sent and the next thing I know I was attached by a large plant with water, vines, a large flower and little flowers, which shot quills at me. I shot it with my gun, called you and then passed out cold. I think." "I think I know what attached you," the guardian stated calmly. "What?" the little one questioned. "The plant which attacked is called a Lauren (color of death) plant. This plant draws its prey with a enticing fragrance everyone smells something different then uses vines and pelts to push the victim into its mouth. Lauren's have poison quills to help aid it capture its prey. You are very lucky little one. You have learned a very important lesson. Now rest we have to start traveling in a few hours," The leader told his friend. Kat took a deep breath and fell asleep.

As the moon took the suns place in the night sky the two travelers pressed onwards. Kat asked her teacher to tall to her about all the dangerous plants and animals they might find in the forest. Kat was in awe of how many other kinds of creatures there were on the planet. She felt good know that once she was an adult she would be on top of the food chain.

As Kat walked she played with computer learning about her full capabilities. She made lots of holograms and maps. She soon with the help of Zutiyro learned how to do a pulse. Zutiyro would do his best to explain to Kat what a pulse was then he would demonstrate it. "Well a pulse is a way to know what is around you," he began. "The pulse is like a wave. The wave travels and sends back a picture of your sounding and you can set it up so find certain objects. So if I felt I was being followed I could do a pulse and my computer would send a wave. I then would be able to see or my computer could tell me how many, what and how far anyone is from me and how fast they are going,' He finished. "Computer please do a pulse and show me any fish in the river," He said out loud. "Also please show me the map," he added. With in seconds Kat could see a picture of the river and two miles in every direction. She then saw all the fish, different kinds, their speed and much more. Kat was in awe. For the rest of the day Kat played and practice using her pulse.

The two soon adjusted very well to traveling at night a being on their own. Without Hutto both felt fatherless but they soon relied on each other and got through the hard time. Like brother and sister the duo fought their way through the forest and all the challenges in it. One night Kat asked Zutiyro where everyone went when they passed on. He did his best to tell her all the good souls went to a happy place and the lost souls stayed lost till they could find their way to the happy place. He then proceeded to tell her Domatu, Sunyro, Gyro and Hutto were in the happy place. Kat then inquired to her companion why her brother talked about stars. The leader then told the little one the blissful place was above them so the gratified souls could down on them. Zutiyro did his best to answer all Kat questions and guide her to grow up as a true guardian.

Most days they followed the river but every few nights the true guardian gave the student lessons in flying. Kat loved the nights with no moon because she got to take a break from traveling and she got the play games. Kat was very joyful to find out by her computer her day of birth was in a week and on a night with no moon.

As the night approached she was very excited and jumped from tree to tree. "Calm down little one, we still have a long way to go tonight," Zutiyro stated with a laugh. "Can we fly tonight please, please?" Kat asked. "Not tonight, little one, tomorrow" the leader spoke. Kat looked down in disappointment. They walked for the rest of the night and they did not talk much. The next day the two slept and when the sun was gone to sleep, the two rose to greet the night. Kat was very ecstatic. "Why are you so happy Z.K?" Zutiyro asked. "I think you know," Kat spoke with a large smile. "No, I think I know why you are so happy you better tell me," Zutiyro voiced with a puzzled look. "Zutiyro, stop playing you know this is the night of my birth," Kat stated. "Is it? Are you sure?" he question. The little one just looked at her friend and then stuck her tongue out at him. "It must have slipped my mind, I do not what I was thinking," The zato said while looking around the area.

Kat jumped on his lap and voiced, "You did not forget silly. I think you are playing with me, come on its my night of birth you have to be nice to me." Zutiyro smiled then told Kat to close her eyes. As the little did what was asked of her the zato proceed to reach into his pack and pull out a gift wrapped in cloth. He placed the gift on the little one's lap then told her to open her eyes. Looking down Kat saw and gift and then slowly picked it up off her lap. With a smile the little guardian unwrapped the cloth. When Kat saw her gift she gently set it down and hugged her friend. "I will teach you to use it in the following weeks," Zutiyro pronounced to the little one as she hugged him. Holding her new weapon in the fire light she could she the dagger clearly. The guardian told the twelve year old the dagger belonged to her father. He explained how Domatu gave the dagger to Hutto who hid it in the woods by the village before the Qothos came. When they escaped he found the dagger and gave it to his good friend Zutiyro who decided to give the dagger to his little guardian friend. Kat got a big smile on her face and thanked Zutiyro for the wonderful gift. They played a game of koumata. Then Kat asked if they could go fly. After the little one begged and gave her friend sad eyes he finally agreed to go flying.

They packed up, put out the fire and climbed the nearest tree. Kat spread her wings and took flight. The sweet night air ran pasted her face and she took a deep breath. Soon Zutiyro started a game of tag with the little one who happily played. Kat was so happy for the first time in a long time she was smiling and laughing on her day of birth. Kat saw the river and dove down to the surface. She loved the fly directly over the water. Sometimes she would put her hands or tail in the water making waves. Zutiyro came down next to her. They used the air from the moving waters to pick up speed and raced down the river. They came to a waterfall where Kat let her self droop. Free falling down the cliff with the water she got the biggest rush and smile on her face. When she reached the base of the falls she opened her wings caught up with her friend who had went ahead of her. Soon Zutiyro gave Kat he sign it was time to stop and Kat did some last aerial flips then followed her leader to the ground. They began to look for a nice place to sleep for the day. They climbed up a tree and tied some branches together making a bed. They stayed up till sunrise talking and laughing.

Kat was only asleep for a few minutes when she heard Zutiyro call out into the morning air. Looking around she could not see her friend. Kat reached for the dagger on her belt. Jumping down from the tree she scanned the area for her missing friend. — Computer, please do a pulse to help me find Zutiyro, thank you, — Kat asked. Within seconds Kat had a map of the area and saw her friend was by the river. Running to the waterway with dagger in hand Kat called out for her lost companion. Once she reached the river she saw drag marks leading into the moving waters. She drove into the cool water. Her gills and eyelids kicked in and she did anther pulse to find her friend. Following her computer's directions she found herself making her way through a maze of tunnels. The little one became very worried thinking her friend would soon run out of air if he did to get some help quick. After swimming for what seemed to be forever she reached the surface. Jumping out of the water through a hole she found herself in a small cave, which again had many tunnels. Looking on the ground she could see the same drag marks she saw on the riverbank. Taking a deep breath she began to follow the trail hoping to find her friend soon.

Because the cave had no light Kat used her black eyelids, ears and her computer to guide her through the second maze. Kat kept stubbing her toe on rocks so; she took flight and flew down the damp passageways. Her wing tips scrapped the edge of the tunnel. The passageways were getting smaller and smaller. Beads of sweat were starting to form on her forehead when she was forced to run again. Finally she reached an opening. There was a small pool of water in the far left corner and one opening in the far right side. Using her computer Kat scanned for her lost friend. Picking up a weak signal she went right and into the small tunnel. Running, she came to a wall and realized she went down a dead end. Turning around she was confused. How could her computer be wrong? Scanning again she saw she had to go up and straight. Reaching the opening again she took flight and found a third opening. Climbing into the muddy hallway she made her way to one last opening where she found her lost companion.

Wrapped in a kind of silky web her friend was trying to brake free. Hearing a strange noise the little guardian looked up to the ceiling. There she saw little blue, brown and black creatures. Each had five body parts with two, six joined, legs. On their heads were small white eyes and two mouths full of red sharp teeth. They had little spikes coming out of their backs and a little tail coming out of the last body parts with was pointed at the end. — Stop moving, — Kat told her struggling friend with her mind.

Once he stopped moving she brought out her red ray gun and placed it on level three. She then proceeded to cut Zutiyro a breathing hole. Hearing her friend grasp for air she started to focus on the hissing ones above her. Changing her weapons from the red ray gun to the net thrower, the little one started the shoot the little creatures that started to spit at her, which was the silky web stuff. Now the little female new what was trapping her friend. Jumping and dodging the spit, Kat one by one captured the little things. Once she was out of immediate danger she ran to Zutiyro's side and helped him of the web of silk. Soon her friend was free and thanked her for saving him. The little cave dwelling creatures were breaking free of the nets by ripping them with their teeth. The duo ran out the through the underground mud mazes and then dove into the cool waters where they once again made there way through a maze and tunnels. Finally they reached the surface of the water. The two were exhausted and were happy to be out of the danger. Zutiyro decided that they would rest that night. Kat said she was strong enough to travel that evening if they took it slow. Zutiyro patted her on the head and he fell into a deep sleep. Kat soon joined him in the land of dreams but did not sleep deeply.

When the sun was in bed and the night was coming alive the two got up and started walking. Kat asked her teacher if he knew what attacked him. "The little creatures that attacked me are called, snickertwixs (mud water bugs), and they live in large groups. They capture their prey then take them back to the nest and last eat their victim," Zutiyro explained. "Oh, I see, that is two my friend," she spoke. "What do mean that is two?" he questioned. "I have saved you twice, silly," Kat voiced. "I get it, you are right Z.K. I have to be more careful. Thank you again for being there to help me," Zutiyro laughed. "Anytime my fine friend," Kat told her comrade before giving him a hug. The two walked on for the rest of the night and this time when they looked for a place to sleep they decide to take turns watching over the other. Their computers would keep track of time so they did their turns evenly. Zutiyro went first as Kat fell into deep sleep as the sun's light woke up the land.

They took turns during the day and as they traveled at night they agreed they liked their new system. The nights and days turned into weeks and months. Their journey was going on strong and Kat was growing larger everyday. The duo took turns hunting and collecting the meals each night. Most nights they took one small break but every now and then Kat would be up to skipping the nightly break. She was getting use to walking all night and soon it was easy for her to travel all evening with only taking a few breaks.

Moving Sand

After many months of traveling the two could see the end of the forest when they flew. Both grew smiles when the dark tops of the trees ended and they could see a sea of white. Kat could not tell what the white was but would be happy to get out of the forest and not have to worry about its consent dangers.

Soon both held hands as they walked happily out of the forest and entered the sea of white sand. Their challenge would be to cross a bleached dessert. There were a whole new set of skills Kat had to learn and Zutiyro had to teach. They rested the night before they would embark into the sea. That night the teacher talked about living in the dessert. Without question they walked at night and they would have to carry more water because they would not be following a river. They would have less to eat and have to beware of new deadly animals. They would dig a shelter every night at dawn unless they found a small patch of green trees. The two made extra water bottles and filled them. They also packed some additional food for their travel. Out of bark, leaves and other plants then made cloths for protection just in case they would need them. The duo took turns sleeping during the day and awoke at dusk to start their journey.

The first night Kat had lots of fun in the sand it was a new feeling on sand under her feet. Zutiyro did not say anything knowing soon she would tire of it. When ever they came upon new tracks in the sand Zutiyro would explain what made the tracks and what it looked like. Once dawn was coming the two dug a small borrow for the long hot hours to come. Kat did not sleep much her first day in the sea of white. She was not use to the heat. She could fan her wings and found herself panting for the first time. For food Kat had to get use to having a lot of small meals as they ate ever crossed their path. They drink any due they found and drank from any plants they encountered. After a week of traveling the little guardian told her companion she liked the soft feel of the forest compared to the sand. He just smiled and walked onward. The little one questioned the smiling one who just answered back, "nothing Z.K. nothing." She rolled her eyes and took flight. Zutiyro jumped into the cool air and opened his wings. Taking to the air he caught up to the Kat where he proceeded to start a game of tag.

The team laughed and played into the night. Every now and then one of them would swoop down catching a snack to share and eat. When they saw a good-sized plant they would again swoop down and using Kat's dagger cut the vegetation. They would take a much need drink and fill their water bottle as much a possible. Then continue on what seem to be their never-ending journey.

One day while Kat was on her watch her compute informed her, "Kat do you know what happens in a week?" "I am not sure, I know it is not my birthday and not an anniversary of a lost one, let me think," Kat replied. "Does it have to do with Zutiyro?" she asked. "Yes it does," the computer whispered. "Is it his day of birth?!?" Kat questioned with excitement. "Shhhh, yes, Kat it is. So we need to think of a gift to make and give him," her computer stated. "Wow, I will have to think about this one," the little one voiced quietly. After thinking for a while in silence. — I know what I am going to make him, — she mentally yelled. — Are you going to share? — asked her computer. — I am going to make it the day before his birthday so it will not brake while we travel. I cannot wait, — Kat thought. — Hello, are you going to tell me or not? — the computer cut into Kat's mind. — Oh, sorry, my friend. I am going to use my red ray and melt the sand making her something out of gapea, — Kat told her friend. — Good idea Kat. —

— Thank you, I think I am going make his name. —

— What do you mean his name? —

— A symbol which represents Zutiyro, I am going to make a fire and inside of the flames a model of him standing up to face it. —

— Oh, I understand now. Right now it is time to wake up our sleeping friend and you to sleep. —

The little one then woke up Zutiyro and went to sleep with a smile. The days before the leader's birthday went very fast and soon the little one found herself making her friend's gift. Using some of her water and sand she aimed her red ray and shot the mixture. First she made a ball of gapea then she proceeded to carve into the smooth surface. After she carved a zato standing up to the fire she cut a little hoop at the top so he could wear it or tie it to his belt if he wished. Just as she was finishing the finally touches the sunset and her leader awoke. She quickly and slyly hid the small trinket in her back. Tonight was the night she would surprise her companion with a gift form the heart.

The two took flight and Kat had a large smile on her face. "Why are you so happy tonight, Z.K?" he enquired. "I think you know," Kat replied with a giggle.

"No, I am not sure why you are so happy, did have a good dream?"

"No, silly, I know you know what today is stop playing, Zutiyro."

"I am not playing little one,"

"Ok, ok, close your eyes."

"Can we land first?"

"I thought you were the expert flyer. If I can do it my teacher can right?"

"Fine," Zutiyro stated as he turned his body and shifted his wings so he could continue flying backwards. As the leader closed his eyes Kat pulled the carved gapea out from her back. "Hold your hands out and keep your eyes close," Kat ordered. "Should I be worried," he voice as he reached out his hands. The little guardian put the gapea in her friend's hands while shouting, "Happy day of birth!" The surprised zato opened his eyes to see the carved gift and was filled with joy. "How did you kn... never mind. I figured it out, thank you computer," he stated. "Thank you Z.K," he continued before giving her a hug. They flew on and Kat let her teacher look at his knew gift. After he reflected the male landed on the sand hear a patch of plants. Next he cut a small piece of long grass. Last he made the little gift into a necklace. "Would you do the honors?" he asked while moving down on his knees. With a smile the little one put the small and thoughtful gift around the zato's head. Letting the small present rest on his shoulder and chest. The two flew and talked for the rest of the night laughing and playing games.

Kat found that they were always dirty the sand got everywhere. The little one did her best to keep the sand out of her ears so; she would not get an infection. During the day she did her best to sleep on her wing. At night if there were high winds both travelers put cloths on their body to block the ruff sand moving violently with the gale. While kat could navigate in the winds, Zutiyro being a glider had a lot more difficulty. If possible they would fly over the storms. This hostile weather helped Kat flying skills, high and fast winds were very hard to fly in and with a great teacher the two made it through every storm, which crossed their path.

Seasons changed again but not as vividly as the valley. The day of Kat birth was again almost upon the duo. The night before Kat's day they found an oasis and were overjoyed to find fresh water. They also had a small group of trees to rest under. This was the first time Kat spent the day above the ground. The two got their fill of water and wanted to cool off from the hot sun. Diving into the cool, clear water Kat swam in the small pool. Using her blue lids and gills she played under the water. Playing with her wings she found she could faster and speed up very quickly with out any warning. Zutiyro also had fun splashing around playing games while staying cool. He taught the little one some swimming moves but, it was a short lesson so the two could keep playing in the pool. As night approached Zutiyro and Kat could see thunderheads in the distance. "Those are big and dark clouds. Do you think they are coming this way?" Kat asked. "I hope not Z.K. it would not be fun to be under them," Zutiyro answered. "Should we move on then?" Kat continued. "I am not sure, even if we move on the storm will catch up to us sooner or later," he stated while looking off into the distance. "Should we dig a hole?" Kat continued. "No, the trees will provide us cover. We will see," Zutiyro voiced as he sat down in the warm sand. Kat sat with him. They talked and played koumata while relaxing in the dessert. Looking around all Kat could see was a sea of never ending white. Kat turned to her friend and again asked another question, "What do you like the best, mountain, forest or dessert?" "I think I life the forest the best," he replied. The two talked for a while and slowly fell asleep.

Kat suddenly woke up with beads of sweat on her forehead. She had just had a bad dream about Jabo coming after her. She was running away and Jabo caught her lost family and enslaved them. Right when Jabo was going to catch her she awoke from her dream state. She felt a warm, strong and large hand on her shoulder. Turning she could see Zutiyro's smiling face. He asked if he little one was ok she told him she would survived. The little one laid down once more trying to go back to sleep. Kat was again unexpectedly woken up again but this time it was not a dream but her companion waking her. Examining her surroundings see could see the storm was on top of them. The leader was trying to take her to the nearby tree. Grabbing her Zutiyro threw her against the tree. The little ones claws digging into the strong bark. Next the little guardian could feel the strong warrior's body pressed up against her like a strong hug. She was now pinned to the tree. As the winded picked up and the rain fell from the angry sky Kat could feel the zatos muscles tense up and tighten. She hugged the tree for her life praying for the storm to end and her lost ones to watch over her. Kat tried to look up at Zutiyro but sand flew into her eyes. Quickly looking down she closed her watering eyes. All she saw before sand took your vision was her friend face. His eyes were closed and he was grinding his teeth in pain. The little one could not get that site out of her mind. She did her best to wrap her wings around her body.

The two stayed in their huddled position all night as the wind hallowed and the clouds yelled every now and then spiting lighting down to the wet floor. When the storm finally pasted both of the zatx collapsed out of exhaustion. The two slept all day and when the sun was just setting the little one began to stir. When she slowly sat up her body ached and her head was spinning. Once she regained some strength she started to look around for her companion and protector. With a little difficulty the little guardian stood up and started to scan the area for Zutiyro. The little zatz finally spotted a body by the tree she spent the night hanging on to for her life. Running up to her friend she saw he was unconscious and the sand was red by him. She very gently rolled him over onto his side. Then gently lowered him back after seeing the site of his torn up posterior. The wind and the wind carved Zutiyro's back to the bone. The little one saw layers of muscle and a little bits of bone. With tears in her eyes and beginning to roll down her sandy cheeks, she tried to wake her sleeping friend.

"Zutiyro, Zutiyro, come on buddy wake up, please," she whispered as she shook his shoulder softly. After some time passed and made her voice louder the leader slowly opened him eyes. Blinking because of the sun, he tried to look up at his friend. Kat moved so her body blocked the sun's light from the warrior's eyes. "Are you ok, Z K.?" he asked. "Yes, I am fine, how are you?" she replied. "I am fine little one, I can fight this with you at my side," he quietly stated with a smile.

Kat grabbed his hand and told him, "I looked at your back and you look fine. I am sure you will pull through this. I am here can I get you anything?" "Just some water, I am really thirsty," he spoke softly. Without hesitation Kat stood and ran to her pack. Quickly seizing a water bottle she then proceeded to the pool where she filled the container and brought it to her teacher in need. Wiping the tear falling down her cheeks her sat by her friend in pain and repeatedly told him he would be fine. The hours crept by and all Kat could do was make Zutiyro comfortable. The little one tired dress the zatos wounds but, she did not get very far because it was too pain full for her friend. She put a cloth under his body so he was not on the white, ruff sand. She also made a small shelter out or leaves and bark from the trees to block the sun rays to her companion. The little guardian held her friend's hand and talked to him every now then getting up to get water or food for herself or the warrior in need.

Time passed as the two sat and soon the sun was setting. Dusk was falling in and all Kat could hear was the long deep breaths of Zutiyro. The air cooled with rising of the moon and Kat took down the shelter making the leaves into a blanket for her friend who was beginning to shiver. He whispered, "Thank you," to the little one who was working so hard to make him happy. They sat in silence. Kat watched the raising and falling of Zutiyro's chest and soon she could only hear Zutiyro's breaths get slower and deeper. When he started to shift the little one quickly told him to stop but he did not listen and slow sat up with a little bit of help from Kat.

"Zeaytera KatOynera, listen to me, you are not going to be traveling on your own now. You need to always be alert and listen to your computer. Your computer has all the knowledge all the guardians and the history of our kind. You must be brave and face all the challenges. Let your computer teach and train so, someday you will be like me but better. I am so proud of what you have done at your young age. Please never think that the death of your family, Hutto or mine is your fault because it is not. Find a new home and never give up, never stop fighting. I know you can do it not only are you smart but you are strong. Do not pity me but just hold your head up high and keep moving. Thank you for being the little sister I never had and helping me over the years. Your heart is in the right place never forget who you are or where you come from," Zutiyro whispered but was forced to stop when he started coughing.

Kat lowered her friend to his back where she looked down on him with a sweet smile. "I promise I will be a great guardian and never give up my quest. I will find a new home and never forget who I am or my history," Kat stated while grabbing her friends hand. "Thank you, Zutiyro for being my brother, teacher, friend and protector. I will never forget you," she voiced with a smile while helping the warrior drink some water. Again the two sat in silence at Kat was once again hypnotized by the sound and motion of Zutiyro chest falling and rising. The moon went across the deep blue sky and when dawn was upon the two zatx. Zutiyro's breaths were farther and farther apart. When the sun was just starting to wake up the land Zutiyro took his last breath. Kat cried as she said a few prayers for her fallen friend.

She dug a grave for her companion by the tree, which he pinned her against not too long ago. Once she buried her lost guardian she again said a few prayers and thanked him for all he did and last asked him to watch out after her. She then proceed to the pool of water where took a drink and then went for a little dip. After cooling off she walked to a nearby tree and fell asleep.

The White Dessert and an Old Friend

Kat woke up with the setting sun. She stretched and started continued on her quest without a companion for the first time. The little guardian proceeded on traveling at night and sleeping during the day. As she walked or flew at night her computer taught her about the history of her kind. The computer would quiz her and play games with to help her learn. At nights when there was no moon and Kat rested from traveling she played with the gray ball Zutiyro gave her. She was getting better at using her ears and not her eyes. Kat was happy to be able to talk to her Computer as she traveled.

During the day when the little one slept she had horrible nightmares. She always woke up in the middle of the day with beads of sweat and the images of lost ones and being a slave again. Her computer always did the best it could to calm the frighten zatz. Sometimes Kat started her travels early because she could not fall back to sleep. Her body got use to less sleep and she would travel more in one night. Kat loved to fly and her computer gave her a command and she would try to complete. Also every other night when she was on the ground and not flying she started to run. She would try to get farther every time she ran. Most of the time she ran in her four-legged form but, every now and then she ran in her two-legged form. She also found she could hunt better in her four legged-form; her footsteps were more quiet when she walked. She was able to sneak up on her pray with ease.

One night while she was traveling she spotted a shadow in the distance. Her heart jump as she thought she might have found another being. Taking to the air she flew forwarded trying to catch the shadow. But after scanning the land below her but, there was nothing there for miles. "Computer, please do a pulse," Kat asked. Her computer fulfilled the request and the pulse came back to Kat with everything looking normal. With a heavy heart Kat landed and continued to walk in the sea of white. "The shadow was just your mind playing tricks on you. You have been traveling for miles without a brake which, I think you should take one," her computer stated. "Ok, computer, I will take a brake," Kat voiced as she slowed her paced to a stop. She sat in a crossed legged position and reflected on her travels since she left the oasis. She sat in silence clearing the mess in her mind once she felt more relaxed she stood and started to walk again.

"How are you doing Kat?" her computer question. "I am doing fine just thinking," Kat replied.

"You have been very quiet lately. I know you are thinking about something."

"I do not know computer, just thinking about my travels. Will I ever find a home? How will I know when I get there? Have I been doing well in my lessons? Will I ever be a true guardian?"

"Well, Kat, you are not giving very hard questions tonight. Where to begin, lets see, first yes we will find a home it will be great. We will know because we will get a great warm feeling inside and deep down we will know. You are doing great in your lessons you are taking in information every day and once you have the history down we will start your physical lessons. I think for the method you are learning you are doing great. Do not worry once you have completed all your training you will make a great guardian. You will be strong, smart, and the best guardian that ever lived. And because of this you will more than live up to your father's, brother's and every else's expectations. Do not worry about the future just take one day at a time."

"Thank you, computer, you all makes me feel better."

"We are stuck with each other so; we might as well be there for each other."

"Computer, in the history of our kind is there any record of any guardian not getting along with their computer?"

"No, I do not think so but let me check."

"That would not be fun to fight with your computer because you are with them for the rest of your life; I feel luck to have you as a computer."

"Thank you, Kat, you are too kind, I checked my files and I was right there is no record of any guardian who did not get along with their computer."

"When will you have me start my physical lessons, computer?"

"When we get out of this desert and you can answer all the questions I have on the history of our kind and how to act like guardian."

"Oh, I see, well, I cannot wait to get out to this sea of white."

"We will soon enough. One day time, remember?"

"Ok computer. One day at a time."

The little guardian walked till the horizon started to turn a light blue. She then dug her sanctuary for the day. She tried to have a peaceful sleep but again awaken abruptly when Jabo Shot her with a red ray gun, laughing. She lay back down in the sand with her eyes open trying to clear her mind. She found herself once again thinking about family and all their expectations. Finally she drifted back into the land of dreams and did not wake up till her computer gently voiced her to back to reality. Rubbing the sleep from her eyes she yawned and stretched. Crawling out of her borrow she watched dusk turn into night. Like the night before, she continued on her way to find a new home.

Flexing the muscles in her back she took flight into the evening air. Taking a deep breath as she took on the night. She was able to do all the flight commands her computer gave her. The next night she went the whole night running without stopping. Her computer was very proud of her and lucky for Kat the next night there was a no moon. That evening she rested while Kat's computer gave her a test on the history of their kind. Then a second test was on how a guardian should act. Kat aced both tests and both were overjoyed. Kat's day of birth was coming up and both would be happy because she would be twelve years of age. Kat's computer told her that as soon as they reached the end of the desert they would start her physical training. The next few nights went by very fast.

Soon the day was upon and Kat was happy she had made it another year. They wish each other a happy day of birth. Kat ran for half the night and then stopped to reflect on her lost ones. She said a prayer for all the lost family in her life and for her protection on her travels. Then she took flight and flew the rest of the night. When she landed for evening she gazed into the distance and did not see an endless sea of white but, a dark green mass. With a large smile on her face she made her den for the day. When she was done she crawled in and turned into her four-legged form. Next she curled up into a ball and fell asleep.

When she awoke she flew out of her of sleeping spot and into the air. With a large smile on her face she flew towards the green mass and out of the white desert. Switching her eyelids she could see the large dark mass was a forest. "We are going to be in a forest again," Kat yelled into the night air. Landing where the dirt met the sand she turned and looked at the sea of white for one last time. She said a small prayer for her lost friend and then with a large smile entered the forest.

She traveled the rest of the night and her computer told her to find a safe place to rest. When she looked around she saw she was in a very narrow valley. Climbing a tree she could see to the left and right of her were large cliffs. Taking flight she found an empty cave on the side of the cliff on her right. Looking around the cave she could not see any sign that the hollow was in use at the moment. Flying back down to the forest she collected some leaves and branches she then preceded back to the cave where she made a soft nest. As she rested and prepared to sleep her computer told her she would now start her physical training. Life would be harder but she would be stronger at the end. Kat thanked her computer and she closed her eyes to sleep for the day.

***

The format of the book is now going to change for the rest of the main chapters travels she is given lessons on how to be a guardian to make it easier for the reader to under stand the diary well now be in groups of lessons not chapters. Keep in mind she is still traveling and time is still going by as she still is trying to find her new home. Once the lessons are done the dairy will go back into the chapter format and will continue in that format till the end of the dairy. Once the Zeaytera KatOynera passed the first lesson she went to the next one. In short you will get a description of the lesson then one or two exert from the dairy. We feel the dairy would be to repetitive to put the whole lesson section into the novel.

— The Scientist who translated this dairy. ***

Lessons

Lesson One: Tracking

Kat must walk and looked for tracks in her surroundings. When she found them she would hunt down the thing, which made them. She had to find her prey and make sure she made no tracks. Her computer made sure she took every step to track correctly and hide her footpaths. This lesson also focuses on how to build traps and look out for them. She had to find remains from an animal and know what attacked it find out what has been eating the carcass. Kat also had to determine what direction the animal went after it left it's meal. She had to set traps and set them off to test them. She learned how to clean the campsite and set one up to help keep herself hidden. How track after it rains or during all types of weather. And one of the hardest areas to track was water. She could follow her prey for miles without it knowing. Another concept to masters was birds and how to track a nebaywho kapeca (bird of prey). Kat could soon walk without making a sound or sneak up on her prey on land, water or air.

When I woke up I looked as down from my resting place. Seeing the ground below me. I could see the always-moving river. The blue shifting water invited me calling with it's quite flow which had relaxed her to sleep. After stretching I jumped into the deep cool waters. Using my eyes I scanned for food but there was none in sight. I looked under rocks in and small eddies but there was no food to be found. Soon I stopped looking and swam to the bed of the river where I pushed off with my feet. Swimming faster and faster to the surface upon reaching it I flew out of the water and grabbed a branch by where I spent the night. Cleaning up my nest I knew today was a test day. My computer would be making sure I could track anything, anytime and anywhere.

Once my mess was cleaned up I jumped to the forest floor where I crouched low. Smelling the air and scanning the ground I saw small tracks leading into a brush. Quickly I carefully walked to the first track where I picked up the dirt around it and took in a deep breath. Smelling the faint sent of a Katrina Detu, female, with young. Standing I looked over the bush and saw the tracks stopped. Thinking for a minute it came to me. Without hesitation I walked to the right and gazed at the nearby tree truck. There I found very small scratches in the bark and some small chips. With a smile on my face I quietly jumped onto the tree and using my claws slowly, and gently climbed the bark. Following the cracks and chips I soon was by the top of the tree. I spotted a small hole right above a strong thick branch. With all my might jumped to the branch and now hanging by my hand I started to swing. Doing a flip I landed silently on the branch, stood and looked into the little hole. Inside I found a young mother Katrina Detu with two young, males. I did not want to wake them. I slow backed away from the hole and taking flight started my journey for the day.

My computer said I did very well but still left large marks in the tree where I had climbed. I was happy I did well. As I flew I followed the river upstream. Looking down I saw a Jukumoo (small deer). I was overjoyed I found my first meal of the day. I flew into the forest behind the small mammal and walking through the treetops I came to where the little Jukumoo was drinking. When my prey put it's head down to get a drink I jumped onto its back and bit the neck. Breaking the neck in one shift move so my prey never knew what happen or felt a lot of pain. I quickly ate everything from the bones to the brains and moved on with a full tummy.

The wind felt good running through my fur as I flew across the sky. A few hours of flying I landed for my mid-day break. I drank some water from the river and ate some berries I found by the riverside. Lying on my stomach I looked at my reflection in the water. I looked different. I had not looked at my reflection in years. Wow, I had deep eyes and black fur. My white teeth were opposite of my pitch-dark fur. Placing my claw into the water I played with the current making different ripples and designs in the water. Soon my computer told me it was time to move onward on my journey. With a roll of my eyes I was off flying again. My computer and I continued to talk as we flew about life, history and the code. I was always being tested to make sure I never forgot my lessons I had already passed.

I travel onward till the sun was low in the sky where I found a resting spot the cliff side where I made a nest out of leaves and gathered water and food. Once I was set for the night I watched the sun set and the sky change colors. Soon dusk was night. I went into to mode of reflection and peace. As I laid my head down to sleep I said a prayer and drifted into the land of dreams.

Lesson Two: Water

Kat had to be able to swim for long distances without stop and rest. Hold her breath for long periods of time, which was no trouble for the little one. Fight, hide, and trap prey in the water. Hide in the water and hide under the bed of the river, pound, lake or any body of water. She also had to climb a waterfall from the underside. Be a master of water and its world.

I woke once again in the treetops above the clear, blue and ever changing river. With a small smile on my face I stretched and said, "good morning," to my computer. Today would be full day of traveling because it was my swimming test. I carefully untied the branches and unrove my nest. Once I was finish I look one last breath of fresh air and while looking at the sunrise to greet the land, I dove into the river.

Making a little splash my body was now in the water. I started to swim up stream fight the current and trying to keep a good pace. I had a respectable stride going but I found it very hard to keep a fast pace. Soon I came to smooth part of the river and scanned the area. I stopped swimming because I saw a Booruukuu (stone shark). The Booruukuu was waiting for me to move forward so it could get a piece of me. I let the current slowly take me a little ways down stream and once a was a few yards from the predator I swam to the side of the deep river and slow started to climb up stream once again. Soon I was parallel with my prey. I could sharpen a rock and attack the Booruukuu but that would be too easy. I had to attack the sea predator head on. Climbing forward I was now upstream of the Booruukuu. Next I went to the surface of the water and once I was above my victim I swam straight down on top of it. Digging my claws into the gills of the grey and brown creature I pinned the fight one down till it drown at the bottom of the river bed. Proceeding to the nearest eddy I then started to eat my first meal of the day.

After my short break I was moving up river again. Hugging the sides knowing being in the middle was dangerous because being out in the open was not safe. My arms ached but I had to head onward I could not stop. Breathing trough my gills and using my wings under the water was becoming second nature. My eyes with the blue lids on worked great in the wet world. I did a few pulses as I was moving upstream to test and get a feel for what the underwater ones were like. They moved faster and looked a little different compared to the ones on land but I still had no trouble reading the maps my computer showed me. I once tried to use my other eyes lids under the water and it just did not work. As I travelled on my computer talked and quizzed me to help keep my mind off my pain and journey. As mid-day was turning into evening I reached a waterfall.

My last challenge of the day would be to climb the cliff against the water. I swam under the massive current from the landing water and reached the rock behind the falls. Digging my claws into the rock I started to climb. Tucking my wings into my back, now I did not feel as much pressure from the falling water on my back. Step by step I climbed higher and higher. Soon I was high enough where the water could not touch me. Turning my head I could see the sun falling slowly down the sky through the clear water. The crashing water consumed my ears and the cold wet rock was not match for my sharp strong claws. My arms ached as I continued to climb. Telling myself not to give up my computer also gave me words of encouragement as the endless climb march onward. When the sun was gone and the moon was on the rise I was near the top of the waterfall. The liquid force was once again against me and this was the hardest part of the climb. I was tired from climbing and I had to go one on one with the current still strong as ever. Hitting the rock hard and getting a stronger grip I continued up and the battle with the water. After putting with all my might my arms, legs and my head were over the falls. Then my body followed and last my legs. I continued a little ways on the bed of the river till I found a safe Edie and jumped out of the water. I slow walked to the edge of the cliff where I could see was I accomplished that day. Looking where I had to go I could only see more forest.

I went into the woodland behind me and caught a few birds and had my last meal of the day. At the edge of the cliff I made my camp where I fell asleep for some much need rest.

Lesson Three: Endurance

To pass this lesson Kat had to be able to swim, run, and or fly without stopping for a week. Only stopping for food, water or any needs. The computer had her swim for a week straight then run and last fly. When she was in the air or land she had to switch from her two-legged form to her four-legged form on the hour. In the water she could travel the best in her two-legged form. Day and night did not matter she could not stop and if she did she had to start the week all over again from the beginning. Between the three ways to travel she got one day of rest. Below is a small day from each of the different way she travelled.

As I continued up the riverbed the water was getting clear which met the sun was rising for my third day of travel by water. I was tired my like normal my body ached. I was getting use the pain and soon it was always there like a new friend. Lingering in background waiting for me to pay attention to it. I liked to travel during the day because I could see with a little more ease. As I travelled I grabbed fish so I really only needed to stop to go to the Dompoo (bathroom). I took turns using my wings then my legs then my arms. So, my different parts got a small break. I could not fully daydream because I had to be on guard for anything that might attack me. My eyes were heavy and so were my wings. I found myself getting sleepy I jumped in and out of water playing at the surface of the river. Most of the time the splashing did the trick but, today I was really tired and the splashing was not working. I had to think quickly. After reflecting and looking around the river I saw a Yughi (dolphin). I remembered that Yughis are playful. I swam up to the male Yughi and started a good game of Leoi. The young male happily played back. The green and black sea creature was a great being to play Leoi with because they were so quick in the water. I know I improved on my swimming skills after that workout. Soon the Yughi left me and once again I was alone.

I spent the rest of the day talking to my computer and being tested till my mind had it for the day and I just swam in silence. The water became darker, darker and darker as each minute passed and this action informed me the sun was setting. Soon it was night again the water was still peaceful, flowing and cool.

— ----------

The ground moved under my running paws. I was in my four-legged form and jogging at a good pace. I was so happy to get out of the water and onto the land. I was still tired and wanted more than a days rest but had to continue despite what I thought. Night was here and the moon was on the rise. I enjoyed running through the forest dogging the trees and jumping the bushes. As I ran I could hear the familiar noises of the forest during the night. Every now then I roared out and made everything quiet for a while. Then a rowjos (crickets) would start their sweet song again, which was only beginning of a symphony of sounds. For the first time I really saw that my white and red lids kind of glowed because at night I could see the light coming off them on the trees. No one ever told me they glowed and I could not image what they must look like. I would have to find a good reflective lake at night. As I ran I saw a group of skittles (cats). I think they are related to my kind some how because they look just like me when I am in my four-legged form but much smaller and have no wings. I liked to run in my four-legged from because it was more relaxing, easier and faster. On the hour I had to switch forms. I did this by jumping in the air and then changing and I would land still running never stopping.

To me the days went by quicker when I was on land then when I was in the water. I was happy to breath fresh air but my muscles and mind were tired. I continued reminding myself I had to make my family proud. I would not fail the ones counting on me and I did not want to do this lesson all over again. I wanted to prove to myself I could do it too. Those thoughts kept my paws moving when they ached and I was in pain. I stopped to catch my second meal of the day and within ten minutes I was running again.

I herd the sky yell and rain soon was falling down onto the trees and land. The thunder and lighting played in the sky and the rain fell cooling the land the giving life. I ran with a smile. I enjoyed the rain and loved to run in it. The dirt became mud and I brought out my claws for better traction. After the storm passed the sky started to getting lighter and lighter and I knew another day was beginning.

— ------------

My long raven colored wings carried me higher and higher up into the clouds. I was happy to give my paws a rest and now my wings would ache for a change. When I was hungry I would fly over the river and grab a fish or two. The world looked different from above. I liked the change. I could see the river and the different shades of green from the trees. The cliffs made great wind tunnels for me to play and do aerial moves. I found flying the easiest to do for a week. The last day of my endurance was finally here and I was filled with great joy knowing once the sun kissed the land I could take a long rest, if my computer lets me. I know I would get a least a day of rest. I mind was wondering and my muscles ached. The wind felt good going through my black fur. I did flips and dove to the ground and back up again when I need to wake myself. Once I tried to chase a bird but was too weak to keep up with the little fowl. I remembered some of the moves Zutiyro taught me to practice when I was learning how it fly I tried to do some of them. To pass the time I again talked to my computer and had it quiz me to make sure I was still on top of the game. I was a little slower but I still got most of the questions right.

At one point I tried to think about how long I had been traveling. I left when I was ten and I was thirteen now. Three years is a long time to be on the move. I could not believe it had been that long since I had freed myself and said goodbye to the group of zatos. I started to think about them but, my computer quickly told me not to and started going over what the next lesson was going to be about. I tried to listen yet, deep down inside I knew I was not going to remember and my computer would have to repeat the whole speech.

Soon I saw the night was turning into dawn I roared in joy because soon I would not only be able to land and rest but also I would complete another lesson. When the warm sun's rays reached my fur I slowly landed by flexing the sore muscles in my back. With heavy arms and eyes I made myself a small bed in a hole in one the cliff and fell into a deep sleep, which only my computer could wake me.

Lesson 4: Crafting / fixing

Kat had to be able to make something out of her surroundings that could fix any problem that may occur. If something broke be able to fix it or wrap an inured body part. How to make shelter, tools, weapons and anything else a guardian might need while on a hut or home in a village and do problem solving with ease.

I awoke to the sun and started traveling like any other day. I had to walk or run these days because my lesson was crafting or fixing and I need to find my supplies around me. Lets face it there are not many supplies in the air. There was a small clearing in the forest and when I looked up my eyes grew at the sight of mountains. I would again have to travel over peaks to find a new home. I was not happy to see the mountain but, I would not let them stop me. I will face the range and win.

My computer would state any object and I would have to make it out of what I could find as I walked. Or my companion would say an object that was broken and I would have to explain what I would to fix and then make it. During my breaks I made a shelter or at least part of one again out of what was around me. This was an easier lesson than the last on and I was very happy about that.

That day during my brake my computer told me to make a roof for a shelter. I scanned the area and saw a lake, trees, bushes, grass and dirt. I saw big leather looking leaves and picked about twenty of them. Sitting in the long grass it ripped the big leaves into strips and began to weave them into a water tight blanket that was not only very strong but would work for a few months as a roof. Once I had all the leaves woven my computer told me I did a great job and it was time to move onward.

All that day as I walked I had to make slings and splints, medicine and other mixtures. I had to make pots and cloths. I only got faster and faster working with my hands and problem solving. If I did not want to waste the goods around me I told my computer what I would do and how I would do it and most of the time me computer said it was ok but, every now and then the answer was "no" and I had to make what my friend asked me too. Rain again fell from the sky today and as time moved on I had a harder time working with the wet and slippery plants. I did find new uses for mud and some kinds of plants, which made me happy. Now that I knew I would be going into the mountains again I started to gather supplies I would need to live. Making new and stronger cloths and bedding for the cold nights. I started to dry berries and collect nuts. which make a great small meal on the go while climbing the snowy peaks.

As the day was coming to an end I fell into a deep mode of reflection and prayer. I found myself looking up trying to find the stars but the trees blocked my view. I wondered if my lost ones were really looking down on me and guiding me. Would I ever find home or a new group of beings to live with and be happy? All I could do was pray and hope for the best. My computer brought me back to tell me to find a place to sleep for the night. Knowing I would soon be sleeping on hard rock for a while I made a nice soft hammock in the treetops. I prayed for that night not to have any bad dreams but to sleep peacefully. I seem to have a bad dream every night. I always awoke in a cold sweat hearing the laughing of Jabo or the cries of lost one. I took a deep breath of the forest air and let the sound of the waters flowing, insect chirping and the calls of the night animals rock me to sleep for another day was done and a new was on its way.

Lesson 5: Hunting and Capturing

In this lesson Kat must be able to hunt and capture any prey without hurting or cutting it in any way. She must track the animal down then pin it to the ground for a minute and last release the prey without harming it. She must also do this action quickly and without her computer's help. At least one of the animals Kat takes down must be bigger than her in weight and body.

I had rested all day and night was here. I was ready to hunt and take down my prey. I was hungry and on the prowl. Using my tracking skills, I found the trail of a young male Veryku (a small type of dog). I knew verykus had big ears and were very hard to hunt because they could hear whatever was sneaking up on them. I decided to go for it and hunt the male. Changing into my form-legged form I began to hunt.

Smelling the dirt and wind I found the veryku's sent. Hiding in the treetops I jumped from branch to branch following to small trail of footprints. Soon I came to a small pond and there on the edge drinking was the Veryku. The little mammal was green and black with deep brown eyes. It had white tips of fur on the top of its ears. The little one looked nervous. I licked my lips and watched my prey for the right time to pounce. The Veryku looked up and moving around his ears in different directions listening for the forest creatures to change. When he let his guard down and lowered his head for a cool drink of water. I silently jumped into the air and landed on the little male. Digging my claws into his flesh I bit the neck snapping it before my prey could make a sound or even find out what attacked him. I picked up my prey with my jaws and climbed a nearby tree. There I ate my first meal of the night knowing I have to master the power of moving in silence. After I finished my supper I jump down from my resting place and was looking for my next prey.

This time I would go after a Jezika (unicorn), and I would not hurt it. My goal was to take it down without harming it and when I captured the mammal let it go to live another day. I would be working on my capturing skills not killing. Because I just ate I could not eat another meal. I started by finding the tracks of my next prey. I walked back down to the pond to look for footprints. The pool looked like a place where lots of animals went for refreshment.

Soon I found a faint track of a young female Jezika. I was on the trail and found the sent on the dirt and grass of the golden meadow. I soon found some dropping and I knew I was on the right trail. I would soon fine my prey and come out the victor. I stayed low to the ground and soon found myself weaving in and out of trees of the nearby forest. I came across the river again and looking down stream I saw my prize. There in the bank of a small eddy was the brightly colored mammal.

The Jezika was a good-sized female was beady black eyes, which were bright and full of life and joy. Her horn was a gold color and was a spiral. It looked about 18 inches long. I would have to be careful because the horn could really hurt me. Her hooves were also golden and her tail and main a sliver-white looking, which matched the sparkles in the water from the moon's rays. The Jezika with the glittery main looked around and was full of energy. I decide I would chase after the female and then trip her. Next I would pin her to the ground. I would trap her but I would not use my claws.

I went a little ways up stream and then crossed the river. Once I was across safely I changed into my four-legged form and slowly started down stream where soon the Jezika was in sight. My eyes never left the goal. I moved in small sessions. When my prey looked down I went a little closer then stopped then a little closer. I was soon a few feet away from my prize. Right when I was about a pounce a bird started to call out into the air. The female was startled by this and took off running. Jumping from my hiding place the Jezika now knew she was in real trouble. She tried to doge between trees and over bushes but I stayed right on her tail. I knew I had to trip her some how, with all my strength. I ran along side the frighten female and I pushed myself against the Jezika. This action forced the prey off balance and fall to the dirt floor. As I jumped on the Jezika I changed back into my two-legged form and grab my pack, which I kept in the space between my wings on my back. I pulled out a rope and tied the female's legs so she could not run. I made sure to keep my eye on her horn, which almost impaled me twice. Once I trapped my prize my computer said I did a good job and I let the Jezika go who took off into the woods at amazing speed.

I walked along with a smile on my face knowing I had done a good job that night. I was not happy with that bird which called out but it was good because I had to quickly change my plan and make it work. After my adventure that evening went by very quickly. When the sun was rising I caught my last meal of the night and made a small fire where I rested my paws and reflected on my day and life. When the sun was on the rise I put out my fire and found a resting stop in the treetops and went to sleep for the day. This was my last day in the forest tomorrow I would take on the mountain.

Lesson 6: Senses

The object of this lesson is to gets Kat's sense in top condition. Her eyes, smell, tasting and touch must be perfected so she can fight, protect and survive. She uses the ball Zutiyro gave her and her computer tests her with other devises like the metal ball. She had to do a number of tests each one on one of her main sense, her computer made a major end test. Once Kat passed all her tests she knew she could always improve but she was considered at the level of true guardian.

I woke up with the sun and start up the mountain again with a steady pace. Today at my break I would be tested on my tasting. My mind was on it all day as I walk up the rocky face and kept my eyes open for a good place to rest. I tried to fly a few times but the wind was always against me and I found it easier to travel by paw. The rocks and snow switched places and I still enjoyed the feel of snow under my paws and it was a lot better than walking on sand for a long time.

Soon when the sun was high in the sky I reach a small summit and there I would take my test. I sat crossed legged in the snow and my told me computer I was ready. Then my computer asked me to make to bowl of neetye (berry soup). I did what I was asked. Once I was finished I put the small meal in two little bowls. Then my computer ordered me to make a small sleeping potion. My computer put out a small arm and took the potion. After I closed my eyes my computer put the mixture into one of the neetye. I had to take a slip of both and decide which one had the potion.

When my computer put its arm back inside it told me to open my eyes and pick a bowl. First I tried the one to my left and took a small slip. Next I sat and thought about it and then tried the bowl on the right. I sat and looked at the two bowls and compared the two tastes. The bowl on the right was sweeter than the one on the left. I thought the mixture took some of the sweet taste away so I told my computer the bowl on the left was the one with the mixture. "Are you sure?" my computer asked. I quickly replied, "Yes!" There was a silent pause then my computer told me I was right. I had passed. I finished the neetye, which was not drugged and went on my way.

I was happy for the rest of the day. I went higher on the mountain and found a nice summit to rest. I built a fire and ate a little hand full of nuts and berries. I had to sleep alone in the snow and I was cold now without another body to help keep me warm. Sometimes I dug a hole in the snow and that seemed to help me keep warmer. I still had really bad dreams but now only my computer would be there to comfort me. The dreams seemed to be getting worst. I could not get rid of them no matter what I tried. The dreams were apart of my life now. I soon fell into a light sleep.

----- —

I had been traveling on the mountain rage for some time now and I was now ready for my computer to test my sense of smell. All day as I walked up the mountain my computer put scents in the air and when I could smell them I had to say what the sent was. I also had to find some kind of prey in the snow only using my nose. I found a small Guupoo (rabbit) in the snow. The little white mammal made a great snack and was tricky to find in the snow because they liked to dig borrows. My computer told me I was doing a great job.

Later when we stopped for the break of the day I sat by a little spring and look down at the surface of the water. This was the first time I had seen my reflection in a long time. I was amazed about how different I looked. I was not a little one but young one and almost a young female. I was going up fast and with a short childhood I could see why. I could not see the scars on my back but tired. I wanted to see why no one liked to look at my back but I could not see that in the reflective surface. After a short break I was climbing again higher and higher and deeper and deeper into the range.

The day moved by quickly and soon the night would be upon me. I made a burrow for the evening and fell into a sleep. Waking with a cry I was a cold and wet. I hugged myself in the snow and whimpered. I had another dream. In this dream Jabo started an avalanche and captured me. After he pinned me to the walls he started to whip me and then Zutiyro and Hutto came in and Jabo killed them with a red ray gun. He started laughing and pointed the gun and me and when he was about to shoot me I woke from my slumber. My computer tried to get me to clam down but I was upset at the fact I had no one and everyone I had ever met was dead because of me. I got up early that morning and prepared for my hardest test for this lesson.

For the next two days I could only travel with my eyes shunt. I made a blindfold out of some cloth I had and made sure I could not see. I had to hunt, sleep, fly, walk and run without the use of sight. I had to use my ears and smell to guide me. I would have to depend on my sense of touch as well. When the sun kissed the land I put the cover over my eyes and headed deeper into the mountain range. I had to walk slowly so I would not fall. In the morning I tripped a lot but by mid-after noon I was doing much better. I kept my ears pricked and moving listening for any prey or predators. I came to a snow filled meadow and changing into my four-legged form I started to hunt any thing that might be hiding in the snow. After searching for a while I was about to give up and move onward but I herd something moving in the grass. Turning slowly and focusing on the sound and then I pounced. I landed on a small mammal I ate it and I continued on my quest.

During the night I travelled in my four-legged form. I would trip more because it was harder. I now had four paws on the ground not just two. I caught a fish and a bird during the night. The time passed quickly and before I knew it the sun was rising to greet the world once again and I knew I was half way done. By the end of the second night I could run up or down the mountain with out all trouble. I found and caught my prey with ease and felt more comfortable without using my eyes. When the sun warmed the land for the second time I took the cover off my eyes. I found a nice place to rest. I rested for about an hour and then was on my way again. I was like the world, always moving and changing. My computer said I was doing great with my lesson and soon I would be on the next one.

Lesson 7: Talking

In this lesson Kat learns how valuable talking or not talking can be. This lesson is to see how long Kat can go without talking. Her computer will try to get the young one to speak. This tool would require great disciplined. Kat's computer tells Kat when she can eat; drink stop moving and when she can talk again. The trick is knowing when the lesson is over or if it is a false end and the computer is trying to hoax her. If she speaks before the lesson ends and the young guardian must start all over again. Kat knew the lesson was over when her computer said a certain order of words.

Ten days have passed since I have stopped talking. I wished to use my voice and sing but I had to hold my wishes. Walking in silence was not fun. My computer only talked when it had an order. I was hungry but could not tell my computer or go get food myself. Finally when the sun was high in the sky my computer told me I could eat some berries and nothing more.

I did so and move down the mountain. "Would you like more food?" my computer asked. I said nothing just continued walking. "Well if do not answer me then that means you do not want any food and that is fine by me," my computer continued. I just remained silent and crossed my arms. "Fine if you are going to get mad. Then I am making this lesson over. You may talk now. You have completed the lesson. Great job," my computer finished. I still did not respond just change into my four-legged form and broke into a run.

The day moved slowly. The hours crept by and with no one to talk to I found myself longing to speak. I held my tongue. "You may stop for five minutes," the computer voiced. I pretend not to hear and kept moving. "You may stop for five minutes," the computer yelled. I still did not listen I just ran faster. Later when the sun was low I stopped for ten minutes to rest my paws. The entire time my computer was yelling at me to move. I did not care I did what it wanted. I walked for most of the night and took another break in the morning and watched the sunrise. The colors of the sky changed from navy blue to light blue, yellow, pink, and orange I always found myself more relaxed after watching the sunrise or fall. After the sun was on its way across the sky, running I moved on my quest.

My computer was not happy that I was not listening and told me it would hurt me. I still did not do what it asked but did my own thing. Then I felt a sharp pain. I computer shocked me! I could not believe it. I mean my computer shocked me! I wanted to ask why and yell but I held my tongue. Later my computer told me to talk or else but, again I just continued on my way through the mountains. About an hour later I felt another pain. This was long and more painful than the first. I wished to yell and scream but, held my tongue. Through the day the shocks got longer and more painful. One was so bad I had to stop walking. By the end of the day each shock that came I fell to the ground and had a hard time getting up and continuing. My eyes watered because of the pain. I tried to pinch them back but they came and slowly rolled down my cheeks. The pains continued into the night. Soon my computer asked, "Do you want the shocks to stop?"

I did not say a word. "If you want them to stop just say the word and I will stop if you do not tell me to stop I will just continue to make the pains longer and sharper," my computer told me. I still did not say anything but let the pains come and go as I walked.

Soon night was with me and I need sleep. I lay down in a small cavern and tried to sleep. I was woken up many times during to night from the sharp pains by my computer. I wished to talk and for the pain to end. Thoughts of my family and friends came into my head and I focused on that thought. The pain slowly died into the background. I stretched and tired to sleep. Soon I was in the land of dreaming waiting for the day where I could talk once more.

Lesson 8: Food

In this lesson Kat could not eat. She could only eat and or drink when her computer told her. She would have to go as long as she could with no food and only a little water. Her computer moved the times between meals in small groups first go a day then a day and half. Then two and half, three days. Once the fast got up to a weak she was allowed very small meal once a day. She also did not travel as much during this session.

My paws were tired and my tummy was in pain. I tired to push the aching to the back of my mind. The sun was on the rise. I continued up the mountain and to give my paws a break I took flight. I saw a large peak in the distance and was not looking forward to climbing it. I could not remember how long I had been traveling but I knew it has been a while. A little over year has passed since the death of Zutiyro. "Computer how old am I?"

"You are fourteen."

"Really, it has been that long?!"

"Yes, you are turning from a young guardian to a true one."

"Thanks for training me computer, do you ever think we will ever find a new home?"

"Your welcome and yes we will find a home. The new place we live will be great."

"I guess you are right."

"You may drink a little from that small spring to the left of you. Just a scoop full from you hands."

"Ok. Thanks computer."

Bending down I took a small slip of the cool spring water and moved on to the big mountain. I could tell I was losing lots weight. I soon moved slowly during to day and took more breaks but kept moving without food. To pass the time and keep my mind off the pain I talked to my computer or played games. I also reflected on my life. I only had a few more lessons to go before I could call myself a true guardian. I also had my computer quiz me to make sure I still was sharp on the history of my kind and about being a guardian. Going to bed hungry reminded me of Jabo. Many nights I went to bed with a whipping and no food. I still had my nightmares and wished them to stop. Soon it was life for me.

The day was coming to an end. I was trying to keep alert but was doing a poor job because my mind was elsewhere. I listened for movement round me and looked for a safe place to sleep for the night. I found another cavern. After building a fire, I sucked on some ice and made a small bed out of what little cloth I had in my pack. I wrapped my wings around my cold body. I did my best to fall asleep to the sounds of my stomach turning on itself.

The night time always seemed to move faster then day. I wonder why but I knew there was no real answer. I again watched the sun rise to relax my tired body and mind. The colors dance across the sky. When the show was over I turned and took I deep breath. I cleaned up my camp and made sure the fire was out and cold. I look around one last time and moved onward I was at the base of the large mountain. I was doing well for my lesson but did not like the constant pain. I made my up the mountain and took a few breaks. By midday I was half way up the mountain. I tried to fly but, the wind was too strong it was taking more work than walking up the mountainside. By night I reached to peak of the mountain. I dug a small hole and like the nights before I went to bed hungry and wishing for a physical friend. I fell into a light sleep and woke a few times over the night from a bad dream or the pain in my tummy. I soon got use to the pain and was getting better at pushing the feeling of pain to the back of my mind.

Lesson 9: Weapons

To give Kat a chance to recover from losing a lot of weight, the next lesson would not be as challenging. She would learn how to make different types of weapons and how to use them. Everything from Kingco (sling shot). moepoe (bow) and Yugis (arrows) to, Comink (spear), Suegoo (daggers), and more. Kat again had to use the elements around her to make her weapons. She enjoyed the break and liked learning how to make new things. She also practiced using her own built in weapons and features.

As I woke with the sun the air was fresh and clean. The one good thing about traveling on a mountain was the good air. I always took in a deep breath before I started the day. I have been learning how the make and use weapons for the last few weeks. I enjoy this lesson it is not to hard physically and I get to learn more about weapons and shooting them. I have now mastered my weapons, which, are made up of my computer and my targeting systems. Today I would be learning how to make and shoot a moepoe and Yugis. I could not wait. I heard form Hutto and Zutiyro my brother was very skilful with the moepoe and no one could beat him.

I could tell this was the last set of mountain because I could see a mass of dark green when I took to the air to just stretch my wings. I cannot stay in the sky for long because of the air and the sleet. I soon found a small lake that was frozen and there was a small grouping of trees by the icy edge. I climbed the tree and found a good branch to use for the moepoe and I looked for a small tree to use for a box.

First I made a box with a lid and blocks inside to hold the moepoe in place. Knowing that night would be a new moon. I could stop to rest even though I had not relaxed in weeks. After I made the box, I shaved the bark off the branch and started to shape it. Once the wood was at the arc I liked, I used my red ray gun to melt to of the ice in the lake. Dipping the moepoe in the new liquid the wood soaked up the water. When I was finished wetting the wood I carefully placed it in the box to dry. I did this many times over the course of the night.

Now that the moepoe arc was on its way it was time to work in the string. I collected the grass I started to make very thin strips and then wove a few of the pieces of grass together to make a very thin rope. I had to stop a few times to check and work on the moepoe. The day was done and night was well on its way. When the moepoe was done I cut holes on each end of each arc. Next I put the string through the two holes and tied knots and made the string tight. I pulled and let go of the moepoe and sting to test the strength of the wood and how flexible the string was. Last I worked on the Yugis. Taking the box I used with the moepoe I made the bodies of the Yugis. I caught a bird for a very late dinner and used the feathers for the Yugis and pointed rockss for the Yugis heads. I craved into the stones making little triangles and use the left over grass to tie them on to the wooden bodies. Soon I was done with my night project I tired out my new weapon. Aiming for a spot on a tree by the time dawn was here I was a decent shot with the moepoe and Yugis not as good as my brother but had a great feeling for the weapon.

I could not carry the moepoe and Yugis with me on my journey because it got in the way so that night I used them as firewood to cook my dinner. I would be out of the mountain rage any day now and could not wait to be out of the snow. I worked on other weapons and making them work. I was very busy and tried out some of my new weapons when I was hunting for a meal later that day. Water was hard to find because the weather was so cold. I had to use my red ray gun a few times. The days were short and I was sick of traveling I could not wait to find a place to live and stay. I decide to keep moving that night and not borrow down in the snow. I watched the moon dance across the sky and the colors of dawn take over the sky.

My arms were sore from throwing and shooting for the last few days. I told my computer I really wanted a break. She communicated to me a great idea. I slowly made my way to soft patch of moss growing under a tree. Resting my back against the smooth bark I closed my eyes and took a deep breath. As I let the air out I opened my white eyelids.

With my white lids in use I truly focused on what I could see and do. I found with concentration I could see great distances or zoom in very closely to an object. My computer informed me over time I would not have to work as hard to zoom in and out on my target. I had to develop my eye muscles. Next I tired my red lids. I could not find a real change. I did my best to change my vision but nothing really happened. My life long friend told me to try flying. We found the wind did not bother my eyes! Like the blue was for the water red blocked the wind in the air. My computer predicted these eye covers would mostly help with sun glare and rain when in flight or running at full speed. We decided to try them out the next day we were on the move.

I landed by a cave and decided that was a good place as any to sleep for the night. I collect supplies and prepared a meal. When my tummy was full I sat in a near by river to try to relax my sore muscles. Letting the river run by me I did my best to do some meditation and push all my pain and stress away. I pushed all of it in the river and let those thoughts drift away.

Later that day I look time to study the dagger. I sharpen the bladed and studied the handle. I did not like having the weapon hang from my belt. I made a leather covering for it. It was a strange feeling knowing the history of this weapon even though I have never used it. The family chips gave me the full story. The dagger was not anything special when my father was it's owner. It was just in the family for a few generations.

After my last meal of the day I put my green lids into place. I could see heat. Cold things were a different color than warmer and still a different shade for hot. If it were cold out nothing with a heat signature, as my computer called it, would be able to hide. Hunting would be easier if need be.

Last to try was my black eyelids. This one is very hard to explain. My computer called it an interface. I could see the world around me a new light. If needed a dark cave would become magically brighter. I could also see numbers my computer calculated. Distance, plant and animal species, targets verse allies, how thick or thin an object was and even predictions are all examples of some of the details I could see. I found these eyelids the most helpful. Like everything I would need to do some more practicing to make these abilities second nature.

Lesson 10: Fighting

In this lesson Kat learned how to fight. All different styles and where the body has weak points. She learned how to fight with weapons and how to fight without out weapons even if her challenger did. She acquired knowledge in how to defend herself and how to disable a fighter without killing the attacker. She again practices the use of her weapons in fighting.

Her computer was able to make a hologram of a challenger of all sizes and strengths. She was able to physically fight theses 3-D computer made fighters. They could hit Kat back and cause her pain. Her computer controlled all aspects of the aggressors.

I was happy when the sun kissed the snowy peaks. This was the last day I would be in the rage. I would enter a forest once more and have to change my sleeping habits. I would again travel at night and not day. I made my way down the pass as my computer explained the new way of fighting while showing my models and moving pictures of how the fighting was done. When I came to a good breaking point in my journey I would stop and practice the new or the fighting style I was working on at that time.

As I walked I could start to smell the scents of the forest and a smile grew on my face as I broke into a run. Within the hour I walked from snow to rock to a dirt floor. I would now not have to worry about food and I could fly when I wanted too. I would travel till the next no moon night then rest. I found some fruit on a tree and after looking at it I realized what kind of fruit it was from my training. I dug into the soft yellow and red fruit, which was called a dollies (kind of like a mango). I was joyous to eat real fruit again and my senses were overwhelmed. The dirt felt great under my paws. The ground was no longer cold but warm as I continued to find my new home.

The sun fell and rose three times before the new moon was with me. I stood by a small clearing made up of long golden grass. There was a small lake in the distance. I took and deep breath and faced my challenger: a level black young true guardian zato who was a light grey with some white highlights. Moving my body into a defensive position and awaited for my competitor to attack me. When he did so I fought back strong and hard. When he ran at me with his hands coming at me, I leaned back putting my body weight on the back of my paws and with a smooth action I jumped over the attacker running full speed at me. Doing a clean flip over his head once landed I moved to a crouching position when I proceed to trip him. Hearing him fall on his back I ease off him giving my attacker a chance to leave me before I really got mad.

The male stood up and faced me once more and as he started to jog to me he pulled out a Comink with a sharp blade on both ends. Jumping from side to side I dodged to blades. Pulling my wings out of my back just a little to aid me in getting more air as I jumped but not too much. I did not want to slow my backwards jumps. I started to take smaller and quicker jumps and with all my might on my last jump I pulled my wings out and took to the air. Without hesitation, so did my zato. I knew I could take him is the air because my wings were cable of doing more than his could so, I landed to give myself a challenge. Landing I quickly ducked and rolled out of the way as the fighter flew at me with the blade. He landed a few feet away from me. I went running at him and when he stuck out the blade to cut me I jumped and used it as a step. I flew over the grey one and grabbed his back. Putting him in a choker hold I held him till he passed out cold.

Once the fight was over my computer told me I did well because of the victory or if I did not win it would tell my good try. Next we would sit and watch the whole fight. My life companion would stop and show me where I could change and do better or where I did very well. That way I would learn what I needed to work on and what I did right. Next my friend would teach me something new if I was ready. Even though I still had much to work on but my computer decide to teach me something new for that day.

I was surprised to find out about a glad in each of my fingertips. My claws were like needles. My life long friend explained the liquid in the glad was toxic and extremely powerful. Just one drop could knock another out for up to an hour but in most cases a few minutes, any more than a drop would kill the recipient. Although I have had the glands since birth only with the last few months had the glad started to fill. The drop could come any of my claws.

I was shown a hologram of zatx and it was white with black spots on its parts of its body. Each black spot was a point on the body where the body was weak. My favourite spot was on the middle of the shoulder. This was a hard skill, which I would have to practice for many hours before I would have it down and ready to perform in a real life situation. The rest of that night I practiced releasing my venom on the black spots.

Later that week I tried the move in an easy battle and I am sad to write I did kill many of my attackers. I found I had applied too much force in my hands pushing out too much venom during the battle. Soon I finally got it was overjoyed and jumped into the air as my attacker disappeared. My computer told me I did a good job but, like always got back to teaching me and pointed out where I need to work. Over the next few days I found I had the most control in my index finger and thumb. I had to exercise bringing out my claws without letting the toxins flow.

After talking to my computer I asked about what would happen if the venom was ever consumed or if I ever injected myself? I had immunity of course but we were not sure what would happen the toxin was ever consumed. We decided to test out our theories. Using my scanners I found a pytrek (marmot) and Caolu (wolf). First I stunned the pytrek using my venom then placed the little mammal near the caolu. After the predator ate it's meal I waited and no harm came to the caolu. I also put my toxin on some leaves and watched a Hyproxi (deer) feast and again no harm came to the unknowing animal. After I killed, cooked and ate the hyproxi it was back to practicing once more. As the sun rose that morning I found a nice place in the treetops to rest and spent to day in and out of sleep.

Lesson 11: Torture

In this lesson Kat learned how to get information out of anyone. How to cause great pain without killing one and how to keep the one being torture alive for long periods of time. She learned how to torture with a lot of physically pain but also how to trick the mind to get what she wanted. This would be a hard lesson because Kat did not like to cause others pain but, it was a lesson she would have to face and pass.

I was getting use to sleeping during the day and moving during the night. I still had my nightmares it did not matter if I slept during the day or night. I did not know how to get rid of my dreams my computer had no answer for me and I just prayed and did my best to face them. Now that I was in the forest traveling was easier to me and I now was in the middle of my lesson on how to torture. I leaned how to hold a part on one's body to cause them great pain but was not that hard for me. I could find points on the body where with little effort or if I hit it at the right angle the bone would brake. I work hard to get the right grips and holds on the models my computer made me. I learned how to use to elements around me to aid me in getting information.

Cold or hot water could help change minds. If I made the beings really cold they might talk or if I made to too hot they would have a hard time focusing and might give me the information I wanted. Some plants or mixtures of plants could help me. I learned how to make a tonic, which made the one who took it very relaxed and willing to talk but it took awhile to work.

I learned how to cut the body where it would hurt but not bleed as much as in other places. This was a hard lesson about how to hurt others. As I reflected I realized I every lesson I was more like my father, brother, Hutto and Zutiyro. I was doing this for them and for me to prove I could do it. My computer also put in a scenario where I captured a group. In this part of the lesson I was to learn how to turn the group against each other to get any information I needed. The next part on the lesson I had to torture a little zatz who was still very young. This was hard because I did not want to hurt the little one but if I could not play with her mind I would have to cause her pain. In other cases I had to be intimidating to a large male this was hard because I was still somewhat small to a large full-grown zato. I had to cause him pain in order to prove my point.

As the sun rolled high in the big blue sky, I stopped to get a drink by a small eddy in the river. There I caught my last meal of the day, which was a fish. I made a small fire and cooked it while I relaxed. Looking at the forest around me I loved all the colors of the woods. I enjoyed listening to the forest noises. Each group of calls were like little quizzes to me. How many calls could I name? I enjoyed this game because it reminded me of Hutto and Zutiyro and when they had to tell me all the animals and plants now I could do it on my own and I felt proud. I also enjoyed the smells of the forest more than the mountain or desert there was more in the air. There seemed to be more life around me. There was more to do. I did not like having a hard time seeing the moon and stars but I knew they were there. Time passed more quickly and I was having fun traveling in the wood. I had to watch out for more danger and I had to sleep lightly because I was by myself but life was good.

Realizing I had been walking of a long time I climbed a tree and took to the air. Rising over the treetops and following the river. The twisted path of the river cut its way through the dark green blanket of trees. Doing some flips and aerial moves I stretched my wings. I saw the sky start to become a lighter color and day and night met. Once dawn was well on it way I found a nice place to rest within the treetops. Like how I started my day I took a deep breath. Closing my eyes I tried to get some well-needed rest. Knowing what my next Lesson was.

Lesson 12: To survive being tortured

In this lesson Kat had to take all the ways she learned how to torture others and use them on herself. Her computer made her very warm or cold. Also the computer use Kat's weapons on her. Her computer would talk to her playing with Kat's mind. Kat knew to mind her computer if it talked in her native tongue but if her friend spoke in the tongue of the Qothos Kat was not to mind. It was important for Kat to understand what it feels like to be tortured so she can relate to what she might have to do to others someday. Once she passed this lesson she would be one step closer to being true fighter in the sense she could handle was her enemies throw at her. Out of all the lessons this was the one she travelled the shortest distance.

I was so happy to be done with another lesson. I ran and flew hard all night out of joy. My next lesson would be really hard my computer warned me as I flew. As night was turning into day my computer asked me to find a cave. After looking for over an hour I finally found one. I flew down and made sure the little cave was not someone's home. The cave was cold and empty. Next my computer had me make a strong net. After the net was complete I made a layer of dirt and leaves to go over the woven ropes. Last I made a ropes with little starts (bells) tied to them. Before I hung the net I made several buckets and a cup. I filled over half of the buckets with water and the ones that were left with some berries and other small types of food. I place all the buckets in the cave. Once I was done with my projects my computer asked me to hang the large leaf net in front of cave trapping me inside the dark place. Then I tied the ropes with the starts on them about an inches off the ground walking deeper into the cave my computer told me this would be a very hard lesson for me

My computer told me to lie down on my back and look up at the top of the cave. Then my computer proceeded to tell me that I could not move from this spot no matter what until I heard the words, "This part of the lesson is over." I could not move. I did not like the sound of that. I had been moving almost every day since I started traveling and now I could not move for any reason. This was not going to be fun.

I sat in silence for a while focusing on the task at hand. The net made it so no one would come in and irrupt my training and in case anyone did the starts would ring. The net also served another propose it blocked the sun's light. I could not tell if it was day or night. This made the time go by even slower as I laid on my back reflecting and wondering how long I was going to be in this cave.

Soon I started to talk to my computer who happily talked back as if nothing was going wrong. Then without warning I was not aloud to talk to my computer but only sit in silence. Next the familiar pain of hunger set into my tummy. I could handle this pain I had already passed that lesson. I wanted to move and stretch but, sadly I could not. I muscles ached and wished to move. I just lay there trying to think about what I could do. I sited to guardian's code and soon I fell asleep. I awoke quickly to a sharp pain. My eyes opened and watered. I almost sat up but I did not seeing I was still in the cave and I remembered I had to stay on my back. My computer had shot me with my red ray gun on a low but still painfully level. My computer told me I could get up and be free if I stated out loud my name and rank. I reminded quiet. Though out my time there my computer cut or shot me but I did not say a word only spit. My computer also made it very hot or cold for me but I still could not move. This was not fun at all and I wanted to be over as soon as possible.

Later I had a new pain but I knew what this one was. I was not happy about it. Now I knew why my computer told me we could not talk. I bit my bottom lip as I tried to think of a way to get rid of this new pain. There was only one way and I did not like it. I had to go Dompoo really, really bad. I started to think that no matter what I was going to have to go and lie in my own waste. This was part of the training and my computer would wait for sure till I went but how long after would I have to wait. I just relaxed and let myself go and the pain was gone. I was unhappy and did not like the smell. I would have to get use to it and I realized if all the others before me could do it so could I. The next time I had to go I just went there was no point in causing myself more pain.

During the periods where there was nothing going on I wonder what time it was but I could not tell. Time was at a stand still then my computer ordered me to close my eyes and I was not to open them unless the part of lesson was done. My eyes close was like a blindfold. I could turn my head from side to side so I did this every now and then but this did not matter because I could not see anything.

As time passed I had to push the pain of my aching muscles to the back of my mind and just lie there. What else could I do, not much. My computer use its small arm and every now then gave me water and if I was lucky some food. Now that I knew what the buckets were for I wondered really how long I was going to be in this cave. I did not know if I got more water and food than need or just enough. I did know the longer I was in this cave the water would slowly lose its good taste. I drifted in and out of sleep facing all the tests my computer put me though. I would pass this part of the lesson there was no way I would want to do this over again. I knew I had been in the cave for more than a day or so and my wings were now starting to really ache. When I could not stand the pain I just tired to sleep because that was the cure for my pain.

Lesson 13: Control

In this lesson Kat must be able to control her anger and emotion in times of battle or conflict. Whether she dose not talk or is very forgiving; Kat must remain in control of herself. Her computer will try to make her mad and hurt her and Kat must remain clam. The computer has the power to trip Kat when she is running, flying and swimming.

I was so happy to out of the cave. I was very weak and did not have much muscle so I had to move very slowly. I first decided to get some fresh water and food. I tried to catch a fish but I was very tender. There were sores on my wings from not moving and being in my back for so long. I washed them in the river and later choose to give myself a nice long bath. Then without warning my computer tripped me. I slipped under the surface of the water. Coming back to the surface I asked my computer to be careful and it was okay.

I ate some berries and found nuts. I really wanted some meat. I craved it. I made a trap in the river and finally after waiting for what seemed like forever I had some meat. I did not bother to cook the fish but ate it when I caught it. My prey tasted very good and hit the spot. I was not happy when my computer told me I had to start moving again. With a roll of my eyes I started my way along the river.

I was very pleased to be moving again and not on my back but I was in a lot of pain to walk. The sores did not look good and whenever I took a break I would clean them. I asked my computer if I could fly but there was no answer. I asked my computer why it was mad and if I could do anything. Still there was no answer from my friend. "Well I am here for you if you ever need me or want to talk," I stated as I flexed the muscles on my back finding out they were very weak. As I walked I moved my wings trying to work my muscles all over again so I could fly. I felt like I was in training again. Then again without warning my computer tripped me. I fell to the dirt floor. My hands caught me from doing a face plant. Once again I asked my computer why it was upset but, sadly, there was still do answer. I repeated my offering of help.

We walked in silence for the most part of the day. My computer every now and then would trip me or shoot me with my red ray gun. By the early evening I was very tired of being tripped and shot at but I remain clam. The last time my computer shot me I asked if I was doing something wrong and stated that if I hurt anyone I was sorry and that was not my intention. If you would tell me what I did wrong I will do my best to work with you and solve the problem. Not to my surprise there was no answer.

Soon the time had come for me to catch my last meal of the day. I was still very weak and sore do I decide to catch fish again. Making a trap in about an hour I had a good meal. This time I took the time to cook my meal. I sat in the treetops eating and watching the sunrise when my computer finally talked.

I almost broke into tears as my friend told me I was failure and my father was nothing and weak. One by one my computer went though everyone I ever knew and yelled at me telling me all the ones I have cared about were not good zatx and were weak. I kept my emotions and just sat listening to my computer. Once my computer was finally done yelling I just took a deep breath and told my computer I was sorry it felt like that but, I feel like have done a good job growing up without a normal life. I looked up to my family and friends and was delighted to be like them. I went on to say how what the computer has said hurt me but was an opinion. This was really hard for me to do without getting very emotional. When I was done I told my computer I was going to bed and wanted to be left alone. I needed to cool off from my heated words. After about an hour I was finally clam and was falling asleep and my computer shot me with my gun. This was going to be a long lesson, but not as long as the last one, happily. Taking a deep breath I tried to go back to sleep.

Lesson 14: Muscles

In this lesson Kat must build up her muscles from all the lessons before this one. She must work hard and become very strong. Building the wing muscles too so, she can take flight from the ground.

I was joyous, cheerful excited, and happy. This was my last lesson. I could not believe it and I had come so far. And to make things even better this was an easy lesson all I had to do is work on my muscles. I was so happy I could not take the smile off my face. The next few weeks I would feel like I was done with my lesson because I would just be doing what I had been doing since the beginning of my travels.

The day started like all the others I got up, cleaned up my site and headed onward. My sores were almost gone from two lessons ago. As I walked I moved my wings working on my back muscles. The days were going by so fast and I mainly just traveled all day. When I was in the air I had to start slow and I would carry a rock in my hands. This way I was working on my arm muscles while I flew. Most nights I went to bed very sore but I was content. As I flew I could smell new scents in the air. I was happy to be in the air again. I did moves and quickly got back into the grove of flying. About midday I landed a little ways from the river at a lake. The lake was so reflective and peaceful. I picked up a large rock and started to walk into the water. I walked across the lake under water carrying the rock. I was very tired after I was finally done but I once again took flight by climbing a tree.

I loved looking at the world from above. Later I landed and changed into my four-legged form. I ran through the forest dodging the trees and jumping over bushes. As I ran I talked to my computer I was happy we were on good terms again. We both did not like when it was being mean to me, but, I learned a lot. As the ground moved under my feet and the day was turning into the night I still ran I was just in the mood to run. Soon I stopped for some food. I caught a few birds they tasted very good. My muscles were coming back and I was getting strong again this made my heart sing.

I decide with the help from my computer to sleep or at least try. I found a small thicket of bushes and laid down to rest. Sadly my sleep did not last long. Like most of my slumbers Jabo and the other Qothos awaked me. I had a cold sweat and a beating heart. I took a few deep breaths as my computer talked to me trying to comfort me. I did not want to sleep so I found a small clearing in the woodland and started to do some excises. I was growing stronger every day but like all things I need rest. This was going to be a battle for me.

I worked on my back muscles more that day and by the next sunrise I could take flight by jumping off the ground. I was almost back to where I was before the lesson started that took my strength. Life was good I just wish I had a friend there with me. I loved having someone to talk to, my computer, but to have a physical buddy to play games and run with would be even better. I could not wait till I could find a home and a group to live with and grow. Then I wondered what my new friends would look like and my home too. I asked my computer if I could have a hologram over my computer on each arm so no one could see them. If I found a group and they did not have computers I do not want to be more different. My computer agreed and made a hologram. Now I had to get use to not seeing my computer and using them with out seeing them. I had to practice but soon I could use my computers and pulses when I could only see them. The pulses maps went into my mind where I could just picture them instead of having real picture appear in front of me. I was almost done with this lesson then finally I could call myself a true guardian.

Out of the Woods

I woke up and was happy to now be considered a true guardian. I was so joyful to be done with all my lessons and I was stronger than ever. My computer was very proud of me and was cheerful to be done testing me. I was walking when I saw a very small pool of water on the ground. Getting down on one knee I cupped my hands and picked up some water. Bring it to my lips I took a nice refreshing drink. The water was surprising sweet; this was not water. Looking around I saw a flat long green vine wrapping a nearby tree. Dripping from the vine was the clear, sweet liquid. I carefully climbed the tree and found at the top a group of Linsays. Linsays are one of my favorite flowers. They are purple and blue with dark green vines. The flowers soak in the suns rays and turned the light into a sweet liquid. The water type liquid gives the ones who drink it energy and when the flower is out of water if grows more. Linsays are great plants but are very rare. I put some of the sweet water into a bottle and walked on with a smile on my face. I was having a great day.

As I ran I was full of energy thanks to the sweet water. I caught a great lunch and was back on my journey. As I was walking I could hear the sounds of the forest and I could see all of the colors. The dirt was warm under my paws and was soft I loved to sometimes take it slow and just take in all that is around me. I found this a great way to reflect and relax from the long and never ending trip to find a new home.

I was now on top of the food chain I can remember when I was afraid that something would try to attack me but now I was older, wiser and bigger and I do not think anything would try attack me. I could relax a little but I would always ready for anything that might try to challenge me. Over the past few years I have work hard on mastering all my skills. I could now fight using the toxin without fear of killing and new how to use all the weapons in my computer. I had also watched the family chips my father had left me. I knew every word by heart. Reflecting I recalled on the mental skills I possessed. I had not thought of them in years. After a conversion with my computer we decided to find a way to work on those abilities next.

I decided to take flight and spotted a large green mass ending and a sea of a white color or yellowish color. I did not know what to feel I did not want to be in the desert again. I liked the forest but that would mean I would be farther on my journey. I would take what ever comes. I landed and walked on the forest floor just in case I would not be on dirt for a while. I was walking at a good pace. I strolled into the night and listened to the night sounds. Naming all the different animals. I walked in peace and I soon found myself very hungry so I stopped to catch a meal.

I caught a mammal called a BurQuo (black elk). The BurQuo was a large meal but, I ate it all so I would not waste any thing. With a very full tummy I headed onward in the darkness. When night was turning into day I continued walking. I did not stop at all that day. I stopped to eat and take a few very short breaks. Soon when night had fallen again I took flight and flew over the trees trying to get a better look of what I would be traveling over next. Lucky for me it was not sand but a large meadow of long golden grass. I would enter woods again soon. I was so happy that I would not be in a desert again. When I reach the meadow I realized there was no moon that night so I would stop here for the night. I found a nice tree where the forest and meadow met. I tucked my wings into my back, made sure my computers were hidden by the holograms, kissed my metal heart and looked up at the stars. I thought I could smell smoke in the air and wondered if there had been a thunderstorm off in the distance that had caused a fire. I was exhausted and just did not care. Sitting against the tree I took a deep breath and fell into a deep sleep, which I need.

I was in a very deep sleep when I felt something touch my shoulder. I jolted awake. My body ached from all the work, traveling, and constant testing and questioning. The sun was just rising in the Eastern sky. Looking around to see what woke me, I froze. I pushed my back into the tree as my eyes widened. I eyes locked on the two being standing before me.

In Kat's eyes she was considered a true guardian. The young female passed at the tests set before her. The book for the most part will not be in dairy form from here to the end of the book. If Kat is by herself and is the first person that is a good sign the passage is taken almost straight from the diary. The authors choose to write the majority of the book in third person. Once reason they made this decision was because a change in language. The authors would also like to express although it is not written Kat is having constant conversations with her computer. Some are recorded in the pages that follow but most are not. At this point Kat is sixteen years old.

Part III: Home

A Long Day

Kat looked at the two beings staring at her. One was a tan color with a white underside and the other was a very light red with very light yellow patches of fur. They both looked to be male and both looked just like her brother. A smile grew on her face as she realized her journey was over and she found life. Quickly she stood up to greet the two strangers but as she did this they moved into a defensive position and held tight to their shafts. Kat backed to the tree and stated calmly, "I am not your foe. I am a friend. I come in good spirit." The two males looked at each other in disbelief as Kat looked at them. Her face turned from excitement to a puzzled fear. The two male started to talk to each other but Kat could not fully understand. They seemed to be talking in her tongue but only using root words. She never even thought about a language barrier. Kat bit her bottom lip as she thought how she wanted to handle their meeting.

Then the red one turned to the zatz and spoke. The only word she could pick up was clan or tribe. Looking down in thought. She tried to understand how to talk to the two who were looking at her. Finally she said, "No clan." The two seemed to understand because they started to talk to each other quietly and quickly. Then the red one turned to the guardian and started to talk again. He pointed to himself and stated, "Tom-Tom" then he pointed to his friend and voiced, "Atom" and last he pointed to her. The guardian figured out what the red male was doing. He was stating their names so Kat could then proceed to tell them her name, "Zeaytera KatOynera." They both looked at each other. So Kat then quickly stated, "wondrous one" and they both nodded their heads. They understood her!

Kat had to talk in roots and could understand part of the conversation. If the two males talked very slow then Kat could pick out the a few words and the more the two talked the better Kat got an understanding their "root" tongue. Tom-Tom asked Kat to come with them by turning his body and pointing for her to follow. The zatz was hesitant, she was not sure what they were fully saying and her gut was telling her to be careful. Then a third male came up from across the meadow and started to talk very fast to the other two. As they talked they pointed to Kat who soon felt very uncomfortable.

The third male looked angry. He was a dark sliver color with darker blue lines going down his body. Kat backed closer to the tree, which caught the attention of the infuriated male who seemed to yell at Kat who just looked confused. Then Atom turned to Kat and pointed to the grey one and stated, "Blazer." Then Blazer looked at Kat with eyes full of anger. He then pulled a rope out of his pack and started for the guardian. The zatz voiced, "NO," very loud and clear! He did not listen but continued to walk towards Kat who jumped back and got into a defensive position. The three looked at each other and laughed. Kat did her best to tell them she did not want to fight but the warrior would if the three really wanted. Blazer whispered something to the quiet one, Atom, who went running off across the meadow.

Blazer now turned his full attention to Kat who was ready to fight if they really wanted to get their asses kicked. Blazer gave Tom-Tom an order to get Kat. The little fighter again stated, "NO," to the attackers. She then tried to say, "no, fight, friend," but, they were not listening to her. Tom-Tom continued in Kat's direction.

Without a warning the male sprang at Kat who with one graceful movement moved to the side letting the pouncing one fly past her. Next the fighter turned her back so she was facing both of the males at an angle. She did not want her back to Blazer or Tom-Tom. Tom-Tom who did not look too happy started to walk up to Kat again. He made a hoop in the rope and got ready to try to get the zatz. When he threw the rope at her, Kat grabbed it and pulled as hard as she could bringing the male to the dirt floor. Next she heard Blazer start to laugh. Tom-Tom got up shaking the dirt off his coat. Kat did not like this fighting. The two males exchanged words and Kat tired understand it. Tom-Tom was telling Blazer if it was so easy to catch the female then he should do it. Kat looked at Blazer who rubbed his hands together and started to move in her direction.

The strong male came at Kat with a series of kicks, punches and more. The female fighter blocked all the attacks with great speed and with ease. Finally Kat got a punch out and hit Blazer who stumbled back with a surprised look on his face. The two males looked at each other and both headed in her direction. The guardian got ready and when the males worked as a team to fight her, she did her best to block the attackers. Kat did! Her training had paid off. With ease she pushed both the males back and did not even break a sweat. The two attackers were very surprised. Both caught their breath and came at Kat for round two. The zatz did a number of flips and jumps again she beat the two males proving they were no match for her.

As she was watching the males catch their breath she heard a familiar sound. She quickly turned and grabbed the flying teeka (dart) out of the air, which was heading for her back. Atom, the one who shot the teeka, face went blank at the site of his weapon being caught. Hearing the sounds of footsteps behind her Kat crouched to the ground and as both males went running past her she put her legs out. This action tripped the attacker who fell face first into the dirt floor. Kat could then hear a different noise. Looking up she saw there were a lot more than three attackers.

A large group of the males were gathering at the site and sounds of their friends fighting. Looking around she saw the group grow. She could not believe there were so many. She then looked at Tom-Tom who was looking at her expressions. Kat's face was in a shape of awe and fear. Turning to him she did her best to say she did not understand what was going on and she did not want to fight, but she was interrupted with a strong male's voice coming from the group. Then members from the group came and tried to capture Kat. The young guardian who was full of fear did not know what to do but because she did not want to be tied up she fought. As attackers one by one came after Kat, she knew it was going to be a long day.

As she fought the aggressive members from the crowd would randomly shoot teekas or cominks. Kat dodged or caught the weapons and then she used them against her challengers. Each time an attacker fought Kat and lost they would back off to catch their breath and then would come at Kat again. The female fighter was not getting any breaks. As the day went by Kat was getting tired of fighting and was get dehydrated.

At one point a large blue male with black spots came running up to her and he had a dap (shaft) in his hand. He started to attack the young female and she blocked his blows with her arms. Lucky for the guardian, with the roaring crowd and noise coming from the fighter no could hear the wood hit her metal computer. The fighter felt no pain as the wooden pole struck her and this action puzzled the attacker who out of frustration only came at her with more of his brute strength because he was hitting her harder. This made his blows slower, which gave the female the advantage. Moving faster she tripped the blue and black male with his own dap and sent him to the ground. Kat grabbed his weapon, which she used on the next aggressor and to hit away any flying objects thrown at her. The next challenger was red and also had a dap. The two attacked each other. Blocking and hitting, the female soon out moved the red opponent and grabbed one of the flying teekas and threw it at the red one who soon fell asleep.

As the day went on Kat started to use more harmful blocking techniques so, when she could, she would push on the pressure point on the shoulder and injected the warrior with her venom and the fighter fell to the ground out cold. The first time all the fighters witnessed this combat skill they backed off while looking at their friend on the ground. When attackers saw he was still alive they looked at Kat who was catching her breath. Before long the attacks started again and Kat would just knock out all the males and females who tried to take her down to the ground.

When evening was coming Kat was sick of fighting and brought out her claws and started to cut and break bones. When the moon was on the rise she was fighting a young female when she heard something above her. Quickly doing a flip she landed on a flyer's back. Grabbing his wings she pulled with all her might and made him do a flip and crash into the ground. Jumping off the fallen flyer she continued to fight the challengers on the ground. Still having to fight the ground fighters, flying weapons and now flying fighters. She was getting really fed up of being attacked and was ready to stop.

Then she realized the group did not know she had wings. The next flyer that attacked she would use him or her as a push off and take to the air. The beads of sweat fell from Kat's overworked body as the fight went into the night. Finally a flyer came down to take Kat. She jumped to the side and back over to get on the males back. As she landed on the male she put her weight into his back causing him to do a flip and as the action took momentum Kat forced the male into the ground. Kat opened her wings and took to the night air. She heard many grasps and awes as she took flight. Many of the others also did. Many nets were dropped on the tired fighter who used her claws to break free. She now had to fight in the air, which was easier for her to do and this gave her feet a rest. She still had to dodge weapons, which was not fun. Her computer helped her by giving a warning when someone or something was heading her in direction. Then she started to fade because of fatigued and dehydration.

When dawn was on its way Kat was in pain and wished for all the fighters would stop and leave her alone. A few times during the night she saw Atom, Tom-Tom and Blazer. She went hard on Blazer but tried to be kind to the other two. As the sun kissed the shadow filled land it brought light and warmth. A team of flyers took a few nets, flew at the fighter and tried to capture Kat. The guardian was too tired to dodge it. She hit the ground fast and hard. Now her head hurt and this pain made her livid and her eyes turned black. With a small new burst of energy she fought out of the net and the black eyes did help because some of the aggressors backed off at this new sight that filled them with fear.

The major of the group could not see Kat's eyes and did not understand why they had let the female go free. The strong male's voice came over the mass again. The group backed off and made a circle around Kat who now stood in the middle shaking very thirsty and in need of a break.

She had been fighting almost a full day. Taking slow, long and deep breaths they all stood in silence. The only ones who were moving were a few members who were taking the wounded back to wherever they lived. Kat slowly and carefully tucked her wings back into her back as she looked over her body checking for major cuts. There were none. A few scratches but nothing too bad and worry about.

Once she was done Kat started to look at the group their numbers never seemed to change even though she had been fighting and taking many of them down and out of the fight. The zatz's head was spinning and she did not know what to do. Finally the little fighter called out to the group, "Sue keymetu, gijuga sunkruu easma mattatee rowloe. Sue nequka moosawta teansa." When she finished the new one to the land looked at the group who by the look on their faces did not understand her. Kat then remembered she had to talk in roots. The one in the middle then voiced, "No, fight. Confusion. No rope, no cage." The guardian was getting no reaction from the group.

After another short moment of silence, a very large, strong, male stepped forward towards Kat. He had fierce golden eyes full of sprit, and patched colored fur of grays, blacks, tans and light sliver, strong black wings coming from his back and sharp white claws. He stood across from the shaking one with a smile on his face. "Are you ready to go down?" he asked. Kat caught almost every word spoken. The guardian shook her head no and slowly got into a defensive position. He laughed like the others before him. He came at her at full force and she dodged and blocked his attacks. She was slowing down.

She would not be able to keep up with this strong male. He had a different style of fighting than the others. His blows were harder to beat and quicker. Her arms and legs were getting heavy and she could not keep up with him. Looking up at him she could see he was still strong. Both of them knew who was going to win and after a few minutes of fighting the male connected with Kat. The guardian fell to the ground.

The male backed off as the crowd cheered and then Kat stood up slowly. She then got in her same position and the male turned to her and question, "Again?" Kat did not move but stayed still. Like before the male came at Kat and they were fighting again. Soon Kat could not do any flips, which meant she could not get into the air. Because Kat was so weak she missed a block and was again hit and fell to the ground.

The patched furred one yelled, "Rope," and a friend tossed him a rope. Kat stood and backed away and again stated, "No." Like before no one listened to her. The two started to fight once more and this time when Kat hit the ground the male jumped onto her back. He proceeded to tie her arms and legs together as the crowd cheered and walked in closing the circle. Kat was still awake when they tied her body with many ropes. They put a stick through her arms and carried her off across the meadow. The rope and stick pinched Kat's arms and legs. Some members of the group even went so far as to put a cloth inside Kat's mouth and blindfold her eyes. The group marched back home talking and laughing.

Soon Kat could feel the air and scents in the air change and the exhausted female knew they were underground, which she did not like because it reminded her of the Qothos and her eyes began to water. Kat felt a sharp pain on the back of her head. The members untied Kat's limp body and moved her into an empty room.

Who are you?

When Kat awoke she was attached to a cold stonewall with black, hooped, metal chain. Her head was spinning and her stomach was turning on itself, she needed food. As her eyes focused she realized she was in a dark room lit by fire. There were a few sets of chains. Kat was in the middle. There was a barred door, which was the only way out of the caged room. Feeling the back of her head Kat could feel a cut and dried blood. Grief came over her when she realized her dagger was now missing and possible forever lost. Kat sat in silence with her computer.

During her long battle Zea and her computer observed all the ones she fought did not see any computers, were in four-legged form, or shared some her different features. She wondered if they had noticed her gills and was pleased she had the hologram over her computer. Zea would do her best to see what physical features these new ones had, then do her best to hide her differences from them. The guardian could not tell if it was day or night but drifted in and out of consciousness. So she asked her computer who informed her it was night.

The door of the cell opening awakened Kat as a female walked into the fire lit room with a male who pulled on a set of chains that tighten Kat's restraints. She now could not move her arms. Kat's eyes focused very quickly and she saw a young female who was holding a tray with some food, and cloth. The young one knelt by the chained prisoner and looked at her. Finally the young one spoke, "Can you understand me?" When the she finished speaking the guardian looked down in thought then raised her head and nodded. A small smile came to her face as she began to speak again to Kat, "My name is Sweet Water and I am one of the doctor's aids. I am going to look at your wounds then give you some food." Kat could not fully understand what the young one was saying so she replied, "Kata? Yught bootika vealghoti. Missuy kindky rian." Sweet Water just looked a Kat then shook her head, "I am sorry I do not understand." The chained one tried to tell the young one in root words, "Sweet Water, friend, pain, sorry." The aid smiled and started to look at Kat's cuts. She explained what she was doing the best she could.

As Sweet Water dressed Kat's wounds the chained one looked at her. She was a very light greenish-gray. Her kind eyes were a yellowish-green and she had the gliding wings. The wings themselves were black but the fur holding them were the same color as her body. Her tail was a little smaller than Kat's and when the young one was done looking over Kat she started to give her some soup. Because Kat's hands were tied she could feed herself.

The prisoner tried to smell the soup and with a small laugh Sweet Water voiced, "Good, food." The guardian looked at the one in front of her then at the soup and last opened her mouth. The warm liquid felt very good to Kat's tummy and made her feel better. "Thank you," she voiced to the young one who smiled and said, "welcome."

As the two sat together Kat's ear pricked when there were three voices coming from outside the cell. "I want to see what group did this to all the wounded upstairs," a male stated. "How bad did they get beaten for their actions and what clan is the group from?" a female asked. "You will see, not beaten to badly and we do not know the clan yet" a second male voiced as the group appeared.

Kat looked at the three who were staring at her. Kat still could not fully understand the conversation they had but she was sure they were talking about her. Upon seeing them Sweet Water got up and backed to the wall while bowing. "Well?" the male said quite upset. "You are looking at the group." the second stated calmly. "That is not possible! One young female could not beat all those up stairs and not have a major wound or even ability to do such an action" the first male stated. "I watched the whole thing, you believe what you want but she is all that we have," the second told the group. The female quickly voiced, "Come," while she motioned everyone to come outside with her. As they asked Sweet Water questions about what she had been doing with the chained one. The guardian looked at the group. The first male was tall and slender. He had a dark tan fur with a black underbelly coat and green eyes. The second male was red with yellow and a black marking with deep brown almost black eyes and was well built. The female had a greenish-cream cream. She had light blue eyes and was a good size a little bigger than Kat. The chained one just sat and relaxed while trying to pick up the new language.

When the group was done talking the female and tall male came into the small room looking at Kat. The male turned to Kat and started talking very fast, "Who are you? What clan are you from? Why are you here? Why were you fighting? What are you speaking? What are you doing? How did you learn to fight like that?" Kat sat there bewildered not knowing where to start. So she voiced back, "Sorry, no, understand." The male looked very unhappy and rolled his eyes looking at his female friend.

The female crouched down on her knees and turned to Kat while saying, "My name is Kortne and this is Hunter." She paused allowing Kat to think then went on to ask," Where do you come from?" as she pulled out a map. She placed a map on the ground and handed Kat a rock. Kortne also had a rock and placed the rock on a place on the map and stated, "Home." Kat then took the rock and threw it as far as she could out of the room and voiced, "home," then looked at the two who were puzzled.

Then Kortne pulled out a cloth and it had all kinds of symbols on it in different colors. "Which one are you from?" Hunter asked. Kat looked at the symbols and did not recognize any of them. Finally the little one pronounced, "No, sorry," while she shrugged her shoulders. The two talked as Kat tried to listen and understand but they were talking so fast. Finally the male turned to Kat and asked, "Name?" without pausing Kat gave them her name, "Zeaytera KatOynera." The two continue to look at the chained one who then stated, "Wondrous one." They nodded and the female then asked Kat how old she was. Kat had to think then gave them the number sixteen. Then the guardian started to ask questions, "Why am I in chains, where am I, who are you? Why are we fighting? She continued asking questions till the Hunter yelled at her. They did not understand her and they were confused with the whole situation. They started to talk again but soon they left Kat was again left alone with her thoughts.

Time drifted by with Kat sleeping on and off during her wait to see someone. She was thinking how ironic it was that she wanted to meet new beings and when she did they caged her. She did not understand how everything got so mixed up and went wrong. She did not want to be in a cage but at least she was meeting the strangers and finding out about their way of life. Kat did not know what a clan really was or what the symbols were.

She was thinking about what happened for a while till her computer broke the train of thought in her head, – You were captured but, you did a great job fighting you are strong like your father. He did just what you did but Jabo helped bring him down and out of the fight. I am very proud of you –. A smile grew on Kat's face because she did not even think about the battle or how well she was fighting. She thanked her computer for the kind words. The both talked about the fight and that they were finally done with there long journey. Together they figured out each one of the symbols must be a clan whatever that was, maybe their word for village? One of the clans might be willing to take Kat in to live with them. She talked to her computer till she fell asleep.

The next time the door opened Kortne, a well built male who was a dark brown color with light blue markings and a third in chains walked into the room. The new prisoner was a smaller male who was a dirty orange color with white marking. The dark brown male chained the smaller fellow to the wall next to Kat. They exchanged some words and the male left. Kortne handed Kat some water who thanked her and watched her walk out of the dark room then shut the door.

Next Kat turned her attention to the new face next to her. He was looking at her with deep dark blue eyes, which looked tired. Kat looked at the water and took a long drink. When the cup was about half gone she offered the rest to the new one even though she really wanted it. He said, "Thank you," and took the rest of the water. Kat pointed to herself and said her name. The blue eyes widen and he choked on the rest of the water. When he regained his breath, he started to talk very fast. Asking her questions. He went too fast and Kat shook her head saying, "No, fast…Yes, slow." He took a deep breath and slowly asked Kat, "Do you know what you are speaking?"

"Home, tongue?"

"Where is home?"

"Far"

"You are specking an old language not spoken here for years. I have never heard it out loud. I have only tried to translate it and write it. Who taught you how to speak this tongue? Ummm…Teacher?"

"Father"

"Who is your father?"

"Domatu"

"What clan is he or you from?"

"Clan?" Kat tried to speak the new word but it came out slurred. Then Kat continued, "Name?"

The orange one looked down in embarrassment realizing he just started to ask question without introducing himself. He told Kat his name was Sparrow. Kat smiled. Then told Sparrow, "Travel, alone, long, where, here?" Sparrow stated thinking trying to piece together the roots Kat had voiced. When he finally understood he turned to talk and told Kat, "You are in the Shadow Kat's den. They are one of the biggest clans, which is a large group of Kats who live together. We are called Kats and there are many different clans in this land. The land's name depends who owned the land. You are in Shadow Kat's land. I am from the Cave Clan."

They sat in silence for a while for Kat to try to make sense of the information given to her. Finally she looked up into the blue eyes and asked, "why you here?" Sparrow half smiled as he shifted in his chains. "Well you see," he began, "the Shadow Clan captured me to talk to you. My job is to study the history of our kind. I study your language and try to understand it. Everyone thinks I am the best. So, if I do well with you by helping you learn our language then they might let me go home." When Kat pieced this together most of what he said and she felt very guilty that she had caused him pain.

She once again looked down in thought trying to think of the right words to say, "Sorry, help Sparrow." The new friend smiled and voiced, "I am going to try to teach you our language but, I need my notes to help you so I am going to try to go get them. I will be back, I hope." Kat smiled, watched and listened as Sparrow called for Kortne who came and took him out of the room. The guardian took a deep breath in the little room, as she looked around, once again alone.

Not a lot of time passed by before Hunter came into the room with a frown on his face. He had a small tray with some soup and bread. The male sat across from Kat and asked her what clan she was from and why she had no marking. When Kat told him she did not understand he took a bite of food. Kat realized very quickly he was going to eat all her food. She did not comprehend all his words but knew he was not going to help her. The zatz turned her head and closed her eyes. Hunter started to yell at her and threw the food on the ground while storming out of the room. Kat just looked at the wasted food on the ground. She watched the soup soak into the dirt floor and she soon drifted asleep.

The guardian awoke with beads of sweat coming down her forehead. Her surrounding might have changed but she was still the same and her nightmares were still strong in her mind. Her ear pricked as she heard footsteps coming, but they passed her cell. There was no time for her while in chains. Not seeing the stars made Zea very hopeless. Her computer could tell her how long she had been on the dirt floor but in a way the little one did not want to know.

She fell into a mode of reflection and prayer. She asked her lost ones to help her in this hard time and she thanked them for helping her this far in her life. Zea snapped out of her trance when the door opened and Kortne walked in with some water. The guardian thanked her as she downed the water. When Zea looked into Kortne's eyes she could tell the light blue kat wanted to help her. Soon the zatz was left to herself again. She was thinking and the word 'kat' was a form of the word zatx. Somehow the kats and the zatx were related. Kat had found her home now she had to make it hers.

The next group to walk into the cell was Kortne, Hunter, a well-built female and Sparrow with a great smile on his face. He carried with him a book filled with papers. A smile grew on Zea's face to see her friend. He was only chained at the foot this time he could move more now. Everyone left the room and Sparrow moved across form Kat while stating, "Your name means 'wondrous one'." She smiled and said, "Yes."

"That took me all night to translate your tongue it is very hard to learn. I have a question for you."

Kat nodded.

"What do you want me to call you because I am sorry but I can not say your name. What call you?"

Kat sat and thought she could be called Kat, but that would be to confusing. After thinking she gave Sparrow an answer, "Zea."

"I have been thinking on how to teach you. So, I have decided to write words and letters out for you."

"Thank you"

"These are our letters," he said while he handed her a piece of paper. She looked it over and smiled because now things made sense to her.

The two talked for hours and Sparrow taught Zea how to mainly speak their tongue. By the end of three sittings she could speak, write and read the new language. Sparrow was taken out of the room and Zea could hear and understand what was going on outside her room:

"She is amazing I have never seen anyone who is as smart and quick as she is, I am without words. I have done what you asked me too. She can speak, read and write. I wish I could stay and learn from her but, if I can go home I will." (Sparrow)

"We will see if you can go or not, that is not my call. Take him to his cell" (Hunter)

"Go get him." (Unknown male)

The group walked away and the silence took over the space. Zea was so happy she could understand what was going on around her. She smiled as she drifted into sleep. Zea awoke when Kortne walked into the room with some food. As she fed Zea she told her, she was going to be meeting "him" and she must be on her best behavior. And as she walked out she voiced, "Good luck." The guardian just sat there wondering who "he" was. A few minutes later the door opened and five very strong male kats walked to a certain spot in the room. Zea was thinking they were possibly a group of bodyguards. Once everyone was in their place Kortne walked into the room and preceded to the left of the door. Then he walked in to the room as Zea looked up in wonder.

The First Meeting

Walking into the small, dimly lit room was a very strong male Kat who gave a motion with his hand and the closest Kat to Zea raised her to her feet. The two looked each other over in silence. The male was taller than Zea and very strong broad shoulders, he had very bright golden eyes witch seemed to light the room. Zea could see the firelight reflection in the black part of his eyes. His coat was orange with a white underbelly. He had stripes the color of black starting from his back and going down to meet the white part of his fur. The black rings on his tail matched the color of his wings and he had some white on his face but most of the fur was orange. The male did have some stripes on his head pointing down to his cold black nose.

The new Kat paced in front of Zea with his arms behind his back looking at her. The guardian just looked at him wondering when the silence would be broken and she would finally know who was pacing and observing at her. The chained one-eyed Kortne, who was looking at the floor she was standing very still and quiet. After time had past the male stopped pacing and faced Zea who looked up at him from her deep green eyes.

Finally the waiting was over and he spoke, "Well, little one, you have caused a lot of trouble. I do not know what clan you are from but, I suggest you tell me right now before I become angry." His voice was low, deep and very solid. Zea took a deep breath and replied, "I am not from a clan, like I have been trying to tell everyone I have been traveling and I am not from this land." "I do not think this is the time for games. Where are you from?" He voiced very loudly. "I told you. I am not from this place, I have been traveling for a long time. I ran away from my home. I have never seen a clan in my life except, this one and I have been in here the whole time," Zea also voice strongly but not as loud. He went on, "No one cares if you ran away from you clan, I just want to know where you were born."

"Fine, but, you are not going to know it because my land is not yours. I am from the Villa turuku Yaottyro (The village of Bright Star). I do not know how to translate because your tongue Villa turuku does not exist and in my tongue clan does not exist."

"Who is your father?"

"Domatu"

"What does that mean?"

"Bear"

"What clan is Bear from?"

"His name is Domatu. And he is from the same place I am from."

"Well, little one, it seems we are getting no where. And I thi..."

"I have a name and I do not even know yours. I believe it is rude not to introduce yourself when you walk into a room," Zea interrupted. The male quickly turned his head and looked at the chained one sharply. "You are strong and very spirited but, you do not know your place," he told her. Zea quickly answered, "How am I to know my place if I do not know who you are?" "Everyone knows who I am," he proudly stated.

Zea cupped her hands and slid them down her face. She looked down then slowly looked up while taking a deep breath and restated, "Like I have been saying, I am not from your land. I do not know your ways, your kind, or who you are!" The male looked down one could tell he was frustrated. "You are very stupid, he began, "and very good at acting or very lost and smart. I feel like I have been very patient with you; I have killed for less. Now this is your last chance, I am going to ask you a question and you better tell me the truth." "Sure why not, even though I still do not know your name," Zea replied.

"What is your name?"

"Zeaytera KatOynera"

"How old are you?

"I am sixteen years of age."

"Who taught you your tongue?"

"My father, Domatu and my brother, Gyro"

"Who taught you how to fight?"

"Gyro and my friends, Hutto, Zutiyro and others"

"Ok, ok what is the meaning of all the names?"

"Why? I gave you the name. You do not call my friends and family by the meaning of their names. In my eyes that is disrespectful."

"You do not talk back to me."

"Why not?"

His eyes filled with rage and he and looked though Zea and yelled at her, "Because, I am the leader of this clan and you will show me respect. That is why and you will do as I say." Zea just looked at him calmly and asked him, "What is your name because I do not know what to call you. Unless, you want your name to be, "you" what do I call you?" He continued to look at her and then turned away as he did he voiced, "My name is Dark Flame, but you will call me Master." Without hesitation Zea told Dark Flame, "You will never be my master. No one will ever be my master. I will call you by your name and nothing different. I have no master!"

Dark Flame did not seem content with the chained one's answer. After pacing he finally spoke, "You will learn your place little one or I will have to teach you the hard way." Then he looked at her one more time thinking how the little sixteen year old fought over half his forces and lasted so long. The leader left the room and his guards followed him.

Zea was left with Kortne who walked over to her slowly. The guardian sat down in the dirt holding her head in her hands. "I am not sure what you are thinking" Kortne broke the silence. "I am just trying to understand what is going on right now, I was traveling one day and the next I am in chains. I do not know the language and I do not know anything about the way of life in this new place. Then this male comes in and starts getting furious at me. I have done nothing wrong. I was attacked first I was defending myself the whole time. That is what I am doing." "You live your life the way you want but, be careful about who you pick your fights with around here," the helper spoke softly to Zea. The green Kat left the room and the guardian was left with her thoughts.

– Computer, do you think I am doing a good job so far?– she asked her friend. – Yes, Zea, you are doing well. There is a lot going on and you do not understand all of it so, yes you are doing a good job. – her friend reassured. Zea tried to lie down and sleep but was not able to sleep much. She had so much on her mind and if she did fall asleep Jabo was there to keep her company. When the guardian was left alone and there was nothing to do she reviewed the new language she had learned from Sparrow and did her best to make sense of her life.

The next time the door opened Hunter walked in with a smile on his face. Zea did not know if this was a good thing or bad. He walked up to her and spoke, "Good first impression with our leader. I cannot wait till I can take you to the other room and make you suffer." Zea just smirked and looked away from him. "What are you smiling at," he questioned strongly? She said nothing but turned to look at him. Becoming angry he struck the chained zatz across the face, he laughed and Zea spit at him. He was about to hit her again when Kortne and Sweet Water walked into the room.

"What are you doing," Sweet Water called out into the room. Hunter stopped turning to look at the two females to staring at him. "I was helping her learn a lesson," he expressed as he left the room. Both females looked at the chained one who just glazed down while moving her jaw. They stepped into the room. Sweet Water observed Zea's cuts while Kortne started to talk to Zea about what was happening as she set out the chained one's food. The guardian thanked them for the food and kindness. Sweet Water told the young one her cuts were healed and she was going to be just fine.

After she had some food in her stomach the prisoner felt much better. She asked the two if she would ever see the light of day again. The two looked at each other and soon Kortne told Zea it was up to her and her actions. The two females left Zea again who fell asleep on the brown dirt floor. Because to Zea there was no time she got bored a lot, there was nothing for her to do, but just sit and think. She felt very unfortunate and wished to free. She did not like to be caged again her dreams were getting worse because the chains reminded her of the Qothos.

When the guards walked into the poor lit room Zea knew who was coming in next. Dark Flame walked in and up to Zea then stood right in front of her this time. He grabbed her chin and moved her head to the side getting a good look at her. She at first tried to fight, but soon just went along with him. She just looked into his eyes, while he asked, "Have you changed your mind little one?" Zea replied back, "Why would I change my mind?" He let go of her and she gazed down while moving her jaw. "I would like that you do not hold my face like that I do not like it," the chained one stated. "I will do what I wish," he voiced to her. "You do not respect me. Why," she question?

"I do what want and I do not see a reason to respect you. You are a trouble maker."

"If you do not give me any respect. Why should I respect you?"

"I am the leader of this clan an.."

"Not my leader," she interrupted he slapped her across the face and turned his back. She spit at the ground after moving her jaw. Zea then told the leader he had no respect for her so she would not give him any. He laughed at her while he asked her, "You think you have power?" He continued to say, "You have no power because you are nothing and you are mine." She said nothing but viewed the ground.

He once again grabbed her chin and moved it from side to side looking at her. Once he let her go she spit at him. He wiped the saliva off his cheek and proceeded to strike the chained one who fell to the floor. Slowly Zea got to her feet where she just stood there. Dark flame who was full of rage yelled into the room, "You must learn your place and now I am going to have to teach you how to act." Upon finishing he told his guards to grab the prisoner and follow him as he walked out of the room. They placed ropes round the guardian and even put a cloth in her mouth. The group pushed the fighting female out of the room, down a hallway and into a different chamber, but this one had a system of chains and pulleys.

After she was chained up she was facing the group. Dark Flame looked into Zea's green eyes and voiced to her, "If you get on your knees, pray for forgiveness and if you tell me I am your leader. I might just go easy on you for your punishment. If you do not I will make you suffer." Zea made only one sound and that was spit leaving her mouth and landing on the leader's chest.

This action did not help Dark Flame's mood and he ordered his guards to tighten the chains. Once they were done Zea was facing the wall and she knew what was coming next. They were going to whip her and she knew what that pain was like. Next she heard the familiar sound of the whip crack and some laughs from the group. The zatz had not felt the whip for so many years now and she knew the first strike would hurt but she would be able to take the pain for a while. Then she thought about it, they have never seen her back, the artwork of scars. She wondered what they would think when she opened her wings.

After thinking the guardian thought she wanted to show the group her wings not let them find her artwork. Zea without warning felt the barbs of the whip rip into her back. The pain cut her thoughts and she lost what she was thinking. When she heard some members of the group laugh she opened her wings. Silence took over the room.

Next Zea could hear some of them whispering and the whip dropping. The guardian then felt warm hands touch her back and upon feeling that she shut her wings on the hand. Dark Flame yanked his hand out from the trap and had his group unfold the chained one's wings. Once they were done the leader was in awe at the artwork. A part of him was in disbelief and trying to think about how the young one got so many scars. He felt her back again and was not sure what he wanted to do.

Zea continued to fight the ones who were trying to see her back. The group got her wings open and saw the full artwork on the little one's back. Dark flame broke the silence, "What happened to you?" There was no answer only stillness. Zea wished she could have seen their faces when she opened her wings and in a way she wished she could see the artwork herself. The next sound the guardian could hear was the group walking out of the room. She was left there with the cold chains and the stone walls.

Now that she was alone the guardian looked at her situation and tried to find a way out of her chains. Seeing the network of chains and pulleys she started to think of how to get loose. Standing on the tips of her feet she made some slack with the metal rope. Grabbing the extra slack with the rope she jumped and pushed off the wall. Landing on her feet her back was now pressed up against the cold wall. With all her might she ran forward. The chains held her back making her fall on to her back. Getting up quickly the Zea ran again trying to break a chain or a pulley. She was weak from a lack of food and not being able to move. Finding herself on her back again she got up and tried once more. The fighter kept doing this hoping to break free.

Soon a figure stood in the doorway and before Zea could get up from the ground the kat was pinning her down saying, "Oh, no you don't. Stop! You do not want to hurt yourself." The guardian now recognized the kat. He was the same one who took her down when she first came to this new land. He called out some names and soon he was not alone. The small group worked to restrain the zatz. Zea fought against the kats and the last thing she remembered was a large pain to her head. She was out cold.

When Zea woke up she had a chain on each arm and leg. She was stretched out with the pulleys and chains and there was no slack for her to move. Not much time had passed before Dark Flame walked into the room. "Well aren't we the fighter. You do not give up do you?" he began. There was no answer from the female warrior. "Where did you get all those scars?" the leader continued, "So, you are not talking anymore. Lets see if we can change that." He called out a few names and in walked in a few males. Each of them took turns beating the guardian and despite the pain Zea did not make a sound. Tears ran from her eyes as she was kicked and hit. The male kats laughed as they hit the zatz. When they were done they left the room but, as Dark Flame was walking out he stated, "Maybe this well loosen your tongue."

She was left to herself and then shortly after the silence was broken when Sweet Water and Kortne came into the dim room. Sweet Water dressed Zea's wounds as Kortne gave her some water and a little food. As the females were leaving the room Zea whispered thank you under her breath. They turned looking at the chained one, smiled and left.

A few minutes later a very strong male walked into the room Zea had never seen before. He was orange, black and white. He looked like Dark Flame but, the colors were switched around in his fur. He was mostly black with orange stripes and some white patches on his head and other places. His eyes were a bright golden color and he looked into the deep green eyes of the chained one in front of him. He broke the quiet by stating, "So you are the one Dark Flame has been talking about. How can you be dangerous? You are so beautiful." She did not speak a word but looked into his eyes. "Why are you not talking to me, what have I done to you?" he questioned. The male went on, "I am being rude my name is Pyro and I am not sure if I really know your name." The zatz cleared her throat and voiced, "My name is Zeaytera KatOynera."

"You are talking now that in nice."

"Who are you? If you do not mind me asking."

"I am the son of Dark Flame soon to be leader of the Shadow Clan."

"I am daughter of Domatu and I am from a very far away place from this land."

"Where did you learn how to fight like you do?"

"My friends taught me before they left me."

"You are so beautiful, does your name mean, 'pretty one'?"

"Well, you are charming. My name means 'wondrous one'."

"Thank you," he told her as he started to stroke her cheek. Zea turned away not wanting this attention. "You do not like?" Pyro asked. "I do not know you that well and this is not the time or place," the guardian whispered. He was disappointed but looked at her again, stroked her on the cheek, gazed into her eyes and told her, "Till next time." Pyro walked out of the room with his head high and his tail moving from side to side. Zea shook her head and spit at the ground once again alone. All she could think is, what just happened?

Her body ached and she drifted in and out consciousness as time passed. Soon Dark Flame walked in once again with a smile on his face. He voiced to the chained one, "So, against my wishes you have met my son. Did you like him?" There was no sound from the zatz. "You are still not talking, you did not learned your lesson yet?" He paused, "Am I going to have to teach you another lesson?" There was another pause then he spoke, "I do not want to do this but you must learn your place." He called his guards and they came and turned her around so she now faced the wall. Next Zea could hear the crack of the whip and the sound of the group laughing. The guardian felt the whip tear into her back. She did her best not to focus on the pain in her back but as the tears fell from her eyes all the childhood memories came back of Jabo and his temper. Right before Zea passed out her computer tried to comfort her. Finally the pain ended as she was out black.

She awoke on a table chained down at each leg, and arm. She was in a different dirt room. Her back was on fire and she wanted to have water but like usual she was alone. Pulling up hard on the ropes and chains that were holding her down she had no slack. Later she fell asleep.

A Break from the Darkness

When the guardian awoke her back was on fire. The hard wooden bed was not the most comfortable thing for her to sleep on or spend all her time lying and being pinned to. Zea's tail was free and still strong but her arms and legs could not move much. The room was all dirt and there were two fire torches on both sides of the doorway. As the zatz pushed on her restraints her friend spoke to her, – Zea, listen to me. You are wasting your energy. You need to relax and remember your training. You can beat this just relax.– The fighter took a deep breath and relaxed. Then she told her computer, – Thank you. I know I can always count on you.– –We will get through this but one day at a time.– the computer told its friend. –Thank you computer. We will get through this.– The two talked for the while till Zea fell asleep.

The door opened and Kortne and Sweet Water came into the room they were once again there to help the prisoner. Doing what they normally did, Sweet Water nursed Zea's wounds as Kortne gave her some water, bread and a little bite of soup. The guardian thanked the two who were helping her. Kortne did not look happy. When Zea asked her what was wrong the green Kat gave her a cold look. As she went back to work she voiced, "You are not being smart, every time you see Dark Flame you insult him. Are you trying to get yourself killed? I do not know what you are thinking but your choices are not good ones." The zatz turned to her helper and told her, "I am doing the best I can. I will not be a slave to anyone and especially if the one who wants me to serve him from a cage and beats me. I would rather die then to have him as master."

"If you would just give Dark Flame a chance, he can be a nice guy. If you follow his rules he is a great leader and cares about the clan."

"I am sorry, Kortne, but I will not be a member of a clan that hurts others for their benefit. They hurt sparrow just to get what they wanted. I do not want to be a part of that so if I am not a part of the clan, Dark Flame is not my leader."

"You are so stubborn," Kortne yelled as she quickly walked out of the room with the tray and bowls, leaving Sweet Water and the zatz alone. As

Zea closed her eyes she whispered, "I am sorry." "She just does not want to see you get hurt. She likes her clan but, she does not like to see others suffer when they do not have too," Sweet Water murmured. "I do not like to suffer but, I will not be a slave and just let them chain me," Zea stated. "I do not know your past, but there must be a lot of pain. I think what you are doing is brave but, be careful. I will not see you for a while your wounds are almost healed up completely. I do not how you heal so quickly but you do. Good luck and I hope not to see you too soon," the nurse told Zea. Sweet Water picked up her supplies and left the room.

Again there was no time to Zea. Every now and then someone came in and changed the guardian's waste and fed her. She missed looking at the stars and fresh air. Finally one day Dark Flame came into the room. "Have you learned your place and do you like your new home?" he stated with a smile as he walked up to Zea. There was no answer. "I have put a good portion of my time reflecting, little one. I have decided that I will let you join my clan even though you attacked my family. If you join of course you will be let go as soon as you say the words. We will teach you all you need to know and all the pain will stop to everyone's joy," Dark Flame voiced to his prisoner. To his disappointment there was no answer. The leader continued, "If you are not with me you are against me I will treat you like you are an enemy." Zea remained silent and just turned her head away from the Kat. He reached down and grabbed her chin forcing her to look in his direction. "Do you not understand what I just offered you," the leader asked Zea very strongly. The zatz still did not say a word just fight against the hand, which held her. He let go of her and started to walk round the wooden bed.

As he walked Zea quickly moved her tail causing him to trip and fall to the dirt floor. This action made his blood boil. The leader quickly grabbed some wooden hoops and a hammer. Dark Flame proceeded to make sure his prisoner could not move her tail. "I am very disappointed in you. I will now treat you like you have been acting. I hope you know what you have lost," he yelled as he walked out of the dim room. The fighter moved her jaw and did her best to relax. She would not join this clan it was against her ways and the code.

Dark Flame came in later and told her things were going to change for her. She would be getting little to no food till she talks. He also blindfolded her. Kats came in less and less to take care of her. She just wanted to be free and did her best to try to think and find a way out of her cage. Because she was getting less food and she was getting weaker and thinner.

The next visitor to come to see Zea was Pyro. She was not too happy to sense him. He walked up to her and carefully removed the cloth from her eyes. This was the only time she got a break from the darkness. He always had a little food for her. Zea liked what Pyro did for her but she did not like that he was falling in love with her. "How are you today?" he asked sweetly. Zea did not respond. "Ooooh, come on, little one, please talk to me. I will give you some food," he tempted her. He then hung a piece of meat in front of her. She till did not talk. "Do you want to play a game?" he asked. The guardian turned her head away from her visitor. "You know little one I think your attitude is why no comes and sees you," he whispered as he walked to where she was facing. "I am sorry. I will not call you little one but your name is so hard to say. I always mess it up will you please say it again" he asked her. The guardian then whispered, "Zea."

"I like the sound of that, Zea, Zea. Zzzzzea. May I ask you another question? If you do not mind how old are you?"

"I am seventeen."

"You are lying. You told my father you were sixteen."

"Time as passed since then."

He walked in silence around looking at her. Thinking about her words. Next he asked, "How do you know what day it is? I mean if you know when your birthday was." She turned to him and said, "I am good at counting."

"What do you count?"

"How many meals I get, different cloths, change of the guards out side my cell. That is what I count."

"Can you really count all those things?"

"I do not have much to do in this place."

He smiled and looked at her while he stopped walking. He looked at her beauty and saw how thin she was getting. He saw her deep green eyes and fell into them as he talked to her. Then one of his friends came in telling him it was time. Pyro looked at Zea one more time before he carefully put the blindfold back on the zatz and left with his friend. Zea did not like that he liked her but he was nice to her. There was nothing she could do at this point so, she just tried to relax and sleep.

As time passed the ones who helped the fighter got to know her started to realize how amazing she was. One day Dark Flame and Pyro came to see what Zea was capable of even though see was in restraints. As they stood in the doorway they saw that one of her hands was loose. Without hesitation Dark Flame yelled at the group, "Why is she loose what is the meaning of all this?" One of the guards tried to calm his leader and once everyone was ready they got Zea prepared. "She can tell where everyone is in the room even after we move and she has the blindfold over her eyes," the guard said.

He motioned for everyone to be quiet and he moved in the room. Once he stopped Zea's free hand pointed to him. Then another guard gave her a small piece of food. Then two guards moved and the guardian pointed to one then the other. All the Kats thought this action was great and amazing but, to the one who performed it, the action was easy and boring. Her training was much harder than what she was performing now. They asked her to play their games of finding and pointing till they could not think of any more ways to challenge the female.

She did not miss one. Both Dark Flame and Pyro were astonished at Zea's actions. They both wondered how she learned how to fight and all her skills but if they asked they knew they would get the same vague answers they got earlier. Soon Dark Flame told the group the fun was over for today and there was work to be done. The main guard retied Zea's arm to the wooden bed. They all left and she got a break from the games. Zea was left to her thoughts with the lifetime companion. They talked till once again the guardian fell into a sleep.

She awoke gasping. Trying to sit up the restraints held her down to the bed. Tears rolled from the guardian's eyes from under the cloth. Like many nights before this one Zea had just awoken from another nightmare. They were getting worse now that she was in a place that reminded her of the Qothos and her childhood with Jabo. As she lay down on her back she tried to think of the best way to escape. Pyro coming into the room interrupted her thoughts.

Her head followed the male moving around the small room. He stroked her leg and then slowly moved up to her stomach. Moving up between her breasts and up the neck. Soon he was gently stroking her face. Zea tried to move her head away from Pyro's hand. The Kat broke the silence, "You do not like?" The guardian stirred then spoke, "I do not know you that well and I do not feel comfortable with you touching me." "Be mine," he whispered. "What?" she asked. The visitor carefully removed the cloth from Zea's eyes and turned to her.

Getting down on his knees he whispered, "Be mine, I love you. Come, be my meka (girlfriend) and me your meko (boyfriend). Maybe later we can be maskas (husband, wife) but, I love you and I can get my father to let you go please give me a chance." Zea was quiet. She was thinking about what the male next to her was asking of her.

Finally after some thought she turned her head towards him and whispered back, "I am sorry. I am sure you are a great Kat but, I cannot be apart of a clan like this one." He stood up while stating, "But, Zea you are noting giving me a chance and you are not giving my family a chance. You have only seen the bad part of the tribe. You must give me and the clan a chance and show you the good parts." Zea closed her eyes and stated, "I have told you my answer. I am sorry but, I do not want to be member of this clan and I have told you many times why. I will not pretend to be something I am not." Pyro now started to walk around the room. He was not happy with Zea's words and was not sure what to think or do. Soon he carefully covered the guardian's eyes with the blindfold and left the room.

After that meeting, Pyro did not come and see Zea as much but every now and then he would show up with some food and to give her a break from the darkness. Pyro was the only Kat the guardian talked too. They were short talks but they spoke to each other nonetheless.

The only other one Zea really had contact with was Hawk who came to feed the fighter every now and then. They did not talk much but Zea soon could tell when Hawk was in the room by her footsteps, smell and sometimes voice. Most nights Zea wished to see the stars and to be free. She did not feel complete when she was tied down to the wood bed. As time passed Zea got used to Pyro's visits.

One night they were talking when the male asked, "If you could be doing anything right now, what would you being doing?" The female took a deep breath and answered, "I would be in the meadow outside lying in the grass looking at the stars because I do not know any other place in this land and I miss the stars." "Why do you like the stars?" the leader's son questioned. "They have special meaning to me from my past," the guardian whispered. "Do you know if there is a moon out right now?" The young one asked. "I do not know, wait. How do you know it is night out right now?" Pyro inquired. "I can tell because you always come to visit me at night," the zatz told him. "You did not answer me. How do you know what time of day it is?" the male asked. "I can tell because of the scents in the air, the temperature in the room, when the guards move outside and other things as well," Zea replied. Pyro took a deep breath and told Zea he would never fully understand her but he still loved her. He placed the cloth back over the female's eyes and left the room.

Later that week Pyro came and had a short conversation with Zea and as he walked out of the room he told her there was no moon that night. A small smile came to her lips when he said this to her. He had remembered. As she laid there in the darkness the guardian recalled the scents of flowers and dirt on Pyro's fur. More than ever she wished to be free but there seemed to be no end to the darkness and her entrapment.

Days and weeks went by and the guardian remained on her back. Her wings ached from not being able to move. She did her best to move her arms and legs whenever she could so she would keep some muscles strong in them.

Then one day Pyro walked into the room. He was moving more quickly then normal and when Zea's eyes were free he looked down at her. He looked worried. "What is wrong," the zatz asked promptly. He shut his eyes and looked away from the female. Then he spoke, "My father is growing inpatient with you. I am worried that he might do something to you. I really do not want him to hurt you. I think it is because you do not talk to him and he wants answers." "I am sorry but, I will not give into your father and let him win," Zea voiced. "This is not a game. This is your life. What if is tries to kill you," he told the guardian. The zatz voice was calm, "What ever Dark Flame has planned for me I will face it and if I die so be it. At least I will die with honor and not pretending to be something I am not. I will not disgrace my family and my kind. I am sorry if this hurts you and I do not want to end my life but if living by my code means I will die then I will. I made a promise and I will not break this promise to myself, my family, friends and the code." "There is nothing I can do that can change your mind?" he asked quietly. She shook her head no. He looked down in disappointment as he placed the blindfold over Zea's eyes. As he walked out of the dim room he told the guardian, "I will do my best to change my father's mind or make him go easy on you. I will talk to him but, please,

please stop spitting on him it makes it very hard for me to help you. Oh, by the way the moon is full tonight." Then he was gone till the next visit in a few days. As Zea was left alone a smile grew on her face hearing Pyro's words.

Switch

The days went by and all Zea could think of was when Dark Flame would come into the small room again to try to teach her a lesson. She felt like she was in the cave all over again but, this time she was there against her will. She was losing a lot of weight but was doing well. Since she was taken in all they were feeding her was water, bread and a little soup. The guardian was very glad she had someone to talk too while she was trapped. She communicated to her computer when she was alone and they chatted about all their adventures so far in their short life and how to escape. They were speaking one day and Zea started to ask her computer question about itself. Such as what sex it was or if it had a name. The computer told its friend that it had no real sex but could take one on and could do the same with a name. After much talk the two decided that the computer was a male but could not pick a name. By the end they felt like they were one in the same so for now the computer would be male but remain nameless.

One day Dark Flame walked into the room with all his guards. Zea mentally pictured where each guard stood in the room and where the leader was walking. He was pacing trying to think about what to say to his prisoner. The black female could recognize the next footsteps to enter the room. Dark Flame stopped in his placed and turned to the doorway. The leaders voice cut through the room, "Get out now!" "Please, may I stay," the one in the entry way pleaded. "You heard me the first time Kut (boy). Leave now," the father yelled to his son. With that Pyro left the room making his hand into fists as he walked down the hallway.

Now Dark Flame turned all his attention to Zea who was looking up with the blindfold still covering her eyes. He continued to pace. Besides him the room was still. Suddenly the leader stopped and looked over Zea. After taking a deep breath he broke the stillness of the room, "You have been trying my patience and I soon will not have any left for you. Weeks have gone by and you have not learned your place even after I have tried to teach you." The guardian did not say a word. She just sat there motionless as if she was in the room alone. He started to pace again but he stopped shortly and ripped to cloth off the zatz eyes.

Once he was looking into the deep green eyes he stated, "I will give you one more chance little one before I will let go in a very painful way which does not need to happen. The next time I come in if you do not speak and cooperate with me I will be forced to give you a final lesson which will end in your death. You will mind and respect me or you will die. In my eyes the choice is simple so I will not give you a long time to think. I have to go out of camp for a while and when I return I will be able to give you my full attention." He covered her eyes when he realized she was not going to respond to him. He quickly walked out of the room and his guards followed. Silence took over the room and yet again Zea was left to her thoughts.

One evening while the prisoner was resting familiar footfalls came into the room. The male walked over the Zea and slowly removed the cloth from her eyes. After a few blinks she whispered, "Thank you." "What brings you to my room?" she continued. Pyro leaned against the wall and slid to the dirt floor. While rubbing his head he voiced, "My father is driving me crazy." The female remained quiet.

"I mean, lately I have disagreed with all of his decisions."

"Have you tried to talk to him?"

The dark male laughed.

"You have met him."

"As you say I have only met one side of him,"

Now the Shadow Kat was silent.

"If you really do not like your clan why stay? Can you start your own clan or join another?"

"Join another??!! I would never lower my rank. Right now I am in the most powerful group not to mention second in command. Starting a new clan would be…"

Stillness took over the room.

"Pyro, I do not know your customs. I only have my beliefs and to me power is not everything."

"In this land powder is needed to survive. Over time you would learn this fact. I am trying to help you. That is why you should join forces with me."

"I do not agree with the morals of this clan"

"We can make a few changes."

"No more kidnapping, torturing, bullying and ma.."

"Zea, you are taking all the fun out of life," Pyro interrupted. The female just took in and let out a deep breath. Pyro tried to continue his logic but the zatz was not very talkative. "Fine, Zea. I will give you some more reflective time. It is getting late and I have a busy day tomorrow," the male said voiced as he replaced the blindfold. "Till next time," the guardian responded.

– There must be a way out of this trap,– Zea said to herself. – First, you must relax, take and deep breath and lets think, – her computer told the guardian. Zea tried to break the wood and ropes holding her. Then she realized her arm was almost free not because she broke the wood but her hand was so thin she could almost pulled her hand out of the small hoop. Digging into the wood with her claws she tried to make the gap bigger so she could be free. Her fingertips began to bleed from the splinters cutting her flesh.

After Zea worked for about an hour her hand, throbbing, was free. A smile came to her face as the guardian used her free hand to release the rest of her body from the wooden bed. Once she was out the guardian tried to walk but was really weak. Zea started to do exercises. –What are you doing?– her friend asked. –I am trying to work up some of my muscles in the short time that I have. I cannot just walk out of here because I am weak and not ready but, if I workout before Dark Flame gets back I might have a chance,– Zea replied. –I am proud of you. That is a great idea,– her friend stated to the guardian.

When the fighter heard someone coming she quickly jumped back into the wooden bed and retied herself up but still leaving one hand loose. Every chance she got Zea would free herself and workout. The guardian felt more alive now that she was able to move. Now the trick would be getting out of the underground maze and to fresh air.

The days seemed to go by more quickly now that Zea had something to do besides lay down and look into the darkness. As each day went by she knew her time was running out and the guardian needed to think of a way to leave this place of death. Once Pyro walked into the room and saw that Zea looked different. As he walked around the prisoner he looked over her body. Zea moved her arm so it did not look loose but tight against the restraints. The dim lighting was working for her. Pyro's words broke into the air, "There is something different about you but I cannot place it. What are you up too?" The guardian said nothing only shifted her weight. "You are not talking to me today?" he asked. Zea remained motionless. He reached over and carefully removed the blindfold from her eyes. She blinked letting her eyes quickly adjust to the new light. "Is that better?" he questioned. The guardian nodded while looking at Pyro. "How are you today Zea?" he enquired. "I am doing well, thank you, and yourself?" Zea spoke. "My father will be home any day now and I will not be the clan leader anymore so, that saddens me but, just the sight of you makes me feel better and the sorrow leaves me."

"You say sweet words, Pyro."

"Have you been thinking about what I asked you earlier?"

"My answer is the same. I am sorry. I do not want to hurt you."

"Then do not, Zea, give me and the clan a chance."

There was a silent pause as the guardian took a deep breath. Then she spoke, "We are going in circles. My answer will not change." Pyro also took a deep breath creating another pause. "I am sorry to hear that. I wish you would think about my offer but I cannot make you do anything. I have a lot of work to do before my father returns. I will see you later," he stated softly. "Yea," she whispered as he carefully placed the cloth over the guardian's eyes. Then he looked at her one more time then he sighed and walked out of the room locking the door behind him.

Zea worked harder and harder with each passing hour and soon she felt like she was a lot stronger. Finally the guardian came up with a good plan on how to escape from her captors. Zea went over her plan with her computer and reviewed it again in her mind. Soon she knew every step and her computer felt like her friend could escape from the Shadow Clan. The next time someone entered the room she would try her plan and she would try to free herself from the grasp of the clan. She took a deep breath and relaxed getting ready to go into action.

Then a familiar male walked into the room and walked around Zea. He started to feed her some soup and bread. Between bites Zea asked her feeder, "where is the normal one who feeds me?" The male cleared his throat and whispered, "Hawk is busy today so, since I am a high and trusted member of the clan I was given the job of feeding you." Then Zea recognized him. "You are the one who took me down that day when the clan took me," she stated. He chuckled and spoke in a soft voice, "Yes. I am the one." "Are you a strong fighter because I noticed you fight different from the other members of the clan?" she questioned. There was a long silence then the male whispered to the guardian, "I am a very strong fighter. I am not sure who is the best in the clan but Dark Flame is very good. Pyro is growing stronger every day as well." Zea nodded her head.

When they were finished he stood and as he did Zea spoke under her breath. The male could not hear and asked what she said. The guardian repeated herself still very quiet and under her breath. He leaned down close so he could hear her soft words and as he did she repeated but this time in a whisper, "Sorry." When she finished speaking for the third time with her free arm the guardian reached up and applied pressure on his shoulder and released a drop of venom. Zea hit her mark and the male fell to the dirt floor passed out cold. Upon hearing his body fall without hesitation Zea freed herself from the wooden bed and placed the Kat's body on the bed.

Just as she was checking to make sure the male was tied down he started to stir. When he realized he was in Zea's place he began to fight the restraints. She moved to his head and placed the blindfold in his mouth so he could not call for help. She looked into his eyes and repeated her words, "I am sorry." The guardian then paused and spoke once more, "I do not even know your name but, I am sorry and I hope nothing bad happens to you. I also hope you understand but, I need to break free or I am going to die. Good luck strong warrior." Zea took a deep breath and slowly opened the door, looked in both directions and for the first time walked out of the dim room locking the door behind her.

The hallway was also dark and lit with fire touches. She hugged the wall and moved very slowly. The guardian was praying she went the right way as she made her way through the maze of dirt walls. Her computer helped guide the guardian with pulses, but did not want to do too many because her energy was running low. When Zea came across another Kat she silently knocked him or her out and put the body in a room or in a dark corner. Soon she could smell the sweet scent of the outside world. She quickened her place and broke into an up hill run towards the exit. Again if she came across anyone in her way she fought them but, she was happy she had the gift of surprise.

Soon the scent of trees and flowers were overpowering and she could not wait to climb out of the dirt. She brought out her claws for traction and tucked her wings into her body. Taking a quick, short jump she landed bringing herself to a stop. There was a large group of Kats standing outside blocking her way to freedom. There was a lot of mud –It must have rained earlier,– she thought to herself. Zea rolled down on the mud floor, now her fur looked a dark brown color not black. She then arched her body and moved to the hallway. Zea was in view of the Kats and she yelled in a deep voice, "The prisoner has escaped. She is running the opposite direction." The Kats came running down the hallway and passed Zea who looked down acting like she had just been fighting. Once the group was gone she ran as fast as she could out of the Shadow Clan's lair.

The sun was out and she looked down to block the light. The sun's warm rays caused her to squint. The guardian did not know which way to run. Running to the shade of a tree she paused for a moment letting her eyes adjust to the outside world. Hearing the sound of footsteps she turned her head in the direction of the sound. A group of shadow Kats came running out of the maze and the male that beat her when she fought the clan. He spotted her and then pointed to her. Zea broke into a run as the group followed her.

In her mind the guardian was running for her life, she was afraid if they caught her Dark Flame would kill her. She was fast but she was also growing very weak. Soon she found herself in a meadow and she turned her head to look back. There was no sign of the group chasing her. Suddenly Zea ran into something and fell to the ground. Looking up she met eyes with a very strong male with deep blue eyes. She began to crawl back and away from him. He just looked at her in silence then he moved his eyes and gazed across the meadow and saw the group heading for their direction. Moving his head he spied down at the zatz who just looked at him and whispered, "Please, help me." He gazed at the brown female with deep green eyes pleading for help. He shifted his weight and pointed into a patch of long grass. Zea nodded while very quietly moving to the long grass where she laid low and slowed her breathing. The guardian stayed motionless while she watched the group come up to the strong blue-eyed male.

"Have you seen anyone come this way?" the male Zea knew and who was leading the group asked. "I have seen many come this way," the blued eyed male answered. "Have you seen anyone come in the last few minutes?" he leader asked impatiently. "No," the blues eyed Kat replied. The leader moved into the others male's face and spoke to him low and strong, "I better not find out that you lied to me, Bear. That would be a poor judgment on your part and you would risk war between our two clans." Bear shifted his weight and restated his answer, "No." The leader looked at him coldly, gave a signal to the group and moved on to hunt for their prisoner. Once they were gone Bear looked at the patch of long grass and motioned to Zea it was safe to come out of hiding. The guardian stood and faced her savior. She smiled and gave him a sign of respect. He still stood in silence looking at the odd stranger.

The Clan of Dark Star

Zea looked at Bear he had deep blue eyes, was well built and his fur color was a dark, reddish clay color with black marking on his head, back and tail. He had a white cream-colored belly and chin. He was looking her over as well. Finally he broke the silence, "What are you waiting here for? Go home you are out of trouble." Zea looked down then slowly looked back at him while stating softly, "I do not know where to go but, I cannot go home." He gave her an odd look and spoke, "What clan are you from?" "I do not have a clan." She paused and put her hand out while stating, "Sorry I have been rude. Thank you for helping me, my name is Zeaytera KatOynera." He looked at her hand then back up to her face but did not but reach his hand out to greet hers. "Are you a Colin (loner)?" he asked. "I am sorry but what is a Colin?" she responded. "I do not find this conversation very funny," Bear informed her. "I am sorry. You have already saved my life. I do not dare to ask any more of you," Zea said as she showed another sign of respect. The male just observed at her with an aggravated look.

The male crouched down and continued to work. The exhausted female did her best to hold back her tears and fear. She started to look around. She knew the way she came and was not going to return. Shaking the zatz took a few steps then stopped and continued looking left and right. Zea shifted her weight for the first time in a long time she was unsure of herself. Her body ached and she was tired. Bear looked up and saw the young female having a mental battle. He watched as she stumbled to the ground and fought to stand again. Then he realized if she really had escaped from the Shadow Kats the female would be weak.

"Wait," Bear called. Zea turned to face the male. He could start to make out her fur color by the tear trails. "I need to finish my work and then I will find you a place to stay for the night," he told her. The guardian's face turned from fear to pure joy. "I do not know what to say but thank you," She responded. Zea carefully walked over to the male and sat down. As her adrenaline came down the female had a hard time staying conscious.

When Bear was done with his work he helped the female to her feet. They began to walk. The male had to support Zea as they moved forwards and asked her questions to help her stay awake. "What do you mean you were not born in my land?" he asked. "I have traveled here from beyond the mountain range," Zea answered. "There are no clans over the mountains do you mean the flat cliffs West of here," he told the female. Zea paused her mind was fuzzy and she was tried to get her barring. –No,- the computer helped. "No, I do not know what you speak of. I know there are no clans over the mountains. I came from a very large Villa. A Villa is a very, very large clan made up of hundreds," the female informed.

"You are telling the truth aren't you," Bear whispered. "Of course I am why would I lie?" she stated. "I am not from your land. I ran away from my home, traveled a long time and when I reached this land the Shadow Clan imprisoned me. Once they found out I could not fully understand your language they captured, Sparrow from the Cave Clan. He taught me your language. I do not know how long I have been underground with the Shadow Clan but I know it has been a while. I just escaped and now you saved me," Zea continued. "That is quite the story," the male responded.

As they walked Bear could see how thin and weak the female really was. The weight of the mud was not helping. As they were walking up a small hill Zea's computer voiced in her head –I am sorry friend but we cannot go much further.- -Thank you computer- the zatz answered. "Bear, I am sorry but I am very light headed and .." the young female started but was cut off when her tired body finally gave out. Bear quickly caught her and with a sigh picked her up in his arms and continued on his journey. He finally reached a river where he carefully waded into the water and lowered the limp body.

The mud started to fall off in the moving water. With the change in surrounding Zea was snapped back to reality. Bear almost dropped the surprised female. "Clam down, it is okay," Bear voiced strongly. The computer was told the zatz the same message and she quickly regained control of her emotions. Bear helped her wash off the rest of the mud. The zatz also took the opportunity to take a long, needed drink. The male was astonished with the amount of earth on the little female and how black her fur really was.

Dusk was on its way and Bear knew he had to get home. "It is getting late so I guess you are coming home with me tonight," the male stated. Zea did not know how to respond. "Thank you again for helping me, words cannot express," she whispered. The two moved onward towards safety.

Soon they reached their destination. In a large meadow on the outskirts of a forest and by a river a clan rested. There were a grouping of huts and a fire in the middle burning bright. Bear called out to his friends who came out to greet him. Zea saw there were guards who walked round the perimeter of the camp and they just waved to Bear and continued to keep watch. Very quickly the guardian noticed that the clan was all males. She stayed close to Bear as they walked to a hut for the visitor to sleep and they stopped every now and then because one of the clan members wanted to talk to Bear. Finally they reached a shelter and they walked inside where it was quiet.

There was a small cot against the far wall and a wooden table with a chair. Zea sat on the bed while Bear pulled up the chair. He took a deep breath and began, "I now have to go out and explain why I brought you back into our camp. As you noticed this is an all male clan and you already know my name is Bear. I better not find out that you are a good actor and you are lying to me." "I give you my word I am not lying to you," she affirmed. "State your name again," he asked.

"My name is Zeaytera KatOynera."

"And where are you from?"

"I am from Villa turuku Yaottyro. Which I think translates to the really, really, big clan of Yaottyro or Bright Star. I have traveled a very long time but I came from the narrow valley and from over the mountain rage."

"Okay, do not leave this hut. I will be back soon." He took a deep breath and stood up now looking down at the little one before him. Bear left the room as Zea thanked him for his kindness. The guardian was now alone and free. The cloth on her back felt very good compared to the hard wood. She was so tired when she laid down to wait for Bear to return she fell into a deep sleep.

The sunlight hit Zea and she awoke from her sleep. When she opened her eyes she saw water and a small meal on the table. The guardian slowly stood up and walked to the table where she sat down and slowly began to eat. When the zatz was just finishing her meal there was a knock on the door and Bear walked into the room. "How did you sleep, little one?" he asked. "I slept well, thank you. How are you this morning?" she questioned. "I am doing well." He moved to the bed where he sat. "What to do with you," he whispered to himself. "I am sorry if I am causing you trouble. I will leave if you want just point me in a good direction," Zea told Bear.

"I cannot have that on my mind now can I. If what you say is true then how are you going to join a clan if you do not know our ways?"

"I do not know. I guess I will have to find a clan that will take me in and teach me."

"That will not happen."

They sat in silence then finally Bear spoke, "Come I wish you to meet someone." He came to his feet and headed for the door. Zea followed the Kat out of the hut and into the light. They strolled across the camp and as they walked the guardian looked around her happy to be outside and free.

As they walked all the males in the camp looked up to see the new one and then turned back to their work. Soon the two reached another hut where Bear knocked and waited for them to be called into the room. When they heard a voice call, "Enter," Bear lead the way into the hut. Upon entering the room Zea could see a tan and white colored male with deep brown eyes working at a table. He looked up seeing who was coming to see him. He stood to greet his visitors. Walking up to Zea he put his hand out for Zea to take as he stated, "Hello, my name is Dark Star and I am the leader of this clan which is named after me. I can see you have met my second in command and best friend, Bear. What I understand is you are not from this land and you do not have a clan." "I am pleased to meet you. This is true. I am not from your land so I do not have clan. I just escaped from the Shadow Clan."

"The reason we have a hard time believing you is because in our history no one has ever escaped from the Shadow without some help."

"I am telling you the truth. I fight differently and was brought up in a different way maybe that is why I could escape when no one else ever has."

"That could be true."

The three stood in silence for a while till Zea for the first time in a while broke the silence and asked the males, "Do you want me to leave? I mean the camp not just the hut because I heard what the Kat who was tracking me told Bear about causing a battle." The males looked at each other and then down at the ground in thought. They asked Zea to leave while they talked and the guardian did what they asked. Once she was outside everyone stopped and observed at her. She loved the feel of grass under paws and not dirt. She sat on the grass outside the hut and let the sunlight bathe her.

After some time passed both Bear and Dark Star came out of the hut. They looked at the guardian who stood upon seeing them. Bear walked over to Zea and told her to come with him. They left the camp and made their way to the river they started to collect water. Bear was being very quiet as the two did the chore. The Kat would look up at Zea every now and then. "Why do you look at me so much and get all quiet around me?" she asked. "Never mind, please just keep working. If all goes well today I will tell you tonight," he replied. When they had enough water the two walked back to camp.

Once there, Dark Star asked Zea to come into his hut because they needed to talk. Zea followed the leader into the hut and he took a seat at his desk while the guardian stood in front of him. He took a deep breath and started to talk, "From what I understand you and I are in a unique situation. Here is what I have decided. You may stay with my clan despite the danger you bring with because of the Shadow Clan. You will live with Bear and we, as a clan will teach you the ways of our land. As you stay with us we will try to find a clan where you might be able to join. Do you understand all that I have told you?" "Yes, and thank you. If there is anything I can do to repay your kindness I will do everything in my power to do so," she answered gratefully. "All I ask of you is to show respect to all in the clan and do your best to stay out of trouble. Do you think you can do this?" Dark Star asked Zea. "Yes, I will do my best to fulfill your wishes," Zea told the leader as she showed him a sign of respect. "Very well then, Bear will be waiting for you outside and he will take you into his care. I will see you tonight at dinner," the Kat spoke to her. She smiled thanked him again and told him she would see him at the last meal of the day. The guardian left the hut with a smile on her face and she went off to find Bear.

Bear was not far from Dark Star's hut and when he saw Zea. He walked over to her and reached out for her hand and smiled. She took his hand and they walked to his hut. When they got there Bear walked in first. The zatz saw there was a main room with a very small fireplace, table, desk, chairs and some shelves with supplies on them. She also saw a smaller room to the left. Bear walked over and told her she could look inside the smaller room. Gazing in Zea saw a large cot, a very small dresser, a chest, and a long pole witch went along the ceiling of the room. On the pole was a large cloth, which divided the room into two. Bear told her this is where they would sleep as he walked over to his bed and pulled the chest our from under it. Once the chest was open he pulled out a hammock and placed it on the bed. Next he took everything out of his dresser and moved the hammock and dresser to the other side of the room and made Zea her space. She helped the best she could and thanked him when he was done. Last he told her that they needed to have a conversation and they moved to the main room where they both sat down facing each other.

"The first thing I am going to tell you is," he began, "you remind me of someone I once knew so, that is why I was looking at you. Also you can trust all the members in this clan. I trust them as if I they were my brothers. In addition like you I was not born in this clan but was able to join. With every clan they have a symbol, which the members wear to show they are a part of that tribe. If you noticed the Shadow Clan all had the symbols burned into their skin. In this clan we have a band, which is placed on our arm. That is why when Dark Flame's group members look you in they search all over your body to find out what clan you might be a member of. Do you understand what I have been telling you so far?" he finished. "Yes, I understand everything so far and things are making more sense. What clan were you a member of before you came to this one?" she asked. " I was from the Black Forest Clan and I left because I lost someone. I did not want to be a part of that clan and this one just seemed to fit me and I was very lucky they let me join," he answered.

Then Bear went on to say, "Do you mind telling me a little about your past?" Zea was quiet, shifted her weight and looked up into Bears deep blues eyes. After the short pause she spoke, "I do not like to talk about my past but I will tell you all that I feel comfortable telling you." After taking a deep breath she began, "I come from a very, very, large clan called a villa and there was one leader and the name of the clan was after the leader. My father was the first ranking warrior and I guess you could say he was second in command. A few days after I was born a different race came and took over our villa. They were called Qothos after a large battle they won and I was put into slavery. Years later I escaped and the few that were left started a surprise attack. Now that we were free the ones that were still alive started to make a new life and the only problem was I was the only female in the new form group. Two of the males who had worked with my father took me under their wings; I was not in my teens yet. They took me from the group because the other males were planning their future without a thought of my quality of life. Over the years I lost my two friends but I went over two mountain ranges, a desert, and two forests or valleys. When I arrived here the Shadow Clan took me in and now I am and here with you."

Bear was quiet thinking about the story Zea's life. He turned to his new friend and asked, "So how long were you traveling and how old are you now?" "I think I was traveling about six years I just turned seventeen," she answered. "Well, little one that is an amazing story. You have been through a lot and you are still very young. We must go now, the time has come to go to dinner," he stated as he stood up and started to make his way to the door. They walked out of their home and made there way to the center of the camp.

There was a large feast for the clan, everyone took some food from the table then would sit around the fire. Bear told Zea to sit where she wanted and try to make new friends. The guardian was a little hesitant but she found a spot by the fire and began to eat her last meal of the day. Not much time passed before two young males who looked her age came and sat next to her. They acted like they were brothers by the way they were talking and playing. One of them had dark green fur with light gray and dark blue streaks down his back and a yellow underside, which matched his bight eyes. His friend's fur was yellow with a green underbelly, which went from his chin to his tail. His eyes were bright like his friends but they were all white but the black slits from the pupils.

When they both took a bite of food Zea turned to then and stated, "Hi, my name is Zeaytera KatOynera. How are you tonight?" They looked at each other with a laugh then the one with the bright golden eyes spoke, "My name is Roberd and this is my friend Robby. You are the one from afar right?" "Yes I am," she answered. "Do you speak a different language?"

Robby asked. "Yes, I have a different tongue then spoken here," Zea replied. "What do our names mean?" Roberd asked with excitement. The guardian gave a small laugh and looked down in thought trying to translate to two new words. Finally she came up with the best answer she could, "I think Roberd means, 'tenacious or fearless' and Robby your name means, 'risky or risk taker'. That is the best translation I can do for you." The two males laughed and went back to eating and Zea did the same.

The meal was made up of meat, plants, bread and drink. The food felt good in the guardian's tummy. She talked with the Roberd and Robby and they played games after they were done eating. Others joined in and soon almost everyone in the camp was playing a great game of Tulu (played with a ball and two teams). For the first time in over a year Zea was smiling and having fun. Her heart sang with joy because she was no longer alone. Once the moon was high over the camp the game was stopped and the clan went to sleep for the night.

Bear and Zea made their way back to the hut where the zatz went to the hammock and the Kat went to his bed. Fire torches lit the two rooms. Bear got up and put out the fires then divided the small room into two with the cloth and at last got into his bed where he fell asleep. The guardian had a hard time falling into the land of dreams. There was so much on her mind and she was so excited. Finally, she drifted asleep. She awoke to Bear standing over her asking if she was okay. The guardian sat up in bed and wiped the beads of sweat from her forehead. The zatz was breathing hard and she was shaking. "I am sorry. Ever since I could remember I have had nightmares," she whispered. He held her and felt her body slowly stop shaking. Then he whispered, "Come on little one." Picking her up he walked to his bed where they both lay down and fell asleep.

One of the guys

Zea woke with the sun and left her friend sleeping. She went for a run around the camp. After moving everyday for years it was hard for the guardian not to move. After a brisk run she walked to the center of camp where a few Kats were making the first meal of the day. In total there were about fifty members in the clan. Zea asked if she could help with making the food. They said sure and the guardian joined the workers. When the meal was ready one of the cooks sounded a horn and slowly all the clan members came to get some food to start their day. When Robby and Roberd came to get their food, Zea told them good morning and asked if she could sit with them. They smiled and told her she was welcome anytime. After everyone got their food, Zea put her meal together and went to go sit with her two new friends.

The two males were talking about a gathering coming up in a few days. Zea asked what they were talking about. Then Robby turned to the zatz and told her, "Soon we are going to visit the EnyoRhea Clan which is made up of all females. We hope to find some nice Kats who are willing to have some fun with us. We get together at least once a year to show that our clans are friends with each other and to make our friendship stronger." Zea nodded and told them good luck. They both laughed to themselves again and went back to talking and eating. Once they were done eating Zea went down with five others to the river to wash the dishes from the meal.

The five she walked down to the river with were, Rock, Nathan, Lighting, Star and Fire Hawk. They laughed as they did their work. Zea was so happy she found a group who were cheerful and good-natured. She still did not fully fit in and when she was thinking of her differences the guardian realized the clan did not know she had wings. Everyone she saw so far had wings but they were for gliding not flying like her wings. She decided she would show Bear the next time they were alone. A voice cut into her thoughts, "What's wrong little one? You got really quiet all of a sudden." Zea looked up and broke out of her trance. Looking at where the voice had come from the guardian saw everyone looking at her and she said she was daydreaming. She laughed and went back to working. Soon all the dishes were washed and they walked back to camp.

Once there, Dark Star gave her a list of jobs that she could do in the camp and Zea came up with a great plan. She would rotate among the jobs that way she could meet everyone in the clan and learn all the jobs and ways of the clan. He agreed with her and decided she would start tomorrow.

That night when Zea was alone with Bear in the hut she told him she needed to show him something. He looked at her and she gazed down at the floor. "I hope you know you can tell me anything and I will do my best to help," he said. She took a deep breath and asked him to sit. Then she began, "As you know I am a little different, but I am not sure what you know about my physical differences." "I know your fur is very black and I have never seen fur of your color," he stated. She shifted her weight and began to speak again, "Where to begin and how to show you. I think I will tell you then show you." He nodded. "First, I have different eyes. I have five different sets of eyelids. They are different colors, white, red, blue, green and black. Each one allows me to see the area around me a little differently. I will now show you but, please remember I am still me do not be mad or afraid." Before the male could speak she first showed him her white lid then the red next was the blue and green and last was the black. When she was done she watched him hoping for a good reaction.

He was quiet then Zea broke the silence because she could not take it. "I will go on I am going to show you one more, which is, I have wings," she spoke softly. Upon saying that she flexed the muscles in her back and opened her wings. "With my wings I can fly not just glide," she whispered. Then Zea sat down and waited for his reaction and stillness took over the room.

Zea then stood and flapped her wings showing him that she could move them easily. He witnessed the female raised herself off the ground and then slowly back to the land. She told him it felt very good to open and move her wings. "Let me think just a minute, little one," he voiced to her. She tucked in her wings and walked out of the hut leaving her new friend to his thoughts. Once outside she looked for a place to sit nearby. Her heartbeat was in her ears. –Did I make the right decision?- she pondered. – You had to tell some one. It was only a matter of time- the computer responded.

Gazing across camp she saw a shadow in the distance moving towards her. Then Zea saw who the shadow was. Walking around the camp was Dark Star who was making his rounds. "Hi, little one, what are you doing?" he asked. "I need to give Bear some space. I think you should go talk to him," she replied. The leader looked at her then up at Bear's hut. "Before you go, can I ask you a question?," Zea spoke softly. "Sure anything," Dark Star answered. "Why does everyone call me 'little one'?" A smile grew on his face as he chuckled he told her, "I think there are two reasons. One, you are a little one because you are young and second, I think it is because you have a very hard name to pronounce." The guardian also smiled and said, "Thank you, Dark Star, I will be outside the hut if you want me to come in after you talk to Bear." The leader smiled, patted her on the shoulder and made his way into Bears hut. Knocking and the walking into the still quiet home. Zea paced outside the hut waiting for something to happen.

Finally, the door open and Dark Star asked Zea to come into the hut. Upon entering the guardian started to speak, "I want to say sorry I should have told you before you let me come into your clan. I am sorry." The leader took a seat next to his friend and told the zatz, "What you look like should not determine if you are in the clan or not. Do not worry yourself. Now, please if you are willing, let me see what you showed Bear." Zea took a deep breath and then restated and showed both males in front of her what she had done earlier. First opened her wings and took herself off the ground then back to the floor.

"Whoa," Dark Star expressed when he saw the little one's white lids. Next to follow were her red ones. "I cannot hold my blue ones for very long." Zea voiced. "Why?" Dark Star questioned. The female explained they were for the water. After the blue ones were in place she quickly moved into her green. "Wait, could you keep your head still and look towards the door then the bedroom and last the far window," The leader asked. Zea did as she was asked. "What? Crazy," Dark Star gasped. "What?" the zatz quickly responded in a worried tone. "I cannot see your pupils. We cannot tell where you are looking. Your eye only has one color," Dark Star explained. "Oh, okay, well I guess the only one left is my black ones," She stated. Bear shifted uneasily. Zea let her black lids come into view. Bear shuddered as Dark Star leaned back. "I told Bear each eye covers gives me a different type of vision," the guardian said.

Once she was done the stillness was back in the small room. The guardian became uneasy and started to pace because of the tension in the room. Finally, Zea broke the silence, "Do you two want to see anything again or want me to explain anything over again. I will leave again if you want me too." Dark Star stood up and walked the zatz to her bed. Then before she lay down for the night he placed his hand on her shoulder and looked into her watering eyes. Next he told her, "Thank you, for being honest with us. From now on you can show your wings to the other clan members but lets keep the eyelids between the three of us till I can think of a good way of sharing your features with the clan. You did a good thing tonight and you are still welcome in our group. Now you get some sleep," rubbing the top of her head. As he walked out of the room and back to his friend he turned his head and smiled at the little female. The guardian closed her eyes and tried to fall asleep for the night.

She awoke during the night when she heard Bear climb into his bed. The guardian looked up and thought about what had happened earlier. Very quietly left the warm bed and went outside of the hut. Leaning her back against the wall of her new home she looked up at the stars. A sight she had not seen for a long time and tears came to her eyes. Thinking of her family the guardian found herself in prayer. Looking at the stars always made her think and fall into a state of reflection. –Are you ok?– the computer asked her friend. –I am ok, I am just thinking,– she replied. –Do you want to talk about anything?– the guardian's friend asked. –No, I am just thinking if I did the right thing tonight.– Zea told her friend. –If I may say, I think you did do the right thing because what if they found out about your difference by surprise it would look poorly on you. If you tell them this action shows that you are honest and not trying to hide from anyone. You did the right thing Zea,– the computer voiced in her mind. –You are right. Thank you computer. I am going to try to get some sleep now,– she told her lifetime friend as she stood, stretched and walked her to bed. She closed her eyes and did her best to relax.

When the sun kissed Zea's faced she awoke and went for her daily run around the camp. She again helped the group who were working on the first meal of the day. The group changed everyday so every morning Zea was able to meet a new crowd but this morning was different. Today for the first time the guardian had her wings visible for all to see. The female decided that she would always be at an angle where no one could see the scars on her back. Her computer helped her accomplish this by using pulses. She was a little more timid than usual because she was not sure how the group was going to act upon seeing wings that were not visible the previous day.

The guardian slowly moved towards the group and as she did she saw that Robby and Roberd were there as always smiling or laughing. She walked up to them as if nothing was different and asked if she could help. They looked at each other and Robby said, "Sure." Zea worked in silence while she could hear the two males whisper to each other. They were trying to figure out if they had ever seen her wings before and both were very confused. Finally Roberd just turned to Zea and asked, "Did you have those wings yesterday?" His buddy punched him in the arm after he finished speaking. The guardian took a deep breath and told her two friends, "Yes, I had them but you could not see them. I can hide them if I wish or have them out for you to see." "Really?" Robby questioned with awe. "Yes, I will show you," she voiced with a laugh as she took a few steps away from where the Kats were standing. Zea then proceeded to show the two males and everyone who was there her wings. She folded them and placed them in her back, then brought them back out again for all to see. Everyone just looked at her. The guardian broke the silence, "See, it is very simple." With a smile the zatz walked back to where the males were standing and started to work again. Robby was the next to break the silence, "That was buoghti (awesome, cool)." Everyone laughed and started working on the meal again.

For the rest of the day Zea did not see Bear. She was very nervous about not talking to him and finding out his full reaction to knowing her differences. That day her job was working, as a guard and she would be shadowing one of the main warriors who walked around the outskirts of the clan's home. She was walking with a male with light gray fur and green eyes. He walked with a spear in his hand. The sun was beading down on them and the golden grass in the field gently moved from side to side in the cool breeze. At first they walked in silence. Finally the male spoke, "How long were you traveling to get here?" Zea looked down in thought before answering. "I left my home I think when I was ten and now I am seventeen," she stated. "That is a long time and you were alone?" he asked. "I was alone for part of my journey. When I first started out I had two male friends but they died a little over a year a part. Have you been in this clan all your life?" She replied and questioned. "Yea, I was born in an all female clan and when I was old enough I joined my father in this clan. That is the way a lot of us are. Very rarely if one of our members falls in love with another they will move to a clan where they both can be together but, like I said that is rare," he voiced. "I hope I am not being rude but, what does your name mean?" he continued.

"My name means Wondrous One."

"What does my name mean?"

"I believe your name, Nathan, means 'Eagle Warrior'."

"That is really cool."

"What?"

"That you know a totally different language."

Zea smiled. They spent the whole shift talking and getting to know each other and when their work was done they continued talking. Soon dusk was upon them and they had to get ready for the last meal of the day. The guardian headed back to the hut where she slept and she was not sure how to feel knowing there was a good chance Bear would be in there. The guardian knocked on the door. Hearing nothing, she slowly opened the door and walked into the dark room.

In the middle the room was a table with a few candles, plates, cups and food. Then Bear walked in from the room where they slept. He carried a pot, which had steam rising from what ever was in it. Seeing her, he smiled and placed the pot on the table and gave her a motion to take a seat across from him. "I was thinking we would eat by ourselves tonight, if that is ok with you," Bear told Zea who agreed with him as she took a seat. The Kat told the guardian what the different types of food were on the table and then they started to eat.

After they started their meal Bear started to speak to Zea, "If you do not mind I would like to tell you about myself." "I would love to hear about your past," she replied. He took a deep breath and began, "I was born to Andrew and Karai. My father was in the Dark Clan and my mother was from the EnyoRhea Clan. They fell in love and both left their clans so they could be together. They joined the Green Water Clan where I was born and had part on my childhood. My mothered died when I was little because she got sick and there was no cure. My father could not live in that clan. Everything there made him think about Karai so we left and became Colins.

Later as we were walking in the woods we had a run in with a group of Shadow Kats. After fighting and running we escaped and ran into another group who were members of the Rock Clan. They took us in to their group and we were both happy again. I learned how to fight, hunt and gilfting (reading, writing, and math). I grew up in the clan with many friends one of them being Snow Flake. As time went by we fell in love and before I knew it Snow Flake was my partner for life."

Bear paused to take a slip of water and when Zea looked up she could see his eyes beginning to water. Then he started to speak again, "A little more than a year later my love was with child. I had a little female and we named her Sun Ray. She looked just like you, Zea, but her fur was not as dark and her eyes were a golden orange color and did not have all your physical features. She was strong and beautiful.

Sadly, Snow Flake died giving birth to my daughter. We were content and living well despite our loss. Then one day as we were walking with a group of friends we were jumped by a large group of the Shadow Clan. We all fought hard and won the battle but with a heavy loss. My two good friends were killed and my daughter. Like my father before me I could not live in a place where everything reminded me of my loss. I once again became a Colin.

Living off the land and watching my back I had to remain very strong and a good fighter. One day while I stopped by a river for a drink I met Nathan. He saw that I was tired and unhappy and he took me to his Clan. There I met the group I am with now they kept an eye on me and slowly we gained each other's trust. I quickly became a friend of the clan. Dark Star and I became very close. Later I asked to be a member of the group and after some tests and work I was a part of the Clan.

From that point in my life I have not looked back, I have been blissful and I have made new great friends. The longer I have been here the better my life has became and now I am a high-ranking member of this Clan. Now you know about my past and life. Do you have any questions for me?" Zea took a moment to think about what her friend had just told her. "I really do not have any questions but, I want to say thank you for trusting me and telling me about your life," she answered.

Bear took a deep breath and wiped the water from his eyes. "Anytime you want to talk about it I will be more than willing to chat with you. Also when you are ready go talk more about your life I will be here for you. I want to tell you I should have talked to you earlier about what you showed me last night. I was just in awe and amazed. I am not mad at you because you did not tell me sooner and I do not think differently of you because you are diverse only that you are truly great, brave and strong," he voiced to his friend. "I have to tell you," he continued, "I think that you can fly and not just glide is different but that is good thing because you can do things others cannot. I do not fully understand the whole eye thing but I have never seen anything like that in my life I will get used to it. Just because your eyes are different does not mean your personality is different. Do not think that because you are diverse that you are not a good being or not welcome in anyway here in this clan."

Zea looked down taking in what her friend was saying. They continued to eat in silence as they thought about their actions. Finally the guardian broke the stillness, "I want to show more difference but I also want you to get a chance to get used to my eyes and wings." "You should do what ever you feel comfort doing but, I think it is a good things to let thing sit before you stir things up again," he stated. The female nodded and proceeded to finish her meal in good company.

The next day she would be going to collect supplies from the surrounding area. This would be the first time she left the safety of the clan since she came to the tribe a few weeks earlier. Bear was a little nervous but knew she was with a good group. There were only a few Kats in the clan Zea did not know a lot about yet and Josh was one of them. He had pinkish red fur and dark purple eyes. In the guardian's tongue Josh means 'pretty one' which was rarely used. Josh was well-built and a little shorter than normal but, he was still taller than some females. He loved to play and joke with the others around him. He was a little slow to start to play with the new comer of the group but by the time the sun was high in the sky he was coming around. Zea who was use to being around males had no trouble keeping up with the pink one's jokes. They were collecting a type of wood and plants. Soon everything needed was gathered and they headed back to camp. When they got there Zea's fur on the back of her neck stood when she saw who was in the camp.

There in the middle of camp was a group of Shadow Kats, a very large group. There leading them was Dark Flame and to his side was Pyro keeping his eye out for anything. Nathan without hesitation took control of the group. They all couched down in the meadow grass and the leader told half the group to go around to the other end of camp. Zea was to go with them. They set off keeping low to the ground and not talking but using hand gestures. Once they were on the other side of camp they waited for the other group to make their move. As the guardian waited she saw Lighting signing her to stay here and not enter the camp. She was not pleased but she would follow his directions.

She watched as the group leave her alone in the tall grass and entered the camp. She crept forward so she could hear what everyone was saying in the camp. With the sudden arrival of the rest of the clan both groups shifted. Dark Star with Bear at his side faced Dark Flame with Pyro by his. The Shadow Kats must have found out that Zea was staying there and wanted her back. She would die before she would let them take her into their world again. She leaned up against one of the huts listening to the leaders talk.

"Do you have her here, yes or no?" - Dark Flame

"Why do you care?" - Dark Star

"She was ours first we found and took her in and if she is a Colin then you have no ties to her." - Dark Flame

"She is not an object. If she is a Colin then your right she has no ties even to you." - Dark Star

"I am telling you we want her and if you hold her from us you are risking a fight." - Dark Flame

"Do not threaten me. I know many clans, which would back me up and we would both loose fighters in a battle, which does not need to happen. If you cannot contain your prisoners that does not mean you can throw a fit if one escapes. I am telling you this meeting is done. If the one you talk of is with our group there is nothing you can do about it and do not come into my home to bully me" - Dark Star

"I do what I wish and there is nothing you can do to stop me," Dark Flame stated while turning his back and leading his group out of the camp. Dark Star's Clan did not ease up until the outsiders were well out of sight. The leader called out Zea's name who came out of hiding. She was not pleased to cause the clan problems. Once she was in front of Dark Star she got down on one knee and stated, "I do not want to cause the clan any trouble if you want me to go. I will understand and I am sorry for what I have done." There was silence and then after looking around he placed his hand on Zea's shoulder. After asking her to stand up he told everyone to go back to work because there was much to do before nightfall. The guardian was very quiet for the rest of the evening.

That night Josh, Roberd, and Robby were sitting together talking and laughing. Zea was eating near them but, was not in a joyful mood and did not join in with her friends. At the end of the meal they came over and tried to cheer the little one up but she just stood up and walked to her bed where she tried to fall asleep.

Bear came in later that evening and did his best to talk to the zatz but she was not in the mood to talk about anything. Picking up on this the Kat let the little one be. He slowly walked to his resting spot where he proceeded to fall asleep. That night he ended up going to visit the little one again because Zea was having another nightmare. Shaking and sweating the male held her trying to give her some comfort. "Thank you, Bear, when I was traveling there was no one there to physically hold me. I am sorry if I woke you," she whispered. "Do not worry about it," he whispered back. After time had passed she fell asleep again.

All Bear could do was try to understand what happened to the little one to make her have so many nightmares. He had not seen the scars on her back yet. The guardian was doing a great job of keeping them hidden. No one had really seen Zea use her wings. The guardian also did not like to talk about her past which, the others noticed. If they asked her about her life she was very vague or told them she did not want to talk about it. Once the male made sure the little one was asleep he walked back to his bed where he fell back into a restful sleep.

The next day Zea got up like she always did and went on her morning run around camp. As she ran something was different, everything was quiet. She ran faster and kept her eyes and ears alert. Then the female asked her computer to do a pulse who was more than willing to help. When Zea got the picture back she saw that there was a large group hiding in the long grass. If she continued on her path then she would run into a trap and be surrounded. The guardian stopped stretched and ran in the opposite direction. Then she heard an all too familiar voice. Looking behind her Zea saw Pyro and his gang joining him from all directions. "How did you know to turn around because you always run this way?" he asked. She gave him a look of puzzlement. "You have been watching me?"

"Yes, once I found you. I did not want to leave you. I told you that I loved you and I will not let you go again."

"Pyro, I am not ready and I do not love you. Do you know anything about me?"

"Well, no, not really but, Zea, you never gave me a chance. You just ran away?"

"What do you want me to do? Your father was going to kill me. I was not going to just lie there and wait for my death."

"Zea, please give me a chance we can meet once every few days and get to know each other."

"I will think about it Pyro but, right now I need to leave."

Zea turned and began to walk away from the group. One of them ran in front of her. She glared at him as she stated very strongly, "Get out of my way. I do not want to fight." All he did was smile and the guardian tried to walk around him but he moved back into her path. She turned around and looked at Pyro. She looked at him seeing if he was going to do anything. After waiting and seeing no reaction the guardian spoke to the leader of the group in a low and strong whisper, "If you are trying to be my friend you are doing a horrible job by letting your colleagues treat me this way." Upon ending the fighter flexed the muscles in her back allowing her wings to come out of their hiding spot. Taking to the air Zea flew back to Bear's hut where she opened the door and walked into the dark room.

There Bear looked up seeing his friend come home. Zea quickly pulled her wings back into hiding as she took a seat at the table. "What is wrong? I have never seen you here at his hour," he asked. She looked down and took a deep breath. Finally she spoke, "Sorry, Pyro likes me and I just found out he has been stalking me. I am a strong fighter and I am almost sure I could beat him but I do not like the knowing that he is watching me. I do not know what to do." Bear took a seat next to his friend and stated softly, "Pyro has his way with words but he is not with a good group. I would not get involved with him. If he does confront you do not fight him because that action could create problems with the two clans. If anything happens you should just fly, walk or run away to our camp or to who ever you are with and make sure you are not alone." Zea looked up into his deep eyes, which comforted her and thanked him for his kind words.

"Do you mind if I express something to you?"

"Sure Bear"

"You say you are sorry a lot. I can tell you have been through a lot and I am not sure about your past but one of the first words out of your mouth is sorry. You are strong. You escaped from the Shadow Kats and traveled here on your own. Do not ever apologize for who you are. You can show respect without saying sorry. In another way saying that word too much makes you seem weak. If you want to be a member of a clan you must not appear weak. And a member of Dark Star Clan, even a temporary one, is proud, has self-confidence and we do not apologize unless truly needed. Do you understand?

"Yes, I will do my best to choose my words more carefully. Thank you."

"Everything will be okay."

The two hugged. They walked out of the hut together. Walking to the first meal of the day Bear told the zatz he was going to tell Dark Star about her run in with Pyro. Zea agreed and got a plate of food. Joining her friends she ate her meal with a smile on her face to be among peers.

The days went by and soon the time had come for the yearly meeting of the two clans: the EnyoRhea and Dark Stars. That night the two would meet and have a great feast. The two groups will play, dance and eat. This would be the first time Zea would see another full clan. This year Dark Star's clan would have to go to the EnyoRhea's land the year before the females had to come to their territory. No one was doing their job that day all they could talk about was what were going to do that night. The zatz was excited to make new friends and meet females. She had never been around females for a long time or a large group of them. She enjoyed talking to all her new friends about the fun they were going to have that night then it dawned on her, who was going to stay and watch over the camp.

The guardian walked over to a group of males who were making gifts for the other clan. Reaching them she sat down facing her friends, Josh, Robby and Roberd. Watching them finally the zatz spoke, "I have to ask you Kats a question if you do not mind." They all looked up at her and Roberd answered her, "Sure." "While we are away who is watching the camp?" the little one questioned and with a smile Josh responded to her, "We take turns and every year few members stays behind to watch our camp. If there is trouble the ones who stays behind will throw a special log into the fire which changes the smoke and sends us a signal that we must return to camp." "No one has every tried to enter our camp while we were away," Robby joined into the conversation. "Yea, who would be dumb enough to attack our camp? That would cause a battle," Roberd added. "Oh, I see and who is doing it this year?" Zea questioned.

Again the group of Kats looked at each other and Roberd looked and started to tell Zea as the others went back to work, "This year Krist, Tristan, Colt, and Tanner are staying behind. I think Krist is the only one you have not met. He has been out of camp for a few days and he is kind of an outcast. Not because we make him one but he wishes to be. He is a great fighter, teacher and friend but, has a tattered past. He just needs his time to himself." "Yea, a lot of time sometimes," Josh chipped in with a grin. "Where is he now?" the guardian questioned. Robby looked up to answer the zatz, "right now? He is most likely in his hut which is the last one on the left." Now he was pointing in direction of the one in question's hut. Zea thanked the males for helping her. Standing she said goodbye and ran to her hut.

Once she reached her hut she saw Bear who she asked if he would walk her down to the river. With a smile he said sure and after Zea grabbed a bowl they were on their way. Reaching the bank of the flowing waters the guardian filled the bowl with sand. Bear gave her an odd look and then she piled more sand into the bowl. She gave him a smile and they walked back to the hut. "I have to go talk to Dark Star I will be back soon," Bear told his friend who smiled and said, "I will see you later have fun." Now that the guardian was alone she let her computer be visible. The zatz then proceeded to melt the sand with her red ray gun and made gapea. She made two small shapes one was a triangle with a heart inside and one was a flower called a Moei (like a rose). The triangle one was for Bear and the Moei was for the leader of the EnyoRhea Clan. Zea wanted to thank Bear for all his kindness and the leader just for meeting her. The gift was a sign of kindness and hopefully friendship.

The EnyoRheas

As day turned into dusk the clan packed up and set off for their destination in the nearby forest. The guardian was full of excitement and wonder, as she got closer to the other clan. Everyone was jumpy and could not stop smiling. Soon Zea could see the firelight through the trees and bushes. The smell of food and smoke grew stronger with every step they took. The group suddenly came to a stop and Dark Star stood in front of them. He looked at his clan and after taking a deep breath he spoke, "Listen to me. Have fun tonight but be careful who knows if there is anyone out here that would be dumb enough to try something. If you want to leave to go home you must have a least two others with you. No one gets left behind. If one of you wants to spend the night then do so but you must find a least two others who are doing the same. When you get back to camp I would like you to sign in so I know who got back. On my desk in the middle hut is a piece of paper. When you get home write your name on the document. If you know someone who is going to be spending the night here then put a mark by his or her name. I hope all of you have a great time and I will see you all tomorrow." He smiled and proceeded to lead his clan to the new camp.

As they walked Zea looked at Bear. He laughed and told the guardian, "Tonight I will not leave the camp without you. You can go off by yourself but do not leave unless you are with me." She nodded and stayed by his side as the group walked into a residence full of cheering females. There were a little more in this tribe and were all very happy to see Dark Star' s clan. The two leaders walked up to each other and embraced with a handshake and hug. Once this action was done the two groups joined and fun and play began.

Zea stayed next to Bear's side walking next to him while looking all around her. She could not see any huts where the females might sleep. After doing a pulse to fully understand her surrounding, the fighter realized the main portions of the clan's structures were above her. The female's huts were tree houses.

Near one of the fires she spied Josh, Roberd, and Robby who were already entertaining a few of the females. The two leaders were talking and Bear and Zea walked over to the food to get their last meal of the day. Many of the EnyoRheas came up to talk to Bear as the two friends were eating by one the fires. Each time one came up Bear he would introduce Zea who would shake their hands with a smile. Over the roar of the crowd Zea heard her name. Looking in the direction of the call the guardian spotted Dark Star looking at her. After making eye contact with the leader he motioned for the zatz to come to him. Zea told Bear who nodded. Next the guardian stood up and made her way to Dark Star. As the female walked her mouth became dry.

He was still sitting with the leader of the EnyoRheas. She was all white but had black stripes, which were down her back. Her eyes were a golden color and she was grinning as Zea extended her hand to greet her. They shook hands and then Zea took a seat next to Dark Star. "Dark Star has told me a little about you. Good job on breaking free from the Shadow Clan," the leader exclaimed. "Thank you, it was very hard but I was extremely lucky that I ran into Bear and to be accepted by Dark Star and his Clan," Zea replied. "Sun Flower, Zea has never been or even seen a Clan of all females," the male voiced. "Is this true?" she questioned the guardian who nodded to answer. "Dark Star did not know about this but, I wanted to give you something just to show you friendship from me," the zatz told Sun Flower as she reached into her back to get the Moei made of gapea. A smile grew on her face as the guardian did his action. Dark Star and Sun Flower looked at Zea's cupped hands and wondered what she had hidden.

The new friend looked at the guardian as she opened her hands showing the Moei. Both leaders looked at each other puzzled on what the flower was made out of and how it might have been crafted. Sun Flower carefully took the gift from Zea's hand while saying, Thank you." "I hope you like it. I do not really know you so I just made a Moei. If you drop it the Moei will most likely break but if you put it in sunlight you will see

Tattimoepoe. They will get hot and can start a fire so be careful," the guardian said with a smile. "I am sorry but what is a Moei, and Tattimoepoe?" Sun Flower inquired. Zea looked down in thought and finally did her best to answer the EnyoRhea, "A Moei is a type of flower from my homeland and Tattimoepoe are colors in the sky after rain. There is an order of colors. I think the order is red, orange, yellow, green, blue and purple. Sorry I am not sure how to explain." "A rainbow," Dark Star voiced. Sun Flower smiled and nodded in agreement as Zea just looked at him while shrugging her shoulders. "This is truly amazing. Thank you Zea," the female said. "You are welcome and I am glad you like it," Zea smiled. The three of them talked for a little longer about Zea and how she was living in the male clan. Once they were done Zea left the two leaders to walk around the camp to meet some of the EnyoRheas.

Taking a deep breath the guardian walked over to a pair EnyoRheass who were laughing and talking by a fire. One of them was a pinkish color but had a sliver tone. Almost like a metallic pink and her eyes were a deep green. The other one was a very dark blue almost a black - violet and had golden eyes which shown through her dark fur. Her white teeth opposite of her night colored coat.

The two were sitting by each other giggling and looking at all the males, which had entered their camp. They were one of the few females who were not talking to a member from Dark Star's Clan. Zea cautiously walked up to the two talking friends. The guardian smiled as she walked into the firelight and extended her arm to greet the friends. They looked at her trying to place who she was. Zea brought back her arm while saying, "I am staying with the Dark Star Clan." The two looked at each other then back at the new comer. The zatz felt out of place and did not know what to do. At a loss the outsider said she was sorry for interrupting their talk and began to walk away back into the dark.

Just as she was about the leave the light she heard one of the Kats called out to her. A grin grew on her face as she again walked up to where the EnyoRheas were now standing. "Have a seat," the one with the green eyes stated. The guardian did as she was asked and looked at the two who were giggling. "What is your name?" the dark one asked. "My name is Zeaytera KatOynera but, almost everyone calls me Zea," the zatz answered. "May I ask your names?" she continued. "My name is Liz and this is my friend Sarah," the golden eyed one voiced. "I have never heard a name like yours before who are your mother or father," Sarah asked. "My name is not in your tongue in your language my name means 'Wonders One'," Zea replied. "What do our names mean?" Liz questioned. The guardian looked down in thought thinking of the best translation. Finally she spoke, "Well, the short name Liz means 'Aurora' and there are many different meaning for the name Sarah, but I think the best translation for your name the way it is spelled is 'Sparkle'."

The two friends laughed and looked at each other thinking about the new meaning to their names. "Do you like your Clan? What is it like to be an EynoRhea?" Zea inquired. The duo stopped laughing and looked at the outsider and after a small pause Liz spoke, "We are a very tight group and we are a group of mothers, daughters, friends and more. We have each other's back and we do not let just anyone join our group. She must have certain physical and mental physique. I love my Clan and would not leave for any reason." "Oh, I was just asking. I do not know a lot about the clans here in this land. I am sorry if I offend you," Zea voiced softy. "You did nothing wrong. We are just have strong feelings for our Tribe," Liz told the guardian. Zea smiled. The three talked for a while about the EnyoRhea Clan. Soon two of Zea's friends from Dark Star's Clan walked over and asked if they could talk to Liz and Sarah. The two females giggled, stood up and joined in the two males in dancing and playing. Again Zea was alone but was content to have made two new friends.

As she walked around the camp she found a lone female painting the scene around her. She was very strong and looked well built. Her fur was mainly gray but had some white parts too it. Overall she looked like a maine-coon. The painter's eyes were nice light blue which had some yellow slits that gave her a lighter yet fierce look. The blue eyes darted from the paper to her friends eating, dancing, playing and laughing by the fire. Zea walked up to the painter looking at her work. The colors and shapes were just right and the artist did a great job capturing the group in front of her. "Nice work, I like your painting," Zea whispered. "Thank you," the artist said. "I like to draw and make art. I made a Moei for Sun Flower. A Moei is a type of flower. She can show you later," the guardian said. The painter stopped working to look up at the one talking to her.

She just realized that the female she was talking to was not of her clan. "I am sorry I was being rude. I am not a member of your tribe. I am staying with Dark Star's Clan and my name is Zeaytera KatOynera but, almost everyone calls me Zea," the zatz voiced. "Hi, my name is Avis. I am pleased to meet you," the artist stated. "You have a different name," Avis continued. "My name is not of your tongue. When translated my name means 'Wonders One.' I am still learning your ways here in this new land. I traveled here from my home," the guardian told her. "I bet many have asked you this but, what does my name mean?" Avis asked with a half smile. "Yes, many have asked me but it is no problem. Your name has different spelling and meaning in my native language I think is 'Sara.' If you change just one letter your meaning changes drastically. My tongue is a very hard one to teach and learn," Zea spoke with a smile.

The two talked for a long time as Avis painted. They discussed again about the EnyoRheas and a little about the guardian's past but like all the other times this topic came up she was very vague. When dawn's light was just waking the land Bear came up to his friend and asked if she was ready to leave. Bear, Dark Star and Zea were the last to leave the camp if they were not sleeping over with friends. They walked back to their home and when they got there Dark Star went to the middle hut to see who was home that night. Bear and the guardian went to their hut where they got ready to sleep. Then each went to their beds. Soon were both in the land of dreams.

Clans and the Opening

The fighter woke up a few times during her sleep. When mid-morning was turning to late afternoon she left her resting spot and went for a run. As her paws hit warm grass the guardian's mind drifted to last night. A smile grew on her face thinking about her new friends and about the female camp. As she came to the end of her run she bumped into Josh who was also running through the camp. He asked if he could join her and she agreed happily. They ran and the sun beat against their faces. Zea asked her friend about what he did last night and all he could do was smirk and laugh. He finally said, "I had a lot of fun with my friends and the EnyoRheas." Zea smiled and they continued running and talking. Once they were done they joined a main group who were making the one of the meal for the day.

Bear joined Zea once he had his food. They sat off to themselves so Bear could talk to his roommate. He wanted to ask about her meeting last night with the different EnyoRheas. As they ate their meal Zea explained about the two main talks she had and about the three new friends she met. Then the guardian asked Bear what he did last night. He told her he met with the leader, Sun Flower, and old friends he talked to each year. They were both happy the other had a great night. Dark Star interrupted the two's discussion. "I wish Zea's company," he spoke softly. The zatz stood up and joined the leader in walking to the middle hut where they sat down to talk.

"I had a nice long talk with Sun Flower last night and that Moei you made was not only beautiful but also amazing. I have never seen anything like that in my whole life," he began with a smile. "I am glad you had a good night last night too. If you wish I will make you something like I made Sun Flower, just tell me what shape you would like and I will do my best to make it," Zea also stated. "That would be great. I will think about the shape and tell you later, but the reason I asked to see you is after talking to Sun Flower I do not think I can get you into the EynoRheas Clan. They are a very tight group and do not wish to go to war unless there is no way out and then they will fight. With the Shadow Clan after you, Sun Flower feels it is too risky to let you join their group at this time. I was told they will keep an eye on you and see how you are adjusting to this new land. If they feel that the Shadow Clan has lost interest you would be a good addition to the clan. They will most likely let you join. When I have to send anything over there I will ask you to do it with another and I will continue to look for a good and safe clan for you to join. I am sooo sorry, Zea, I know you had fun last night," he spoke softly while placing his hand on her shoulder.

The female did not say a word. "Do not worry about it little one, you are a great fighter and thinker. The EnyoRheas have lost an amazing chance to be lucky enough to have you in their family. We will find the right clan for you. Just give it time. You are among friends," the leader voiced soft but strong. Zea looked up into his kind eyes, "Thank you, Dark Star," she whispered. "Now, do not linger on this go explore," Dark Star stated. She got up while giving him a sign of respect and ran out of the hut looking for something to do.

The sun was out and the cotton clouds slowly drifted in the sapphire sky. At the end of the North side of camp there was a Kat working very hard. He was making something. She decided that she would go and try to help him and meet him because she did not recognize him. His fur was a very light golden color he matched the light amber grass of the meadow perfectly.

Hearing her footsteps the worker looked up to see who was coming his way. Seeing her he looked down and went back to work. Zea walked up to him and spoke, "Hi, I do not think we have really met, I am sure you have heard of me. My name is Zea. What is yours?" He stopped his labor and looked at the smiling female. His eyes were a metallic steel color but as his head moved the eye color seemed to change to a greener tent. Zea had never seen eyes like his before in her life. "I am very busy right now Zea, if you do not mind I would like to get my work done," he stated strongly. "I am sorry, if I can help I would me more than happy to do so. If I may, before I leave you, may I please get your name?" she asked. The male sighed and said quickly, "Everyone calls me Krist." "Oh, well thank you, Krist, I will leave you to your work," the guardian spoke lightly.

Then she turned and began to walk away but, then she rotated quickly and told him, "By the way if you are trying to build a roof or part of a wall I know a tighter weave you can use to keep the rain from leaking into the dwelling. If you ever need help or want to know I will show you." The female then walked away hoping to meet Krist again soon.

During the day Zea helped groups with their chores. Because this was the day after the meeting of the two clans everything was relaxed. The next day everything would go back to normal. Zea was playing with some dirt and water when a shadow loomed over her. Looking up the guardian could see Krist looking down with cold eyes. His fur was a different color now in was an almost black. The only reason she knew who he was because she saw his eyes. The zatz smiled sweetly and asked, "How are you?" He continued to look down at her and he broke the stillness by asking her a question, "Will you come and show me the weaves you were talking about?" "Sure I would be happy too," Zea stated while standing up to walk with hopefully a new friend.

As they walked the guardian noticed the males coat changed depending on what light was shining on him. She was amazed with his coat. The hairs were kind of clear so the suns light reflected off them. When there was no light his fur looked black because the absence of light. When the two reached Krist's hut there was a pile of long leaves and some longs grasses wove together to make a rope. They sat down next to each other and Zea began to teach the Kat how to do different weaves depending on what the finished product was going to be. He seemed happy to learn something new and to have company. "How did you learn all these?" he questioned. "A friend taught me," she whispered.

"I heard you traveled a long way to get to our land."

"I traveled for a long time this is true."

"Were you alone?"

"For some of the way. In the beginning I had two companions but, they passed and I had to continue on my own."

"Did you like being alone?"

"I was alone for a good part of my childhood. I did not like traveling alone but I got use to it. I found it ironic that every night I wished to meet **another** being and when I did they locked me up and beat me."

"I know what it is like to be alone."

"Really, if I may be bold and ask. What is your life story?"

He was quiet for a little bit and they wove in silence. The male proceeded to clear his throat and then he began to tell Zea his life story,

"I was born a Colin. Both my mother and father could not find a home they both fit into and live happily. Later in my childhood my father became very sick and soon he left my mom and I. Then because we did not have a strong male we had to stay hidden and always moving. Then the Shadow Clan took us in by force. My mother did not want any harm to come to me so we joined that clan. I spent most of my childhood there.

A few years later my mother passed and I was alone. I did not have a lot of friends and everyone always looked at me differently because of my fur and eyes. Soon everyone called me Krist and I am not sure why but, I cannot remember my real name and now Krist is my name. When I became of age I left the Shadow Clan late one night so they could not stop me. I had always acted like I was happy but, I was really not. I was alone and soon I was used to it.

The life of a Colin seemed to be the life for me. I did try to join a few clans but because of the Shadow Clan and my past the group I tried to join did not want me. My father did not have the best of reputations so that did not help me. I was a young male and drinking water from a small eddy when I fell into trouble. Dark Star saved me despite not knowing who I was. He let me come back to the Clan, he was not the leader back then, where I was given good food and some time to rest. The leader at the time took pity on me and let me begin the process of joining the clan.

They were very hard on me because of my background but I stayed and passed all their tests. I remain in this clan. I still am used to being a Colin so I do not have the best of social skills, but Dark Star says I am getting better. I do not know why I was born with a clear coat and metallic eyes but they have caused me so much trouble because I am different. I do not like being different because I cannot fit in and others treat me differently."

"I know how you feel, I lost my mother and father at a young age, I had a run-in with the Shadow Clan and I have many different physical features," Zea told Krist gently. He looked at her with watery eyes and look of wonder. "I do not talk about my past a lot. My childhood is very painful. I have not told anyone the full story of my life," the guardian spoke softy. "In my tongue your name, Krist, means 'suffering.' That seemed like an odd name for a mother to name her child. If you watch and look at me I am different my wings and parts of my body. I will show you something but you cannot tell anyone," she continued. He met at her eyes and then spoke very strongly, "I give you my word. I will not tell a soul." She stood and asked if they could go into his hut.

Once there she told him to sit on his bed. Then she stood across from him and said, "What I am about to show you very few have seen. You can touch but just be careful." He nodded Zea turn her back to her new friend and opened her wings showing off her artwork of scars. She heard the male make a small gasp. Then the room fell silent. All that could be heard was the two souls breathing.

Krist slowly stood up and walked to the guardian. Reaching out he touched her back feeling all the scars. He could not believe what he was seeing. Zea broke the stillness by saying, "Most of them are from my childhood and a very few of them are from the Shadow Clan." He was still and quiet for a long time. After he was done feeling he went back to his bed where he took a seat. Zea brought her wings in and turned to face her friend. She whispered into the calm air, "I do not know what my scars look like because they are on my back. I can only guess what they look like by everyone's reaction." Then the guardian heard Bear call her name. She told Krist she was sorry but had to go and see Bear. He understood and she ran out the door to meet up with her other friend.

Bear wanted her to help him make a run to a neighboring clan so she could meet more friends. She was very excited and knew she had to be careful for the Shadow Kats. They both packed a bag full to clothes, a little food and bedding. Once they were done packing the duo walked to the middle hut where Dark Star was sitting and working. He was happy to see them enter the small room. The leader gave his friend a scroll as Zea watched. "Be careful and on guard. I would like you back in four days if not sooner. If I do hear from you we will start taking action. Have fun and I will see you soon. Oh, and Zea I know what shape I want. If possible I would like a sun," Dark Star voiced with a smile. Bear shook his friends hand and began to walk out of the hut. Zea shook the leaders arm, gave him a sign of respect and winked as she left his presence.

"What was that?" Bear asked the little one with a laugh as they left the camp. "What?" she questioned innocently. "Why did you wink at Dark Star?" he inquired. "Well, he asked me to make him something," the guardian spoke playfully. "And what are you going to make him or am I never to know?" the male questioned. "Dark Star wanted something like the thing I made you but in the shape of a sun," Zea voiced happily. "I must have missed something because I do not know what you made and gave me," the Kat spoke calmly. "This," she whispered as she stopped, pulled the little triangle with the heart from her back and showed it off for her friend to see. Bear picked up the gift and looked at it at all angles. Puzzled he was not sure what the gift was made out of. "I hope you like it. I made the shape of a triangle because you are strong and the heart because of all the kindness you have showed me. I gave one to Sun Flower in the shape of a flower, and now I will make one for Dark Star in the shape of a sun," the guardian stated joyfully as she continued to walk. The male caught up and joined her as the walked into the forest. He thanked her after he stopped looking at it and put the gift in his pack for safekeeping.

They walked in silence for a while till the guardian broke the calmness, "Can I ask you a favor?" "What can I do for little one?" he replied. "Can we fly? I have not been in the air in such a long time," the guardian requested. He was quiet for a while then said, "Sure, why not?" A smile grew on her face. When they reached a small clearing in the woods, Zea brought her wings out and flexing her muscles brought herself off the dirt floor. The male just watched, wide eyed seeing the female do this action effortlessly.

Bear began to walk to a tree when he heard his name. Looking in Zea's direction he spotted her open hand. Looking at her grinning face he shrugged his shoulders and took her arm. With all her might the guardian threw her friend into the air where he took flight. They climbed the sky and Bear then again realized the female's strength and differences. Watching her fly and do patterns in the sky he knew were impossible for him a smile grew on his face. Zea made sure that as they flew her friend did not see her back. After sometime passed Bear told Zea they had to land and make a good and safe camp for the night.

Landing the duo made a fire and laid their bedding side by side. As Bear collected firewood, Zea caught two birds for them to eat. After they were done with the last meal of the day the guardian cleaned up the mess from their food. Then she walked to a nearby rock, which faced a meadow. Looking across the moving sea of grass see saw a very peaceful place and got a warm feeling of home. She knew this was her home now and she now needed to find a clan. As the gently, warm breeze kissed her face the guardian found herself looking at the stars and her eyes began to water. Zea began to whisper prayers in her native tongue to her lost ones.

Her ears pricked when the sound of footsteps were coming in her direction. Turning the guardian saw Bear coming. He sat next to her holding her trying to understand why his friend was in tears. Looking at the meadow then the stars and last at the little female. "What is wrong?" he asked. She looked at him and then gave him a hug where then the returned the hug. Finally she broke the silence, "I think I am ready to show you more differences." "Whenever you are ready," he calmly stated. "I have showed you my wings and eyelids right?" she quietly asked. "That is correct," he replied.

While Bear continued to sit on the rock Zea jumped down from the rock on to the soft of the golden grass. Then she turned to face him while wiping the water from her eyes. After taking a deep breath she began, "Another difference I have is…" She stopped.

The guardian opened her wings and using them she jumped up onto the rock next to Bear. "I would rather tell you about my past in full detail then show you another physical difference," Zea whispered while looking at the ground. "Whatever you are comfortable with doing. If you want you do not need to tell me anything tonight," he voiced softly.

Zea proceeded to sit down next to her friend and speak, "I was born daughter of Domatu and Sunyro. My brother, Gyro, was about 18 years of age. My father was in charge of all the warriors and was great friend of Yaottyro who was the leader of the villa. I was very loved and a few days after I took my first breath of air my villa was taken over by the Qothos. I was put into slavery.

Shortly after our enslavement my father passed because of a poor choice I made. About two years later my mother fell to the same fate of my poor choice. Then four years later my brother was taken from me. The

Qotho who owned me was named Jabo. He had a mate named Uta and together they had a little one named Draco.

I found a way to break my braces and chains and I started a rebellion. The night of the escape Jabo ran out of the hut to see what was going on in his camp. His father was the leader. When rebellion began and Jabo exited the home I captured Uta and Draco putting them in chains. I left to join my kind in the fight. I ran into a Qotho named Moojigo and after he threatened me I fought. What I did not know was this was the leader of the camp and Jabo's father. Jabo then came out of nowhere. He told me he was delighted about me killing my family and I lost control. My rage took over I killed Moojigo, Jabo and many others but the main two I feel the most bad about killing was Uta and Draco who were behind me when I killed Jabo.

I woke up later under a tree. I had passed out and a friend had saved me. There were not many of us left after the attack and I was the only female in the group. Not long after the escape I left with two friends Hutto and Zutiyro. I traveled for many years. Hutto was the first to fall then Zutiyro. I was on my own again and I worked on my skills, fighting and mental. Later, the Shadow Clan captured me after I fought for a day. I escaped and ran into you." "Wow that is quite a story," he told her. "I am not done I have another thing to tell and show you," she whispered. "You do not have too," he spoke softly. "I feel like I need to tell you so you fully understand about my childhood and my nightmares," the guardian stated gently. "I am here for you, it will be ok," he told her while placing a hand on her shoulder. She again took a deep breath and wiped her tears.

"When I was in slavery Jabo did not always treat me well. I do not how to explain but he punished me a lot and took his anger out on me. I guess the best way is to show you," she voiced as she stood. Before turning around she spoke one more time, "You can touch." Zea then proceeded to open her wings for Bear to see the artwork on her back.

She stood there as Bear looked at all the scars on her back and he stood. Like all the others he was in awe to think about how young she was and how much pain she must have gone through. He reached out and carefully touched her back and wings. The nightmares and the way she always kept her wings in made more sense to the strong male. When he was done feeling the artwork and stepped back Zea brought her wings into their resting spot in her back. Then they both sat down on the rock.

"I was told the ones we lose look down from the stars. They talk to us but in signs not in a certain tongue. That is why I look at the sky a lot and pray when I do so," she whispered. The guardian watched the golden grass wave in the night air and listened to the sounds around her. She waited silently till Bear was ready to talk. "Dark Flame and some of the other Shadow Kats know about my back. They just do not know who gave me the scars. Dark Flame himself added to my back and wings but not much. He was mad because I would not talk to him and give him respect," Zea added.

Time passed and the zatz knew they had a day of traveling so she told her friend, "You do not need to give me a response. I will not be hurt or mad and if you need more time that is okay too but I am going to sleep. We have a long day of traveling tomorrow so are you going to join me?" she stated with a smile. He looked up into her deep green eyes, smiled and said "yes" as he stood. Holding hands they walked to their beds to get some much needed rest.

The sun kissed her face waking the guardian. Stretching she stood and set out to collect some food. Finding a nest with six eggs the female took three. Quickly returning back to where she had stayed for the night Zea rebuilt the fire and started to cook the eggs for the first meal of the day. As the food cooked she cleaned up her bedding. Soon the eggs were ready, Zea took them off the fire and placed them onto two large leaves. Next she picked four, what looked to be Lukeies (like oranges). In the cups they brought from camp she squeezed two of the Lukeies making juice and cut the remaining fruit for eating. Once her meal was ready Zea woke Bear up who was surprised that the little guardian had done all the chores. They ate their meals with smiles. Bear cleaned up his mess and the two made there way for the other clan after they put out the fire.

They walked all day only stopping once for Bear to get a drink from a passing river. As they walked Bear broke the silence, "Thank you for sharing with me last night. I could tell that was not easy for you do. I am very sorry you did not have a normal or happy childhood. If there is anything I could ever do please let me know." "There are still some differences I need to show you, but the time will come for that. I wish I could walk with my wings free but the scars bring me so much attention that I do not need or want," she replied. "This is true. I think when you are ready you should ask Dark Star to call a meeting and at the meeting you should say something simple. You could say, on my back I have many scars and they are from my childhood. I know it is a sight at first so I wanted to show you. I am not sure how you want to do that Zea, but I am here for you on what ever you decide," Bear voiced. "Thank you, I will think about it," the guardian spoke softly. They continued on their journey.

When day was turning into night they reached the other clan. The camp was by the side of a large rock face. The cliff gave the group protection. When Bear and Zea were close to the camp they entered a meadow of very tall green grass. Feeling uneasy the guardian started to use some of her training. Using her ears, as they walked Zea suddenly heard a movement in the grass, very quiet but there. She stopped. Bear looked at her, "Come on little one it is getting late," he started. "I hear something, we need to get out of the long grass. I do not like being in this meadow," she voiced strong and soft. "Then lets move onward," Bear also stated strongly. The guardian moved forward but did a pulse to make sure her ears were right. Then the picture came to her and again she stopped moving. Kats surrounded them in the grass. There was one very close to Bear. "Why are we stopping again?" he questioned. Without hesitation Zea ran and jumped into a large patch of long grass. There she landed on one of the Kats. Pinning him down he tried to fight back but was no match for the guardian. Seeing this all the other Kats who were hiding jumped out of their resting spots. Bear was in shock with all the action.

Regaining his train of thought he quickly ran over to Zea and picked her off the fighting male who stood up and backed off to join his fellow clan members. They all were looking at the newcomers. Bear raised his hands to try to calm the group down, "We are here as friends. There is no need to fight. This is all a misunderstanding. I am Bear from Dark Star's Clan and this is Zea a good friend who is a little jumpy. I am sorry for the confusion, but I am here to give your leader a message from mine," his voice breaking the stillness. Everyone relaxed and one of the Kats walked over to Bear who extended his arm in greeting. Everyone laughed at the whole situation. Staying next to her friend's side Zea walked into the new camp with the new group of Kats.

The guardian watched as some of the members of the group came up to Bear and it was clear they knew him but had not seen him in a long time. With no warning the crowd parted and in the middle stood an older male with a female by his side. The male had brown fur with a hint of tan and also had very small white patches. His eyes were a very light green and the way everyone was acting Zea got the feeling he was the leader. The female next to him had very light blue fur with very dark eyes.

Bear showed the leader a sign of respect which then the guardian followed her friend's example. After seeing that action the dark brown kat standing in front of them came alive and walked up to Bear giving him a hug while laughing. "It has been too long my old friend how are you?" he asked turning and walking with Bear. He must not have seen Zea who started to follow the two males. They were now engaged in a conversation. The blue female looked at the guardian. The zatz felt very uncomfortable so picking up speed ran to Bears side for his safety. She did not want to start fighting again and get in more trouble. The leader, Bear, the female and Zea walked in to a hut on the far side of camp.

Once inside the four of them sat in a circle and for the first time the leader saw Zea was present in the room. He looked at her and stated, "Why, hello there." The guardian smiled and replied, "Hi, my name is Zeaytera KatOynera." "Well that is a different name and why are you here with Bear?" he questioned the fighter. "Right now I am staying with Dark Star's Clan because I have no other place to live and stay," she answered. "Zea, is staying with our clan right now because she not only does have a clan to call home but also she had a run in with the Shadow Kats. I am here to give you this (handed the leader the scroll) from Dark Star," Bear joined in the conversation. Bear turned to the guardian and asked, "Zea will you go outside if you do not mind because I need to talk to Blizzard alone." Blizzard then asked the blue furred female to go with Zea and make sure there is no trouble. The zatz left with the female so the Bear and the leader could talk.

When Zea was outside she looked around the camp seeing that the camp was co-ed. Most of the members were outside their huts looking at the far hut where the guardian was standing. Taking a deep breath she turned to the blue one and voiced while extending her hand in greeting, "Hi, my name is Zea, what is your name?" She looked at the zatz then her hand and back up at her face. The new comer brought her hand back and looked away and at the onlookers. Feeling very out of place Zea wanted to get out of the center so she walked away from the hut where the blue one remained.

The camp was over all very quiet and still. Zea walked around the camp but no one was really coming up to her. Finally she found a small pond where she sat down looking at her reflection. Hearing footsteps she turned seeing a male walking in her direction. He had green fur and then Zea recognized him, he was the one she jumped on in the grass, which his fur matched. He sat down beside her and she looked at him through her deep green eyes. "Hello, my name is Snake. I am sorry to bother but, I was wondering how did you know where we were in the grass because in all my years no one has ever just found me in the meadow?" he asked. Zea smiled. "You are not bothering me. I have been trained very well on the skills of tracking and hunting. I am sorry I did not know what was going on and I was not trying to hurt you or start a fight," she spoke softy. "I am not mad. I am amazed you found me in the long grass," he stated. "Thank you, for not being mad at me. Is everyone else angry at me because it seems like everyone is mad at me?" Zea asked. "Our clan has been having some trouble with outsiders lately so we are not very trusting with newcomers.

By some of my clan member's reactions after seeing Bear, you might have guessed that when he was little this used to be his home. You seem like a nice Kat but, you are a little different," he said. "There you are," Bear voiced as he walked up to where the two were sitting. "Come on little one, Blizzard would like to see you," Bear voiced kindly while reaching out his hand. Zea stood up and joined her friend walking to the far hut.

Once they got to the hut Bear knocked on the door and they both entered when they heard a voiced ask them to come into hut. The duo walked in and took a seat across from Blizzard. "Hello again Zea, sorry I was being rude to you earlier. I am sure others have told you that we have been having trouble with outsiders lately. You are welcome to stay the night with us and after this talk I will introduce you to the clan. If you are a friend of Bear's you are a friend of mine," the leader told the zatz. Zea smiled. "I am sorry I attacked one of your members in the grass," the female said. The leader smiled and voiced he was not mad and knew she was only watching after her friend. Once they were done getting to know each other the three of them walked out of the hut where the rest of the group was waiting.

Blizzard introduced Zea to the clan. After the leader's speech the group relaxed and started to warm up to the newcomer. That night as they were eating dinner many of the members came up to meet the new female. Everyone was very nice to her and as Zea walked around the camp she saw a lone female. Walking up to her the guardian saw the loner was a whitish-gray color with black spots. Her eyes were a crystal blue and they were watery. "Why are you by yourself?" Zea question. "I do not know," the spotted one responded. "My name is Zea, would you like to get some food with me?" the guardian asked. A smile grew on her face as she stood up and stated, "Sure, I would love too. My name is Rain." The two walked over to where the table was and got a bowl of food then proceeded to one of the small fires where they sat down to talk and eat.

Rain told Zea she did not have a lot of friends and she just moved out of the hut where her mother and father lived. The guardian listened to the female speak and then told her new friend she escaped from the Shadow Clan and ran into Bear who took her into his home. They were soon talking like they had been friends for a long time. Soon the moon was high in the night sky and the time had come for everyone to sleep. Bear came for Zea who went with him with a smile as she waved goodnight to her new friend. That night the guardian had another nightmare as she slept under the stars. Bear awoke and comforted the little one who was shaking. Finally she went back to sleep.

The next morning the sun was out and the camp was in motion. Blizzard came up to the guardian and told her she was welcome back anytime. With a smile the two visitors finished their business then got ready to leave the camp. Before they left Zea found Rain and told her she would come back and visit if Dark Star let her. They said their goodbyes and Zea left the clan with Bear and they headed home.

"How was your time in the Mountain Clan, Zea?" he asked. "At first I was not happy and did not like the camp but, after Blizzard introduced me to the group and everyone was nice to me I had fun. How was your time there?" she replied. "I had fun seeing old friends," Bear answered. "Can we fly?" Zea questioned with a large smile. Bear laughed and told her they could fly. Flexing her muscles the guardian took to the air and proceeded to give her friend a hand so he would not have to find a tree. Once they both were in the air Bear asked to talk to the little one.

"What you shared with me the other night was not easy and again I wanted to thank you for putting yourself out there and trusting me. I am truly sorry you had to feel that pain and even at such a young age. I cannot even begin to understand what your childhood was like but I hope you never feel bad about waking me up at night with your dreams because I am here for you. Whenever you are ready to show or tell me something new I will be here for you."

"Thank you Bear, for understanding. Soon I will go into a little more detail about my time in the slavery. You can just glide not fly right?"

"Yes, that is correct. I cannot fly like you. I bet you could make it back to camp in one day if you were not with me."

"I bet I could but, I like taking things slow so, I can see your land."

"Our Land" Bear corrected.

They both smiled and flew towards their home. When the sun was high in the sky and Bear needed a drink they stopped along a river. They were a little downstream from a waterfall and they were at a small eddy. They sat on the green, soft grass in front of the calm circling water. "Bear, did you like the Mountain Clan when you were a member?" Zea asked. "Yes, I enjoyed my time there and made many friends but, when I lost my loved ones I could not live there with memories everywhere I looked and took my leave," the male answered. "Oh, I am sorry you had to leave," the guardian voiced. "I was content to leave. The timing was right for me and I am truly happier in Dark Star's Clan. His clan fits me better and think if I had not left I would have never met you," he stated. A smile grew on the zatz's face as she watched her friend get up and make his way to the water's edge where he bent down to get a drink.

Without warning a hand came out of the water grabbing the strong male and pulled him into cools water. Zea quickly stood realizing her friend did not fall in but was forced under the clear, blue, liquid. The guardian dove into the water. As her body hit the water her blue eyelids fell into place. Doing a pulse and looking around for her friend. There was no movement but, the reeds moving in the current. There hidden near the bottom of the bed there was a very small hole and a string of bubbles was leaving the entrance.

The fighter swam for the cave and entered ready to fight. There she saw a strong male holding her friend trying to force him in some kind to underwater cage. As Zea reached for her friend someone grabbed her leg and she was dragged out of the dark cave. Turning Zea saw three males coming in to capture her. Placing her body into a defensive position the guardian got ready to fight the males. As each one fought her she matched their moves and overcame them. A fourth watched the guardian fight and was amazed by two main things. One was the little female not once went to surface to get fresh air or had an air pocket and the second was the little one's grace in the water. She was obviously comfortable in the water and under the surface.

Once Zea beat the three males she did a pulse and found the forth watching her. Making eye contact she signed for him to come out and fight.

He did so the two began to battle. He swam at her with much speed and force but with one graceful movement Zea sent the challenger down stream.

The guardian then focused on saving Bear. Racing back to the cave she reached in grabbing who ever she could see when it was not Bear she knocked him out and with all her might threw him onto the river bank so would not die. Now once again she returned to the dark opening on the base of the river and reached in to find her friend. Freeing Bear she carried him to the surface where he grasped for some much needed air. Zea tossed him onto the soft grass and made her way to the riverbank.

Just as she was going to pull herself out of the water a pair of hands grabbed her shoulders forcing back into the cool liquid. The guardian was not pleased with this action. Turning, it was her old friend she had sent down the stream. She smiled and got herself in a defensive position. Out of the corner of her eyes the zatz could see more underwater challengers coming in all directions. Zea cracked her neck and signed for the fight to begin and it did. Each time someone fought her she would send him or her flying out of the water. The guardian was hoping Bear was up there to finish the job or at least tie them up so they could not fight again.

After time had passed and the guardian had been fighting for a while she looked up and saw there was now only one competitor left. The same one she had sent down river seeing him see smiled and prepared to fight him just as they were about to go at it they heard a sound in the water. Both looked at the maker of the sound and the male backed off from Zea. She gazed at another male who had been watching the fight. He gave them a sign to let the female go and leave the water. The male did not look content about this but let Zea find her way to the surface where she took in a large breath of fresh air. Next using her wings she flew out of the water another new sight for the ones in the river and Bear to watch for the first time in his life. Seeing someone fly out of the water again showed Zea's wings did not only set her a part but allowed her to do more than what was considered normal.

Landing next to Bear she asked if he was all right. He did the same. They both smiled realizing they both had the same answer. Looking around Zea saw Bear did tie up the fighters she had thrown out of the water. "I guess you like the water," Bear stated. "I have spent sometime in the water before and I guess I know how to swim a little," she voiced with a smile has her blue eyelids left leaving her normal green.

Bear and Zea started to group the fighters when they heard a voice come from the water's edge "Where did you learn how to fight and hold your breath like that, little one?" Turning Zea saw the same male who had told the other male to leave. He was a dark green color with blue stripes. His fur pattern was the same of a tiger but, with green and blue not orange and black. His eyes were black with dark blue lines. "Why do you ask? I do not even know who you are," she replied. "My name is Tim and I am the leader of this clan. I ask you because what you just did amazed me and I have never seen anything like that in my whole life and I have been in the water since a little one much younger than you," Tim stated as the fighter Zea now knew as the downstream warrior came to the surface of the river. Bear stepped forward and voiced very strongly, "Why did you attack us we were doing no harm."

"You are in my territory."

"We were getting a drink and then to be on our way home. You could have asked and not just pulled me in and try to cage me."

"Anyone who comes to my falls gets the same treatment. You were lucky you were with your little friend or you would be in my keep."

Bear rolled his eyes and told Zea to stay with him. She looked up at him and then back to the water where more clan members were appearing. There were males and females. Bear turned and began to walk away from the river and Zea followed him while turning her head to look at the water clan one more time. "Wait, please. Can we talk?" the water leader yelled. Bear stopped in his tracks thinking about what he wanted to do. Looking down at the guardian then turning back at the river. "I guess this would be good for you so you can meet a new clan," the male whispered to the little female. The duo walked back to the eddy in the river where the others waited. Bear and Zea took a seat under a tree in a nice soft patch of grass as the leader and a few members of the water clan came out of the river.

They faced each other in silence till Bear broke the stillness, "Are you going to talk because you did ask us to join you?" "I am sorry. I am trying to think of the right words to use," the leader said. "I will start. My name is Zeaytera KatOynera. Right now I am not a member of a clan but, I am staying with Dark Star's Clan with Bear," the female stated. "Why do you not have a clan?" the downstream fighter asked. Before Zea could respond the leader spoke, "As I told you my name is Tim and this is my second, Blue Fire. He is being rude and I apologize for him. I am the leader of the Green

Falls Clan. I would like to say thank you for meeting us and I hope there are no hard feeling about what just happen between us." Bear shifted. "I hope I did not hurt any of your members but, they were attacking me first," she voiced. "There was no harm done," Tim spoke softly. "Where did you learn how to fight and move like that in the water?" the leader continued. "Well, I am mostly self taught," the guardian spoke in a low voiced. "How are you self taught?" The leader repeated the question. "I do not know. How else can I put it, I was for the most part self taught," Zea voiced a little louder.

The others looked at her trying to understand how the little one was self taught. "Are you looking for a clan to join or are you staying in Dark Star's Clan?" The leader asked. "Yes, I am looking for a clan to join but, I am still trying learn all of the ways of this land," Zea responded. "We have to be on our way back home. If you want you can come to our clan if you want to talk to Zea more or Dark Star but, like I said we must be on our way back to camp," Bear stated as he brought himself to his feet. The guardian followed his lead, "It was nice meeting you," she voiced. "You are welcome back to visit anytime," Tim enunciated. The duo went on their way back home.

When they could see the smoke from their home and when they could see the huts smiles grew on their faces knowing they were finally home. Once there they met with Dark Star. Telling them everything from meeting the Mountain Clan to the Green Falls Clan. After the leader got the report he let his two friends go and see the rest of the clan.

As they were leaving Zea turned to Dark Star while saying, "Can I talk to you when you have a few minutes?" He smiled and said, "Sure. Why, lets do it right now if you are ready." Bear looked at her and seeing her face he knew what she was going to do. He whispered low, "Do you want me to stay?" Zea shook her head no. He smiled and left the hut to see his friends but, as he did he told Zea, "I will be here if you need me afterward." The guardian smiled and again nodded.

Once she was alone with Dark Star the zatz moved the two chairs in front of the leader's desk. He got up and helped her move the room around. Taking a deep breath the female cleared her mind. She asked her friend if he wanted to sit and he did so. Again the guardian took a deep breath letting the air fill her lungs and letting it exit.

Opening her eyes she began to speak softly to her friend, "While I was with Bear I shared with him about my past and there is a part I also wish to share with you. Before I left my home I was a slave and my master did not treat me kindly. He liked to make himself feel better by hurting me. The reason I keep my wings in so much is my master left his mark on my back. I wish to be able to walk around camp with my wings out but I do not want a lot attention for it. So, I was wondering if I could just show the whole clan at once so that way everyone knows and can talk about it then and there. If you do not mind I will show you my back now." Dark Star nodded while giving her a look of puzzlement and compassion.

"You may touch if you like, everyone seems to want to anyway," Zea stated as she turned her back to the leader. Taking a deep breath the guardian flexed the muscles in her back releasing her wings from their resting place and revealing her artwork of scars.

Dark Star was in shock. He did not know what to think or feel. His mouth drooped as he stared into the little ones back. Shaking his head the leader then stood and slowly walked over to where the female was standing. Like all the others before him, he reached out and gently touched Zea's back. After sometime had passed and the guardian could not stand the silence anymore she moved her wings and turned around to face her friend.

"Do you like it? Do you think it is a good idea?" she asked. He looked at her with watery eyes, "I cannot even image what it was like for you growing up but for what it is worth I am sorry. Yes, I think it would be better to let the whole clan know at once. That way everyone has the same story and there is less stress on you," Dark Star started voice sweet and low. She smiled then said, "Thank you." "When would you like to share this with the clan?" he asked. "As soon as possible if that is okay with you," she answered. "How about tomorrow night?" Dark Star questioned. "I think that would be great," Zea replied. They said their goodbyes then the guardian left the hut to see her friends.

The air was fresh and light. The sky was turning dark with the coming of night and the sounds of laughter came from the members of the clan as Bear told the story of when he and Zea went to the Mountain Clan. How the little one jumped in the grass on one of the guards. Everyone was happy to two travelers were back safe. Not much had changed while they were gone. Josh, Robby and Roberd were sitting by the fire talking with their meal and Zea asked to join them. They all said, "Yes," at the same time and laughed. The guardian joined in as she sat down to eat.

Later she went to bed but the next night's events were on her mind. She tossed and turned all night long and could not wait for the sun to kiss the land once again. When dawn was well on its way Zea got up and went for a morning run. To her surprise Krist was also out running. He joined her and both with smiles went for a run as the sun was rising. "How are you?" she asked her friend. "I am doing well. I am sorry I did not talk to you about your back," he replied. "I am not mad and I understand. Tonight I will show the whole clan that way I can walk around camp and not worry about my scars," the guardian told him. "Really, good luck. I know that will be hard for you," he spoke softly. "I am sorry you did not have a good start on life," Krist stated. "I am just doing the best I can but, you do not need to feel sorry for me," she said with a smile. "Anytime you want to talk I will be here for you. I now consider you a friend. We can be Colins together living in clans," Zea continued. Once morning was well on its way the two runners were back in camp and working on the first meal of the day.

The rest of the day Zea helped with chores and had fun talking and playing with all her friends in the clan. Soon evening was on its way and the clan was sitting down to eat the last meal of the day. As the little female ate she was very quiet and nervous. Josh noticed the guardian not being as playful and asked how she was feeling. The zatz told him she was doing well but explained to him he would find out later why she was so nervous. He was not happy with her answer but would have to live with it because that was all she was going to say. Soon the time came and Dark Star called Zea to come talk with him.

Walking over to where he was standing he asked her again if she was ready and willing to share her scars with the group. After taking a deep breath she told her friend she was ready. He stood on a table and got the clan's attention. Soon all the eyes were on the leader. He began, "Good evening. I hope you all are doing well tonight. As you know for a while now we have been sharing our camp with a new friend. Tonight she would like to share something about herself with you. I ask that you give her all your respect for this is very hard for her to do. So, here is Zea." Stepping down the leader helped the guardian onto the table as the crowd cheered.

The female cleared her throat and put up her hand signaling she was ready to speak. The group became still. Zea shifted her weight and began, "Hi, I hope you all are enjoying the last meal of the day. As you might have noticed I am a little different from you guys, physically." "I hope so," Roberd yelled from the crowd breaking the tension.

After everyone laughed Dark Star pulled the group back and asked the female to continue. Bear walked up to Zea side for support. Again she took a deep breath and spoke to the group once more, "One main difference you might have noticed is my wings. I can pull them in and out of my body and I can fly not just glide. You might have also noticed I keep them in my body a lot. This is because I have some scars on my back that I am not to happy or proud about. I am hoping to show all of you at this time my back so that way no one is whispering behind my back.

Now we can all talk about my scars here and now to get all the questions out in the open for everyone to hear. They are from my past and I do not like to really talk about how I got them but they are now apart of me. So, I guess all that is left to do is show you." Her heart raced. "It is ok, Zea you can do it," both Bear and Dark Star whispered to Zea. Members of the group were whispering and the guardian could hear some giggling as she turned her back to the clan. Taking a long deep breath she held it in till she let her wings and breath out at the same time. The crowd fell silent. Holding her wings up high the female let the clan see her artwork. When some time had passed Dark Star told Zea she could stop if she wanted in a whisper. The guardian turned and faced the group once more and stated, "thank you for your understanding." Then Zea stepped down and stood next to Bear who comforted her, "You did a good job and I think you did the right thing."

The leader broke the silence, "lately some of the watchers have seen some Shadow Kats in the distance. I would like everyone to be on guard and also if one leaves have a least two friends with you. Do any of you have any questions?" There was only silence. "I will be around if anyone needs to talk, other than that every have a good evening and thank you that is all for this meeting," he finished.

The rest of the night Zea was very quiet and distant. She was looking into one of the fires hypnotized with the fame's dance. When the female felt a hand on her shoulder. Looking up she met eyes with Roberd. "We are going to play a game would you like to join us?" he asked. A smile grew on her face as she stood and joined her friend. They walked to a field where a good number of the males were playing. Roberd started to explain the game and Zea recognized the game. The game was Leoi but they called it gimme. They played into night and Zea forgot all about her back. They laughed, played and enjoyed the company of others.

Which One?

As weeks went by Zea got used to living in a clan. Dark Star asked her travel with messengers so she could meet other tribes. There were so many she was learning a lot in a short time. She was very joyful that she was not alone and was starting to adjust to the new life style.

One morning when Zea was running and she could hear someone behind her. Coming to a stop the guardian turned around to see a familiar face. "What do you want?" she asked quietly. "I just wanted to see you. I should not be out here alone but, I wanted to see how you were doing," he stated. "Pyro, I am fine. I do not know why you want to come see me if you are going to get in trouble and I am not willing to be with you," the guardian told the Shadow Kat. "If you ever need a place to stay I know hiding places and I will keep you good company," he voiced to her. "Thank you, Pyro, I must be going right now," the female voiced strongly. "I hope to see you soon," he said as he turned and ran off into the bush.

Zea continued on her run and as she jogged she thought it was odd that Krist was not with her. He did not meet her this morning. The female headed back to camp where it seemed very quiet and there was no group making the first meal of the day. Looking around and not seeing anyone she started to feel uneasy. Hearing a twig snap on the ground behind her she whipped around to see Bear with a smile. "Where is everyone?" the female asked. "Now!" he yelled. Everyone came out of their huts or from hiding yelling, "Surprise or congratulations" Zea was very lost and did not understand what was going on in the camp.

Dark Star walked up to the guardian and while giving her a hug stated, "You have been with his for a year." – Computer is that true? – she asked very puzzled in her mind. – No, you have been here for a half a year this day– the computer answered. "I am sorry Dark Star but, I have not been here for a year but only a half of one," the zatz stated quietly. His faced changed from a look of joy to puzzlement. "How many days are in your year?" the leader asked. "7,300 days are in a year. Why how many are in yours?" Zea questioned. "There are 3,650 days in a year," Dark Star voiced. They looked at each other is disbelief at their discovery. After some talk they found out that one year of Zea's was two to the others. She would be aging slower and live longer than everyone else. This did not make the guardian feel cheerful to find another difference. They had a good celebration that day despite the new information about time.

Later that night when Zea was alone with Bear she asked if she could share more with him. He of coursed agreed. They sat on his bed and began to talk. "I have told you about my back, my eyes, my past and my wings," she began. Taking a breath a silent pause took over the room. Then the guardian spoke, "I think tonight I am going to tell you about two more things but they are both very big and different in my eyes. I am just hoping that after I share myself with you that you remember I am still the same."

As the female stood and faced her friend he voiced, "Zea, you know you can trust me. I will never leave or treat you different because you are diverse." "Thank you, Bear, after I show you the first one and you think that is enough please tell me and I will wait for another night to share with you," the female replied. "I will be honest with you," the male said as he sat up on the bed to give his full attention to Zea.

The guardian again took in a deep breath and voiced softy, – I do not know how to say it so I am just going to do it. – "Ok," Bear voiced not realizing the last words he heard did not come from Zea's lips but her mind. A small smile grew on the guardian's face because he had no clue her mouth never moved. Trying again she moved a little closer to her friend, – I am trying this again because I do not really know how to put this action in words without seeming crazy.– He observed at her with a puzzled look. Zea did not know if he realized she was not using her voice to talk or if he did not understand what she was trying to share. Bear broke the still room, "What?" She smiled again while stating with her mind, – What do you not understand?– He looked at her and was not sure what to think or say. Finally he broke the stillness in the room. "Are you doing what I think you are doing because I am a little lost," he asked her. The guardian smiled and stated to him softly, "I am talking to you through my mind." "Well you do it again?" the male asked. – Sure, what would you like me to say,– Zea spoke mentally. A smile grew on his face as he looked at her. "How did you do that? You are amazing. This is, I mean, I am speechless," Bear voiced. "I was just born with it and my father and brother helped me developed my skills. I can talk to you, read your mind or send you pictures in your head, but I would never read one's mind without asking them first," the zatz told her friend.

"What am I thinking right now?" the male asked. "You are thinking about the fire and now you are thinking about a green meadow which leads to a waterfall," Zea paused, "Would you like me to continue?" she finished. "No, that was good," he spoke with excitement. "I am glad you like this gift I have. I have not used this ability in a long time. I think with practice I could do more. I hope you do well with this next difference because this one is going to be very hard for me to do," the guardian told him.

"You do whatever you feel comfortable doing," he whispered while placing his hand on her shoulder. She looked down while he tried to comfort her. He could see the smile and joy leave her face and the fear on the unknown come into place. Soon she looked up into his blue eyes and found safety. Taking a deep breath Zea stood up and walked across the room from Bear.

He shifted his weight on the bed and looked at the black one who was standing in front of him. "Like I said this is very hard for me and I really again do not know how to explain this so I am just going to show you," the female stated to the room. "Take your time," Bear voiced softly. The little one shifted her weight and she said, "Here I go." Then Zea proceed to show her friend how she changed from her two-legged form to her four-legged form. He watched in silence as she talked to him while in her four-legged form and then how she could move her wings. She continued to show him that she could fly in her four-legged form and how she could change back to her two-legged form.

Once the guardian was done presenting Bear her different forms she sat crossed legged on the dirt floor looking at her friend who only sat there thinking about what he just witnessed. Stillness took over the room. The little one waited for a response from her roommate. After Zea waited very patiently she stood up with watery eyes. The female did not like waiting in silence for a response from her friend. Seeing her standing in front of him he smiled and opened his arms. She hugged her friend and they sat in silence for a while till he released her. They locked eyes and hugged again. "Everything well be okay, thank you for sharing with me," the strong male reassured her. "I never thought you could change your body like that," Bear stated.

"I have been able to do that too since I was born too."

"You are definitely different but you are amazing."

"Thank you, Bear, you always make me feel better."

"You should get some sleep, little one."

The guardian gave him one more hug then got up and went to her bed where she laid down for the night. Zea awoke to Bear standing over here asking if she was okay. She had yet another nightmare. She got another hug from the warrior and they fell back into the land of dreams together.

The sun seemed to rise quickly that morning as Zea ran on her morning jog with Krist. They talked about the night the EnyoRheas would be coming up for the yearly visit. The guardian realized that her running partner did not go last year. She smiled as he told her stories about past meetings and all her friends. When the two returned to camp they helped with the first meal of the day and went on with a normal day's works.

The zatz was helping one of her friends fix a hole in one of the huts when she heard her named called. Quickly the guardian stood and ran to Dark Star who was waiting for her. "Good morning," the leader spoke. "Good morning," she replied upon reaching her caller. Zea followed Dark Star though camp till they got to his work hut where they walked into the small room. The leader took his seat behind the desk and motioned for Zea to also sit. The female looked at her friend and around the room as she waited for him to speak to her.

Finally the stillness was broken, "Well, my friend, it seems other clans are interested in you. I have received a few letters and massages asking to meet with the two of us. I have decided to have a large meeting with all those who are interested in you. They will each have time to speak to you and then you can pick one. If this is okay with you," Dark Star told the guardian. Zea looked at her friend and then decided that the leader's idea was a good one. They talked where and when the meeting would be and then they both went back to their work for the day.

Later that evening Bear was sitting next to Zea as the group was eating the last meal of the day. "How is everything going?" the male asked. "I am doing well and I have had no problems lately. Do you need to talk to me?" the female replied. "No, maybe later but, not right now. I was just checking on you and making sure you were doing well with the clan," he voiced to the fighter. She smiled and told him, "Everyone is being nice to me and if there was something wrong I would tell you." He also smiled and pulled her close and started to push and poke her. Playing back the she laughed and broke free running from him. He pursued and a great game of gimme started.

They played into the night and soon Dark Star told the clan the time had come to stop for the night. They all stopped under the moonlight and went to their huts for the night. Once there Zea and Bear got back to their hut they each laid in their beds and talked. Bear told Zea he thought about her back and her differences.

Then he asked her a question, "How did you stay under the water so long when you were fighting the Green Falls Clan?" Zea was quiet trying to think if she had ever told him about her gills but she could not remember finally the guardian spoke, "Well, as you might have guessed it is another difference. I have a set of gills by each of my ears." "Can I see?" the male asked. "Sure," Zea stated as she stood up and made her way to where her friend was lying. With the moonlight the little zatz pushed her ears and her fur back so the inquisitive Kat could see her gills. After he got a good look he let her go and she sat crossed legged on the dirt floor. They talked about the guardian's differences for a while longer before they went to bed.

The next morning Zea awoke with the sun and ran on due filled grass. The sky was just turning from pinkish orange to a light blue. Within minutes of running Krist was by her side jogging on the emerald green field. They asked if they each had a good night and stories of the past. As they ran Zea got an uneasy feeling and asked her computer to do a pulse for her. When the picture came back she could see there was a group up ahead. "I think we should stretch and head back because I have an odd feeling," Zea told her running partner. "Sure," Krist answered. They stopped, stretched and moved back to camp.

Like before Zea could hear the footsteps behind her and the familiar voice of Pyro calling to her. When Krist heard the other male's voice he quickly turned around to confront him. The two males faced each other and there was a lot of tension in the air. No one spoke; only the sound of the air moving could be heard. Pyro was not alone he had five friends with him and this fact did not seem to matter to Krist who was not going to let the other male push him around and tell him what to do.

Finally Zea broke the silence, "Both of you stop it. Krist, lets go back to camp and Pyro leave. Please." But, both heated males paid no attention to her. They only looked into each other's eyes in a dead cold stare. The guardian grabbed Krist's hand and tried to get him to leave with her but he did not move. Finally one of the males spoke," What are you doing here?" "That is none of your business, Matakai (one who dishonors a clan)," Pyro stated coldly. "I did what I had to in order to live and be happy," Krist replied. "I suggest you do what you do best and run away from the group," the leader's son retorted. Hearing the cold words leave Pyro's mouth Zea became saddened and upset.

While holding her friend's hand the guardian whispered into his ear, "He is not worth this and you know it. Please, lets go back to camp. I think he likes to upset you. Please." Once hearing these words his cold eyes shifted to meet the little one's deep but warm green ones and he closed his eyes, took a deep breath and spoke softly, "You are right." They both turned and began to walk back to their home. Seeing this made Pyro's blood boil and he quickly moved in front of their path.

This action did not make Zea happy and before Krist could make a move the zatz walked up to the troublemaker. Looking into his eyes she voiced very strongly, "I would not do that again if I were you. I am not in the mood to play this silly game with you and I think you should leave. Come Krist lets leave this place." Turning her head Krist joined her. They both once again started to head home.

"Zea," Pyro yelled. The duo did not stop moving. "Zea, wait I need to talk to you," the Shadow Kat called into the air. The guardian paused, turned and told Pyro, "I will not talk. You have lost my respect and I think you should go home as well." Within minutes the two were home and Zea went off to help with the first meal of the day while Krist went to talk to Dark Star.

The rest of the day Zea did not know what to think. The picture of Pyro and a fight breaking out replayed over and over in her mind. As mid morning turned to day she laid down in the green sea of grass, which lined the camp and began to think of the future. Taking in a deep breath the guardian could smell the smoke, flowers, scents on the wind and the fragrances in the air. Her ears pricked and moved back as the sound of footsteps came closer. Turning to see who was coming to join her she met eyes with Bear who was smiling and proceeded to take a seat next to her.

The two sat in silence till Bear finally broke the stillness of the peaceful scene; "I heard you had a visitor this morning." "Yea, Pyro is still lurking near camp. I do not know what to do. I have told him I do not want to be with him but I think his feelings blinds him. I did not want a fight to break out this morning but Krist was so mad," she voiced slowly. "I think Krist has befriended you which is very rare action to see him do but, I think he was trying to protect you from Pyro. He does not like the Shadow Clan," Bear told Zea. "Was Dark Star mad?" the guardian asked. "No, he is not pleased with Pyro and is unsure on the future. I know for a fact he is not angry at you. Do not worry about it little one if there was a problem Dark Star would talk to you and we would all work it out till the problem was gone," he replied. A smile grew on the guardian's face knowing her friend was really getting to know her.

Bear once again broke the silence, "How do you feel about the meeting coming up where you will pick a clan?" "I have many emotions. I am nervous because this will be a big choice, happy to be finally on my way to joining a clan, and sad to leave all my friends here in this great camp," Zea stopped. "Do not worry. I am sure you are always welcome here in this clan. You could come visit us whenever you had free time. I bet that is what all of us here would want and even if they do not I do care. I want you to come visit me and I wish you to promise to come see me," Bear voice grew stronger with each word. Standing with a smile the guardian stated, "Of course I will come see you." After Bear stood they hugged and hand in hand walked back into camp.

The rest of the day flew like the shifting wind and soon the last meal of the day was upon the camp. Zea sat with her friends, Josh, Robby and Roberd who were all laughing and joking around like normal. "I am excited about tomorrow," Josh whispered. Upon finishing his words all the others looked at him causing him to cup his hands over his mouth. "What is he talking about? What is going on?" the female inquired looking from male to male. The trio looked at each other wondering who was going to tell the female about the next day.

Finally Roberd rolled his eyes and whispered into Zea's ear, "Because Dark Star and Bear's birthdays are so close together we as a clan have a big party for both of them on the same night. As you might have guessed tomorrow is the day we as a clan have decided to have the celebration. I am guessing why you have not heard about this is one you are not a true member of the clan yet, sorry, and because you are always around Bear so it is hard to just pull you aside. Bear might find out when we were going to have the feast." "Oh, thank you for telling me, Roberd," Zea voiced softly. The small group continued laughing and telling jokes.

Soon they started to talk about stories from their past. Zea always felt a little out of place when this topic came up because she was very vague with her sharing and did not have any good stories to tell the group, but the guardian loved to listen to the funny memories. As they were laughing Zea's eye caught her friend Krist sitting by himself a little outside light. Standing the zatz told her friends she would talk to them later and proceed to join her friend who was sitting in the cold.

"How are you?" she asked as she sat down next to her friend. "I am doing well. Why did you leave the fun and come sit with me in the cold?" he inquired. "I wanted to talk to you and I think speaking with you is just as much fun as talking to everyone else, never doubt that. I enjoy chatting to you and I always sit with them. I did not see you all day today and I wanted and needed to talk to you," the guardian told Krist strongly. "You are too kind to say such words and thank you. I will never doubt myself like that again. Thank you for sitting with me I enjoy your company. What did you want to talk about?" he questioned.

"Well, I am not sure what you have heard but I have a big choice coming up in a few days."

"I think I heard something about a meeting."

"Yup, I soon will not be living here and I do not know what I am going to do but I know I am going to miss you and the others."

"I am sure you will be fine."

"I know but I will miss you and want to talk to you."

"Well, maybe we could meet once a month and we could talk and catch up at this reunion."

"I like that idea. I would love that."

Both smiled and hugged. "We will decide on a meeting place after you pick a clan," Krist told his friend. "I have to go down to the river to get some sand would you like to join me?" Zea asked. "Sure," he said while standing and extending his arm to help the zatz up off the dirt floor.

The two made their way slowly to the river where the female put some sand in a bowl. Krist watched her and wondered why the little one wanted sand. As they made their way back to camp Zea stopped to look at the sky. There was no moon that night and the stars were out shining for all to see. "Why do you look at the stars so much?" Krist asked quietly. "They remind me of my past and lost loved ones," she told her friend. "Why do you need the sand?" he question. "I am going to make a gift for Dark Star. His party is tomorrow with Bear right?" the zatz asked. "Yes," he stated has they walked back into camp. Krist then went back to his hut and Zea to hers. She laid on her bad and tried to think of what gift to give to Bear.

Her roommate was not home yet but out playing with the other members of the clan. – What do you think would be a good gift for Bear?– she asked. – I am not sure. Do you want to make him something or do something for him?– the computer responded. – Well, I gave him gape. – she voiced mentally. – What if you made something for him that would help him somehow– the life long friend spoke. –I am not sure computer, maybe I could make him a new blanket or bed. – Zea told him. – Or you could make him a meal of new food,– the computer advised the young female. – I like that idea, thank you, computer– Zea said. What to make him the guardian asked herself as she walked out of the bedroom and into the main room. Where she walked to the corner with the bowl of sand. After doing a pulse to make sure she was alone and then proceeded to bring her computer into view. Zea then made a sun for Dark Star. When she was finished the guardian hid her computer and the little trinket for the next day. Zea then walked outside the hut and looked for her friends.

The majority of the clan was by the main fire talking and playing games. A few of the older members were discussing amongst themselves and the leader and his close members were also in a group talking. Bear was in this assembly. The female decide to join her friends by the main fire and she sat next to Josh and Robby. Roberd was on guard that night and could not join in with the fun. They joked and told stories by the warm fire. Hearing her name being called out the guardian looked in the direction of the caller. Seeing and locking eyes with Dark Star she excused herself from her friends and joined the leader's group.

Taking a seat next to Dark Star and across from Bear, Zea looked at each member in the group waiting for one of them to speak. Soon the leader spoke to the group. "We have two large events in the next few days. They are of course the meeting with the EnyoRheas who are coming here this year and the meeting with different clans for Zea. I am not sure how many clans will be at this meeting and I am still thinking of a good spot to have this gathering but I will find one. I am not sure if the Shadow Clan will be bold enough to show up at these events or if Pyro is daring enough to show his hide as well. I do know we must be very careful with these events because not all of us will be on guard. I will address the clan but we all know what happens when the EnyoRheas come or any group from outside the clan. I think we should all be on guard this week because all that is going to happen."

All of them agreed and Zea remained silent listening to the members of the group voice their say on what should happen in the following days.

Dark Star turned to Zea and stated, "How would you like the meeting to go? Would you like to be alone? How do you want it organized?" After looking down in thought she answered, "I think I would like each group to talk to me alone. Then I would like to make my decision. If one of you would like to be with me that would be fine with me." "I think this is a good idea, but we must think of a good place to have this meeting," Bear voiced.

They all talked well into the night on this problem and decided that the groups would stay with the clan and would be in numbers of two. They would each get a chance to talk to Zea then on the second day the female must make a choice. Then she would leave with her new clan mates. With high hopes Zea would pass all the clan's test and join within a few weeks. After the talk was done they all went to their huts for some much needed rest.

With the sun coming Zea awoke and went for her morning run. Soon she came to the river where she decided to take a swim. Diving into the cool blue water she used her blue lids and used her gills. The water felt very good and she played in the weightless world. After time passed she came to the surface and met face to face with an old acquaintance who was waiting for her. With a roll of her eyes she went back under the surface and made her way to the riverbed.

Once there the fighter pushed off the floor and swan to the air. Opening her wings for speed and for flight she reached the water's end and took to the air. Flying up and into the clouds the cool wind dried her fur and the female headed back for the ground. Reaching the tree line she landed in a graceful motion bringing her wings back into their resting spot. "Everything you do amazes me," Pyro yelled above from a nearby tree. "What can I do for you today?" Zea asked. The leader's son jumped down from the tree to face his love.

Upon reaching her he spoke, "I think I will be at that meeting you are having in a few days." Turning to face him they locked eyes. "I do not think that is a good idea. I will not be picking your clan. I have told this and nothing you could ever say will make me change my mind. I will not be a part of a clan that hurts others for fun or to make itself stronger. I am sorry but my answer will always be no," the zatz spoke very strong. "I am sorry to hear that but I am not the kind that gives up easily," the male stated while walking a circle around the female who watched him with hawk eyes. "I will not change my answer. I do not think you should come to the meeting," she voiced. "Then let my turn be now," he suggested.

The guardian looked at him giving him permission to go on with his speech. Pyro cleared his throat and began, "The shadow Clan will always be a bad clan if someone like you does not join. We need strong ones like you to help change it from inside to the outside and make it greater than ever. I think this would be smart because you have already made friends in other clans and once they see you with us then they will see that the whole clan cannot be bad if you are with us. And if ..." "Pyro stop," the female interrupted.

"You must realize once I join a clan I must follow the leader to the death it is a very serous action for me. If I join now your father will be in charge of me and I do not like his morals. I will not let him be my leader. And if you want your to clan you change so much you should stop wasting your energy on me and try to help your clan. You are strong but you need to work to lead your clan. Me joining the group will not just magically change the ways the tribe or the views others have of the family. You are sweet to try to persuade me but I will not change my answer," the guardian told the Shadow Kat.

He looked down in disappointment and then looked back into the female's deep dark green eyes. "My feelings for you will never change. Every time I see you I fall more in love with you and I will do anything to have you," Pyro voice as he walked to a nearby tree and took to the air. With a roll of her eyes Zea walked back to camp where she joined in with the first meal of the day.

The day went by very quickly and soon mid-day was turning into night. Zea had really kept to herself all day and left the safety of camp a few times to gather food for the small treat she would be making for Bear. While the sweet bread cooked the smell wove its way through camp and all were wondering what was cooking. Zea kept the food hidden by her bed once the project was finished.

When night fell the clan surprised both males with a feast and celebration. Both Kats were happy and thankful the night was full of games, gifts, laughter and stories. Zea gave Dark Star his sun and he was quite happy with it and thanked her with a smile. The whole clan had fun that night and when the night was over Bear and Zea walked to their resting spots.

Once inside the hut Zea asked her friend to sit at the table. She then proceeded to retrieve the food by her bed. The female placed it in front of her friend who looked at it and all the colors. "What is this little one?" he asked. With a smile she told him it was a poi (like a cake) and he should eat it but she also told him it was very sweet. The male took a few bites and fell in the love with the sweet tasting poi. He had tasted sweet bread before but nothing like this. Once he was done they both went to their beds and fell asleep. Zea awoke with Bear standing over her. "Its ok``ay Zea you are safe," he whispered. She wiped the beads of liquid from her brow and hugged her friend. He rubbed her back until she was back in the land of dreams.

The next two days went by very quickly and soon the sun was setting and the EynoRheas were on their way to the camp. All the males were excited and happy to be able to see their friends. Dark Star addressed the clan moments before the females entered the camp. Again the night was full of joy. Zea saw Liz and Sarah walk into the camp together. The guardian greeted them. They were all joyful to see each other again. They all sat down to eat together. They were all having fun talking and playing when Roberd, Robby and Josh came up and asked to steal the females away to dance. With a giggle the two females joined the males and Zea was left to find more friends.

The zatz ran into Avis who was talking to some of her friends. The painter was happy to see Zea. Nathan joined Avis and the guardian who were talking by one of the fires. Soon they were all full of food and games took over the two clans. Zea took a break for water and ran into Sunflower who was pleased to see her. The guardian gave the leader a sign of respect. They talked of Zea's progress with the all male clan and living in a new land. After the two caught up the little female joined in with the games again. The two clans played long into the night and soon dawn was upon them. With heavy eyes Zea went to sleep.

The sun rising came too fast for the little one but like always she went for her morning run. The fresh crisp air filled her lungs and gave her energy to take on the day. The warm star, which lit the sky felt good on her face. Once back in camp the guardian helped make the first meal of the day and when it was ready sat down to eat with her tired friends.

The next few days went by very fast and Zea was full of excitement and fear and soon the day of the great meeting came. All the clans who wished to talk to Zea were in camp and ready to meet with the female. They would all have a chance to speak with Zea. The first two to go were from the Red Water Clan. They were very kind and told Zea she was welcome to visit anytime. Next two were from the White Meadow Clan then the Rock Clan. Snake and Ice came from the Mountain Clan. They explained to Zea she would have to work to enter their clan and if she did not pick their clan that day then she would never be allowed to join but still she would be welcome to visit. Then came the Green Falls Clan and they said she was welcome anytime as well and they hoped to be friends. No matter what clan she joined. There were a few others and all the clans were very nice and seemed to really want meet Zea. When the last group was done talking to the guardian she was left alone with her thoughts. Soon Bear came into the small hut to talk to his friend. The zatz told him all her feeling about each clan and he gave her his opinion. They talked for a while and then once again the raven colored female was left to her thoughts.

The next day when morning was turning to midday all the groups met in the middle of the camp. Zea walked out of the middle hut and faced everyone who was waiting for her answer. Taking a deep breath she stepped forward and with a smile began to speak, "After much thinking and comparing in my mind I have chosen to join the Mountain Clan if they will have me. The other clans were great but I feel that I would fit in the best in the Mountain Clan. I want to thank all of you for coming and caring. I hope we can still be friends even though I will not being joining you. I hope you all have a safe trip back to your homes and thank you once again." The two from the Mountain Clan came up and embraced their new sister member as the other groups gave their respect and left the camp.

That night was Zea's last night with Bear. With heavy hearts they went to their hut for the last time for quite awhile together. Sitting on Bear's bed they held each other and talked. The strong male stated in a shaky voice, "I am going to miss you little one and the clan will not be the same here without you. I hope you know you are always welcome here for safety and or to visit."

"I will miss you so much Bear. I will come visit you and the others. I would not be here without you because you saved me and helped me when it seemed like one else would. Thank you."

"No matter what anyone says you will always be my friend and it would be my honor if you would be my daughter."

"No, no Bear the honor would be mine to have you as a father."

The two hugged in tears now that they were considered family. Zea and Bear now had a family again and both were very happy to have each other. "No matter what anyone says you are amazing and a great fighter," Bear voiced strongly. "Thank for everything Bear you are a great warrior with a strong heart," Zea told her father. The duo was silent for a while till Bear broke the stillness, "You are astonishing. You never cease to make me think and surprise me in every way. Thank you for telling and showing me this because that has been on my mind," Bear laughed. "I am glad you like my differences," Zea smiled as she gave the male a hug. The two talked long into the night and soon watched the sunrise together. Zea gave him a hug and told him she had to go run around camp for the last time.

Running out of the hut the guardian met up with Krist who was very happy to see her. "I am going to miss you, Krist," the jogging female said. "I think I have found a great meeting place for us to see each other once a month," the male excitedly told his friend. "Where?" she asked. "In the forest there is a small cave about a mile North from the Green Falls Clan. I know this meeting spot is closer to my clan than yours but I am sure you can travel faster than me," he stated with a smile. She laughed and agreed. Then the young one asked, "When would you like to meet?" "I was thinking about the time and how it is different for you and me so I was thing since you look at the sky so much we would meet every four nights with no moon" he suggested. "I like that idea so every forth no moon I will meet you at the cave," the zatz agreed. They stopped running, hugged and went back to camp where everyone was waiting for her.

As the guardian ate her first meal of the day every member came up to her at different times to say goodbye for now and give her respect. Last to come up to Zea was Bear and Dark Star. The leader told the guardian how cheerful he was that they were friends and how she was welcome in his clan whenever she wanted or needed to come. He told her he would miss her and respected her for her bravery and honesty. They hugged and the zatz moved onto a tearful Bear. They hugged and said goodbye as a father and daughter. The three walked out of the camp with smiles and tears. Soon the guardian attention went to her two new friends walking with her and thinking of her new home.

The Mountain Clan

When the three entered camp the clan cheered at the sight of their new "sister." Blizzard opened his arms and welcomed the young one into his camp. They went to his hut to talk of all the things to come.

Once there they sat across from each. The leader began to speak to the excited female, "Welcome to the Mountain Clan. I hope you enjoy living here with us. Tonight I will introduce you to the clan and tomorrow we will make you a hut. Right now lets talk." In the small room in the back of camp the two discussed all the rules of the camp. The leader also told the guardian the steps she would have to do to be able to join the clan. She was overjoyed and excited to join a new group. Once they were done talking and all the questions were answered the two walked out into the night air.

As the clan of about 65 sat down to eat the leader stood beside them with Zea at his side. "Good evening, Let me introduce you to our newest friend of the clan. This is Zea and tomorrow she will start the process of joining our clan," Blizzard began but was cut off with everyone's cheer of the news. "Zea is from Dark Star's Clan and does not really have a true clan. If all goes well, we will be her first one. I would ask you all welcome her and share in her differences and similarities," the leader continued and then turned to Zea while placing a hand on her shoulder, "Welcome once again to the Mountain Clan, sister." There was a loud cheer as the zatz smiled and thanked everyone for their welcome. Then they all sat down to eat and tell stories. When the meal was done Zea walked around and met many members of the clan. When the moon was high in the sky the Guardian went to a hut to sleep for the night.

When the sun kissed Zea's cheek she awoke, stretched and began her day. She walked around camp but because the camp was carved in to a mountain there was no real path to run around the camp. Talking to one of the guards she decided to run around the meadow but to remain in view of the grass guards. With the sun warming her back she took off across the meadow to start her run of the morning. When the little female returned more members of the clan were up and preparing the first meal of the day.

She helped where she could while talking and making friends. One of the males she met while they were making the food was a light blue with lighter green eyes. His name was Ken. The light blue male was very kind and soft spoken. Ken had been in the Mountain Clan his whole life and lived with his mother because his father was a member of an all male clan, The Bassoon Clan, which was a few days walking North. He was a very joyful and was strong male who loved to play games. The young male made the guardian laugh and smile. Soon the clan sat down to eat the first meal of the day.

That day Zea's job would be to collect supplies to make herself a hut. With a group of five they set out to chop wood and gather grasses for the roof. Once they were across the meadow they entered the forest where the group would look for strong wood. As Zea was picking large foliage to weave later her ears pricked to the sound of footsteps.

Turning her head to greet her visitor, she was surprised by seeing a familiar face. "What are you doing here?" she questioned boldly. "I am here to see you," he replied. "I am sorry but I have to go," the female stated as she began to walk away from the male. "Wait," he voiced. "What do you want Pyro?" Zea inquired. "You moved to the Mountain Clan that is an okay choice. I had to work hard to find you but, I am happy my work paid off because I found you," the male spoke softly. "Pyro, I do not know what you want but, I am leaving right now. I do not want to be with you," the strong fighter told him. "I just want to be your friend," the leader's son said. "I am sorry, but we do not have a healthy relationship and I do not think you should keep just showing up to talk to me," Zea told him while she looked around for a member of the Mountain Clan. "I am sorry you feel that way but, I love you and I will continue to come and see you. I have to go my father wishes to show me something and I am excited. I will come see you later, have a good day," Pyro told Zea as he disappeared into the green brush. This did not make the guardian happy and she returned to her work. Soon the group was done and they head home talking and laughing.

Once the group returned to the camp Zea started her work on her new home. She started by trying to find a good safe spot to build her home. As she was walking around camp she saw Rain who was again by herself. "Hi, Rain, how are you?" the guardian asked. "I am doing well. What are you doing right now?" the female questioned. "I am trying to find a good place to build a hut," the zatz replied.

"I know a great place; next to mine on the edge of camp where the meadow and the mountain meet. There is a small pool of water there and I think you would like it."

"You think so?"

"Yes, Zea, I do. Come I will show you."

The two walked over to where Rain's hut was located and the both females agreed this would be a great spot for Zea to build a home. Zea began by digging a perimeter for her dwelling. Next she cut the wood and built the frame. As the day went by the guardian was very focused and did not stop to rest. When the sun was setting the little worker was just tying the last knot for the roof to the walls of her new home. The female took a break to eat the last meal of the day and when she was done the zatz made a hammock, blanket and pillow so she could sleep in a bed that night. Everyone was impressed that the little worker was done with her home by the end of the day. That night Zea slept in her own room for the first time since she had found the Kats. A smile grew on her face as she closed her eyes to sleep for the night.

Zea woke with the rising of the sun and went for her morning run. When she returned she again tried to help with the making of the first meal of the day. For the first week Zea would be shadowing different members of the clan to see what she would like to do for a job. Everyone took turns guarding but there were many other jobs to be done.

That day she would be watching and helping a hunter named Elisa. She was a deep red with a hint of cream white on her underside with blue-green eyes. "I heard you speak a different language," Elisa stated as she was climbing the mountainside with Zea. "Yes, I have a native tongue. I had to learn yours when I was taken in by the Shadow Clan," the guardian respond. "What does my name mean?" the red female asked. "I am not sure why everyone asked me that question. I find it funny that everyone wants to know, but to get to the point, I think your name means original beauty," the guardian spoke with a laugh. "Really, I like my name in your tongue," Elisa said with a smile.

"What are we hunting for today?" the zatz asked. "We are hunting for Randys. They are medium sized reptiles with a tough blue skin and deep green eyes. There are sometimes called 'bad terrors' because they like to attack anyone who is walking on the mountain for no real reason. They are hard to skin but the meat is very tender and good. They are very strong flyers with sharp teeth and talons, a forked tongue, a long slender tail with a small triangle at the end and a snout with two little holes at the end for a nose. They walk on six legs and have a good-sized wing-span. They vocalize with a girlish like call or laugh and like to sing. They do have a high-pitched scream when they dive at their prey. A large group of them have been known to kill a Kat," Elisa explained to the inquisitive young female.

"Where do they like to live?" Zea inquired. "Randys like to dig into the rock face of a cliff. They build a nest but luckly for us it is not too deep in the rock," the red one answered. The two talked more about the Randys till they reached the edge of a cliff. "Here is the tricky part we must climb down the rock and catch us a few Randys. We need ten of them," Elisa told Zea. "I think this well be fun," the guardian stated as she began down the cliff. The red one followed.

Finally they reached the nest site and Zea watched Elisa do the first one. She reached in and said, "The trick is getting the head. You can snap the neck or at least keep the mouth shut." Then she pulled out the one she killed by snapping the neck and put it in her bag, which was on her back. Suddenly the duo heard a scream and turning they saw a Randy heading right for them. "I got this one," Zea called out as she released her grip from the rock. Opening her wings the guardian took to the air. The Randy started to chase the guardian who loved to be in the air again. Doing an aerial flip the Randy found itself as the prey.

The blue reptile was quite surprised to see how fast and agile the female was in the air. Within minutes the fighter caught up with her prey and she grabbed it with a simple twist the creature was lifeless and the zatz put it in her bag. She caught four more in the same matter. Elisa liked having Zea in the air to watch her back. When they caught all the Randys needed they headed back home.

That night Zea talked and made more friends. She found a female named Jenny who had a yellow coat and brown eyes. She was in charge of all the food. The next day the guardian would be making food for the group all day. Later that night after the last meal of day Zea worked on making things for her home like a table, chairs, shelves, etc. That night Zea had a very strong nightmare and she awoke with a pounding heart. Wiping the beads of moisture from her brow, she stood, up and walked around. The female got a drink of water from the cool pool outside her hut.

Once outside she looked around and saw Blizzard's second in command, the light blue female. Zea was not happy that she did still did not know her name. The guardian thought this would be a good time to ask. When the blue one saw the black one approach she was surprised. "What are you doing up at this hour?" the tall female asked. "I did not want to bug you but, I was wondering if I could know your name?" the zatz asked. "Oh, my name is Storm." the second stated softy. "Thank you, Strom, I will leave you to your work. Have a good morning," the new comer stated as she walked back to her hut. The zatz laid down and tried to get some much need rest.

The morning came very fast and soon the sun was greeting the day and Zea was off for her run. Next she joined the food worker and began to work for the day. All that day she cooked and talked with the new friends. Zea was very good cook and did not need much instruction. Everyone was again amazed with the little female. Over the next few days the guardian farmed, built, fixed, planed, wrote and much more. Soon Blizzard asked her what job she liked the best and Zea told him she liked to fix problems. The guardian enjoyed problem solving and meeting different members of the clan. He smiled and at the last meal of the day he announced to the clan Zea would be one of the two fixers among the camp. As usual there was a large cheer followed by laughs.

The weeks went by very fast for the young guardian and soon she was well known and loved. Her best friend was Rain and when they were not working they were playing. They were seen as sisters and Zea confided in her. Rain could not imagine what Zea's childhood was like but she did whatever she could to help. When the guardian had nightmares Rain did her best to comfort the shaking female. The zatz was so happy she found a close friend.

Over the next few weeks the strong fighter also worked with Snake and other main guards to help them on their fighting and tracking/ hunting skills. Zea was doing well fitting into the group. Soon everyone knew she had scars on her wings and that she was a little different but the one who knew her the most was Rain. Although she did not know all Zea's secrets like Bear, Rain knew more than everyone in the clan. Like the guardian and Krist discussed they met on the planed time. Everything was going well for Zea but she did miss Bear.

Finally one day Zea asked Blizzard if she could visit Dark Stars Clan. He smiled and said sure but she must be back in three days. With a grin the guardian left the hut and went to her home to pack. As she was packing Rain knocked and came into the small room. "I heard you are going to Dark Star's Clan," she began. "Yes, I am Rain. I cannot wait to see my old friends," the zatz told her friend. They talked till Zea was done packing and then they hugged and the guardian was on her way to see her friends again.

Old Friends

As Zea walked away from the Mountain Clan the guardian felt strange. The female did not like leaving her home but was very excited to see her old friends again. The guardian left the meadow and entered the forest. The blanket of green blocked the sun's rays from warming the fighter. As she walked she found herself along a river and she stopped to get a drink. The clear waters refreshed the young fighter. Then the zatz continued on her way to see her father.

Zea's ears pricked with the sound of footsteps coming from behind her. – Computer, will you pleas do a pulse?– she asked her life long friend. – Sure.– the computer answered. Then the picture came back Zea could see she was surrounded by at least 20 kats. The fighter slowly stood and began to walk to the nearest tree. Then a familiar face appeared from the high branch of the tree.

Jumping down Pyro met eye to eye with the female. "What do you want?" the fighter asked. "You," he voiced strongly. Upon the ending of his words the group he was with went into action. The guardian moved into a defensive position and waited for her first attacker. To the guardian it felt like all 20 attackers came at once. Fighting all the Shadow Kats, Zea was not pleased with Pyro and soon could feel ropes against her fur. Bringing out her claws to rip the leashes she could not help but scratch the aggressors.

Then out of the corner of her eye the zatz could see a flash black. Before she knew it Zea had a friend helping her fight Pyro and his gang. The fight was over faster with help and soon the only one left standing were the two black ones and Pyro. Breathing hard the guardian manage to say, "This is over Pyro, leave. I do not want to see you. I do not love you and I will never join your clan!" "This is far from over, my love," he yelled as once again he disappeared into the bush.

Now turning to her helper, who was also panting, the guardian asked, "Thank you, if you do not mind who are you?" "Hi, my name is Damon," the male stated. As the female looked at him she could see he was very well built and had black fur with spots like her father's and his eyes were such a bright white they seemed to be glowing. "Why did you help me?" the zatz asked. "I am a Colin. I do not like living in large groups and I do not like it when the big clans attack the 'little ones'. I heard and saw them attacking you and seeing you were alone and smaller I decide to help," the Colin voiced. "Thank you, again Damon. Do you live only in the woods?" the fighter asked.

"Yes, I just go where I wish. I have a few clans where I can go if I need but I really do not like to go into tribes. I enjoy living as a Colin and there are other Colins out here who are my friends. I am happy. Are you a new Colin or do you have a Clan and just out here for the fun of it?"

"I came from a far away land and when I got here the Shadow Clan took me in by force. I escaped and ran into Bear from the Dark Star Clan. He and Dark Star took me in and I lived with them for a while. A few months ago I moved in with the Mountain Clan and right now I am trying to join the Mountain Clan. I have been a 'Colin' for most my life. Right now I am traveling to see Bear because I miss him."

"I see, you are a different one."

"You are uncommon in my eyes"

"I am sorry but I do not think I caught your name."

"I am sorry, I forgot. My name is Zeaytera KatOynera but most of my friends call me Zea."

"Now, that is a unusual name."

"Thank you, I guess. You have a nice name."

"What language is your name in because I do not understand."

"Yes in my land I spoke a my native tongue but here I had to learn your language. My name means 'wondrous one' in your tongue."

"Will I guess I learn something new everyday."

"I am sorry to cut it short but I have to get going. I hope to run into you later or next time I am traveling."

"Yes, I hope to see you again too, it was nice meeting you."

"Yes, you too Damon, and thank you, bye"

" Bye."

Zea jumped to a high branch of the tree above her, opened her wings and took to the air. Once flying over the land the guardian felt more relaxed and clam. She loved the feeling of the wind weaving through her hair. The fighter could relax knowing she was most likely the best flyer in this new land. Looking down Zea could see her destination was coming up quick.

Looking up the guardian could see a group of jezebels. They were pink and peaceful, graceful flyers which fed on honey and fruit from trees. They had pink feathers and purple eyes. They were also very friendly and helpful creatures. The flyer flew upwards and joined the jezebels who were a little startled. They danced across the sky and played with the wind.

Soon Zea was over the Clan of Dark Star. She left the jezebels and made her way down to the land below her by diving. Reaching the dirt floor she razed her wings and landed in the middle of camp to everyone's surprise. The clan was just sitting down to the last meat of the day. Bear jumped up from his seat and hugged his daughter. The female was overjoyed to be with her friends again and they all sat down to eat, talk and laugh.

The daughter sat by her father all night and he would hug her many times. After everyone was done eating a game of gimme broke out and everyone felt like nothing had ever changed. Soon the moon was high in the sky and everyone turn in for the night. Zea joined Bear and in her old hut and they stayed up late talking about what they had been doing since the guardian left camp. Bear had stayed the same and was still happy in the clan. Zea told her father about all the friends she made and how she was fitting well with the clan. He was blissful to hear of his friend's success. Then the fighter told Bear about her last run in with Pyro and the help from Damon. The father was not pleased to hear about this and did not know what to say or do.

The guardian told him she was strong and could fight him easily but just did not like the feeling of being watched or being stalked. He told her to tell Blizzard when she returned and to her best not to travel alone. They talked for a while longer and then fell into the land of dreams.

The next morning like she always did Zea awoke with the sun and she went for her run. A smile grew on her face to see Krist waiting for her. They laughed and ran as the sun slowly rose in the sapphire sky. They had seen each other a week earlier in the cave. "I miss our runs together," Krist told his friend. "Me too," the female agreed. When the two returned to camp Krist went to his hut and Zea went to help make the first meal of the day.

Once the clan was up and ready the guardian joined Josh, Robby and Roberd eating. They were still the same, telling the same jokes and having fun. When they were done the zatz walked to Dark Star's hut. There she talked to the leader and caught up on everything. He too was not happy to hear Pyro was still giving her trouble and gave the same advice Bear did. Soon the sun was high in the sky and Bear asked Zea to go down to the river with him and of course she agreed and they left for the cool waters.

Once there they swam and Bear asked to see Zea's gills and how they worked under the surface. The father was amazed with his daughter. After they played for a while the duo headed back to camp. The guardian could smell the familiar scents of smoke from the fires now being started in the camp.

Entering her old home Zea looked around to see everyone working like normal. Zea sat down by one of the fires to rest and watch the flame. To her surprise the guardian realized all her friends were circling her. Looking all around she saw them holding hands and walking closer to her. When Zea was encircled the group stopped and began to chant something Zea did not fully understand what they were doing. Then it dawned on her. A smile grew on her face and began to tear because of the joy in her heart.

When the clan finished Dark Star stepped forward and voiced loudly so everyone could hear, "I think we are a few weeks early but, on behalf of the Clan I would like to say, happy birthday." The guardian jumped up and hugged the leader. To everyone's delight the party began and there were stories, games, food and more. This was the little one's first birthday party and she so full of emotion that all she could do was tear. That night she did not sleep but played till the dark night was starting to turn lighter shades of blue.

Just as the sun's light washed over the land the guardian was running with Krist. They had fun laughing about how the others made fools of themselves. When they got back to the camp they hugged and said their goodbyes. Then Zea ate the first meal the day with her friends, packed the little gifts and tokens from the night before and said goodbye to her friends. Giving a tearful hug to Dark Star and thanking him for everything the little female moved on to her father where like before they hugged and gave their respects. Last Zea was on her way back home with high hopes and a singing heart. As the guardian flew home she talked to her computer and both were joyful to be in this new land with friends.

Remembering

As the sun was just beginning to set in the now changing colored sky Zea landed back home in the Mountain Clan. Everyone greeted her and asked how her travel was. The warrior asked to see the leader of the clan as soon as he could find the time. After seeing the look in her deep green eyes he told her to meet him in his meeting hut in 20 minutes. She nodded and went off to talk to her friends and have the last meal of the day.

That night Zea decided to sit next to Helena who had a purple coat with brown eyes. She loved to act and play games. The guardian thought her personality fit the meaning of her name, which was "star". The purple kat told the guardian all about her childhood. When about 20 minutes had passed the little female politely excused herself and made her way to meet Blizzard.

When the female reached the hut she knocked on the door and waited till she heard the leader welcome her into the small room. The hut was warm and cozy. The leader stood and gave a motion for Zea to sit across from him. She did as was asked and cleared her throat. "What can I do for you little one?" Blizzard asked calmly. "For a while now Pyro, from the Shadow Clan, has been stalking me. He always shows up when I am running or doing a chore and when I was traveling to the other clan he approached me again but this time was different. I have told him many times I do not love him and never want to be with him or his clan but he tells me he loves me and I should be with him. Well, this meeting for the first time he attacked me with 20 of his fellow members. I fought back and won with ease but this worries me because he has never attacked me before and I do not want to put this clan in trouble," the guardian explained.

Blizzard sat there soaking up all the information and when he was he ready spoke to the female, "I knew taking you in that we might have trouble with the Shadow Clan. I do not want you to worry about the clan. We are behind you. I wish you not to go running or anywhere alone. I wish you to have at least one guard with you when you run in the morning and when you are out doing chores be within a few feet of another worker." "I will do that and thank you, Blizzard," Zea stated. The female stood and made her way back to her home for some much needed rest.

There the guardian saw Rain waiting for her. They hugged and were overjoyed to be together again. Rain was the first real female friend Zea had ever had. They both went into Zea's hut to talk of the guardian's travels.

The young female talked about the party and the games. Rain hung on her every word. "When is your birthday?" the listener asked when the story was done. "In three weeks I will be 18 years old," the zatz voiced. "Wow you are young" Rain exclaimed. The guardian laughed, "Well, how old are you?" "I am 21 years old," the friend answered. The two laughed and talked into the night.

The next few weeks went very quickly for the fighter. She continued to fulfill her role as a camp fixer. The female did her best to learn everyone's name and role within the camp. She could not believe how far she as come. Her goal of being a member of a group was in sight. The warrior wondered when Blizzard would start her trials. The best part of the last few weeks was no Pyro!

Zea woke and found snake also just rising. The female asked if he would like to go on a run with her and with a smile he agreed. The two jogged across and around the meadow. When they returned both runners got their first meal of the day and went on their various paths for the day. Zea's day was full of fixing huts and other objects. When the day was late a little one came up to the guardian and asked if Zea could make a gift for her to give to a mother. The guardian said, "sure" and asked what kind of gift the mother wished to have. The little one, Moondust, asked to have something different but beautiful. Then the zatz asked Moondust what the name of her mother was and the little one replied, "Sunbeam." The fighter smiled and told the little one she had the perfect idea.

Then Moondust ran off to play. Zea walked to the back to the camp where it met the mountain. There was a lot of sand and the guardian collected some in a small wooden bowl. Next she went to her hut where the different one could be alone. Once in the safety of her hut the guardian brought her computer in to view and proceed to make a sun out of gape for Moondust. When the sun was finished Zea wrapped it in soft cloth and went to the last meal of the day. There she found Moondust and gave her the small gift. The little one was overjoyed and loved the gift. With a smile Zea watched Moondust run off to play and see her mother. The zatz sat down and ate the last meal of the day with Rain who talked about her day. When the time had come the clan cleaned up and went to sleep for the night.

Zea lay down in her bed and looked up at the roof of her hut. She could not sleep. – What are you thinking about?– her friend asked. – I think you know what I am thinking about Computer, – the guardian mentally voiced. – You should not worry about that, like I have told you before that is not your fault, – the life long friend stated. – I do not care what you say, my father's, mother's and a little of my brother's deaths are my fault. I hope that I can someday forgive myself for these actions and maybe someday when I meet my family again they will forgive me as well,– the female continued. – Jabo, used you and ...– The computer started. – I will not talk to you about this subject anymore if you will please stop,– the zatz interrupted. – If you wish. That was really nice of Dark Star's Clan to throw you a party. Does anyone here know when your day of birth is?– the friend asked. – Only Rain.– Zea mumbled. – Do you think she will do anything?– the computer questioned. – We will see my friend, we will see,– the young female sighed. – You should really try to get some rest, Zea– the computer pleaded. – Okay, I will try to sleep,– the guardian agreed as she shut her eyes and did her best to clear her mind.

The morning came fast for the little one and she rose with the sun. As the guardian walked to the edge of camp to her surprise Snake was there waiting for her. "Would you like to run with me?" he inquired. "Sure," Zea voiced as a large smile grew on her face. The two friends ran across and round the meadow and were laughing and talking the whole way. Zea was overjoyed she had a buddy to run with in the morning. When the two got back Zea went to her hut to get ready for the day.

Once the first meal of the day was ready the guardian woke her friend up and the two went to eat. Just as the guardian was finishing her meal Moondust and Sunbeam came up to her. "Good morning," the little one chirped cheerfully. "Good morning little one," the black one laughed. Then the zatz gave the mother a sign of respect. "Can I help you, Sunbeam?" the guardian asked respectfully.

Both females sat down next to the guardian and Rain and then Sunbeam spoke, "I wanted to thank you for making that gift for my Moondust. May I ask you what it is and how you made it?" Zea smiled and told her, "It is called gape and I guess you can say the sun was made out of sand. I have to make the sand very hot then it melts and I can shape it into any shape. Gape breaks very easily and can be very sharp but is very beautiful. If you ever want another one or a replacement I will be more than happy to make one for you." "Thank you," Sunbeam stated as she stood. Zea gave her a sign of respect as she left.

"Why do you give her so much respect?" Rain questioned. "I was taught that all elders should be given respect because of their age, experience and wisdom," the guardian replied. "Oh, I understand. Where you came from there are a lot of rules and ways to act?" the spotted one continued. "Well, when I was growing up there were a lot of rules but, I have been taught a certain way to act and I do not see them as rules or a way of life. I see what you call rules as a part of me. I think showing respect should not be seen as something you should or have to do but what I want to do and just do without really thinking about it," the black one explained.

Zea loved to have deep conversations with Rain. She felt closer to Rain and was getting used to living with females. Rain could relate to some of the problems Zea had because she was a female. The whitish-gray Kat with black spots loved to talk with her black friend because she learned a lot and finally had some one to talk to other than her reflection in the pool outside her hut.

"What was life like back in your home?" the spotted one inquired. "My life back home was not what you would call normal. I will tell you but please keep this between us. Is that okay?" the guardian began. "I promise," Rain whispered. Zea took a deep breath, smiled and started, "Where to start? I think I will tell you about my "clan" before I was born. We lived in a very large clan made up of 2,000, I think. There was one leader and everyone kind of acted like you would act here but there were just little differences.

A few days after I came into the world a different race called, Qothos attacked, and they took over our clan. I was put into slavery. Finally years later when I was older and stronger I escaped and traveled here to start a new and better life. So, as you can tell I did not have a normal childhood because I was a slave." The two sat in silence until Rain broke the stillness, "I am so sorry Zea, and I had no idea." A smile grew on the guardians face when she saw the compassion from her friend.

"You do not need to feel bad for me or bad for asking about my past. Now you know why I do not talk about my past a lot or tell funny childhood stories," the zatz again explained. The two talked for a while longer until Rain told Zea about her childhood, "I was born here in this clan and to my mother, Nighthawk, and my father, Trio, and I have a older brother, Gecko. He disappeared a few years ago and no one really knows why. Most of the clan thinks he ran away but I know he would never do that but I do not now what happened. We were very close and he watched out after me. He left I think about three years ago and I have really been alone ever since well until you came.

My childhood has been normal in every way except for Gecko missing. Just before I met you my mother and father told me I was old enough to be on my own so they helped me build this hut and then I moved into it. I still see my parents but they live across camp and I just feel alone sometimes but not since you came. I am so happy we are friends." When the older female finished speaking she hugged the younger one and laughed. "Thank you for sharing with me, Rain, I am joyful we are friends too and I will be more than comfortable to help you find your brother, if you would like me too," the black one voiced strongly.

"Tonight my mother and father asked me to go to their house for dinner would you like to come?" Rain asked. "I am sorry but unless there is a strong reason for me to go I have to do something tonight," the guardian spoke softly. "No, I do not think my parents had anything planned and I told them I would go so, I guess I will see you later and I know there will be other times for you to come over to eat with us," the spotted one voiced. "Thank you Rain, I hope you have fun tonight and I will see you later," the zatz wished her friend. The two hugged and Rain left the hut to join her family. Zea sat in the room as the cold, dark and stillness crept in to greet and keep her company. After thinking for a few minutes the guardian knew what she wanted to do. Standing the zatz took a deep breath and went to find Blizzard.

Upon finding him she asked if she could climb the cliff and sit on the edge because she need time to reflect. The female also expressed to the leader that if there was trouble she would simply fly off the cliff and come back into the safety of camp. After hearing what the little one had to say Blizzard agreed with her. After giving him a sign of respect and thanking him the guardian made her way up the rock face.

Once the zatz reached the top of the climb she took in a deep breath letting the night air fill her lungs. Then she began to shake and cry in the moonlight. – Everything will be okay, Zea, do you want to talk?– the computer comforted. – No, no one remembered. – the female cried. – I know, I know, but, the other clan did and I that is more important because they were with you longer. I think Rain just had a lot going on today and forgot. You are still new to the clan and not everyone really knows you that well. – the computer explained. – I also feel so bad and alone sometimes and I do not care what you tell me their deaths are my fault all of them.– the young one voiced. – Zea, stop. Do your best to control yourself. – the life long friend soothed. The shaking female stared to rock and fall into a mood of prayer.

Soon she was calm and looking at the sky with tear filled eyes she wondered if her loved ones were there watching her. The female sat still in silence of a long time. Soon the moon was setting in the night sky and she stood. Zea said a final prayer asking for forgiveness and guidance from the wise ones from the past. After much thinking Zea realized that she never celebrated her day of birth the real first party was with Dark Star's Clan a few weeks earlier. To her it was not a big deal that no one really remembered her day of birth. "18 is not that important of a year, I guess," the zatz whispered to herself as she jumped off the cliff and took to the air.

After landing the female made her way to her hut where she looked for the small gifts from the all male clan. Krist gave her a book to write her thoughts down but the male did not know about her computer. Zea would draw or find another good use for it. Robby, Josh and Roberd gave the zatz a necklace they all worked on together and Bear and the leader of the clan gave the guardian a dagger and holder for protection. After looking at her present the 18 year old was blissful to know she was loved. After packing all her gifts the little one went to bed for the night.

Finally

The weeks seemed to fly by for the guardian. Every time Blizzard asked Zea a question about how the camp life was or any rule the female gave him the correct answer without pausing. He was very proud of her progress. Many times he asked the fighter to give lessons to some to the guards. The zatz of course helped any clan member who asked. As time went by she became more comfortable with the clan but they still did not know a lot of the female's differences and past. Overall many of the clan members did not really ask Zea or really get to know her they just saw her as a friend.

For the most part the zatz was happy because she did not need to talk about her past but was a little troubled that no one in her clan really wanted to get to know her. The only one who really asked was Rain. Rain knew about the scars and a very vague outline of the guardian's life. With their late night talks and living next to each other the two never seemed to be apart. Soon many of the members were asking if Zea would make them gifts for each other. And this helped Zea to recognize everyone in the clan.

Snake enjoyed running with Zea every morning and he liked talking to her but did not ask her a lot about her past his questions were about how to fight. One of Snake's best friends was Treble. He was a dark purple color with orange eyes. Treble loved to play games which involved fighting or wrestling. The fighter loved to play games with the males at night. Some days went by slow while others ran like the wind. Gradually the guardian relaxed and did not really care that no one in her new home forgot about her day of birth but she still was mad at herself about her past.

She felt like she should have prayed more or did more on her day of birth. The female's life long friend did her best to tell the guardian that everything in her past was not her fault. The zatz spent many nights crying in bed and hoping for the future to come.

One morning when Zea woke up she went for her morning run and then went back to her hut to get ready for the first meal of the day. The day was going normal, the sun was out, every one was happy and there was no outside trouble. Zea decide to go to the nearby river for a swim and the female asked if Snake and Treble wanted to go with her. They were off guard duty and had nothing else to do so with great smiles they joined the little one.

As they walked on the green sea of grass they talked and laughed. The guardian was happy she made close male friends in the camp because the zatz was used to living with males. When they reached the moving waters the guardian climbed a tree and dived in to the wet world as the two males watched her grace. Soon the three were in the water playing games and laughing. Treble got out to lie down in the warm sun. The two others stayed in the water to play. Every now and then one of them would spray their resting friend who laughed and threw rocks or dirt back at his attackers. The trio laughed into the evening.

Zea and Snake went to take one more dive down to the river bed before heading back to camp as Treble stood to stretch. When the guardian came to the surface of the water her expression moved form joy to fear and anger. There to greet her was Pyro and a group of his friends who were holding Treble. The Shadow Kat smiling to see the black one. "What are you doing?" Snake yelled. "You, stay there, Snake, or your friend will pay for your mistake," Pyro ordered.

Treble struggled to brake free but was punched in the stomach and held in place. Zea was very troubled with Pyro and his actions. There was silence for a while till Pyro broke the stillness, "Are you happy to see me, my love?" Both of the Mountain Clan member's faces turned to puzzlement to hear the other male's words. "I am not your love and to be honest no, I am not pleased to see you. Why won't you just leave me alone?" the guardian voiced very strongly. The male crouched down so he was closer to the female and spoke, "I will never leave you, Zea, I love you and someday you will see that you love me as well."

The zatz was very angered by the leader's son action. "What are you planning to do? Have us sit in the water till it stops flowing or are you going to do something?" the guardian asked sarcastically. The male stood and started to pace. Zea could see that Snake was growing tried of swimming. "Pyro, if you want to talk to me fine but, can you let my friends go or at least out of the water?" the female asked. The male laughed. The guardian swam over to her friend and helped him tread in the water. "I am done with this," the tired female whispered.

With all her strength the fighter threw her friend out of the water and on the opposite bank of where her other friend was trapped. Landing next to Snake the guardian checked to make sure he was feeling well. After she looking over at her comrade who as sitting on the ground and regaining his strength, the female then turned to face the other group across the moving waters.

Pyro crossed his arms and looked at the fighter who opened her wings knowing that now Snake would see her back. she felt that getting to Pyro was more important. Seeing her scars Snakes eyes widened but he knew this was not the time to say anything, as he tried to stand. Once Zea was on the ground she brought her wings back into their resting spot. Now Pyro and Zea were face to face.

"Pyro leave, I really do not want to fight right now," the female ordered. "I do not think you are in the position to be giving me orders. I think you should be trying to make me happy not upset me," the cocky male stated calmly. In one quick and graceful move Zea tripped the male and forced him onto his back. Next the guardian pulled out the dagger she received from Bear and placed it gingerly under the Shadow Kat's chin.

To everyone's surprise the leader was down and looking around at his friends for help and then at the one holding him. The guardian then yelled to everyone around her, "Move and I will kill him." Now turning her attention to the striped male she voiced in a very low and strong, "Tell me one reason why I should not end your life right here, right now." Pyro remained calm and was not even trying to fight his way free. With a smile he whispered back, "I know you, Zea, you would never kill me unless I really did something wrong. There is some silly rules you follow about killing in your little code. You will not kill me, hurt me but not kill."

Silence flooded into the scene and soon all that could be heard was the moving water and the air moving in and out of the fighter's chests. Finally Pyro spoke, "I believe the move is yours." "A trade, you for my friends," the female told him. "I do not think I like that trade, little one," the striped one stated. "I am sick of your games, Pyro. I wish for them to end so I do not need to worry about you," the zatz told the leader. "All you need is to agree to come with me and all the games will stop all I want is you," he spoke while finding himself lost in her deep green eyes. "Goodbye, Pyro," the guardian stated as she pushed on his shoulder while releasing a drop of venom and watched his body go limp.

Now standing the other members quickly became upset and began to yell. The one's who were holding Treble started to tie him when Zea's voice cut the air, "Your leader is only sleeping. Release my friends before you do something you regret and make me mad." The other Shadow Kats did not move. "Fine, have it your way, we will fight or ...," the female stopped to think. Walking over to Pyro's now resting body Zea picked him up and walked to the water's edge. "I am now going to throw your leader into the water. You have two choices you can save your clan member or fight me because once I release his body I am coming to help my friend," Zea spoke loud and clear.

Upon finishing she dropped the unconscious body into the water. "Your crazy," one of the Shadow members called out as he released his grip from Treble and dove into the water. Others followed his lead. As soon as the coast was clear Snake made his way across the river and joined his two friends who were happy to be out of trouble. Snake and Treble helped each other back to camp. Zea told them she was going to stay a few paces back to make sure they were not followed. The guardian climbed a nearby tree and watched the Shadow Kats find and save their leader. Once Zea knew that Pyro was not in major trouble she took to the air and joined her friends who were almost home.

When the trio reached the camp others came to help take Treble to the doctors while Snake and Zea went to talk to Blizzard who was not pleased to hear of the Shadow Kat's actions. Once Zea was out of her meeting with the leader of camp she went to get some food. Rain was waiting for her outside and greeted her with a large smile. As they sat down to eat the guardian told her friend all about her run in with the Shadow Kats.

The next few days went by very slowly for the young female who still went on her morning runs with Snake but they were shorter. A few days after their run in with Pyro, Snake stopped running and asked the female a question, "I am sorry if this is rude but it has been on my mind for the last few days. How did you get the scars on your back?" The guardian half smiled and did her best answer her friend, "Well as you might have noticed I do not talk about my past a lot. This is because I did not have a normal one. I would ask you not talk about this to anyone. Well, to answer your question, when I was growing up I was a slave and my master did not treat me well. He liked to take his anger out on me and that is how I got the scars." "I have seen them before but never that close. I did not realize you had so many and most of the time you walk around camp with your wings hidden so I forgot you had them," the male explained. "Yea, I do not really like to talk about my past so I keep my scars hidden from the world," the zatz told her friend. The two talked for a while longer and then continued on their run.

Life seemed to be going smoothly till one afternoon Storm came up to the working zatz and asked to see her. With a smile Zea put her project away and joined the second in command. They walked to the edge of camp where Rain was waiting like always she had a smile when she saw her friend. The three of them were going to the river to collect some plants. Zea found it odd that Strom was joining Rain and her but the female was happy to have the chance to get to know the second in command of the camp.

As they worked Rain talked like normal but Strom like usual was very quiet. Zea wished she could break the barrier and become friends with Strom. – Maybe she is worried that because you are a strong female you might take her place in the clan?– the computer placed in Zea's mind. The three continued to work until all the plants that needed were collected and then they headed back to camp. Where everything seemed to be normal.

Zea went back to her project as Rain and Strom went straight to Blizzard. The guardian did not like the thoughts, which came running through her mind. – I am sure everything is fine and Rain is your friend. I do not think she would keep anything from you that would hurt or affect you in a major way. I think you should do your best to relax,– the female's life long friend spoke calming her racing heart and mind. The female busied herself in her work.

Later that night there was a large feast and everyone was sitting together as a clan. This action happened every now and then to show unity among the members. When everyone was almost done eating Blizzard stood and got his clan's attention. Once the group was silent he began his speech, "As you know we have been honored by having a young female stay here with us and pledge to become a member. After much thinking and talking the clan and I have decided to allow Zea to become a member of the Mountain Clan." Now turning to Zea he voiced, "Over the past few mouths you have proven yourself and have overcome many problems. Would you like to become a member of the Mountain Clan?" With tears in her eyes the guardian accepted the gift of membership. That night there was a great fire, games, stories and the highlight for Zea was when she stood in front of her new clan and Blizzard placed a band around her arm. The guardian was overwhelmed with emotion. The clan celebrated long into the night.

The next day Zea went for her normal run and went to work after the first meal of the day. The zatz was happy to finally be a member and although everything seemed to be the way it was before she joined. The female did notice she got more smiles and the clan seemed more open with her. Now that she was a Mountain Kat she had to have guard duty and luckily she was able to take her time when Snake was there. As the sun moved across the sky, Zea worked.

When she was taking a small break for some water the female looked at her new band. The band was brown and made from Randy hide. In the middle was the Mountain Clan symbol and it was tied about her arm with a traditional knot. Zea thought one was not supposed to take the Clan marking off ones body. "Hi, Zea what are you doing?" Rain interrupted the guardian's train of thought. "Nothing, just thinking and working. What are you up to this fine day?" the zatz asked. "I am coming to find you. I just wanted to talk and play," the friend explained. "I see, and what would you like to talk about?" the new clan member question. "Well, I would like to know your opinion," Rain started as Zea put her work down giving the talking female her full attention.

"What do you think is more important, friends or family?"

"That is a good question. I think good friends are like family and I would have a hard time choosing who would be more important. I guess it would depend on the situation on who I would choose but over all to fully answer your question I guess I would have to choose family because your blood comes first."

"I see your point. Did you know we are getting visitors tomorrow?"

"No, I did not but, before we change the subject why are you asking me about friends and family? Is anything wrong?"

"No, I was just wondering. I like our little talks. Tomorrow a few Kats from the Cave Clan are coming. They wish to tighten our bonds between the two clans, I think. Also they wanted to talk to Dove."

"Is Dove the one who writes the history of your clan?"

"Yes, She only does our clan. What are you doing tomorrow?"

"I guess the same thing I do everyday, have fun and work."

The two talked for a while longer as Zea worked on her project. When the guardian was done and walking around camp checking some of the huts for weak spots she heard her named called. Turning the little female saw the familiar smile of Snake and Treble was by his side. With a grin the zatz greeted her two friends and Snake began to speak, "Zea, could you come help me with something?" "Sure, I will do what I can," the female strongly stated. The three walked to Snake's hut, which was a little larger than normal because he taught a lot of the young ones in the camp how to fight and he needed room for lessons.

Once inside they moved to the fighting area. The green one turned to the black one and inquired, "How do you fight so well, I mean how did you knock out Pyro without even striking him? The guardian brought her hand to the back of her neck where she rubbed her neck then slow moved her hand to her face as she looked down at the dirt floor. Finally looking up at her curious friends brought her hand to her side. "I can tell you how I knocked out Pyro but I do not know how I would teach you," the fighter began. "What do you mean you do not know how to teach us?" Treble called out into the room. "Well, why don't we start with pressure points and move from there" the female suggested.

The two friends looked at each other. "How did you practice?" Snake asked Zea who smiled and did her best to explain, "I practice with my teacher and we had special tools to help me work on my technique." "Can you make those tools here?" Treble asked. Zea was not sure what to say, "I am not sure if I can I will do my best to think of a way to teach you but please be patient I will to my best to solve this problem. In the mean time I can teach you other fighting moves." The two males were happy with the fighter's solution and wanted to learn more fighting skills. Zea would stand in the middle of the room and one at a time the friends would take turns play fight the female who helped them grow in there fighting skills.

The next day came fast for the little female and like always she went on her run, got some food and went to work. As the sun was dancing across the sky Zea looked up to see a familiar dirty orange kat walking her way with friends. A smile grew on her face as she stood to greet her old friend, "Sparrow!" "How are you? I see you have done well for yourself since the last time we met. Come we must catch up with each other. Can we go to your home?" the Sparrow asked. "Sure," the female voiced as she led the way to her hut. Once there she set up the table and chairs so everyone could sit.

Around the table was Sparrow, Dove, a white and black male kat who was young and Strom was standing in the doorway. She asked to see Sparrow who stood and join her. They went outside to whisper with each other. As they did this Zea turned to the black and white one and introduced herself, "Hi, my name is Zea. May I ask who you are?" A very large smile spared across his face as he spoke, "Hi, my name is Zaann. I am Sparrow's apprentice." "I see and you are from the Cave Clan as well?" the female asked. "Yes," he answered. "How are you Dove?" Zea asked to quiet one. "Well thank you," she responded. The guardian saw that Zaann could not stop smiling.

Finally she broke to stillness to ask him why he was so joyful. The bi-colored kat told Zea he was excited and before he could continue Sparrow walked back into the room. He did not look too happy but his mood seemed to change once he sat down and faced Zea. "So tell me what have you been up too lately?" Sparrow asked. "Well, Dark Flame did not like the way I was acting and told me that if I did not do what he wished he would take my life. I craved into my wooden bed and freed myself. I escaped and ran into Bear. He took me in and soon I was living with Dark Star's Clan. They helped me and taught me more about this land. Then ago weeks I joined this Clan and a few days ago I was accepted into the Mountain Clan. What have you been up too?" Zea told her old friend.

"After the Shadow Kats let me go I went home and worked so if met you again I could ask good questions and hopefully learn and fill in some holes," the orange one spoke. "I am sorry to be rude but I have work to do is there a reason I am here?" Dove cooed into the conversation. "No, I just guessed you might want to know some of Zea's history for your records," Sparrow explained to her. "If I ever get caught up I will have to sit down and talk to you Zea someday," the female voiced as she stood and headed for the door. "Thank you but I must be going," she stated as she left to room. The two males turned and looked at Zea who just shrugged her shoulders. "Can you state your full name for me?" Sparrow questioned.

"Zeaytera KatOynera."

Zaann face just grew with excitement. The guardian laughed. "What is so funny," the orange one inquired. "Your friend, Zaann, he is so happy," she answered. "You will have to excuse him like I was before he has never heard your tongue spoken before just now," Sparrow explained after looking at his excited friend. Sparrow placed some books and papers on the table. The fighter started to look though them. She saw that they were broken pieces of what life was like in the villa before the Qothos came. "Not to be rude but I have been comparing you to all my work and there are a few differences I would like to talk with you about," the orange one began. Zea nodded.

"In my books it states that there are fighters. Are you a fighter?"

"Yes, I am."

"All my fighter pictures and texts have wings but you do not?"

"Oh, I do have wings," female stated and then proceeded to bring her wings out of their resting spot. Both of the male's faces lit up and both of them laughed with excitement. "Not many of us can hide their wings like I can but, both my father and brother could not hide their wings. I am little different but a lot of my friends from my childhood had wings. Some did not have wings and some did not look like me but they walked on all four," the guardian continued. "Yes, I read about that the difference in the kinds of ... Zatx? Is that right?" Sparrow agreed.

"Yes, that is what I would call myself."

"So, I am guessing you can fly and not just glide."

"Yes, you are correct."

"Now, you had to go through training to be a fighter?"

"Yes, I had to pass many lessons to be a 'fighter'. A master teaches the beginners and we started at young age."

"What was the hardest one?"

"Well that depends on how you look at it. All the lessons are hard and changeling. Myself I did not like the one called control but I am stronger for it."

"I am sorry to be rude but can I heard you speak in your tongue?" Zaann added. Zea laughed and rolled her eyes. Next she turned to him and asked, "And what would you like me to say?" The male quickly went into deep thought. Finally he broke the stillness, "Can you say? Hi my name is Zea and I am happy to meet you." The female smiled, " Mootue, Thaieyy oith ithee ithe Zeaytera KatOynera cookto upteneded bunnit cooruu geccctoa satr." "Wow, thank you," the black and white one stated barely able to sit down he was so overcome with joy.

Both Zea and Sparrow laughed. Next the orange one pulled out a different book and stated, "This is my big question for you, this is my book about fighters and I keep finding holes I hope you can fill." The male opened the book to a marked page, which had pictures of past 'fighters'. As the female looked her computer could match the picture to a name from her database and tell Zea. Who then could say the name out loud to the males whoes mouths dropped. When the fighter had named all on the page Sparrow spoke again, "How, do you know there names it took me years to only get a few of them and I was not even sure I was right? To my point of showing you this page, Sorry," he paused and then started again pointing to one of the pictures, "Almost all the fighters have different colored bands about their wrists. Why do you not have them and what are they?"

Zea was at a loss for words she did not know what to tell her friend. Right when she was going to speak Rain walked into hut to invite the trio to dinner and before the males could say anything Zea stood and voiced, "sure." The four of them walked to the main fire where the majority of the group was waiting. Zann and Sparrow were not the only members from the Cave Clan visiting the Mountain Clan. The visiting group sat together next to the high-ranking members of the clan where Zea and Rain sat at their normal spots at the end by a smaller fire.

They talked about Zann's reaction to Zea and then Rain told her friend she thought the black and white male was cute. The guardian told her friend she should go talk to him after the last meal of the day. She laughed and said, "No." "Why not?" the zatz asked. "I do not know?" Rain replied. "Fine I will get him to talk and you can come with me. Then you can start to talk to him and then I will slowly leave that way you can get to know him," the fighter explained. Rain just giggled.

After the meal was finished games started. Zann came up to Zea and Rain to talk to his new friend. "Hi, Zann, this is my friend Rain," the guardian stated. "I am pleased to meet you," Zann voice as he made a sign of respect. Just as the zatz planned her two friends began to talk and when they were comfortable she slipped away to talk to her friends.

Snake was on guard duty and the fighter decided to join him. When the group started to calm down the female left her friend and headed to her hut. On her way she met Sparrow, "There you are. I have been looking for you. I was wondering if Zaann and I could stay with you tonight." "Sure, come on I will set up your beds," the black one voiced. As Zea lay down for the night she was worried she would have a bad dream. Taking a deep breath she closed her eyes and bravely fell into the land of dreams.

"Are you okay? Zea, Zea?" Sparrow whispered to his friend who had just awaked from another nightmare. "Yea, I am okay. I just get nightmares. Sorry if I woke you and thank you for helping me," she whispered as she whipped the beads of sweat from her brow. "That must be some dream," the orange one spoke. "Yeah," Zea half laughed. The two went back sleep.

The next morning Zea rose with the sun and went for morning a run with Snake. When she returned to her hut both males were gone. Zea picked up the floor and put away her bed. Next she joined her clan for the first meal of the day.

Rain was sitting next to Zaann and Sparrow was talking Blizzard. Zea joined Ken who was happy to see her. They ate and talked. Once they were done they both went on their various paths for the day. The day went by fast and she was hoping Sparrow would not ask to see her. –What do I if he asks me about you?– the guardian asked her friend. –Well, you can tell the truth and ask him to keep it a secret or you can try to avoid the question and try not to answer it,– the computer voiced. –I can tell them a half truth like they are to show rank,– the female stated. –You could,– the life friend agreed.

"Hi, Zea," a voice broke her train thought. Turning Zea greeted her visitor with respect. "How are you today, Blizzard?" she questioned. "I am doing well. You seem to be hard at work," he began. "Yes," the female agreed. "Did you have fun with Sparrow and Zaann?" the leader inquired. "Yes, they are both good kats. I am happy I got the chance to see Sparrow again he really helped me when the Shadow Clan had me," Zea voiced. "That is good. I am just coming to check on you and make sure you are doing well with the clan," Blizzard spoke. "Thank you, I am doing well and feel safe here in camp. I am sorry if I am causing trouble with the Shadow Clan," the guardian said as she looked down at the ground. "Do not worry about it, Zea, you are with us and you are safe. I am pleased you feel safe," the leader told the female. When the leader left the fighter went back to work. That evening Sparrow came up to Zea to talk. "How are you doing today?" the orange asked.

"I am doing well. You must have been busy today" the female smiled. "Yes, I have had many meeting today but I am done and that is a very good thing. Sorry we could not finish our talk yesterday. I have to leave tomorrow to go home. I hope we can talk again some other time so I can fill in my holes. If that is okay with you."

"Yes, I would like that a lot. I hope you have a safe trip tomorrow and if you ever need something I owe you so do not hesitate to ask."

The two shook arms, which was a honor for the orange one. Before he left he voiced to the female, "Thank you, Zea I cannot express how amazing you are and how much your help means to me." "You are welcome, I will see you soon. Say goodbye to Zaann from me," the guardian called back to her friend. The next few hours went by fast and Zea was happy she got a chance to say goodbye to her friend when she did. By the next morning the group from the Cave Clan was gone.

The next few days Rain seemed distant like something was on her mind. Zea did not like to see her friend worried. The guardian tried to get her friend to talk but she would try to change the subject or was never in the mood. All the zatz could do was comfort her friend in need and hope she would opened up soon. Finally Zea got worried and went to talk to Blizzard. He too was worried about Rain and asked to see the female.

The guardian paced outside her hut waiting to see her friend. Finally when the moon was high in the sky Rain returned to her home with tired eyes. "Are you okay, Rain?" the zatz asked. "Yes, I am okay, but I really do not want to talk to you right now. I will tell you soon," the spotted female whispered. "I am here for you Rain if you ever need me you know this right," the black one voiced. "Yeah," Rain spoke softly. The two hugged and then they went to sleep.

The next morning there was mist in the air and it was a crisp. Zea went on her daily run with Snake and then went to work. Rain did not come out her hut that day but Blizzard and Storm did go visit her. That day Zea was checking huts and making gifts for her fellow clan mates. She was very uneasy not knowing what was bugging her friend. That night was her meeting with Krist.

After dinner she took to the air and headed to the old cave to meet her good friend. He was happy to see her and she told him about Rain. Krist explained to the guardian how life was back in Dark Star's Clan. The zatz was thrilled to hear all her friends were doing well. After they visited long into the night the two friends went back to their homes

The next day the sun was out and after Zea's run she got a good first meal. Rain was there. A smile grew on the guardian's face seeing her friend out in the sun. "Can I sit here?" the zatz asked Rain who nodded and stated, "Of course." As the two ate Zea's mind raced with questions to ask her friend but knew that Rain would talk when she was ready. "Zea, I am sorry I have not been talking lately but, there is a lot going on and I do not know how to tell you. I think the best way would be tomorrow we will go for a walk and that way just you and I can talk and get what is on my mind all out into the air. If you do not mind to wait one more day?" the female explained. "I would wait as long as you needed. Tomorrow would be great and if not I can wait. I am here for you whenever your ready," the zatz comforted her friend. Tears came to Rain's eyes. They ate the rest of their meal and then went to work.

The day like the ones before seemed to move very quickly. The young female liked being in a clan and to be a part of a group. She enjoyed being busy and having a job working with others and her hands. Soon the moon was on the rise and Zea, Rain and the clan were sitting down to eat. Blizzard stood and did a katraci (toast) to the young guardian stating how much of a help she as been and a good clan member. Everyone cheered and the zatz thanked her clan mates with an open heart. That night Rain asked to sleep in Zea's hut. The guardian could not say no to her friend and they both stayed up late talking about nothing laughing until the moon was slowly falling to the ground.

When the sun kissed the black one's face she awoke and went for her run with Snake. He seemed to be quiet that morning but she got him to laugh a few times. When the first meal was done Zea packed a small pack of food and prepared to leave with Rain who was just coming back from a meeting with Blizzard. With a smile Rain helped Zea finish packing and then the duo were off for the day.

Walking out of the green sea of grass the guardian heard her named being called, "Zea, Zea." Facing the camp once again the young females saw Snake running towards them. "Can I help you?" Rain asked when the green one reached them. "I just wanted to give this to Zea," Snake voiced as he handed the black one an object wrapped in cloth. "Sorry it's so late but I am slow and did not have a lot of time," the guard explained as he started to walk back to camp. Unfolding the gift the phrase, "Happy birthday," was burned into the cloth. Turning the female ran to Snake and gave him a hug thanking him for his kindness. "Have a good day Snake, I will see you later. Lately you have been quiet we can talk later on if you want. Thank you again," Zea told her friend who just half smiled turned and waved goodbye to his friend.

The guardian placed the gift in her back between her wings for safe keeping with her dagger, ran forward and caught up to her walking friend. "So, what do you want to talk about?" the zatz started. "Not yet," Rain whispered. The two walked in silence for a long time and soon they came to a break in the forest where a small lake rested. Rain stopped walking and took long cool drink. The guardian followed her friend's lead.

Once their throats were wet again they continued walking. Soon Rain broke the silence, "Would you mind if we jogged?" "No, I would love too," the guardian smiled and the duo picked up their pace. About mid day they stopped at a small meadow made up of long green and golden grass. There are large rocks scattered in area. Rain seemed to looking around the sea of grass. "What are you looking for, Rain?" the zatz asked. "A place to sit," the white and black spotted one responded. Finally after a few minutes Rain decide to sit between to large rocks at the edge of the meadow.

Once sitting Rain cleared her throat and began to speak, "You know a few days ago I was asking you about family and friends?" "Yeah," the zatz said. Rain looked at her friend and who began to speak again, "Well, a few days before I asked you that question I found my brother..." "That is great. Wow, where is he?" the black one interrupted. Before Rain could tell Zea the answer the guardian heard footsteps. Looking up standing behind her was a smiling kat.

The guardian stood full of anger. "What do you want?" the zatz yelled. The male walked up to the two females while stating, "I just want to talk to you and Rain." Pyro snapped his fingers and the grass came alive. Within seconds Shadow Kat surrounded the two females with their leader laughing in the middle. The guardian did her best to stand in a good position to protect Rain.

Pyro snapped his fingers and once again the kat moved again but this time to attack the duo. Zea did her best to fight the kats but had to stop when she heard Rain's cry. Looking over in her direction the hairs on the back of her neck stood on end at the sight. The leader's son had a knife to the female's throat. "Stop fighting right now or Rain will pay for your actions," Pyro ordered. Once Zea stopped fighting a few of Shadow Kat came and grabbed her holding her and tying her in place.

Soon Pyro called out, "Stop." The kats stop and looked in his direction. "My friends what you are doing is an act of war. Untie her. Now Rain I wish to talk to you." When Zea was free she stood still so Pyro would not hurt her friend. "Bring him out!" Pyro yelled. Out from behind a rock a few Shadow Kats were holding a skinny male. Rain began to cry at the sight of seeing her brother. "Now Rain," the striped one began again. The male continued, "If I am not mistaken this is your brother. Quite a while ago he came in to my possession and I would like to know if you would like to trade me something for him." "I have nothing but myself. I cannot hurt my clan but I can give myself to you," Rain cried. "No!" Rain's brother yelled. "Quiet Gecko," the leader yelled. Upon his words ending the kats holding Gecko punched him to correct him. "Stop it," Rain screamed.

Pyro raised his hand and everything was quiet once more and Zea was not sure what she wanted to do. Taking a deep breath she spoke, "Pyro can I speak with you please." He smiled gave the knife to one of his males who continued to threaten the spotted female's life as Pyro walked to the guardian. "Take me," Zea whispered. "What?" the male asked. "I will take Gecko's place. You let both of them go and I will come with you with no fighting and I will not fight to escape but I am telling you now if there is a door unlocked or a rope untied I will leave but I will not break myself free or try to escape until I am safe in your clan's camp," Zea voiced coldly. "You would do that for Rain?" Pyro asked. "Yes, she is my friend and I know you know I always keep my word I will not fight until I am in chains or caged back at your home. Just do not hurt my friend or her brother," Zea stated.

"Very well, I like this trade and I FINALLY have you," the leader's son called to the air. The Shadow Kats tied Zea with ropes and chains and placed her in a cage. Once she was locked. Pyro turned and looked at his prisoner and stated, "Promise me." "I promise to everything I stated to you before," the female said as she looked away from the male. "Yes," he again stated to the air. Then he walked over to Rain where the knife was taken away and he voiced, "I told you everything would work." the guardian's ears pricked up and she turned to look at Rain who was in tears.

"My plan worked. You got your brother and I got my Zea. I knew that if I did this my little one would fall into my trap. Thank you Rain it was my pleasure working with you. Now for our deal, because you brought Zea to me I will give you your brother. Release him! And because you got Zea to come into my grasp I will make a deal we discussed that the Shadow Clan will not attack the Mountain Clan for 20 years. At the end of that time we can try to make another deal but until then our two clans are at peace. I have talked to my father who has agreed you and your clan is now safe," Pyro talked with Rain who could only cry. When Pyro and Rain shook hands Gecko reached them and they embraced each other.

Zea's heart broke she was at a loss of words. She could not explain her emotions of being betrayed. Her eyes watered and all she could do was look at Rain who was hugging her brother. "Lets go we are losing daylight," Pyro commanded. As Zea was being carried off she looked at Rain with such sadness and fear. When Rain saw her friend's face she felt her heartbreak and she again began to cry once more. Zea watched as the brother and sister holding each other started home. Zea closed her tearing eyes knowing she was now going back to the place she feared the most and back into the hands of Dark Flame and his son.

Back into the Darkness

Zea watched the trees go by as the group headed home. Once there, without a fight the guardian kept her word and walked into a cage where she was chained to the wall. A few minutes later Dark Flame walked in, there was a great smile on his face. "Long time no see, little one," he stated calmly. "I am clan member now. If our clans are at peace then how can you keep me in chains?" the female asked. "You poor, silly, female. You were never a real clan member," he laughed as she ripped the band off her arm.

I started talking with Blizzard and then Rain a long time ago as soon as I knew that was the clan you were joining. You picked a very weak clan to join. They would much rather have protection than you. Once I knew you were joining a weak clan it was just a matter of getting them to deliver you, Rain and Gecko was my chance. Lucky for me I had him in chains and you happened to pick his clan. Blizzard gave you a child's band because you would not know the difference between a child's and a real band.

Every child in most clans are given bands you can take off and at their coming of age party they are given a real band because at that age they can truly pick their clan. The whole celebration was a cover up to keep you busy so you would not notice the real trouble you were in with me," the leader voiced as he walked around the small room.

Zea was so full with anger and emotion she did not know what to do. Tears ran from her eyes as she clenched her fisted. "I am just tickled everything came together so well. I was worried you would pick up on the unseen meeting or Rain would cave and not go with Pyro's plan. I am very proud of my son he is going to be a great leader. Well, little one, I just wanted to welcome you back to your room. I have many things I must do but I will see you soon," Dark Flame voiced. Then he left the room and Zea was left to her emotions.

The female cried in the caged room. –Zea, do you want to talk? Are you okay?– the computer voice softy. –No, I do not know what to think right now. How could ... did I do the right ... why... I have so many thoughts and emotions in my head I do not know what to do. I just want to scream,– the female told her friend.

–Rain was manipulated just like you. I think. We should be mad with Blizzard who is the leader of the clan. Do you think Snake knew?–

– Yes, but what could he do? One must be loyal to their clan and leader, Rain must have been loyal too but she was my friend and Snake. Could they have told me or hinted to me? If Rain told me the Shadow Clan had her bother I could have helped get him back home.–

–What did Snake give you?–

The guardian paused. Reaching into her back she felt the dagger then the cloth. Unwrapping the cloth the female could see a stone and which was carved. There was a heart in the middle of the whitish-gray stone. On the inside of the cloth was a note to her from Snake. The writing was burned into the cloth and explained to Zea that he was very thankful all of Zea's help. –Do you think Snake found out what Rain and Blizzard were doing this morning and that is why he was acting strange?– the guardian asked her computer. –That is possible,– the life long friend agreed.

–I am so mad. I cannot believe … I mean I do not understand.–

–Zea, no matter what you say or do this situation is not going to make sense. I think you should relax, clear your mind and lets find a way out of this place.–

–You are right, computer, and thank you.–

The guardian took a deep breath and did her best to clear her mind. The zatz rested for a few hours and was interrupted by the door opening. Sweet water walked in with a tray. "How are you Zea, I have not seen you in a while?" the Shadow Kat asked. "I am doing okay despite what just happened and you?" the guardian responded. "Well, I have some food here if you would like it," she explained to the prisoner who took a deep breath and accepted the meal. The two friends caught up and when the black one was done with her meal the Shadow Kat left to do work.

The next few days the guardian talked to her computer and did her best to think of a way out of the darkness. She did not want to get weak again but was at a loss of what to do. Zea considered using her computer but was worried the marking left behind would raise too many question and put her in more danger. The chains, which held her to the wall, were thick and heavy. Every other day the prisoner was given some soup and water. –What if I act very sick and weak? Then when they are checking one me I can fight and escape.– the guardian suggested. –Do you really want to put Sweet Water or one of her helpers in trouble and if you did fight to break free how far would you get? We do not know how many guards are down the hallways and last time you were very lucky not to run into a Shadow Kat. Do you think you will get lucky like that again?– the computer asked her friend. –Good points. I guess that can be a last resort,– the female stated. The door opening and a smiling male walking into the poorly lit room broke the fighter's train of thought.

"Good day, Zea, how are you feeling?" the male asked. "I am doing well despite being here and being treated so poorly," she responded. "How do you mean treated poorly," he inquired. "If you cage me then you are taking away my ability to get food and stay healthy therefore you should be giving me the things one needs to live but you do not. I am not given healthy meals or the freedom of moving for exercise," Zea explained. "You are bring up good points little one but if you do not compromise then you are not helping the situation," the striped one told the female. "What do I need to compromise to be free?" the female asked. "I would like you to consider joining my clan," the leader stated. "But Dark Flame I do not wish to join the Shadow Clan. Where can we compromise?" the guardian continued.

"You join the clan, then you will be free," Dark Flame explained. "I would not get my freedom I would still be trapped here in this place that has only given me pain," Zea voiced strongly. "Awww, this place is not that bad, good things happen here. You met my son, Sweet Water and some of the others have been kind to you," the leader spoke calmly. "Your son thinks that someday I am going to join your clan through him and I am sorry but that will never happen," the female stated while folding her arms. "Last time I checked no one could tell the future. My son has a way with words and I have a way of changing one's mind with actions. We will see if your heart changes soon," Dark Flame laughed. "I will never join your clan or choose to be with your son!" Zea exclaimed. "We will see, little one, a lot can happen in a few days," the leader smiled while leaving the room. The guardian did not like the leader's words.

The next few days were the same. A least once a day a guard came in and checked all of the prisoner's chains and room for any attempts of escaping. Zea did not make the guard's job easy but he got it done. With all the Shadow Kats the guardian saw everyday she wondered where the other fighter was. She hoped that he was not hurt or in too much trouble because he was the one she knocked out and then he did not catch her once she was outside of the camp. Zea did not even know the grey, black, light tan and sliver male's name.

The female started to pace from boredom. There was not much she could do in a cage. Waiting for some action to happen she was sick of being in a pen. Her nightmares seemed to be getting worse now that see was back in an enclosure and was betrayed by her only close female friend. The days crept by hour by hour.

Finally someone came into the room. Zea's eyes grew at the sight of the male. "How are you?" the female asked. There was no answer from the patched colored male. His golden eyes shifted around the room looking for any changes or weakness in the chains. "For what it is worth I am sorry for what I did but I had to escape or Dark Flame would have killed me and I hope you did not get in a lot of trouble," the female spoke. The male smiled. "I am not mad. You did what many others could not. Just never do it again or I will kill you," he whispered. After he looked at the room he walked out locking the door behind him. The female was happy she saw the male fighter again and was content he was not too mad at her or got too big of a punishment.

A few days later the door opened again and for the first time since she was brought to the dark world Pyro walked in with a great smile. "How are you, my love?" the male asked. Zea rolled her eyes and said nothing. "Oh, nothing to say? I thought you would be happy to see me. Does it feel good to be back home in your room," the leader's son stated with a grin. There was still no answer from the one in chains. "You are not talking? Well, I come here to ask you, if you are excited for tomorrow?" the striped inquired as he walked by Zea who just looked at him with a puzzled face. "No, one has told you? Well I guess I will. Tomorrow, Zea, you will be mine. You will love me and we will be together!" the male stated with great excitement. "Well, I have to get ready for tomorrow. I bet I am more nervous then you. I will fully have you soon my love," Pyro voiced sweetly as he walked out of the small dirt room and locked the door.

Zea was left to her thoughts. –What can he be talking about? I will never be with him. What could he be doing to me tomorrow?– the guardian pondered. –I do not know but I do not have a good feeling. I hope you remember to keep your control no matter what he does,– the computer responded. The two talked long into the night trying to come up with ideas of what Pyro was talking about. Finally the female fell asleep with many questions.

When morning came Sweet Water came in and gave Zea a small meal and did not say much. She looked nervous and the guardian knew she was upset about what was going to happen later that day. When Sweet Water left Zea began to pace because there were so many ideas running through her head. A few hours went by and when the door opened the female did not know what to think or do. Guards walked in and stood on the outskirts of the room.

Next Dark Flame walked into the room with Pyro at his side. They both stood in front of Zea then the leader walked forward as his son back away to the dirt wall. "Good day, little one, how are you today? I hope well," the Shadow Kat began. "What is going on?" the female demanded. "I am going to give you a choice and you will give me answer and depending on your selection I will choose my action," the leader continued. Scenes of Zea's childhood flashed in her head and she began to shake. –Breathe, remain in control it is going to be alright,– the computer voiced.

The female took a deep breath and stopped shaking. "Are you ready?," he asked. Zea shifted her weight. The strong male turned and looked at his son who looked nervous. Then he gave all his attention to the one in chains, "My son has expressed a liking to you and he has asked to have you as a partner. As a father it is my duty to say you have my permission to love and be with Pyro but are you going to accept this honor? Without hesitation the female answered, "No." "Very well, I want to make my son happy and I will go a great distance to do so. You have made your choice," Dark Flame stated as he turned and walked out of the room.

All the others remained and Zea looked around the room waiting for an action. About a minute later Dark Flame returned to the small room with a group of guards behind him. They were carrying another prisoner. Zea's fur stood on end and she clenched her fists in anger as they chained Bear to the wall across from the female. Bear was beat up and looked sick and weak. "Now I am going to ask you again, will you accept?" the leader question. "I will not be with your son and do not bring Bear into this. He has nothing to do with my decision," the female yelled. Upon hearing the word "no" Dark Flame gave a sign to his guards who began to hit Bear. Zea became very upset by his actions and began to shake as her white lids fell into place. Some of the guards saw this and became uneasy. "Stop," the guardian ordered. "I will tell them to stop when you say you will be with my son," the leader called out into the room now seeing Zea's eyes turn from white to red. "Let him go," she shouted. Bear's blood fell to the floor. The female's eyes turned from red to green. Zea's rage took control. – I will not lose my father again because of one of my choices,– the female voiced.

The guardian's black lids fell into the place as with all her might she ripped the chains from the wall. "Where are her eyes?" one of the guards asked Pyro who shook his head. The guards ran to restrain the fighter but they were tossed aside because they were no match for the guardian. "Orb aith sito kaito nien," the female stated as she looked over to where Bear was chained and Dark Flame was standing. The computer brought up the red bean gun and powered it up after Zea's command. "Pyro, leave now," his father's voice cut the air. Pyro seeing the guardian with no eyes and his friends now on the floor not moving did not question his father and left.

Zea watched him leave but turn her head when she heard Dark Flame pull out his dagger. He had it pointed at Bear's hard breathing chest. "Back off, Zea," the leader told the female who did not listen. The leader cut the member of Dark Star's Clan who called out in pain. Zea was so full of rage she blocked the moving blade and punched the Shadow Kat. After the blow Dark Flame dropped his weapon and Zea picked him back up by the neck as Bear fell to the floor. The guardian threw the body across the room and followed her prey.

The zatz walked quickly over to the leader and again picked him up the neck. Next she raised her arm so it looked like was about to punch the leader. He could not see the computer's gun pointed to his head, powered up and ready to fire. "Tell me one reason I should not end your life so you will never hurt me again," the guardian voiced low and strong. The males voice was low and weak; "I will kill you for this you rookack (a slang for low, dirt female "bitch")." "Wrong answer," she stated as she released her red gun. Dark Flame screamed.

Then the fighter felt a hand on her shoulder. She dropped the now crying male and forced the other to the dirt floor and right before she could attack he yelled, "Zea, its me, its me. Zea its Bear." The guardian paused and Bear repeated his words. The fighter released her grip and the male slowly backed away and stood. "Zea? Are you okay?" he asked softy. The zatz looked at him with her black, cold eyes and was motionless.

"Come on, you won lets go home lets go please," he pleaded. Zea looked back at her victim who was holding his head. "What did you do to his face with your claws? I saw a light but that was your eyes right? Wait it does not matter please lets leave this place. Lets get out of the dark. I need your help I am cut very deep and I need to get to a doctor, please," Bear explained to his daughter very carefully and soft. She turned and looked at her father who was crying. The guardian had stopped listening to her computer once her black lids had fallen into place. She closed her eyes and tears fell down her cheeks when the female opened her eyes again they were green again to Bear's joy.

The fighter helped Bear out of the darkness. As they walked down the maze of hallways Zea used her sense of smell and pules to find the light.

When they got to the last hallway the patched colored Kat was blocking their freedom. "Do not mess with me, patched one, I do not know your name and I am not in the mood to deal with you or anyone else," Zea threatened. When he did not move the fighters eyes turned eye white. "Move now," the guardian yelled. The fighter set her weak friend on the floor as she faced the male her eyes turned red.

Seeing this the male was not sure what to do. As she got in fighting position her eyes turned black. When he could not see her eyes the male became very uneasy. The male relaxed and stated, "You can go you earned it but do not tell anyone I let you go, I could fight you but you earned it I think." "Thank you," Zea voiced as she picked up and friend and passed him. As they walked by him Bear told the Shadow Kat he would talk to him later. Zea was at a loss why but knew this was not the time to ask. Once the sun hit the black fur the female open her wings and took to the air. The guardian flew as fast as she could knowing her friend had lost a lot of blood and was very weak.

Lost

Landing back in the camp Dark Star and almost all the clan came running when they saw Zea holding Bear's unconscious body. The leader had many questions but saw that the female was shaky and very weak. Dark Star and the others helped the male and Zea to Bear's hut where they were both put in their beds. The doctor looked at Bear first while his aid checked the fighter.

After he saw that Zea had no major wounds and just needed rest he told one of the onlookers who was outside the hut to retrieve some water for the zatz and then let her rest. Then he went to help the main doctor with the fallen male. Roberd brought Zea some water who drank it very slowly and then fell asleep from exhaustion.

A few days later the guardian awoke from her slumber. The guardian sat up in her bed and looked around the sun filled room. She was in her old hut and could hear someone breathing across the room but a large cloth was stopping her view. In the back of her mind the female knew it was her friend Bear. Overall the fighter was strong and was in good health now that she had rested. Standing Zea took a moment to find her balance and wondered how long she had been sleep.

Once she was more awake the guardian slowly made her way to where her friend was sleeping. Looking at him, the zatz could see he was doing well but had a cloth over his chest with a red line of blood down the middle. The female carefully unwrapped the white fabric and looked at Bear's wound. Zea viewed the new forming scar, which ran across his slowly breathing chest. Hearing the sound of a male walking into the hut the fighter covered the chest back up and walked to her side of the room just in time to see Dark Star who was very pleased to see the female awake.

"How are you feeling little one?" he asked. "I am doing well. I just have a lot of mixed feelings right now," the zatz responded. "Well, if you are up to it I would like you too come eat with me and as we do I would like you to tell me what happened because I am at a loss. No one has been able to fill me in and I would go to the Mountain Clan for answers but, I have been to worried to leave the clan behind or send someone out when I am not sure what is happening," the leader explained to his friend who smiled and agreed to join him for the last meal of the day and to talk.

Sitting in Dark Star's meeting hut both the fighter and the leader had a plate of food and Zea began to speak, "Well, I am not sure when the whole thing started or all the details but I will tell you what I know." Dark Star nodded as he took a large bite of his food. "When Dark Flame found out what clan I was joining he started doing everything in his power to get to me. His son gave me a few visits and what I did not know at the time was Blizzard was having meetings with Dark Flame. Long story short, after many meetings the Mountain Clan decided to give me to the Shadow Clan for protection. Because the Shadow Clan's plan, really Pyro's, worked Dark Flame got me and Blizzard and his clan now have 20 years of protection from the Shadow Kats. Here was Pyro's plan, Rain my ..." Zea paused not knowing what to call her.

"Well a Mountain member who I guess was my friend at the time, her brother was missing and like I guess you are thinking Dark Flame had him in chains. Rain brought me to a meadow, Pyro showed up with some of his friends. Rain let Pyro hold a knife to her making me think she was in real danger. They tricked me to take Rain's Brother, Gecko, place in chains. When I got back into my cage I was full of so much emotion I did not know what to think or do.

Both leader and son came to visit me. The are very pleased to have me back in their claws and they are hinting on some big event, which was to take place in a few days. Well when the time came Dark Flame told me to join his son or something bad was going to happen. I said no of course and then they brought in Bear who looked weak and sick. I did not know how long he had been in the hands of Dark Flame but I was not happy. When they stated hurting him and I saw his blood hit the ground I lost control," the guardian stopped talking because her emotions took over as the tears fell from her green eyes.

Dark Star set his plate on the desk and held the shaking female doing his best to comfort the broken female. "You are safe now, everything well be fine, please take some deep breaths and relax," the leader spoke firm but soft. A few minutes later when Zea regained herself she finished her story, "I broke my chains and went to save Bear who was being cut open with a dagger at Dark Flame's hands. I started to attack the male out of rage. I do not know if I killed him that night is blurry but I am sure it will come back to me.

I do know if Dark Flame is still alive because of Bear who came and stopped me from hurting the Shadow Kat any farther. Seeing how weak he was and when I saw his eyes I regained control. We left the dark world where we ran into a Shadow kat and he let us go free. When we were leaving Bear said something to him but I did not stop and find out what they were talking about because Bear was so weak. I landed in camp and I think you know the rest." Dark Star held Zea in silence as he thought about what had happened.

He could not imagine all the pain the little one was in and what battle was being fought in her mind. "Everything will be fine, just relax, little one," the leader told Zea who looked up at him with tear filled eyes. "You think Bear is going to live?" the black one asked. "Without a doubt I can say, 'yes.' He is going to be fine. Bear is going to have a scar across his chest but he is going to live," the leader answered. "Thank you, Dark Star," the fighter whispered. The two talked for a while longer and then they both went to visit Bear.

The father lay on his back with his eyes closed. Dark Star had to leave because he was needed else where in camp. Krist came into the small room a few moments after the leader left. He sat by Zea on the dirt floor. "How are you, little one?" he asked. "I am very broken and do not know what to think to be honest with you," she replied.

"Is there anything I can do?"

"No, I just have to clear my head and then do a few things."

"What do you mean 'do a few things?'"

"I have to go talk with Rain and set everything straight."

"Zea, I do not know if that is a good idea."

"I have to, Krist, if I do not go and talk to them then I will never clear my mind fully. I need to find out why Rain hurt me. I have to think about what I am going to say and I will most likely leave tomorrow afternoon."

"Do you need one of us to go with you?"

"No, I will travel faster by myself and if I get caught it will not hurt the clan. Right now I do not have a real clan. I am back where I started. All I ask is you wish my luck."

"I wish you all my luck and I hope you never forget that anyone here would help you and we are all with you. Oh, and remember do not forget who you are do not stoop to their level."

"I will remember, thank you Krist."

The two sat in silence for a few more minutes and then Krist gave his friends a hug, wished Bear well and left the hut. Zea packed a bag and got ready to leave her home. Soon she was at Bear's side again hoping for him to move or wake. The sun was high in the sky and Zea wanted to reach the Mountain by dusk so she set off to talk and meet Rain.

Opening her wings the guardian took to the air. The sun beat on her back as she few across the sky. –what are you planning to say to Rain, – the computer inquired. "I am not sure yet. What do you think?" The female stated. –I think you should state the code and think about the words you are saying, – the life long friend suggested. Zea took the suggestion and reflected as she flew to the mountain.

When the sun was setting and dusk was well on its way the female landed in the trees, which lined the meadow. Scanning the scene the guardian could see there were more guards than she remembered. Moving along the meadow the black female looked around the edge of camp and could see her hut was gone and a new one was in its place. Hiding back into the trees she again took to the air.

Landing on the mountainside the female quietly climbed down the rock towards Rain's hut. When she was above the spotted ones hut the fighter had to stand still hearing the sound of footsteps. Lucky for the female her coat was black so she camouflaged well into the rock in the night air. Seeing Rain and her brother the guardian eye's narrowed as her black lids fell into place.

"Did you have a good day, Rain," Gecko asked. "I did and how are you feeling?" Rain inquired. "I had a great day," the brother spoke loud. "I am doing okay, I do not like knowing Zea is free. I am worried she is going to come for me," the spotted one said nervously. "Blizzard has more guards on duty and I will check your hut. If you really want you can sleep in my hut for a while or I will stay in yours till you fall asleep," the brother comforted his sister. The guardian watched Gecko walk into Rain's hut.

He came out with a smile and told Rain all was safe. The two said their goodnights and went to their huts for the night. Once the fires were out Zea waited and listened for Rains breathing to change into a repetitive sleep pattern. When the spotted female was sleeping Zea jumped from her hanging spot and landed softly on the sand.

Next the fighter slowly moved into the Rain's hut and then stood over her resting body. In one graceful motion the guardian picked up the sleeping body, forced her to the ground and held her down while covering her mouth as Rain woke. The spotted one eyes widened and she began to struggle but Zea held her down to the dirt floor. "Did you miss me, Rain?" the fighter asked. "Stop moving you know I am not going to let you free," the black one continued. The Mountain Kat ceased her motion and looked up at her attacker with tear filled eyes. "If I let you go do you promise to behave and not scream?" the fighter inquired. Rain nodded yes. Very carefully Zea stood up releasing her grip. The Mountain Kat quick stood and backed quickly to the corner of the room.

"You have not answered my question, did you miss me?" the zatz spoke softly. "I do not know," Rain replied. "All I want to know is why and at any point were you my true friend," the black one pleaded. "I do not know Zea, I felt like I had no other way and I had to listen to the ones I knew and trusted best," Rain cried. "You did not trust me?" the guardian questioned as tears came to her eyes. "Blizzard helped me to see you as a tool and I guess as time went by you went from friend to tool. When I first met you and when you came to stay I would say we were friends but I would never consider us close friends. Please do not hurt me, please do not kill me," Rain cried as she fell to her knees.

"Did you ever listen to me when I spoke to you? I am not here to kill or hurt you. I just want to understand what I did wrong to hurt you. Where I failed you so badly that you would hand me over to my enemy," Zea explained. Just as Zea was walking over to help the Mountain off her knees a male rushed into the room to attack the zatz who flipped and began to fight Gecko. The fight was over in seconds with Zea as the victor.

Using her pressure points and venom Gecko's body fell unconscious as Rain rushed to his side. "He is fine, I only knocked him out cold. I would have hoped you learned something about me but I guess I was wrong. I am going to leave you now but I would like you to know one thing before I leave," the guardian spoke coldly as her eyes narrowed. Rain began to shake in fear and stood to face the zatz. "Rain, I came here to tell you something. I forgive you for all the wrong doing you have done to me. I forgive you for hurting me but if you ever hurt me again I will not be as forgiving. I also want to tell you before I leave that if you ever need my help which I doubt you will with all your 'real' friends I will help you to show my forgiveness and to thank you for at least showing me some kind of friendship. I will leave you now so you can be happy but if I ever did anything to hurt you, Rain, I am sorry," Zea told Rain. "Zea?" Rain called to a now empty room. Before Rain could say anything the guardian was gone and off to find Snake.

The green kat's hut was gone and the guard was nowhere to be found. This did not make the fighter happy. The zatz now found her way to find the leader of the camp. Hugging to inner mountain wall Zea soon found herself outside the male's hut. Next the female crept into Blizzard's room and took the male from this warm bed.

Pinning him down to the cool ground Zea covered his mouth so he could not call out for help. When the fighter was ready she picked him up by the neck. Beads of sweat formed on his brow as the female began to speak, "You betrayed me." "Zea, what are you doing?" the male choked. "You betrayed me," the black one repeated. "What do you want," Blizzard grasped. "Why?" the fighter questioned. "You know that answer, Zea, I betrayed you for the good of the clan. Although you were helping the group we all benefitted more from turning you over to the Shadow Kats," the leader whispered.

"The only reason you let me into your clan was so you could use me?" she questioned. "Yes, who would want you? You are different and no one likes different," the leader said coldly. "Where is Snake?" Zea asked. "He left the clan because we got rid of you. He joined another clan but I do not know which one. I think you should leave," the male responded. "Never, never mess with me again, Blizzard, or I will teach you the real meaning of pain," the female threatened.

The guardian punched the male and called out as he tried to stand, "That is for Bear." By the time Blizzard looked up Zea was gone and in the air. With tears falling from her eyes the guardian found a cliff there she sat by a rock. As she looked at the night sky and the valley below the computer tried to comfort his life long companion. As the female cried all she felt was a lost feeling.

With so many emotions the fighter did not know what do and where to start to clear her mind. Then her ears pricked but it was too a late. Zea was so focused on her feelings she did not hear the dart fly through the air. Breaking her skin the dart hit the fighter's back shoulder. The stinging pain began to spread through the female's body as she stood and turned to see who was attacking her. By the time the guardian faced the tree line more darts were heading in her direction. Because of the first dart Zea could not stop all the darts but most of them. Soon her body felt weak and her eyes tired. As her body fell to the floor slowly becoming paralyzed the guardian heard a group of footsteps. As she broke into a cold sweat, her eyes blurring at the sight of feet and her breathing slowed Zea fell a sleep.

Is This Goodbye?

Zea woke up to pain, ropes and chains. She was wrapped up from neck to ankles and her back shoulder was on fire. Trying to move the female found she was chained to the ground. The fighter's mouth was dry. –What happened?– the zatz asked her computer who answered, –A teeka hit you. Then a group brought you here where they tied you down and left. You have been out for a few hours and the spot where one of the teekas hit you was your back shoulder. You need to focus on healing yourself because

I think you back shoulder is infected or you are allergic to something in the teeka.– –Is that way my shoulder is stinging so much?– the female asked. –Yes, now rest you need it,– the computer ordered.

Just as Zea was closing her eyes a male walked into the room. He came up to the bounded one and checked all the ropes and chains. When he looked at her wound the female sucked in with pain. "Oh my ...," the male whispered before he went running out the door. –That is a good sign,– Zea mentally spoke. –Oh, yes,– the life one said sarcastically. A few moments later the same male returned with friends. "Give me room," one of them called to the room.

As the others backed off the male moved the ropes so he could look at the wound. The female again sucked in with pain as she began a cold sweat. "I have never seen anything like this," he whispered. "I am not from here and I think I might be allergic to what was in the dart," the zatz told the male who said nothing and just continued looking and touching Zea's wound. "I am sure she will be fine. Lets give her some water and let her rest," the male told the others as he stood and walked to the door.

The first male who came helped prop Zea up into a sitting position against the closest wall. Then gave the fighter some water. As Zea looked at the male she could see he had a grey coat with dark blue and green stripes. His eyes were a colorful blue. When he finished the male started to stand as the female stated, "Please help me, and you know my shoulder needs more than rest. At least tell me where I am, please." The male just looked at her with a cold stare and then left the room. –What is his problem?– the black one wondered. –I do not know,– the computer answered. Soon the female fell back into the land of dreams.

Getting slapped waked the guardian up form her slumber. After shaking her head the female looked up and saw a male kat with cornflower blue fur and two colored eyes. His eyes were blue and his pupils were green. As the blue one looked at Zea with a cold stare the female noticed the tops of his ears were black and he had a massive weapon on his arm going down to his hand. The weapon looked like an arm shied with a blade sticking out from the elbow to the wrist and a second blade on over the knuckle.

Now that the guardian was awake the pain on her shoulder kicked in and she started a cold sweat. Finally he broke the silence, "You look rancid." "I am sick from the dart. I have not had a healthy meal since I came here and I have been chained here without freedom. What did you think I would looked like?" the female snapped. The male did not seem pleased with the fighter's actions and in a quick movement he pinned the zatz against the wall while placing his arm blade under her chin. Zea just looked at the male not backing down to his aggressive action. "You are a bold one," he stated. "What is your name? I want to know if you have to change it or not," the male continued. "My name is Zeaytera KatOynera or you can call my Zea," the guardian voiced as strong as she could. "I guess that is a decent name," the blue one thought out loud. "What is your name?" the fighter asked. "Did I say you could speak? I do not think I asked you a question or told you to speak because you are new I will not punish you but next time you speak out of line there will be consequences," he spat at her.

Then he stood and walked out of the room before the female could respond. She was left her thoughts. –What do you think his problem was?– the female pondered. –I do not know but since we have been here there have been no females,– the computer voiced. The two talked for a while before the zatz fell asleep.

Zea was again brought back to the real world by getting slapped. Looking up she locked eyes with the blue male who was smiling. The female rolled her eyes as the male crouched down to her eye level. Her muscles were sore from not moving, her stomach ached and her shoulder was still on fire. The blue one reached over and grabbed the fighter's shoulder to make her lean forward. The zatz sucked in with pain. The male stood and walked out of the room.

A few minutes later another male walked into the small hut. This male had a green coat and blue eyes. "Hello, Zea, I think that is your name. I just talked to my second in command, Erik, and he tells me you have quite the cut on your shoulder. I am Chris and I am the leader of this great group, the Stone Clan," he stated as he walked to Zea and crouched to see her eye to eye. Zea just gazed at Chris while he looked her over and then checked her wound. "I have never seen anything like this," the leader whispered.

"Like I have been trying to tell everyone I think I am allergic to what is on your darts. I am weak and tired. I worried my cut might be inflected as well," the black one also whispered. "Not possible, little one, in my darts there are no poisons," the blue laughed. "I am not from this land therefore I might react to your tonics in different ways," Zea explained. "I think you are tired. You need rest, I will send my joined one to wash your wound," Chris told the female as he stood.

The next one to walk in the room was a female with a dark grey kat with a mottled coat with black. The female has very light green eyes. She knelt in front of the trapped one to clean her shoulder. "Wow, you have quite a cut here little one," she spoke. "Yes, where am I?" the zatz asked. "You are in the Stone Clan."

"Where are all the females?"

"In this clan females are of ... how do I say ... we are of less rank to the males."

"Then why are you here if you are treated poorly?"

"Well, little one, I was born into this clan and I could not leave. All new females, like you, are captured and forced to marry one of the males. Soon they well come in here one at a time and if you do not choose a mate ... then.. well... they will use you sexually till they are done. Next they will wait to see if you are with child. If you are with child they will kill you and keep the baby unless you join the clan and if you are not with child then they will try again and so on till you die. I have seen this happen."

"This will not be my fate. I will not let one male touch me."

"You are strong willed but, your body is weak."

"I will not let this clan take me."

"Good luck, little one, I am done with you. There is not much I can do with your wound. I am guessing soon after I leave Chris will let his males come have a look at you. Bye."

"Wait, what is your name?"

The female stopped and turned. Looking at the black one she stated, "My name is Hale."

The female walked out of the room.

Zea closed her eyes to rest and do her best to force the pain to the back of her mind. –You need to get the ropes off your shoulder every time you move or one of the males move you the ropes dig into your cut,– the computer voiced. The guardian took a deep breath and waited for some action. Finally a brown male walked into the room with a smile on his face.

"How are you, little one?" he asked. The female responded quietly, "I am sick." He talked with Zea for a while but she was not very talkative.

Each male who came in the room was the same. He acted sweet but all their words were fake. Once Zea did not respond to them they became annoyed and their true colors came out for the zatz to see. As the males came and went the guardian noticed a lot of the older males had the same circle scar on their shoulder. Then it hit her, –Do you think? – –Yes, I think you are right, – the computer agreed. The zatz became nervous was wanted her freedom. Then the second to last male walked into the hut. Zea was not happy to see Erik. "Hello again," he smiled. "When are going to give up and leave," the female stated with a roll of her eyes. "You know I hope you do not find this last male to your liking because then I will be the first to have you. Then after you get a taste of me you might want to stay with me. I am not that bad of a male to join with and live," Erik stated as he crouched to Zea's level. "I will not join with you," the zatz voiced. "We will see if you change your mind after I take you," he laughed. "The only thing I will give you is a good beating. When I get better I am going to give you what is coming to you," the fighter spat. "I like you. You are a fighter but sadly unless you join our clan I do not think you are going to feel better," Erik expressed to the black one before leaving her to her thoughts.

When the last male walked into the room the fighters eyes widen at the site. "What are you doing here?" she grasped. "I am trying to join this clan," the green male spoke calmly. "But, Snake, this is not like you. Why are you joining this clan?" the black one inquired. "Think about it Zea," he snapped as he sat across from her. "I am sure you noticed all the scars on the older member but do you realize the roots of this clan?" the guardian questioned. "Zea, do not think I know what clan I am joining? I know this group has roots in the Shadow Clan all the older members are previous guards. What do you think happens when one leaves a clan with ties to the Shadow Kats? Not a lot clans will take you in and I am a Colin. I left because of what they did to you. I never thought I would see you again," Snake explained. "This group is not you. Look how the treat females and are trying to force me to join," Zea told her friend. "I am well aware of how this clan acts. Why are you sweating?" the male asked. "The cut where the dart hit me I think it inflected or I am allergic to what was on the dart. Wait, do not change the subject," the female answered. "I will be right back," Snake told the zatz as he stood and walked to the door.

Snake did not stop even after Zea called into the air, "Wait." A few minutes later Snake returned to the room with a bowl and stone mixer.

Again sitting in front of the chained one Snake began to crush the plants and liquid in the wooden bowl. "What are you doing?" the female inquired. "You know a few weeks ago when you were teaching what do if I or a member in my group get hurt while out in the field?" the green one asked. "Yes," she responded. "Well, this is one of the tonics you taught me to make, now lead forward," the male ordered.

Zea carefully leaned forward as Snake moved the ropes and spread the tonic over the wound. As soon as the fighter's cut was covered the pain went away and she felt better. "Thank you, Snake, I feel much better now," the female told the male. The black one started to tear. "Why are you upset?" Snake questioned. "I am just happy to know that my time at the Mountain Clan was not wasted and you were listening and remembered what I taught you. I am also upset to think you might become a member of this clan. I do not want you turn into one of these males you are not like these guys. I understand there are not many places for you to go but let me help you. Maybe we could leave this place and you could come back to Dark Star's Clan with me," the female explained.

"You were lucky you ran into Bear and he liked you. Me joining would be much different then you staying with them. Dark Star's Clan is very hard to join and there are not a lot of clans I know I can join."

"I know a few clans maybe the Green Falls Clan. I know there are not fields under the water but there is grass. There are good clans out there you could join. Almost any clan could be better then this one."

"I do not know if I can just leave?"

"Sure with me, I will help you."

"If I join Dark Star's Clan and you join another clan how will we remain friends?"

"Just like I remained being friends in Dark Star's Clan while I was in the Mountain Clan. I can visit or you can visit. We will make it work."

"Look this is not easy for me."

"I am not saying this is going to be easy. All my life I have been lied to, cheated, abused, hurt, seen as an object, used and much more. There are only a few in my life I have grown to love and trust but sadly many of them are dead. You are one of the few kats who I trust. If you join this clan I will not be able to trust or see you. If you are in a respectable clan I have a good chance of visiting you and having some relationship."

"You just do not understand," Snake whispered as he stood. Before he could leave the room Zea's voice cut the air, "Snake, I have to leave soon whether you are with me or not. I am sorry but I cannot stay in this place but, for what it is worth thank you and I am sorry if I ever hurt you." The male looked at her with watering eyes one more time before leaving the room. Zea fell into a state of sleep hoping her shoulder would heal now that she had more energy and got some good rest.

Like the other times Zea was awakened with a slap. Shaking her head the female looked up to see Erik's smiling face. The pain in her shoulder was gone. –Is my shoulder better? – the fighter asked her like long friend. –Almost, with the tonic and the good energy you got from Snake I think you are strong enough to leave this place when you are ready, – the computer answered. (Snap, snap). "Where did you go?" the male asked after snapping her fingers at the chained one.

Zea glared at the blue one who always carried his blade with him. "Why do you always have your blade with you?" the guardian inquired. "Oh, you are talking to me now? What kind of question is that? Why do I have my blade? I am the leader of the guards. Why do you think I have my blade?" Erik mocked. "To be honest I think you carry a blade because you lack in so many areas. You might have low esteem or do not feel like a big tough male or like a full fighter so to compensate you wear that blade," Zea voiced calmly.

The male's eyes widened with anger and he struck her. "Wow, you are a tough male you can hit a tied female. Why not fight me like a real male would or are you afraid even with your weapon you will lose?" the guardian told the male in a strong voice. "There is nothing I want more to do than to rape and beat you but, I have orders to follow and I will not fall for your pathetic attempt to escape. I will have you because you have not shown a liking to any male here and no clan members have come forward to claim you but me," the guard answered. "If I say the name of a male who I would be willing to talk to what happens?" the female questioned. "Then I would tell Chris who would think about your choice and talk to that warrior," he explained.

"Snake," the fighter stated. "Snake? Snake! Why him? He is not as strong and is more quiet then most of the kats I know. Why him?" Erik exploded. "I have my reasons," Zea smiled. "You just do not want me to win so you named the first kat who came to your head," the blue one snapped. "You can believe what you wish but that is the male I choose," Zea spoke calmly. The fighter closed her eyes slowly and took a deep breath.

Erik was not happy with Zea's actions. "I will have you," he warned her as he left the room. The black one opened her eyes and began to think of a way out to her ropes. Her computer was tied down and was not able to open any of its compartments. Then the idea hit the guardian and just as she was going into action Snake walked into the room. "Why did you pick me?" he questioned. "There are two reasons. Out of all the males here I would pick you because I know you and trust you. Anyone but Erik he is crazy," she responded.

"You are getting me in trouble. Everyone knows Erik wants you and he threatened to kill anyone who got in his path of getting you. He is very mad at me and I do not know what I am going to do. I told him I was coming in here to make you angry so you would not pick me but knowing you this is not possible. What am I going to do," Snake stated. "Leave with me. Lets run from this place here and now," she answered with full confidence. "Zea, you do not understand please for me and my safety do not pick me," the green one told the female. "What am I not understanding?" Zea cried. Snake looked at his friend with watery eyes and left the room.

Zea was at a loss of what Snake was thinking or doing but knew she had to leave this clan as soon as possible. Now that the female was alone she brought her claws out to play. The white, shape and slightly curved claws slowly grew from the guardian's fingertips. Zea began cutting the ropes and used her teeth to aid her. Soon some of the ropes fell to the dirt floor and once Zea could move wiggled and cut herself free. Now standing on top of a pile of broken ropes and loosened chains Zea took a deep breath and brought her claws back into hiding.

Just as the fighter was about to move Erik came into the room and his eyes widened at the site. "Well, well, well you final grew a brain and helped yourself," he said with a smile. "Erik, I really do not want to hurt you," the guardian voiced as she moved into a defensive position. "I have been waiting for this for a long time," Erik stated in a low voice. Then he ran at the fighter and swung his blade at the black one who ducked the sharp blow. The two began to fight. Erik was very skillful and used his arm blade very well. Zea was surprised that his actions backed up his cocky words and attitude.

Erik was also impressed with the young one's fighting skills. She was very graceful and effective with all her moves. Doing a several back flips the fighter missed the males swing blade. Because Zea did not have a heavy weapon her moves were overall faster and she was able to hit the male a few times. The fight continued and both fighters were not looking to let the other win. Finally Erik made his biggest mistake, when he tried to hit Zea with his arm blade she crouched down and his arm became stuck in a strong wooden pillar. With a smile the guardian made her way back to the struggling one and stated, "till next time," as she used her pressure point and venom to attack. Erik's body fell lifeless and the female un-wedged his arm from the wood. After carefully placing his body on the dirt floor Zea slowly walked to the door.

Looking outside the hut Zea could see the camp looked like any other but the females looked more skinny and rough. Everyone was busy doing chores or talking except for Snake who was waiting for Erik. "Snake," Zea whispered. Seeing the black one free Snake slowly made his way into the hut. "I am leaving now. I need to know, is this it? Is this goodbye?" the guardian spoke in a shaky voice. Searching the room with his eyes the male saw Erik's lifeless body, a broken room and last Zea's face. Gazing into her deep green eyes Snake did not know what to do.

He wanted to be with his friend did not know if he could leave the Stone Clan. "Zea, if I leave it has to be on my own," the male stated. "But ..." the female began. "No, no more. I will miss you Zea, more than you will ever know but, please leave me and let me be," the green one interrupted. "I do not understand," Zea began to cry. "Please for me just knock me out and go from this clan," Snake ordered. "Good luck, my friend," Zea cried as she pushed on Snakes pressure point, released a drop of toxin and watched his body fall.

Next the guardian jumped up onto one of the wooden rafter. After making a hole in the grass roof the female took to the air leaving the Stone Clan. In the back of her mind Zea had a very strong feeling she was never going to see her friend, Snake, again. With a heavy heart the guardian flew home with watery eyes.

Healing Heart

Zea landed in the middle of camp in tears. Dark Star came running from one of the center huts to aid his friend. "What is wrong? Are you hurt?" the leader asked. The black one remained silent all she did was cry. Then the black one felt a warm hand on her shoulder. Looking up Zea met eyes with Bear who helped her off the dirt floor and helped her walk to his hut. Where he sat on his bed with the zatz at his side.

"Do you want to talk?" the father asked. "I do not know? Are you doing well?" the female questioned. "You are very kind for asking. I am doing just fine, thank you but, how are you feeling?" Bear laughed. The guardian looked at her father and saw the scar across his chest. The zatz carefully reached her hand over and felt the male's scar. "Is this what my back looks like?" the fighter questioned. "Well, I have one and you know you have many but, I guess this is what one of your scars look like," Bear answered.

The two talked about Zea going to the Mountain Clan and talking to Rain and Blizzard. Then the two discussed everything that happened in the Stone Clan. Bear did not know what to say to the little one, he knew she had been though a lot in the last few weeks and knew she needed some rest. He left the female to rest and relax. Bear left the hut to talk to Dark Star.

Later that night Zea awoke and made herself another tonic for her wound. She then made her way to join the clan who were eating the last meal of the day. Sitting next to Roberd she asked him to help put the medicine on her back. After the male was done with his task the two of them with Robby and Josh caught up and laughed into the night.

Later when the camp was slowing down for the night Dark Star came over to talk to the zatz. The two walked to Dark Stars main meeting hut. The duo sat down as the leader began to speak, "I know you have been though a lot over the last few weeks, Bear told me about the Stone Clan. I am sorry for what happen but you should have not gone out by yourself. Next time you need or want to go off please tell me and please let one of us come with you." "You are right. I am sorry I left and made you all worry. I will never leave like that again," Zea promised the leader.

"Now that you are here safe I think you should take the next few days to relax and then we will try to find you a clan. I am happy to have you back safe. While you were in the Stone Clan did you meet Erik?" Dark

Star continued. "Yes," the female responded while looking down at the ground. "How is he?" the male questioned. "He is a good fighter but I do not like the way he treats females. He wanted to hurt me but I did not give him his wish. I think he is the strongest in the clan and I do not know why he is not leading but he gave me a good fight when I was escaping. Oh, I have a question, do you know what kind of darts the Stone Clan uses?" the fighter voiced to the male.

"When Erik was very young I knew him and he was always a great fighter but he loved the feeling of having power. I am not sure if I know about the dart but I can find out for you why?" Dark Star inquired. "Whatever was in the dart I think I an allergic to because after one dart hit my shoulder I became very sick and that is why it took me so long to come home," Zea explained. "I will look into that for you but for right now I would like you to rest and stay out of trouble. We have meeting with the EnyoRheas coming and you are welcome to join us. I hope you have a good night. I will see you in the morning," Dark Star comforted the zatz. "Goodnight my friend, thank you and I am sorry, I will see you tomorrow," Zea smiled. The guardian stood and gave the leader a sign of respect and then went to Bear's hut for the night.

Zea woke with the sun and was very happy to see Krist waiting for outside ready to go on a morning run. With a smile the two ran around the camp laughing and talking the whole time. Once back in camp the guardian felt like nothing had ever changed everyone was doing their normal chores and the female walked around camp and help where needed.

The next few days the camp was getting ready to see the EnyoRheas as Zea got some rest and relaxed. Dark Star came up to her and gave her a list of plants that made the tonic, which was on the dart. The guardian gartered the different plants and began to test each one to see if she was allergic to one of them. After seeing each one the fighter found she was not allergic to any of the plants.

Next the zatz made the same mixture, which was placed on the darts. The guardian asked her computer to run tests help her and they found out that Zea's body now had made anti-bodies and that tonic would never work on her again. –This might happen to you every time your body is introduced to a new tonic. I am not sure, – the computer explained. – Because you are not from this land you are more likely to catch any sickness that would be normal to the kats that live here but you might become more ill. We will have to be very careful, – the life long friend continued. Zea sat there and soaked up the new information.

Nathan walked into the small room breaking the young one's thought. "How are you today, Nathan?" the female asked. "I am doing well, I am going out to collect to plants and I was wondering if you would like to go with me?" he asked. "Sure," the zatz agreed. The two left camp with packs on their backs.

Entering the forest Zea kept her ears perked. Giving his friend a list of plants and how much they need of is one, the two stayed in sight of each other and began hunting. As the sun dance across the sky the two worked hard. When they were almost done Zea heard some movement in the trees. Scanning the area the guardian saw nothing. Calling to Nathan he too began to look around trying to see or hear any danger.

–Computer, please do a pulse, – the fighter asked. When the picture got back the zatz could see there were three kats in the trees above them. Walking over to Nathan she told him about the three visitors. "I know who they are and I think we should leave now," the male whispered. "But this is yours clans land why should we leave?" the female questioned. "I know who the three are and I think we should leave now. I will explain to you later why," Nathan told the female has he started to walk out of the forest.

Zea looked around the trees one last time trying to see one of the kats before she left but had no luck. She left with disappointment and caught up to her friend. "I did not like the feeling of someone watching us," Zea voiced. "They were not going to hurt or attack us," the male comforted his friend. "Were they Colins?" the female asked. "No," Nathan responded. The guardian did not like being out of the loop but there was nothing she could do. For some reason Nathan was not going to fully tell her who was in the trees. When they got back to camp Nathan went to talk to Dark Star and Zea went to find Bear.

Finding her father working, the zatz asked if she talk to him. He said, "Sure," and the daughter began to speak, "I was in the woods with Nathan and then three kats showed up and they hid themselves very well. I think they communicated by using animal calls and just sounds. Nathan seemed to know who they were and told me they were not Colins but I was wondering what Clan are they from, if you know what I am talking about?"

Bear stopped his work and looked up at the talking female. "I was hoping you would find out about this clan. I do not want you to be around or even know about them. I would ask that you respect my wishes and do not ask or talk about what happen today. I promise when you and when I am ready I will tell you. I am sorry but I feel this is for your own good," Bear voiced to Zea in a low, strong but clam voice. Again the guardian was not pleased to not understand what was going on but would respect her father's decision. After promising him to agree with his wishes she headed off to find something to do.

The black one walked over to Krist's hut and helped him with all the work that had to be done. Krist talked about his childhood and what it was like growing up in the Shadow Clan. The guardian listened and did her best to understand the Shadow Clan. When the day was coming to a close the two cleaned up their mess and made their way to get some food. When the meal was over the clan went fell asleep.

Zea was joyful to be home and felt like her troubles with the Mountain, Shadow and Stone Clan was just a very bad dream. The days flew by and soon the day of the EnyoRheas was upon the clan. That day like the times before all the males were jumpy with excitement. The guardian was also cheerful for the meeting of the clan because she would be able to see her friends again. The day seemed to fly with the win and soon night was well on its way and the clan was off to see the EnyoRheas.

Dark Star gave the same speech before the males entered camp and Bear told Zea not to leave without him. As the males entered camp the females cheered and the meeting began. There was a great feast and music. Friends sat by the different fires and laughed into the night. Most of the important ranking members of the clans sat together and talked of each other about the other clan's progress in the last few months.

Zea was now a little over 18 and a half. She was growing out of her young one name and Liz and Sarah noticed this when they saw their black friend. They greeted each other with smiles and began to talk of the last year. Like each time before Roberd, Robby and Josh came to talk to the two young females. All were jubilant to see each other. "Do you want to dace," Josh suggested to the group. All the females smiled and laughed. The group stood and began to walk to the main fire where the music was being playing but as they were walking Zea could hear her named being called over the crowd. After excusing herself the guardian made her way to the leaders circle.

Once the zatz reached group she bent down on one knee and showed her respect for the leaders and the elders who were pleased by the female's actions. "How are you, Zea?" Sunflower inquired. "I am doing well, thank you," the fighter answered. "I would like to introduce you to my daughter, Sunray," the EnyoRheas leader told the black one as she pointed to her daughter at her side.

Sunray was a golden color with a white underside. Sunray's coat was splashed with black marking and she had yellowish- green eyes. "It is very nice to meet you, Sunray, I hope you are having a great evening," the guardian voiced. "How was the Mountain Clan?" one of the EnyoRheas elders questioned. "I did very well in the group. I join the tribe and adjusted the clan way of life and regulations. I made friends and I also helped the family by teaching them new fighting skills and ways to build and fix many objects in the camp. Until the Mountain Clan betrayed me I was loyal and was respectful of the clan laws," Zea explained to the group.

"I heard you had a run in with the Stone Clan is this true?" Sunflower enquired. "Yes, while I was there I met Chris, Erik and other clan members. When I regained my strength I escaped and made my way home to Dark Star's Clan," the female told the group. "How do you think you are adapting to this new land?" another elder asked. "I think I am doing well. I am starting to understand the ways of different clans and know the lay of land very well. I also think I have your tongue down and know all of the slang terms," the zatz responded.

The group talked to the black one for a while longer quizzing her on her new life in their land. Zea did not like be questioned but did her best to answer truthfully and with the best answers. Finally the group let the female go and have a good time. The zatz left the group after giving them a sign of respect. Looking around the guardian viewed for a friend. A few minutes later Zea run into Avis who was sitting by a small fire with a drink in hand watching her friends.

Sitting next Avis the guardian began talking with her friend. They laughed and talked into the night. Zea really wanted to join this group and meet more friends in this clan but this choice was not up to her. Soon the dawn was coming and Bear came up to his daughter telling her it was time to leave. The female said her goodbyes and walked back to her home with her father.

The two talked about their night, "I did not like being quizzed like that," the female stated. "Who would?" Bear laughed. The guardian also laughed and hugged Bear's side as they walked. When they reached camp they went into their home and went to their beds. Laid down and fell into the land of dreams.

Like many nights before Zea awoke to Bear standing over here asking if she was okay. The nightmares had calmed down but were still there always lingering in the back of the guardian's mind. Now that Zea was back in a safe place her heart was beginning to heal but her mind still had a ways to go before she would be finally be free. The next step would be to find a clan for her to join and to find a way to save her mind.

Bear sat by Zea's side asking if there was anything he could do. In the guardian's mind she wanted to tell her father about her computer and let him see a visual of her past but fear was stopping her. Her silence worried the father and he did not know what to do. "I am here for you," Bear whispered. The zatz wished to tell him everything. "My heart is healed but I still need to clear my mind. I hope I will be soon be ready to share with you my last difference, but this is my big one, so I am just not ready yet to share," Zea explained to her father who replied, "I will be ready when you are. Take your time and tell me when you are prepared." The two sat in silence in the dark in each others company. "Thank you, Bear," the daughter voiced. "You should try to get some sleep little one," the male suggested. "Soon I will not be a little one," Zea smiled. "Ahh, this is true but, you will always be my little one," Bear told the black one. The two looked into each other's eyes, hugged one last time and went to bed.

A Simple Question

The next few days flew by Zea was falling back into the life she lead before the Mountain Clan. The guardian was blissful but every night and even during the day when she saw that all the males had a bond she did not have. She wanted to join a group, a clan. She wanted to part of a family where she would to be real 'sister' not just there as a tool. Bear and Dark Star knew they did not have to pressure the female to join another clan because she wanted to be in a tribe of her own.

The leader talked with the zatz about many ideas to meet and join a clan. On one of their talks the Mountain Clan came into play. One of the males was going on a long trip and one of the clans he would stop by was the Mountain Clan and then would continue down the valley behind the mountain and he needed at least one other to go with him. Dark Star was not sure if Zea would want to go because of the Mountain Clan.

"If the one who goes on this journey wants me to join him I would be more than happy to do so. If I was to say no to this offer then I would be letting the Mountain Clan 'win' and I would be letting them affect my life and stop me from being content. I will not let them do that to me. I will walk back there and be respectful but I will not be relaxed. If the one who goes does not want me with him there will be no hard feeling and I will still be pleased," the guardian explained to the leader who smiled and agreed. The two talk for a while longer and then leader told his friend he would know in a few days who would be going on the trip.

All the clan members enjoyed having Zea in camp. She was a hard worker and enjoyed working with friends. Bear was still worried about Zea's nightmares and keeping her big difference inside and not sharing it. When the time came Dark Star decided to send Robby, Josh and Roberd on the trip. They left the next day laughing and talking. Zea helped with the threes chores while they were away and the clan was a little more quiet now that the trio was gone. Over all everything was very peaceful and the weather was fair.

Then one day while everyone was busy doing their chores the guards called into the air, "Five heading in, everyone ready, five coming." The all the males in camp went into action. "Zea go into our hut," Bear ordered as he grabbed his blade and ran towards the outsiders. This did not make Zea happy but was not going to fight with her father and quickly made her way to the hut where she peered out the window.

There were three males and two females they looked like they did not want a fight. One male was red with blue stripes and blue eyes while another was back with green strips and yellow eyes. The last male was yellow with orange marking on his face and back with sliver eyes. One of the two females were blue with green eyes and the other was brown with a tan underside and white marking on her face. This female had green eyes.

The black one watched from the window as the outsiders talked to the guards who then were joined with Bear and Dark Star. Then the guardian noticed all five had the same scar they were Shadow Kats. The black one's eyes grew and looked around camp incase the first five were a distraction. The fighter saw that there were still guards all around camp and she felt a lot better. After the groups exchanged words Bear left the assembly and walked to meet with Zea who did not what to expect.

The father walked into his hut and looked at his daughter by the window. "Zea, they say they have a message for you from their leader and will not talk to anyone but you. Do you want to meet with them?" The guardian looked down in thought and then gave the male her answer, "Would it be okay if I just met with one of them?" "I think that would work. If they agree to your request would you like them to meet you in this hut?" Bear continued. "Sure," the female agreed. Bear left the hut to talk to the Shadow Kats then to talk to Dark Star. The two groups talk for what seemed to be forever until the outsiders finally agreed to the zatz request. The brown female stepped forward and walked to the hut with Bear. As the chief of guards waited outside the female walked into the dark room.

The female looked at Zea who waited for the Shadow Kat to say something. Finally the black one broke the silence, "Can I help you?" The brown one just stood there. "If you are not going to doing anything I think I am going to leave or you should," the zatz stated. "Zea?" the outsider finally spoke. "Yes, that is my name," the guardian voiced. "I am here to tell you that my leader wishes to speak you," the brown explained as she pulled a piece of paper from a pouch on her belt. The fighter took the paper and read its contents.

Dark Flame wanted to meet her in the woods in a week alone. Zea did not like the idea. The zatz called in Bear and asked him to get Dark Star. When both males were in the room; the female showed them the note. "I do not mind meeting him but I do not like the place and time," the guardian told them. "Are you sure you would want to meet him?" the leader questioned. "I will meet him. I might be able to get him to back off and not try to get me to join his clan," the female explained her reasoning.

"I guess you can write him a note saying where and when you would be willing to meet," Dark Star told the black one. Zea wrote a note saying see would meet Dark Flame in two days at the cliff that was about a mile from their clan. When Zea gave the note to the brown one without hesitation she left the room and left with her clan mates they started running and disappeared into the woods. Now all the attention was turned to Zea who could not wait for an answer from Dark Flame.

Hours went by and soon the sun was setting. Just as dusk was falling into place five different Shadow Kats came to camp with a message for Zea. A neon colored kat with a neon pink dot on her brow and had blood red eyes. Her name was Tieya and the Shadow Kat gave the zatz a note from her leader. After looking the message over the guardian agreed to the leader's words and let the Shadow Kats go back to their camp.

Tomorrow at midday the fighter would be meeting Dark Flame at the top of the mountain by the Shadow Clan. They were to be alone and have no weapons on them. Zea would do her best to say truthful with her word on the note. Bear and Dark Star did not want the female to go alone but, she told them she could not go back on her word. The three finally agreed there would be a small group of guards at the base of the mountain if the fighter was in trouble she could fly down to them and at least the female would not be walking there alone. Everyone knew that the group would be of no help to Zea once she was on the mountain or if they saw trouble but everyone also knew how strong of a fighter the young one was and if she needed help she could always fly down to safety. After all were somewhat content they went to sleep.

The next morning Zea rose with the sun like normal and went on her morning run with Krist. They talked about the events, which would happen later that day. The male was not joyful to hear of the female's actions but since there was nothing he could do to stop the event he was a positive as he could be and after the run he asked Dark Star if he could be one of the guards in the group at the base of the mountain. The leader agreed with Krist's request. When mid morning was well on its way, Bear, Krist, Nathan, Zion, Polaris and Zea were off to the mountain.

Both Zea's heart and mind were racing as she walked. –I think I know what he wants to talk about abut what do I say? Do you think he is going to try to capture me again? Was this a good choice on my part? – the guardian pondered. –I think you do not need to tell him anything you do not want too. Do not worry about if you made the right choice you are going for it so do not think about the what if's. If Dark Flame wants to start a fight he will not win and you have friends in your corner, – the computer explained.

The group walked out of the forest and into one of the many meadows. The golden sea swayed gently in the warm wind, which kissed Zea's face and the sun warmed her back. Just as mid day was began the group reached their destination. Looking up the guardian saw the top of the cliff. Giving her father a hug she asked the group for luck.

After taking a deep breath the fighter opened her wings and took to the air. All the males were still amazed with the female's flying abilities. Upward the zatz flew playing with the wind and following the rock up to the top where her happy mood dimmed at the sight of her foe. Landing at the edge of the cliff the guardian looked at the male who smiled upon seeing her.

–Computer, please do a pulse, – the zatz asked. When the picture came back the guardian could she the tree line behind the male was coved in Shadow Kats. "I thought we were to come alone," the black one voiced. "You are always so aware of your surrounding," the leader smiled. "You broke your word maybe I should leave," the female continued. "Wait, hear me out, I am getting old and right now I am overall weak. I could not travel here alone without any protection being one of the most hunted leaders in this land. I give you my word they will not come forward," Dark Flame explained. "Very well," Zea stated as she sat crossed legged in front of the leader. All she needed to do was lean back and she would be in the air to make an escape.

"I am very surprised you are meeting with me. I was sure you would have just laughed at my offer and not want to every see me again," Dark Flame began. As the leader was speaking Zea looked at him in full light for the first time. This tiger coat looked old and his eyes still had the sparkle but seemed tried. Well, he only had one eye. A small patch covered the other and now resting from the top of this brow to the bottom of his cheek was a nice clean scar. But the male seemed strong just taxed. "I am not like you. I am more forgiving and I keep my word. You hurt others for your befit while I would never think to do such a thing," the guardian told the leader. "You are what you say. I think if we had gotten off on a better start things would have been a lot different," Dark Flamed dreamed. "Well, they did not. I am sorry to be rude and short but why have you asked me to meet you here on this mountain side," Zea questioned.

"I am growing old and soon my son will be leading the clan. Lately I have been letting him call a lot of the shots and giving him a chance to run things while I am still here and can help. He is still in love with you and I do not believe he will be giving up the chance to have you anytime soon. He liked his father does not give up easily," Dark Flame spoke slowly as he looked at the view.

Again as the leader spoke Zea looked at his scars and images flashed in her mind. The zatz felt apologetic for letting her emotions taking over but thought hurting Dark Flame's eye was an appropriate action. The guardian was angry at herself but could not let her emotions show at this time. After taking a deep breath the female continued listening to the male.

"I wanted to tell you, little one, from fighter to fighter, from a leader looking at a warrior, you have my respect and I think you are a very honest, truthful Kat. I do not give my word very often and show this side of me but, I really am meaning that you are a very smart and talented female," the leader spoke very strongly but low. "Thank you for the kind words," Zea smiled. "There is one real reason I asked to meet you here to be honest. I am asking you from fighter to fighter and I am not trying to take advantage of you but the question is what did you do to me? I mean how did you cut my face the way you did? I have talked to many doctors and none of them can tell me how you did it or even give me a suggestion on what you did. The doctor who looked at me after you left told me it was as if you made your claw hotter than fire. All I remember is you had no eyes but I saw a flash of red before I lost vision in my eye. I know you do not have a lot of trust for me but please ease my pain. This question has been on my mind and hunts me in my sleep," Dark Flame pleaded.

The guardian was quiet and did not know what to say. Finally she broke the stillness, "I cannot share with you how I cut your eye. I have not even told my father and I trust him with my life. I just do not trust you. I think if I shared some of my difference with you it would not be in my best interest," the zatz stated. "Zea, my question is a simple one," the leader told the black one. "That may be true but the answer is not simple," the guardian explained.

"Well where did your eyes go?"

"I had my eyes open the whole time."

"I could not see them. The only logical idea to me is your eyes were closed because you have black eye lids because of your fur."

"Dark Flame, I do not trust or respect you enough to share my difference with you. I only regret loosing control of my emotions. I should have remained in control but you have to admit you were helping the situation. I cannot tell you how I cut your eye all I can do is talk about the future."

"Did you use your eyes?"

"No."

"Your claws?"

"No."

"Then what?"

"I will not tell you," the female stated as she stood in frustration. "What are you? I have never read or heard about anyone ever like you. You say you come from far away, do you come from a place where a Kat can go to in this life," the leader questioned. "Stop, Dark Flame, I am not some greater being. I came from a land like this one just far away and I cannot tell you please understand," the guardian interrupted. "What is there to understand? I am a simple male asking you to heal my suffering. Please...," the tiger coated male begged. Zea stopped the male's speech as her ears moved in the air.

Dark Flame watched this in silence. –Computer, please do a pulse I think there are guest coming up the cliff, – the female voiced. –Sure, – the computer responded. When the picture came to Zea's mind she could see there were three kats climbing up the mountainside. Very calmly the zatz turned to Dark Flame and stated, "Do you know why there are three Kats climbing up the mountainside?" "What?" the male asked. "Are they yours?" Zea inquired. "No, but I am going to find out who they are?" Dark Flame voiced as he raised his hand and one of his guards came running. The leader ordered his member to find out who the three were without them knowing.

"Now were we, what are you?" the leader began. "I am a fighter. Where I come from I am called a guar..." the black one stated. The female stopped because the soldier had returned with information. The guardian could not here what the male whispered but when he left the leader did not look happy. "I am sorry but are time is almost up, little one, I must leave soon. I thought the Kats were sent from my son but they are not of my clan. I wanted to thank you before I leave for meeting me. You truly have a good soul. What were you saying?" Dark Flame told Zea who responded, "Wait who is coming?"

"That does not matter, what were you saying?"

"Why are you leaving, who is coming?"

"You really do not who is coming. I am sorry but I have to go, good luck, Zea," Dark Flame laughed as he stood and started for the woods. "But before I go please, what were you saying?" the leader asked. "I was saying, where I am from I am a guardian," Zea voiced very strongly. "What! What did you say," the leader said very quickly as his eyes widened. Reading his expression Zea became very confused. "Come sir we have to go now," one of the guards warned his leader. As Dark Flame disappeared into the woods his eye never left the zatz. His face never changed.

Just as the Shadow Kats were gone the three kats reached the top of the mountain. The fighter turned to meet the new comers. Three males now stood in front of the young female. Looking the fighter could not see any clan marking on the threes bodies. "How did he know we were coming?" one of them whispered. "I do not know and it does not matter, we must go now," one responded. "Wait, who are you?" the zatz questioned. They just looked at her and without warning the three dove backward over the cliff. When Zea ran to the edge and looked the males were nowhere to be found. The fighter did a pulse and saw the males were under her heading towards the Shadow camp and then she could see a large group by the tree line.

The female turned two the sound of footfalls. Dark Flame was walking cautiously back to where the zatz was standing. Some of his clan members were more visible coming from hiding. She could tell they did not like the visitors. The guardian wondered why the large group would be worried about three outsiders.

"I wanted to thank you one more time," Dark Flame voiced to Zea as he got closer. "It seems we both have our secrets from each other," the leader smiled. "You always love thinking you have the upper hand or you have power over me. We do have our secrets but there is a big difference but I can find my answers elsewhere but you can only get your answer from me. Good bye, Dark Flame," the female stated as she placed her hand out for the leader to shake. After the two shook hands the zatz opened her wings. "You said Guardian, right?" the leader asked as the female's paws left the ground. All she did was smile as the fighter flew towards her friends at the base of the mountain. Landing Zea spoke, "Lets go home." The fighter left the mountain with a simple question of her own and a very confused mind.

A New World

When the grouped reached camp the leader came to ask questions. Zea told Dark Star, "Dark Flame just wanted to know what happen last time I was in his hands." "Did you tell him?" the leader asked. "No," the fighter answered. That night Bear and Zea were sitting at their table eating a meal to themselves.

"Bear can I talk to you about something?" the female question. "Sure," Bear voiced. "I do not think you are going to want to talk about it," the zatz began. Bear stopped eating and looked at his daughter. "When I was talking to Dark Star he asked what I was. No one has ever asked me what I am, so I gave him an answer. His face went blank and he looked surprised. I do not know why and I wanted to ask you but, again I am afraid I am going to upset you," the fighter explained.

"What are you?" the male inquired. "Well, I told him the truth. If I was back home, with all my training, I would be at a certain rank and that rank is called a guardian. So, I am a guardian," the zatz told her father who dropped his fork and looked at the female. "What does that word mean, here?" Zea asked. "Have you told this to any one else?" Bear questioned. "No, I have never spoken that word till today. You and Dark Flame are the only ones. Why?" the fighter continued. "Zea, I do not want you ever to repeat that. For safety never say that you are a guardian to anyone." Bear spoke very strongly. "But, that is what I am," Zea explained. "I am sorry, little one, but for your safety I do not think you should walk around saying you are a guardian. I will tell you soon why but I do not think you are ready and that is all I have to say on the topic," the father spoke very strongly.

"Whether you tell me or I find out later, someday I am going to find out what a guardian is. Do you want to be the one that tells someone or me I meet in passing? I give you my word I will never bring up the topic but I will take advantage of any situation I find myself in and soon I will not be a little one, Bear," Zea stated as she stood from the table and walked out of the hut.

Once outside the guardian walked straight to Dark Star where she asked if she could leave for a few days. He was not pleased with suggestion but after the fighter told him where she was going and why he agreed but asked her to be back in less than two weeks and if she was not back in time he would take action. The female gave her respect to the leader and then headed to Krist's hut. There the fighter told her friend the plan of leaving camp. He too was not fully happy for the little one's choice but did not voice against her and just wished her luck. After a hug the zatz took a deep breath and left the safety of the clan for a few days.

Entering the woods Zea was on her guards with her ears pricked, eyes alert and on her toes. The trees blocked the moonlight. The female felt somewhat at home again traveling at night in the woods. –You know Bear is not going to delighted with you running off into the night, – the computer spoke. –I know he not going to be happy but, I am mad that he will not talk to me. I need some time off and learning about other clans. I will talk with him when I get back to camp. This trip should only be about a week long, – the zatz explained her actions. Soon the fighter reached the river where she climbed a nearby tree and waited for the rising of the sun.

As the sun's light kissed the land Zea jumped down from the tree and headed for the water. Placing her hand in the water the female played with the current. Zea let her white eyelids fall into place and the waters surface turned to glass. Now the fighter could see the one coming for her hand from the underwater world. Just as the kat was going to grab the fighter, the black one reached and caught the others arm. Bring the kat to the surface Zea asked, "Would you be so kind and tell, Tim I would like to see him? My name is Zea."

Releasing the guard the guardian backed away from the waters edge sitting on the cool grass as the guard swam away to deliver the message. A few minutes later a few heads popped out of the water looking at the female resting under a tree. "You are back, I knew you could not stay away from the water," a male called to the female who turned and smiled on seeing a male with the blue coat. He had dark blues in the center of is body and as the fur moved towards his hands, feet and head the fur slowly turned lighter blues till the tips of is ears were white. His eyes were black with purple stripes.

"How are you, Blue Fire?" the zatz questioned. "I am doing well. What are you doing by the river?" the male asked. "I was wondering if I could talk to Tim?" the black one answered. "Sure, do you mind coming to our camp he is very busy this morning?" Blue Fire continued. "I would be delighted," Zea said as she stood. "Follow me," the second in command ordered. As Blue Fire went under the surface, the guardian dove into the cool waters and brought her blue lids into place. The fighter was happy to enter a new world. As she followed the guard she spied the moving current against her black fur.

The two were heading upstream and soon came to a massive waterfall. Diving deeper they went under the falls but not behind. In the rock hidden by the falling waters was a small passageway, which led to the camp. The tunnel was very dark and Zea did a pulse to check her surrounding. There were guards all over in the walls. If anyone tried to come up to camp they would not have a chance. After making many turns and fake doors the two reached the end of the maze. Coming out of a pool or water, the fighter lifted her blue lids and looked around to see fire torches now in a great hall lighted her.

Gazing around the room guardian realized they were under the river. Climbing a ladder the female found herself inside a great hollowed out tree. "Wait here, Tim will join you as soon as he can," Blue Fire told Zea as he was leaving the room. "Thank you," the female called out to the male. Zea shook most of the water off her coat and waited for the leader to see her.

Hearing voices a smile grew on her face. "Why, hello Zea, this is a great surprise. How are you?" the leader asked. "I am doing very well and you?" the guardian answered.

"Also doing very well but I am very busy. How was your time with the Mountain Clan?"

"I was forced to leave the clan because I was betrayed and my life was in danger. I left the clan a while ago and now looking for a real clan to join. I was wondering if I could stay here for a while and see how you run your camp."

"I do not see how that would be a problem. You are welcome to stay here as long as you wish. I will have a bed set up for you. Is there any reason you choose to come to my clan?"

"I remember you were very kind to me and when you came to Dark Star's camp you had a good carefree attitude. You were one of the few leaders who came to the meeting. I love the water. This way I can see if the underwater world suites me."

"This is true. Welcome to my camp. I will have someone show you around camp and I will see you later at dinner."

"Thank you, Tim."

Right after the leader left a female walked into the meeting room. "Hi, my name is Aruze and I am going show you around camp," she spoke with a smile. "Great, I am cannot wait," Zea told her. They left the small room and continued around camp. Most of the ground was covered by sand, rock or dirt. Most of the ceiling was roots and mud. There were many different sized pools where young ones could learn how to swim and others for the guards to practice fighting. There were rooms with many beds, where all the single same sex slept and other rooms where families lived. The camp was very organized and large.

The fighter never expected this the clan to be as large as it was. The camp ate in three rounds and was very active. The little ones had smiles and everyone seemed to be treated very well. One of the last places the female saw was the prison. The cages were fairly large and at that point empty. They did not look that bad and there were charts to show how the caged ones were treated. "We do have many prisoners from time to time," Aruze told the new one. When the tour was done the two females headed to the last meal of the day.

Zea sat next to Blue Fire across from Tim. They all laughed and ate their meal telling stories and talking about the day's events. Soon the time came for the clan to calm down and sleep. Aruze show the zatz where she would be sleeping and told the next morning she was free to walk around camp but to be careful if she goes into a meeting room to make sure no one was using it. She also told the fighter that there were three rounds of breakfast and she could join anyone. The two said their goodbye and after Zea thanked her for everything and sat on her bed.

Zea woke to the sound of laughter. Two other females were starting to play a game of gimme. The guardian watched with a smile as more joined into the game. Soon the whole room was involved and Zea was no exception. After the game ended most of the female went to eat.

In the main dinning room the guardian ran into Blue Fire who was happy to see her and greeted her with a smile. "How did you sleep?" he asked as he sat next to the fighter. "I slept well, thank you, and how was your night?" the black one questioned. "Uneventful," he sighed. "I can give you some excitement. We never got to finish our fight when we first met. Even though I know who was going to win. Without a doubt we both knew I was going to win but I was going to let you try," the female tried to state without laughing. Blue Fire just looked at Zea and then spoke, "We both know, I would have won. You are just lucky that Tim came and stopped me from hurting you." "I would love to give you a free lesson on how to fight," the fighter offered. "I am going to be teaching the lesson," the male warned. The guardian only laughed.

The two finished their meals and then went to the largest pool to test each other. Zea found out that the large pool was able to have a current with help from the waterfall the water looped and created a very strong current. The clan had made a great replica of the river. "Are you ready?" the male asked. "The real question is are you ready?" the zatz responded. The two shook hands and wished each other luck then jumped into the cool moving waters.

Once the guardian hit the water her blue lids fell into place and she positioned herself in a defensive position. Scanning the water the fighter looked for her challenger. Word spared that the second in command was fighting the visiting female and many crowded to the pool to watch and cheer for their favorite. Zea swan a lap around the pool to get use to the current and her surrounding. The guardian looked for Blue Fire.

Then he darted out from a dark corner and went to the surface of the water where on seeing him the on lookers cheered. Zea came to the surface and faced the blue one. "The goal of the fight is to force the other out of the water, you may go over the water, or knocks the other out cold. There are no weapons only the use of the environment and water. Do you have any questions?" the male asked. "No, lets begin this," Zea stated strongly. "Count of three and we will start," the blue one called into the air.

A brown Kat from the crowd started to count and when he hit three both fighter dove into the underwater world in opposite directions. Once Zea hit the far wall she began to scan the area for Blue Fire who was nowhere in sight. Deciding to be bold the guardian swam to the dangerous place in the pool, the center surface and waited for action. Listening and keeping her eyes open the female searched for the other fighter.

Finally the action began when Blue Fire flew from a hidden corner. When Zea saw movement coming down and from the left she took off and a great game of chase was started. As the male followed close behind the female she opened her wings for speed and fast, tight turns. The guardian moved up to the surface where it was the hardest to swim and using her wings in one graceful move did a flip. Now Zea was following Blue Fire who was not elated with this action and headed to the bottom of the tank.

Just as he was going to hit the floor, the Kat did a sharp turn, which helped him gain speed. The turn was no problem with a slight change in her wings. The male quickly grabbed a rock and came to a complete stop. Zea knew she could attack the male but was having too much fun to stop and flew past him knocking him playfully with her tail. Again the female was being followed. Gaining speed again the guardian got ready for her next move. The Kat stayed on Zea's tail and when they going at a good speed the female started to swam towards the surface and just as the male was about to grab the young one's tail she flex her back which made her wings fan out and up. This action made the female stop and move up in the water. As the male pasted the guardian she hugged him to her body while shifting her wings.

Next Zea brought herself and Blue Fire out of the water where she dropped him forcing him to do hit the water hard on his stomach. Once the male was back in the cool liquid the guardian brought her wings in and gracefully dove back into the pool. Where the male grab her and forced the zatz against the wall. Elbowing her in the stomach did not hurt Zea because she was using her gills unlike the male who was holding his breath. The guardian broke free and the fight continued.

When Blue Fire tried to throw the female out of the pool but she used her wings and made her way back into the water before leaving the pool's edge. When an hour or so had pasted Zea was still having fun but the male was growing weak. The guardian did not want the male to drown because he was too tired to swim so she decided to end the fight.

Zea grabbed Blue Fire and took to the air but this time when he and everyone thought he she was going to force him into the water the zatz pushed him to the pool's edge and he was not able to fall into the water. As the female dove back into the water the male landed in the dirt. The crowd fell silent and when Zea came to the surface of the water she made sure the fight was done.

Once seeing Blue Fire sit up and look at her, the black one smiled and made her way to the bank. Climbing out of the water the guardian crawled next to her friend who was catching his breath from the battle. "You are a good fighter," the female smiled. "Thank you," the male stated. "You are very graceful in the water," the second in the command voiced. "If you ever want to fight again or you want to practice I would be more than happy too help and join you," Zea whispered. The blue one smiled and agreed.

Both stood and the crowd parted. Next the two fighters made their way to one of the great halls for some water. As the two ate and drank they talked about their pasted. Blue Fire talked about his childhood and Zea talked about her past in the new land. Soon time came for the fun to end as Blue Fire left to make his rounds Zea was left to look about camp.

The day seemed to go by very fast and the same for the days that followed. Zea met many of the Green Falls members and at the end of the week sat down to talk to Tim.

"How did you like you stay with he in the Green Falls Clan?"

"I had a great time thank you, Tim, for all your kindness."

"Do you think you will be joining us anytime soon?"

"Tim, I am sorry to tell you that I do not think that I can join your clan. This is not because of you or the clan but I do not think I could live under the water and never fly in the air or see the stars. I would not be complete with those two things. There are others but the reason are all for me and not your fault."

"You need to pick a clan that not only works for you but also makes you complete. I understand what you are talking about, only a few can live in our world. Living underwater is very hard and stressful on the body and mind."

"If it was alright with you maybe I can come back and visit your clan a few times a year."

"You are welcome in our clan anytime. I will tell my guards you may come into camp now that you know the way though the mazes."

The leader pulled a small object from a pouch on his belt and cupped it in his hands. Next he showed the guardian what the object was while saying," this is our symbol. You may keep it hidden in your belt or wherever but, when you go in the water wear this and everyone will know you are great friend of your clan and no one will dare to mess with you." Then he placed the necklace around Zea and the female looked at metal symbol and then thanked the leader again for all his kindness. The two exchanged words and then the female said her goodbyes.

Blue Fire and Zea swam out of the maze and back into the main river. As the black crouched on the green bank the blue one looked at her from the moving waters. "I had fun this week. I cannot to come back and see you again," the female voiced. "I had fun too. Come back soon," the male told the zatz. The two said there goodbyes and Zea opened her wings and took to the air. As Blue Fire went back into his world the guardian headed home to Dark Star's camp.

Back in the Woods

Zea wanted to take the night of thinking for herself before going home to talk to Bear. Finding a little clearing not far from Dark Star's camp the female decide to stay for the night. After checking the area the guardian felt it was safe to send the night. The black one made a little bed and lay down for the night.

Zea was sleeping strongly when she felt something around he arms and legs. As the rope was pulled tight the female opened her eyes to find her legs and arms were bound with rope. Looking around a male stood above her with an ax. "Snake!" Zea yelled as the ax started to move forward. The guardian rolled out of the way of the moving blade. "What are you doing?" the zatz questioned as she quickly moved her feet and hands together while bring her claws out to rip the rope.

Once free the fighter stood across from the aggressor. "He says I have to put an end to you to end my suffering," Snake answered. "What are you talking about and who is 'he'?" the black one asked. Seeing his old friend the green one broke down in pain and began to cry. Very carefully Zea sat by his side and tried to comfort him. "Talk to me what is going on? What happen to you?" she inquired. "Like you said I left the Stone Clan but I had nowhere nowhere to go but to be a Colin," Snake cried. "I am glad you left the Stone Clan," Zea told Snake who continued, "I was walking in the woods when I saw him and he started to help me." "Who is he?" the female asked. "I have been living with him for the last few weeks but I have been very unhappy.

I was told if I got rid of you I would be content so I set off to find you. Now that I see you I cannot hurt you or fight you," the green one voiced in a shaken tone. "Can I meet his one who took you into his home?" the guardian question. "I am not sure," the green said as he looked away from Zea. "Please, Snake," the female asked. "Fine but I do not he is going to be cheerful to see you," he warned. "Thank you," she spoke softly. The two walked deeper into the woods.

The night continued and soon the dawn was on its way and the sun was coming to play. Deep in the woods hidden was a small hut. Snake got on his knees in front of the door then called out, "I am back great one." Zea looked at him in puzzlement and then at the door, which began to move slowly. Then the zatz heard a voice, "Why did you bring her here when you were supposed to kill her?" "I am sorry but I cannot hurt her," Snake tried to explain. When the door fully open and a red kat in the doorway stating, "You are weak."

The kat was male and had a beard and green eyes. "Lets see if you should live or die," the red male spoke low. Bring his hands to his face he blew and made a noise and after moving his hands in an odd pattern he brought them away from his face each with a die. Shaking the dice he threw them to the ground and after looking at the numbers he called to the air, "She must leave. She is trouble." "Who are you and what gives you the right to decide the fate of others? The female questioned.

"I am Ryan and this is my part of the woods."

"Snake lets leave this place."

"No, Snake go into the hut and start my meal."

Snake went into the hut while looking down at the ground. "What do you want with him?" the female inquired. "He is mine now you should just go but now I know why he likes you," Ryan ordered. "I will not leave him here in your grasped," the guardian voiced. "You are too late for him. I found him wondering the woods alone. I gave him food and a place to stay. Next I started to teach him my ways and how to live deep in the woods," Ryan explained. "You mean you took advantage of his weak state and then started to brainwash him," Zea added. "Everyday he talked about this female he met and lost. How the female left him. I got sooo sick of hearing about this black one who hunted his dreams and thoughts. I told Snake to stop his pain he must kill the one who brings all the pain which is you," the red one told the fighter.

"You cannot treat him like this and I will not let you," Zea warned him. "What are you going to do?" Ryan asked. "I will take him," Zea answered. "Snake come out here I need to talk to you," the red one called. Snake came out of the hut and looked at both Zea and Ryan. The red male spoke, "Do you want to stay here and be safe. Stay with me who has taken you in bringing you no pain and helping you or will you choose to leave with her. The black one who has left you and brought you pain," Ryan spoke strong and loud. Snake did not know what to do.

"Snake, you need to decide for yourself what you want to do with your life. I never met to hurt or leave you. If you never want to see me again I will understand but this is your choice. You are a strong and smart male..." the female began. "Do not listen to her. She is trying to cloud your mind," Ryan interrupted. "Let him think," Zea ordered Ryan. Silence moved into the scene.

Finally Snake spoke, "I do not know what to do my head is spinning." "What is the hard part of choosing, she causing you pain and I help you," Rain asked. "He is making you a slave," Zea started. "Wait, Snake, I want you to be happy. If you will be cheerful here in the deep wood then stay here but if you want to join a clan then come with me," the guardian spoke. The fighter stepped forward and looked into the green one's eyes and whispered, "Snake, I really want you to be joyful. Are you really happy with this Ryan Kat?" Snake's eyes began to water. "If I hurt you let me set it straight and if you do not want to go with me its alright but you cannot stay here if you are unhappy," Zea explained. Snake closed his eyes as Ryan began to yell at him.

After taking a deep breath he opened his eyes and looked at the red one. Then he walked over to Ryan and punched him. "Lets go, Zea," he stated as he began to leave. With a smile she walked by his side hoping he was not too broken. As they left the woods the green one sat on the ground and held his head. "Now I am where I started," he whispered. "No, you are not. Do you want my help or do you want me to leave?" the zatz asked. "How can you help me?" the male inquired. "I can help you find a clan," the black one told him. "Oh, yeah, what clan would want me? Snake question. "The Green Falls Clan might," Zea smiled. "I heard that name before but I do know where that clan is," the green one said. "Would you like me to show you?" the black one asked. "Sure," Snake smiled as Zea helped him to his feet. The two started to walk to the green waterfall while the guardian talked about the water clan.

Once they got to the waters edges Zea pulled out the gift from Tim and placed it in the water. Two guards came to the surface. "Can I speak to Blue Fire or Tim?" the zatz asked. The two guards disappeared under the cool liquid. A few seconds later a blue male came to talk, "You just cannot stay way from me." "Hi, Blue Fire how are you?" Zea laughed. "I am doing well. What can I do for you," the second in command stated. "I was wondering if my friend could talk to Tim," the fighter asked. "Give me a minute," the blue respond.

Next the leader came to the surface of the water. "What can I do for you little one?" he asked. "I know you have been very kind and giving to me but my friend is looking to join a clan and I was thinking this would be a great group for him. If he could, stay with you for a few days that would be great. If you do not want to do this I will understand because you have already been to kind to me," the female answered.

Tim turned to Snake asked spoke, "Are you sure you want to try to join my clan and are you a hard worker?" "Yes, Zea told me about the clan and I would love to join a group like this and yes, I am a very hard worker," Snake told him. "I think very highly of Zea and I trust her judgment. Snake you are welcome to try to join our clan. I will give you two days to spend with my group and then you must decide if you want to join the Green Falls Clan. You are lucky to have such a great and strong friend," the leader exclaim. Snake smiled and thanked his black friend. As Zea thanked the leader again Blue Fire jumped out of the water to meet Snake.

"Should I stay or come back?" the guardian asked. "I think it would be best if you left and came back that way we come really get to know Snake and he can meet us on his own," Tim told the female who smiled. "I will be back in a few days Snake. You think you can handle it?" the female asked. "Thank you for this chance we will see if I can take the water world. I will see you in a few days," the green one told the guardian as they shook hands. Then Zea took to the air letting Snake meet the Green Falls Clan.

The female was not ready to go back to Dark Star's camp so decided to spend the next few days traveling around the land. This way she could see and learn about the new land by herself. Most of her small journey she was in the air that way the fighter did not disturb other clans and see the whole land by air. The black one saw the whole valley and on her last day at dusk flew to the one of the big cliffs. There was a meadow at the top, which led to a lake and then a forest. Checking the meadow and edge of the forest the guardian found that there was no real sign of a clan near the meadow. At the edge of the cliff there was a tree. Sitting against the tree the zatz could see the whole valley.

If she used her white lids she could see the Shadow Clan's meadow. Zea could see almost all other mountains, bodies of water, forests, meadows and clans. When she tired out her black lids the zatz could add a label to all she viewed. As the sun set the female could see smoke stacks in the distance behind her proving to her that there were clans on top of the cliff but there were at least a day's walk. The guardian looked at the land and was blissful she had found this place. That night she slept under the tree and the stars.

The next morning Zea flew to the Green Falls Clan. Landing on the green bank the brought her wings in and prepared to enter the water. Placing the necklace around her neck the guardian jumped into the cool waters. Getting the okay from the guards the female headed down the maze and found herself in the great hall. Snake was there to greet her. They climbed up to one of the meeting rooms. There they sat down to talk. "Snake, how do you like this clan," the female started.

"I love this clan. Thank you again for never giving up on me. After I am done talking to you Tim is going to join us and then I am going to ask to pledge to become a member."

"I am glad you a happy again and I do not mean to bring back old problems but what was the whole trying to kill me thing?"

"I am soo sorry Zea. When I first saw you I like you. The thought of never seeing you caused me pain. Then when I heard you were joining the group I was overjoyed. I was having the best time of my life spending time with you and learning about you. You are a great teacher. Then I found out what the Mountain Clan was going to do with you and I was frustrated with clan and then myself. I could not stay in a place that reminds me of you so I went to a clan that was the opposite of you so I would not think of you. The last thing I ever thought would ever happened did, you showed up in the clan. All my emotions came back and started fighting with myself. I told myself you would never be with me after our past in the Mountain Clan. Then you told me your thoughts and I started an internal battle.

Next I left the stone clan and longed for a friend. Ryan showed up one day and gave me tonics, which eased my pain and helped me to think less of you. Then when Ryan asked me to do something I found it hard to say no. One day he told me to find you and end my pain by killing you. I was so lost and my head was going crazy. I found you and could not hurt you. My emotions came back and I started to think about all the things you said and my choices in my life. The tonics had been eating at my mind taking my memories away one by one. My mind told me to stay with Ryan but my heart told me to go with you so I went with my heart, you. Look I am sorry for everything I have been... I guess... I was weaker than I thought. I give you my word I will never hurt you again as long as I live."

"I forgive you, Snake."

"Thank you."

"So, you are going to stay here and live peacefully right?"

"Yes, if Tim will let me I will join this clan."

"I am happy you are once again at harmony and I am sorry if I caused you any pain."

Zea stood, looked outside the room and called for Tim who joined them a few minutes later. Snake asked to join the clan and Tim gave him his approval. Once everything was settled. The zatz said goodbye to all her friends again and left the Green Falls Clan. Finally Zea was heading home and she was very tired and was not sure if she was ready to face Bear.

Taking Control

Zea landed a few yards away from camp. Walking into camp everyone was happy to see her returned and in good health. Bear was relieved but upset with his daughter's actions. He continued his work as the female walked to Dark Star's hut to check in with him. "Welcome back little one did you have fun?" the leader asked. "Yes, I helped an old friend who was lost and helped bond my friendship in the Green Falls Clan. I thank you again for letting me go on my journey," the female answered. "Bear was not pleased with me to let you go on your little trip. I think you should talk to him as soon as you can," Dark Star continued. "I will," the zatz responded. "Now, get out and go play," the leader ordered.

The guardian smiled and walked out of the hut. Robby, Roberd and Josh were back from their journey. They all sat down to eat the second meal of the day. All four of them talked about their last adventures. When they were done they all went to work. Zea went to help Krist who was delighted to see her. Once night came the clan sat down to the last meal of the day. Soon time had come for the clan to sleep. The guardian walked to her hut knowing Bear would be there.

Walking into the dark hut Zea looked around for her father. He was sitting at the table looking into the fire. The daughter took her seat by Bear and all that could be heard was the crackling fire. "Bear, before you become to angry at me I must explain this. I have been fighting many battles since I came to this land. Many of them have been internal. I would be lying to my lost ones and myself and I cannot do that. As soon as I was free from Jabo's reign I began training to be a… 'fighter'. I have worked too hard and given too much to hide who I am. Out of respect to you I will not use my word but fighter but to me that is a lower rank and not who I am. If you do not want to tell me want the true meaning of the word or what they are I will understand but only hope to know one day. Just like one day I wish to share with you my last big difference. I needed to get out and away from this camp to clear my mind and realize I must be patient and will know soon enough what a 'fighter' is but please do not tell me to hide what I am because I cannot do it. If one asked me who I am I will not lie. I cannot lie. I am sorry if that hurts you I mean no disrespect. I will use the word fighter unless I am asked who I am and then I will not lie but I will not use the word unless needed for you. Please do not be mad at me or punish me but I will do as you wish. I should have told you I was leaving and for that I am sorry. That is all I have to say right now, Bear," The guardian explained to her father.

He said nothing but only looked at the fire. After a few minutes Zea spoke, "If you did not wish me to speak then I wish to sleep." There was still no answer so the guardian stood and found her way to her bed where she laid down for the night. Zea woke up with a cold sweat and shaking. The fighter had another nightmare about Jabo going after her and her family. Sitting up in bed the female took a few deep breaths trying to clam herself.

The guardian stood and made her way outside the hut. Leaning against the hut the zatz looked up at the night sky seeing the stars and moon. As she gazed upwards her thoughts were racing. Bear, who she was, her past, the Shadow Clan, Snake and more all flashed in her mind and as the night moved forward the fighter decided she had to get some rest. Just as she was standing to enter the hut her ears perked up hearing footsteps.

"What are you doing out hear little one?" Bear asked. "I could not sleep," the black one answered. "Did you have another nightmare?" the father questioned. "Yes," the female responded. "Do you want to talk about it?" Bear inquired while sitting next to Zea who told him, "I do not know." The two sat in silence for a while till the male broke the stillness, "Are you sure you do not want to talk about your dream?" "I do not think it matters. I just have to live to deal with my dreams. There is no way you can picture what I see in my mind, right now," Zea started. "What do you mean, right now?" Bear questioned. "Never mind," the female stated as she stood. "Pretend like I never said anything," Zea voiced as she quickly walked into the hut.

Bear followed the female into the hut and to her bed. "What is going on, Zea?" he asked. "I am not ready to share it with you. I am afraid. My heart races just thinking of it," the black one explained. "I told you that you never have to fear me," Bear told his daughter. "Right now you are upset with me and not fully sharing everything with me. I do not feel ready to share this with you. I do not know what to tell you," the fighter whispered. "Look, a ... a ... 'fighter' is a type of Kat who is always in trouble. There are a group of them and they are dangerous. Many want this group and if ever captured they are almost always killed. They are rebels yet every young male wishes to join the group. I say this because no female has ever joined the group.

The males take advantage of young females like you. To leaders and some groups to be a 'fighter' is not a good thing but to every young male, even me, a dream. That is a fighter and I am not just telling you this so you will share with me but I just did not know how to explain what a fighter is. Why are you called a fighter where you come from?" the father voiced in a low tone. "Are they are good or bad group?" the black one inquired. "They do what they wish but over all I would say they do more good than bad," Bear answered. "Thank you for sharing this with me Bear. I am still sorry I hurt you," the guardian said while looking into Bear's eyes.

"Do not worry about it my little one. I forgive you just never do that again and I hope you learned something while you were out of camp," he comforted. "I did and I promise never again," the zatz smiled. "You need to get some sleep, now rest little one," the father ordered. Zea lay down and closed her eyes as Bear sat by her side till she fell asleep then he too fell into the land of dreams after returning to his resting place.

The next morning came very quickly and like all other morning the fighter rose with the sun. Then she went on her morning run with Krist. "Do you want to stop by the river for a drink?" Krist question. "Sure," the black one responded. The duo jogged to the moving waters where the stopped for a cool drink. The guardian's ears moved to the sound of footsteps. Turning to the sound the female met eyes with a smiling face. The fighter stood in front of Krist holding him back from the new group in now coming from the bushes.

"Let me by," Krist whispered strongly. "Wait," Zea snapped. "How are you my little one?" Pyro smiled. "What do you want?" the female asked. "Clam down little one I just want to talk. Sit down I do not want to start a fight," the Shadow Kat stated. "I am not going to sit or stay here with you. I am leaving unless you start talking real fast," the zatz warned.

"Now, now there is no reason to get distressed. I have just come to give you some great new. I am delighted to tell you that you are now looking at the leader of the Shadow Kats. My father has passed and now I have taken his place," the leader spoke in a loud voice. "Here this is for your leader," Pyro continued while tossing a package at Krist's feet. "Well, I am sorry for your loss and congratulations. I do not mean to be disrespectful but I must be going back to camp," Zea stated calmly. "As you wish, my love," the male told the young female. "I wanted to tell you personally that I now have my own clan. Are you sure you do not want to come visit me for a few days or more?" Pyro asked. "I am sure. I must be getting home now, goodbye, Pyro," the guardian voiced very strongly as she has moved away from the group. "Let them pass," the leader ordered his group who did his command. As the two friends passed the Shadow Kat spoke, "Till me meet again which I hope is soon." The fighter did not stop moving but continued to jog home with her friend by her side as fast as she could.

When the duo entered camp they both went straight to Dark Star's hut where they gave him the package and told the leader about their run in with the new leader. Dark Star asked to be alone and told Zea to find her father and tell him to join him. The female did the leader what was asked of her. Soon Bear and Dark Star were in a meeting as the rumors ran through camp.

Later that day Dark Star called a clan meeting. There he spoke about the death of Dark Flame and that Pyro has asked for a gathering. Zea looked at Roberd who told her a gathering was when all leaders came together to show respect for the fallen leader. Despite what his gut is thinking the right thing to do was to go to the meeting. He explained to the clan that as he was gone Bear would be in charge and he would be taking a few with him. They would leave in a few days. Last he told the group if there were any questions they could come to him. The group left the meeting and went back to there normal chores.

A few days later Dark Star left with a few of his best fighters as Bear was left to lead the group. That night Zea talked to Bear. "What will happen at this meeting," she asked. "All the leaders who go show a respect to the fallen leader and the new one. Knowing he might try something. Even though Dark Flame was over all not a moral kat he was strong and a good leader for his clan therefore should get respect even from his enemies. I am guessing Dark Flame would have been honored if you went but Dark Star felt that it would be too dangerous with Pyro having so much power," Bear explained. "Thank you," Zea stated.

A few days later Dark Star returned and told the group all about the meeting, which went well. There was a great turn out for Dark Flame. The leader also told the clan that Pyro was asking about Zea and was thankful for the respect. Once all the questions were answered the clan went back to work.

Zea did not know how to feel knowing that Dark Flame was gone and Pyro was now leader. Many ideas raced in her mind. Bear noticed that his daughter was troubled and asked to speak with her. "What is on your mind little one?" he asked. "I am worried with a whole clan behind him, Pyro will attack me. There is nothing holding him back now. I also do not have a clan and I wish to join a group more than anything," the female explained. "I am sure everything will be fine. Dark Star is working very hard to find you a good home and our clan will not let the Shadow Clan touch you. Do you worry about what you cannot control? Do not let Pyro worry you because then you are letting him win, he is in your mind," Bear comforted. "You are right, thank you father," Zea smiled before giving Bear a hug. The two talked for a while longer and then they went back to work. Soon the zatz relaxed and was back playing and working in the clan.

No More Males

The next few weeks went by very fast and with every passing day the guardian wished to join the clan. The day of her birth was coming up according to the new time frame. In her eyes Zea would be 18 and half while others would see her as 19. Zea was hoping no one would call her little one. In the zatx culture they are considered little ones till they are 18 but this was a new land. –Computer?- the female asked.

-- Yes,--

--Do you think I should consider myself 19 or 18 1/2 ? —

--you want my judgment? —

-I truly would —

-- All though you are trying to make this land your home and take away as many difference as possible, the fact is we most likely age differently. I think you should count this celebration and your 18.5 day of birth. If you keep up with the new number system soon you will not look your age. –

--That makes a lot of sense. I like your logic Thank you. –

The fighter could not wait for that day to come. The female worked very hard living with all the males in the group and did not think she was missing anything but did wonder what it would be like to live with a female. Her days with Rain flashed in her mind and the sharing of female problems and things that males do not how to deal with made the black one smile. Zea did her best to continue working hard and looking for a new clan to join.

Soon the day of Zea's birth was here and she was hoping no one would mention her age. That day everything was normal. In the morning Krist went on a run with Zea and then after a light meal the clan went into action for the day. Zea went around to different members of the clan asking if she could help in any way and most of them had little chores for her to do. Last the female walked over to Krist hut where he did not have much for the little one to do.

Overall it was a lazy day for the guardian who did her best to stay busy. The female made her way to Pitch's hut. Entering the zatz gave a sign of respect. "Hello Zea how can help you?" the male asked. "You keep all the records and history of this clan correct?" she inquired. "Indeed," he responded. "Have you written about me?" the female continued her questioning. "I have," Pitch answered. "When you write about today what age will I be turning?" Zea probed. "Have not thought about it," the clan member voiced as he pulled a book off one of his many shelves. Opening it he examined his writing. By my calculation you should be 19 but I also recall we found out age differently," Pitch remembered. "I think it would be best if you mark I am 18 and half," the female told her friend. The two talked for a while longer on reasonings and other historical facts.

Later she asked Dark Star if she could go reflect by the river but the leader felt it was too dangerous. After telling one of the guards the female walked into the middle of the golden meadow where she sat down to think about her past. Tears came to her eyes Zea thought about her lost family. The zatz prayed and asked her loved ones forgiveness and for them to watch over her as her life continued in this new land. The bight sun warmed Zea's black body. A few hours later the female finished her reflection and slowly walked back to camp where she continued to try to help her friends.

When night was falling the clan lit large fires and a feast was laid out on two main tables. Once the sun was gone a large celebration was held in Zea's honor. There were gifts and stories. Then a great game of gimme broke out in camp. The guardian had one of the best nights in her life. When dawn was on its way the clan was still playing and having a great time. When the sun was rising Dark Star clammed the group down and the crowd rested for a few hours before work would start again.

The next day the clan awoke slowly. Krist was still sleeping when Zea went for her run so she stayed in sight of the guards. At the first meal of the day the guardian thanked her friends again for the great night.

Midmorning four outsiders walked into camp and after talking to the guards went to Dark Star's hut. Rumors spared who was in camp and Zea became very nervous. Bear found the fighter and began to talk, "I am sure you realized that Dark Star and I did not have a gift for you last night. Well if all goes well then you will get your gift today." "Really?!?" the black one asked excitedly.

As the group was in the meeting Zea could not wait. Finally about mid-afternoon Dark Star came out of the hut and looked for Zea. After finding the fighter he invited her to join him in the meeting. With a smile the zatz walked into the hut with the leader by her side. Sitting on his side of the desk she not sat across a small group of EnyoRheas. One of the EnyoRheas was their leader, Sunflower, who was mainly there to talk to Zea.

"After talking with Dark Star, the times I am spoken with you, Bear and hearing rumors of the land I am here to give you my permission to pledge to join my clan. The real question now is would you still like to try to be an EnyoRhea?" the female leader asked the fighter. "I would be honored to pledge," the zatz smiled. "I have heard you do not have a lot of experience living with females," Sunflower continued. "This is true but I am a hard worker and do not give up easily. I would love the chance too for once in my life live with females but I will miss my friends here in this clan," the guardian responded. The group talked for a few more minutes and then Zea was given a few minutes to say goodbye to all her friends.

A very fast meeting of the clan was held where Zea told the group she would miss them and hoped to visit them sometime in the future. She thanked them for all they had done for her the female spoke very loud and clear. Everyone cheered when she finished speaking.

Last the daughter spent a few last minutes with her father. "I am going to miss you and I hope not to see you too soon," the guardian smiled. "I will miss you too and you come back when every you wish because you are always welcome," Bear told her. "Thank you, I do not know how I will ever repay you for all you have done for me," the zatz whispered. "Just be my daughter and be strong," the father voiced. "I promise Bear, soon very soon, I will share with you my last secret. I will come see you as soon as I can," the black one promised. "Be good," the father ordered. "Always, always," Zea smiled as she hugged Bear. Holding hands they walked out of their hut and walked to the group of outsides who welcomed Zea to walk with them out to Dark Star's Clan.

As the group of five entered the woods they were silent listening for changes in the forest voices. When Zea took her first steps into the new camp the sun was setting. Sunflower called a meeting of the clan. Sunflower stood in front of her peers and told the clan of about 75 Zea was now pledging to join their group. After the speech the group sat down to a feast and then as the group settled down Zea and the leader went to the main meeting hut.

Once in the small room the leader began to speak, "I will be giving you a sister to follow and live with before you become a member. If you have any problems or concerns you can talk to your roommate then if needed come to me. She will give you all the rules and is responsible for you. She is one of my best fighters and trusted friends. Do you have any questions?" "No, thank you again," Zea voiced as she gave a sign of respect. The two left the hut and jump, climbed and glided to a hut across the camp. Here is your home for the next few weeks, good luck and have fun," the leader told the newcomer as she left to do her work.

Zea looked at her new home. The hut looked a little smaller than Bears. The walls were wood and the roof was woven out of leaves. The guardian knocked on the door and waited for an answer. A few seconds later, the door opened with a smiling face. "Welcome, to my home, come on inside," she voiced happily. The zatz walked into the dim hut. Looking around the female could see there was a main room with a hanging fire pit, table, chairs, dresser and a second room with a bunked bed, a chair and a very small table.

The dark furred kat showed the newcomer her warm hut and then they both sat by the fire to talk. "Hi, my name is Liz, I am sure you remember. I hope we will soon be like sisters. I was born here and lived in this clan all my life. As you look at each EnyoRhea you will see each full member has a necklace with our symbol. The younger ones who are not fully of age have an anklet or a bracelet. Also each of the members who are of age to fight have bands around their arm and these bands show the rank of each fighter.

The beads, marks and color show the level and what the fighter has done. Once you become an EnyoRhea then you can start working for your armband. See on mine you can see I have been a guard for five years, been in one war, twelve battles and have been training others for about a year now. My mother is Cricket and she lives a few huts away and my father is from Dark Star's Clan. His name is Lighting. He visits me on my important days and is a good father despite being a few hours away and I know he loves me. I have no sisters or brothers. I have led a normal childhood. How are you?" the kat told her new friend.

"Well, I did not had a normal childhood, sadly. If this could stay between us, but as a child I was a slave and I was not always treated with kindness. Because of my childhood I have nightmares that I must warn you about if we will be sleeping in the same room. I ran away with the help of two male friends and over time the elements took them from me one at a time. Then I traveled here where the Shadow Kats took me then where in time I escaped ran into Bear who led me to Dark Star's Clan. Soon I met clans and joined the Mountain Clan. Blizzard and his group betrayed me. I was back in the Dark Flame's hands where again I had to escape. Dark Flame captured Bear to get me but that only fueled my escape. Once back in safety and rested I went back to talk to the Mountain Clan. On my way home the Stone Clan took me in and I met Erik and Chris. Long story short I made my way back to Dark Star's Clan where I spent the rest of my time till now talking to other clans and helping Dark Star's Clan. Then I came here and now I am with you," the female explained.

"You have had quiet a different childhood. Now I understand why you never talked about your past when to two clans got together. I heard you are good warrior," the dark furred one continued. "Yes, I am a very good fighter. I have been taught combat skills since a young age," the female smiled. The two talked for while longer before the EnyoRhea began to discuss the rules of the camp. The clan was very ordered.

"When you are pledging the others might give you are hard time but its all in good fun and hazing happens to everyone when they are coming of age. Also you cannot be a guard unless you are with another guard. If there are any battles you cannot participate. Also you cannot leave the camp at anytime unless you have my approval or Sunflowers no one else. The others might try to get you to break one to the rules. You should always be one the last ones at the table to eat food and just be respectful which I am sure will be no trouble for you. Your job while pledging will be to help all members with their chores. To be honest with you they will most likely give you the hard or dirty jobs that they do not want to do themselves. That is way the clan loves pledges.

No member should ever physical hurt you that is not acceptable and tell me or Sunflower as soon as possible," Liz informed Zea who listened to all the rules and told her new friend she understood all the guidelines. The two talked for a while longer and then both went to sleep. Zea slept on the bottom bed while Liz climbed to the upper bed. Then both fell asleep.

In the morning Zea woke with the sun and because she could not run around camp she did some excises in the other room. A few minutes later Liz came into the room with a smile on her face. "Are you ready for the first meal of the day?" She asked. "Sure," the zatz voiced. The two left the hut and they headed to the first meal of the day where most of the clan was gathering.

Zea sat where the food was. That way when the food was passed around she would be the last to be served. The zatz found that most of the food was taken but she was happy for what food was left. Then she started her day helping the clan where she could.

Liz was right, the clan loved to pick on the pledges. Zea met another pledge she was from another all female clan across the valley called the Fangs. She was not pleased with the way she was treated and wanted to try a new clan. She had been trying to join the clan for a few weeks now and was use to the treatment but she was glad Zea was there to take a lot of the attention away from her. Although the guardian was doing the grunt work she was happy to get a chance to meet and work with all the different members. The EnyoRheas saw the new female's joyful attitude and worked her harder. With each passing day the zatz met more members and became closer to Liz.

One day she was working with Sarah who was in charge of training the young guards. She was one to the best warriors in the clan. Zea cleaned and set up the fight area and also cleaned the weapons. When there was a small pause between lessons and Zea finished cleaning they sat down to talk. "How are you holding up?" Sarah asked. "I am doing well. I am having fun. I like the labor for the most part and I would rather be working than doing nothing. I really like working with my hands and teaching," Zea smiled. "I have heard of some of your battles and they are great stories. Bear told one of them to the leaders while the two clans were having our meeting. If I remember correctly it was about your first run in with the Green Falls clan," Sarah explained.

"Yes, I have had a few good fights," the guardian smiled. "Have you been in many battles?" Zea continued. "I have been in a few," Sarah answered. Just as Sarah was going to talk about one of her battles a group of young fighters came in for training. The lesson began with Zea on the sidelines and Sarah in the middle. The guardian watched the Kat's fighting techniques and saw the good and bad points. The day went by very fast and soon she was sitting next to Liz eating the last meal of the day.

Another day Zea worked with Taiylight and Mysteaic. They were in charge of scouting the area. The duo roamed around the clan's territory making sure everything was as it should be. Now the guardian would get a chance to see the whole territory and meet two new friends and this made her very happy and excited.

As the trio walked most of the time they were very quiet but they did have a few conversation. Taiylight and Mysteaic made the black one carry their packs. Taiylight was a light colored fur was patched with blues, yellow, pink, orange and purple and her eyes were light gray. Mysteaic fur was also patched but her colors were dark colors of shades of green, tan, black and gray and her eyes were gold and sliver. The two EnyoRheas loved their job on the move everyday hunting.

Zea had not been on the move all day in a long time and she loved it even if she had to carry all the packs. When evening was on its way two outsiders walked into the woods. Quickly and silently the three watchers took to the trees. Mysteaic went to the opposite side that Zea and Taiylight were on as they followed the outsiders. "We allow some Colins on our land but they talk with us and we have a relationship with them.

These two are new Colins or from another clan," Taiylight whispered. The EnyoRhea told the guardian she was to stay in the treetops unless called by name to come out of hiding. Then the zatz watched as the two females circled the two outsiders and carefully talked to each other using hand motions and birdcalls if needed. When the duo was ready they jumped down on the two new comers and forced them to the ground.

After checking for weapons and clan they tied the two up and started asking them questions while Zea watched with open eyes. Within a few minutes the talk was over and the two left the forest while both EnyoRheas returned to the treetops. Nether Mysteaic nor Taiylight told Zea what happen and she did not ask. The time had come for the trio to head back to camp and the next teams of watchers were already out on the territory. By the time the three got back to camp the clan was just sitting down for the last meal of the day. After dinner Mysteaic and Taiylight talked to Sunflower while Zea went with Liz to talk and have fun for the rest of the night.

Zea also had the chance to work with Dream and Meadow who were in charge of food. The guardian worked all day with food. The guardian even had to chance to make some old recipes from her past that the EnyoRheas had never seen tasted before and while most of them were uneasy at first but once they has some were overjoyed to have something new.

Zea showed her new friends how to make new kinds of spices and food. The zatz enjoyed cooking but did not wish to do it everyday because the guardian cooked for most of her childhood for Jabo. The guardian was happy that her new friends enjoyed her cooking. Like many other days that day went by very fast and the zatz had fun meeting new friends.

The next day Zea worked with Sunray who was the doctor of the clan. Sunray has a golden color fur coat with a black stripe down her back with blue eyes. She was very kind and gentle Kat with a loving touch. The guardian followed the doctor around clan for most of day and helped others who were hurt. The zatz also learned how the make tonics with the new plants round her and Zea also showed Sunray some of her tonics. Both were happy to find new ways of helping others. For the fighter the day went by slowly but she did have fun meeting others and helping them but she longed for more action.

Next the black zatz spent the day with Avis who was working on her art. She was drawing mythical creatures for a young female who day of birth was coming up in a few days. Zea had a great time drawing and helping the EnyoRhea clean and hold her paint. "How did you become a member of this clan?" the black one asked. "I was born into the EnyRheas. My mother's name is Nightsong and my father's name is Starfire. My mother lives across the camp and my father lives in a clan a few days walk from here called the Night Clan. I have a little brother, Spider, and he lives with my father. I see him once or so a year. How about you?" Avis spoke slowly as she focused on her art.

"I have no family but Bear. Before I came here I had a mother, father, and older brother but they passed away when I was young. My father was Domatu, mother, Sunyro and brother was Gyro. I miss them but I am glad I had the chance to meet them before they passed," Zea voiced. "Is that way you came here because your family was gone?" the EnyoRhea asked. "Kind of I had more than one reason for travel but yea, I guess. If I had stayed there I would have died or became very unhappy," the guardian explained. "I am sorry for your loss," Avis told the black one.

The two talked all day but Zea did her best to be very vague about her past. They both worked very hard and took a few breaks during the day but Avis's life was very relaxed unless she took too many jobs at once. After a long day of pictures and stories the guardian sat down to the last meal of the day.

As the weeks went by Zea found herself more and more comfortable with the all female clan and soon began to enjoy a life without males but she did miss her friends in Dark Star's Clan. Each night if there was not a game or meeting the guardian spent her time talking to Liz. The EnyoRhea now was use to the fighter's nightmares and helped when she could. Out of all the females the dark furred one knew the most about the zatz's pasted.

Soon the black one felt she would be able to share some of her differences with her new friend. They talked about almost everything. And one night the topic of the guardian's differences came up in the conversation. "I heard you are different physically. I have heard some odd stories," Liz began. "What kind of stories?" Zea questioned. "Well, something about your wings and eyes. Oh, and I heard you can stay underwater for a long time. I mean since I have known you I have never seen your wings but in almost every story I hear you have wings," the EnyoRhea answered.

"Well, where to begin. I hope you know I would like to keep my difference between you and I if that is okay with you," the black one started. "Of course but if I feel Sunflower should know I will tell you," Liz agreed with her friend. "Where would you like me to began?" the guardian asked. "Your eyes," the EnyoRhea responded. "I have five different eyelids and each one is a different color and gives me a different vision. I will show you now," Zea paused.

Then showed Liz her white lid, then her red, next was the blue and last were her green and black lids. After Zea had her normal vision back with her green eyes she continued talking. "My best vision is in my black lids and my blue lids I only use when I am underwater," the zatz explained. "That is amazing. They almost glow, your eyes. Your black eyelids are scary," the dark one spoke as the other laughed. "What next?" the guardian smiled. "Your ... your wings," Liz suggested. "I told you about my past and that is why I keep my wings hidden. I told you about Jabo but what I did not describe fully was how he treated me, which was not well. He hurt me many times and took his anger out on me. My scars cover my back, which was his main way of hurting me.

I will show my wings now but just so you know they are bigger because I can fly not just glide. I guess I will show you now. Oh, and if you want you can touch my scars or not I do not mind but most Kats I show like to touch and I am not sure why," the fighter told her friend as she turned around to open her wings. Zea flexed her muscles and brought her artwork of scars into view.

Silence took over the room as the two stood there frozen in time. Finally Liz moved forward slowly and like all before her slow ran her fingers across the young one's back. After sometime passed Zea stepped forward, brought her wings back into their resting spot and cleared her throat. "I wish to tell and show the clan my back so I may walk around with my wings free and feel closer to the clan but I am not sure how I would bring the topic up with the group," the black one broke the stillness. "Wow,

I had no idea you had so many scars. Your nightmares make more sense now. I am so sorry you had to go though that," the dark furred one voiced.

"I guess I could set up a meeting with you, Sunflower and I and we could talk about your back if you felt safe enough," Liz continued. "Sure, I think that would be the best path to take," Zea smiled. "I will do that for you but, it is getting late and tomorrow is another full day. Thank you for our talk tonight and I will see you in the morning," Liz told her friend as she stood, stretched and made her way to her bed. The guardian put out the fire and went to the land of dreams.

A few days later Zea sat cross from Sunflower with Liz by her side. "Zea shared with me something very personal the other night and she would like to tell you. Later if possible she would like to share herself with the group if you think it is okay," Liz explained to her leader. "Of course, what would you like to tell me," Sunflower voiced as she turned and looked at Zea. "Well, this is hard for me to talk about a lot but before I came here I was a slave I had a master named; Jabo and he did not always treat me well. As you noticed I always keep my wings to my back. I do this because Jabo scared my back over the years I was with him. He liked to take his anger out on me and well, my wings hide my scars well. I guess all that is left is to show you my back. My wings are larger because I can fly with them not just glide," the guardian spoke softy as she stood and took a deep breath as she turned her back not facing her two friends.

After silence slowly crept into the room the guardian took another deep breath and relaxed her back muscles bring her scars into sight. Sunflowers eyes widened at the artwork. "I would like to share my back with the group so I can walk around camp with my wings free and also become closer with the clan," the zatz explained. The room became still. "What do you think of her idea?" Liz's voice cut the air. "I think that would be a great idea. Give me sometime to think how I want to set this meeting up with the group," the leader stated. Both Liz and Zea thanked Sunflower for her time and then they left the hut for the day. Zea felt much better knowing she could not only trust her friends in the EnyoRheas but also began to share her secrets without fear.

Time went by and soon the time had come for the zatz to share with clan her wings. Sunflower talked with the group and told them about Zea's pasted. The leader told her group how the young one was a slave and had a master who was not always kind. Last Sunflower explained to her clan that the black one's wings were different and she had some scaring on her back.

After asking the group for their respect on the delicate situation the leader finished speaking she turned to Zea and asked her to join her in front of the crowd.

When the group as silent and the guardian was left alone she took a deep breath, thanked the group for their understanding, turned around so her back was now facing her friends and once again flex her muscles bring her scars into view. Some in the clan whispered at the sight of the artwork. The guardian felt relived when she was showing her difference to her new friends. The moment had come and passed and there was nothing to take it back.

A few minutes later Sunflower gave Zea a sign telling her she could stop. The black female simply turned around keeping her wings out in view. Next the leader came and talked to the group one more time. Sunflower talked about Zea and how hard it was to show her pain to the group. If they had any questions they could talk to Zea but they must remember to be respectful. When Sunflower had finished speaking the group went to the first meal of the day. Throughout the day a few Kats came to talk to Zea or to show her their respect but over all day was normal and went by fast as usual.

With each passing day Zea wondered if she would be able to join the clan. The young guardian had almost worked with everyone in the tribe. There were only a few who she would not work with such as Sunflower. The fighter also pondered what would happen when she worked with everyone. The zatz felt very lucky to even have the chance of working with the EnyoRheas and hope to join their group despite having no males.

Sunflower thought the little one was doing quite will adjusting to a full female clan. Everything was going as planed. In the back of the fighters mind she began to think of Pyro. No one was talking about the Shadow Clan lately and Zea knew the new leader would most like not attack Dark Star's Clan because of what happen to his father but she still wanted to know what was going on in the troublesome clan.

The guardian felt safe in the all female clan and knew that Pyro would not try to attack her while she was in their company. Liz also told the young one that the Shadow Clan has never outright attacked a member of the EnyoRheas. This also eased the black one's mind. Zea could not believe how far she had come since she came to this new land and all the friends she had made and foes. All that was left for was to fine a clan and that dream was well on its way of becoming true.

A Flirt

One day out of nowhere the other pledge dropped out of the clan. She told the group she loved her time here but felt like the clan was not a good match for her. She thanked everyone for all the lessons they gave her and left. This was a surprise to the whole group who was sad to see their friend leave but content knowing she was going to be happy. That night at the last meal of the day the clan gave a blessing for the lost pledge and then everything went back to normal.

Now that Zea had a chance to work with everyone in the clan the fighter got a chance to decide what job would make her fulfilled in the camp. After much thinking the guardian decided to be a guard, hunter or a fixer. She would do what ever Sunflower felt she would work best for the clan but those were her top choices. After a few days of helping the clan where she could the guardian was place in the fighter team where she would shadow the main group, which protected the camp, the guards, territory watchers, trainers and weapons. The warrior was overjoyed that someday she might be an EnyoRhea soldier.

One evening when work was done for the day Zea was in Liz's hut relaxing when her dark furred friend came into the small room giggling. "What is going on?" Zea inquired. "I just talked to a friend and there has been this male I really like and I found out he likes me as well. Tonight he wants to meet me for the first time!" Liz said with great excitement. "Are you going to go meet him?" the guardian asked. "Well, I really want too but ... I do not want anyone in the clan to know I am seeing him," the Liz spoke while looking down at the wood floor.

"Well, I do not know that many males. I will keep the secret for you. I can go with you and watch your back because you know I am a good fighter. If you want I will not even look at your male," the black one suggested. The EnyoRhea thought about her friend's idea and after a long silent pause a smile grew on her face as she agreed. That night the guardian would leave the camp for the first time in almost a year. After the last meal of the day both females went to their hut to pack and get ready to leave.

Once most of the clan was asleep for the night they set out to meet the male. Zea climbed to the top of the hut with Liz by her side. Then the fighter took to the air and then helped her friend also take flight. Soon the duo was in the air and both were joyful to be free of camp. When Liz felt they were safe from being spotted from the guards she landed and began to walk.

Zea stayed in the air out of sight. When they entered a forest the guardian's flight skills were put to the test as she flew in the treetops silently. Then Liz came to a beautiful waterfall hidden by the trees. Zea was to remain silent and out of sight until her friend gave a signal to come out of the trees. The zatz watched as Liz cautiously walked up to the waters edge and wait for the male. The female wondered why the two wanted so much secretly but she was not going to ask.

A few minutes later a shadow moved in the bushes across the river. Keeping her eye out, Zea watched as Liz called out into the air and a few seconds later a male appeared from the dark. He was a very shady green with black marking throughout his body and a black stripe going from his nose to the tip of his tail. The two kats talked for a long time getting to know each other.

The guardian stayed alert and a little over an hour later Zea heard a noise. Letting her black lids fall into place she could see there as another joining the party. The black female quickly made a bird called communicating to Liz there as something happening. The EnyoRhea talked to the male who answered back while doing hand motions. The dark furred female made another call to her friend telling Zea everything was okay. The two talked for a while longer and then said their goodbyes. Liz ran off into the forest with the guardian running above her in the treetops. Once they reached the meadow the fighter helped her friend take flight and they went home.

The next morning Liz was tired. "How come you are not yawning?" she asked Zea who replied, "I guess I need less sleep." Both laughed and went to the first meal of the day. The fighter joined Sarah for the day. As they talked and worked their friendship grew. Sarah soon saw how strong the zatz was and her great combat skills. The black female helped her friend with her techniques.

During one of their breaks Zea asked her friend what weapons they have to protect themselves. The light colored furred female answered, "We have different kinds of blades, spears, ropes, chains, and darts with tonics. I am sure you have seen all of the weapons that all the clans use. Why do you ask?" "I was just inquiring because we used some different kinds of weapons back in my home and I was just wondering if you had them here in this new land," the zatz explained. "I see. What kind of weapons?" the EnyoRhea asked. "I will talk to Sunflower and see if I can make some for you," the young female voiced. "That would be great," Sarah smiled as the next group came in for their lesson.

That night Zea got a chance to talk to Liz. As they sat by the fire the guardian started the conversation. "How did it go the other night? I did not listen what you were saying to the other male," the zatz questioned. A smile grew on the EnyoRhea's face as she answered, "I like him. I really hope our relationship goes somewhere. He is everything I want in a male and I love his personality." "Can I know his name or is he just 'the male'?" the black one asked. "I really cannot talk about who he is because of his clan," the dark furred female spoke very quietly. "I understand. He is very hansom and you two look cute together," the zatz told her friend who smiled and thanked her. They talked long into the night.

With each passing day Zea felt more at home and her nightmares did not visit her as much and this made both Zea and Liz very delighted. Whenever a messenger went to talk to Dark Star's Clan the guardian kindly requested that the EnyoRheas gave her father a letter, which she wrote. At first the traveling females said, "No," but as Zea became tighter with the group soon the answer changed to, "Sure."

The zatz's day of birth was coming and the female did not know if the EnyoRheas realized her time difference. During one of her many meeting with Sunflower the guardian explained her ageing difference and the leader was amazed at first. Sunflower thanked the little one for sharing the variance with her and then asked her when her next birthday was. Zea smiled as she stated, "I will be the age of 19 in a few weeks. I think three weeks." "In our culture Kats choose their clan as young as 16 and in most cases are settled by 21. You are on a great track. Once a young one as joined a family they are considered of age. At the age of 21 it is rare to be called 'little one'," the friend voiced.

"So, no one will call me little one after I join your family?" Zea questioned. "I guess, if you are of age then if the one who calls you 'little one' if they are not your friend or a respected elder then I guess you could consider it as in insult," the leader explained. "You have done well over that last few months. Keep up the good work, little one, I will see you around camp," Sunflower continued. The guardian gave the leader a sign of respect and left to work with Sarah.

The day went by very fast and soon Zea was walking to the last meal of the day. That night the zatz sat by Avis. As they ate the two females talked about artist's latest artwork. Avis was working on a piece about placing different shapes together and seeing what happens. The EnyoRhea was also trying new colors. "When is your second meal of the day tomorrow?" the black one asked. "I am not sure. I take a break when I feel like taking one," the maincoon Kat spoke. "May I come find you and show you something on my break tomorrow?" the guardian asked. "Sure," Avis replied. After the meal the zatz went to her hut where she talked to Liz about her day and then they went to sleep.

The next day as she had planned Zea found Avis during her break and they walked to the edge of camp where the two females collected some flowers and other types of plants that the black one picked out of the scene. After the plants were collected the two females went back to Avis hut where the zatz spared the plants out on a table. Then the guardian proceeded to show the artist how to make different kinds of paint and colors with the plants. Avis was overjoyed and could not wait to try to new colors. By the time the black one finished her project her break was up and voiced to her friend as she stood to leave the room, "I hope the paints work for you. Please tell me how the colors work at the last meal of the day. Thank you for your time and I will see you later." As Zea ran back to work she could hear Avis yell, "Thank you."

When the day came to a close and the camp was just sitting down to eat the guardian started to think about the last few months. Daydreaming reflections of her life flashed through her mind. –Zea, are you feeling alright? – the computer asked. The guardian shook her head and looked around seeing everyone enjoying the last meal of the day. –Yes, my friend I am feeling well. How are you? – the blacked one replied. –I am doing well. I was just making sure you were okay because you started to daydream and that is not like you, – the life long friend explained. –Thank you for checking on me but, I feel well thank you, – she voiced. After saying a short prayer in her mind the zatz started to eat like all her friends around her.

Just as they were finishing Avis came up to the fighter. "Thank you, the new paints are great. You opened a whole new world of color and texture that I can now use. If there is anything I can do to repay you," Avis spoke with great excitement. "I am glad you are pleased. All I ask is your friendship in return," Zea laughed. The two spoke for a while longer before they went their different path for the night.

When the guardian walked into the hut she called home Liz was waiting for her. "Can we go out tonight? I got a message and my male wants to see me?" the female asked. "Sure," the zatz stated with a smile. "Oooh, thank you, Zea. I will be ready in a few minutes," the EnyoRhea said as she rushed into the other room. The guardian just sat by the fired and relaxed. Like the times before the two friends sunk out of camp and made their way to the beautiful waterfall. As Zea watched from a distance the two lovers played and grew closer.

The guardian also noticed like the time before there was a shadow on the opposite side of the bank. The black female wondered if the shadow knew she was there. Looking at Liz the zatz could see how blissful she was laughing and smiling in the moonlight. When the night was getting late Zea make a call to warn her friend of the time. The EnyoRhea said her goodbyes to her male and took to forest as Zea took to the air. Once they were flying Liz spoke, "Thank you, Zea, you are a great friend to do this for me." "Anytime, you are a great friend to me as well," the guardian explained. When the duo got home they went straight to sleep.

A few more days pasted and soon Zea found herself in front of a fire and talking to Liz. "You know, Zea, I think he is going to ask me," the EnyoRhea said with joy. "Ask you what?" the black on questioned. "I think is going to if we can be maskas as you know we are meko and meka," Liz smiled. The guardian scanned her mind for the meaning of the three words she knew she had heard them before in her time in the new land.

Finally it hit her. "You think he is going to join with you? But what about the secret of your love?" Zea inquired. "Only a few have to be at the ceremony and besides once it is done I can tell my close friends if I get his permission. I am sure I will be able to tell my close friends because all of his will know. We will be more than a couple. We can start a family!" the EnyoRhea voiced. "If you have a boy where will your son live?" the guardian asked. "I am not sure yet. I would give him to a clan that I trusted. I am guessing and hoping right now for Dark Star's Clan but we will have to see. I am soooo happy and thank you, Zea. This would have never happen if you were not here with me," the dark furred female stated before giving her friend a hug. "I am happy to help a friend like you," Zea smiled.

Liz talked more of her male before the two settled down for the night. The both females were grateful to be friends.

A New Way of Life

Soon the Zea's day of birth was only a few days away and her yearly mark of being with the clan was also coming. The guardian was excited for both dates. She did not know what would happen on her day of birth. Zea was now good friends with almost all the members of the all female clan.

One morning when the guardian woke she realized that Liz was already up and gone. The black female did her small workout and then made her way outside the hut. The whole clan looked like they were in a meeting. Zea did not what she should do. She did not know if she should go back into the hut or go to the meeting. Just as the zatz was going to go back into the hut Liz spotted her and gave her a motion to join her in the meeting.

The fighter silently jumped down and carefully walked up to her friend. "What is going on?" the black on asked. "I think Sunflower wants to see you," the EnyoRhea told her. Zea looked in the leader's direction and then turned her attention back to Liz. "Will I be interrupting the meeting?" the guardian questioned. "No," Liz responded. The EnyoRhea smiled as she watched her friend make her way through the crowd and soon was next to Sunflower.

The leader placed her arm around the black one and began to speak to the group. "As we all know Zea has been living with us for some time now. She has been working for clan in many ways and also she has given herself for the tribe showing trust. I have talked to many of you and after having this meeting I have decided that Zea is now welcomed to join our clan. If anyone has a problem please speak now," the leader voiced. Zea smiled as the clan was silent. "Zea, would you join our clan and become a sister EnyoRhea?" the leader questioned. "I would be honored to be an EnyoRhea," the guardian stated. "Now let his day be a day of celebration. There will be no work and only play. Tonight we will feast and have the ceremony of the EnyoRehas and Zea will be a turn warrior sister," the leader called to the group. The family roared. Just as the leader exclaimed the day was full of stories, fun and games and the guardian was the center of it all.

When night finally came the fighter was overjoyed and full of wonder. When the time came for Zea to become a member the crowd encircled the guardian and the leader. "Zea, please stated our clan's code," the Sunflower ordered. "EnyoRheas work for, fight for, love, give, trust, and honor their sisters. Give pledge to their chosen leader and never gives up to weakness. Once an EnyoRhea always an EnyoRhea," the female stated. The group cheered when the zatz finished.

The leader stood behind the black one and the crowd fell silent. Next the guardian felt metal and stone around her neck. The guardian looked down to see the EnyoRhea crest resting on her chest. Last a small, metal pole was placed in a small fire. The weapons maker came into the circle with the pole glowing red with heat. Putting on gloves the EnyoRhea now handled the metal. The leader took Zea's hand as the pole was wrapped around her arm. The guardian closed her eyes but did not make a sound. The band was now a perfect fit for her arm. The band had a spiral at each end so one could place beads on the armband.

Once the weapon maker left the circle Sunflower's voice cut through the air, "Let it be known, Zea, is now an EnyoRhea." The clan went crazy with joy and as tears of bliss ran down the black one cheek the group went into the action. Great fires were lit and games were started. Zea had one of the best nights in her life and one of her dreams of being a clan member came true. When the sun's light kissed the land the clan began to clam down and rest. That day the clan was quiet and rested from the night's actions.

Zea was so happy she could not rest that day. The guardian continued to look at her new necklace and armband. Looking at her new jewelry the simple chain with a circle pendent reminded her of her old one. The zatz made her way to a privet place where she opened a small compartment and pulled out her family chips, the family's necklace and the craved gift from Snake. Holding the objects in her hands kissing the gift form Snake she then placed back in hiding.

Then she looked at the chips as her eyes began to water. After putting them away the fighter grazed at the heart necklace. Studying it the zatz could hear her brother's voice in her mind telling her about the different carving and she began to cry. Zea was caught by surprise as Liz walked into the small room. The guardian quickly cupped the heart in her arm as she hid her computer from view.

"What is wrong, sister?" Liz said with great concern. "I was just remembering some loved one from my past," the black one stated while wiping her eyes. "Are you okay?" the dark furred female questioned. "Yes, I am fine, thank you, would you come with me to get a drink?" the fighter voiced while standing. The two EnyoRheas left the dark room and made there way for a cool drink of water. The rest of the day the guardian was quiet but content with friends by her side.

That night Zea's mind raced with dreams and she did not get much sleep. Liz sat by her side and wished she could understand what the little one's dreams were all about. "Talk to me Zea, what is going on? Why do you shake so? What happened to you when you were a slave?" Liz whispered. Zea looked into her friend's bright yellow eyes and began to speak. For the second time in her new life the guardian told a good friend the truth about her childhood.

Jabo's abuse and the choices he made the zatz make at her young age. Liz was at a loss and did not know what to say as she held the crying clan member. "Zea, I do not think your family member's deaths are your fault. Clam down it is okay you are safe now," Liz again whispered. The good friend did her best to relax the little one down and put her to bed for some need rest. Finally the black one fell asleep and rested.

When the sun's light hit the zatz she stood and began the new day. The new clan member made her way to work after having a small first meal. The day went by very fast and that she was a member she taught classes and was now a guard. She was very cheerful with her job and to be able to work with Sarah and not by her side.

Everyone was delighted to have a new sister and teacher. Later that night after dinner Liz and Zea sat by a fire. "Do you want to talk about anything that happened last night?" Liz asked. "No, I do not know what to say," Zea responded. "Well, if you ever find your words or need to talk I am here for you," the good friend voiced very strongly. "Thank you," the zatz stated. The two sat in silence for a while but both were tried and went to sleep early that night.

Next day Zea awoke to a beautiful day. The guardian stood and made her way to the other room to do her exercises. When Liz joined her in the other room they made their way to the first meal of the day. Zea was very quiet and Liz wished she could help.

During the meal the leader stood and addressed the group. "Good morning my sisters. Today is yet another day of joy for this is the day our newest member is 19," Sunflower told the group with great excitement. Everyone looked at Zea and cheered before singing to her and wishing her well. Zea did not have to work and could do as she pleased. That night there would be a feast in her honor. The guardian thanked her friends and continued her meal with friends coming up to greet her.

During the day Zea laughed and played with friends. When night came there was a great banquet and for the first time the fighter was allowed to sit by the leader. The guardian was not at the end of the table but the middle and everything was a little different. After a toast and a good meal a few EnyoRheas gave the black one some simple gifts. When the clan was starting to calm down the zatz went to talk to Sunflower.

"Sunflower, I was wondering if I could leave the camp for a few hours. I need some reflection time alone. If you say, 'no' I would understand. Last year I found a good reflect spot and it is a safe one," Zea asked. "I should say, 'no' but, I know you are a good fighter and very smart. I will let you go but I want you to check in with me when you get back and be in camp before dawn. I guess this will be your birthday gift from me," the leader answered. "Thank you, Sunflower. I will do all you ask," the guardian told her leader as she got down on one knee and gave her a sign of respect. The fighter stood, said goodbye and left the small room. Taking flight she made her way to the tree on the cliff.

Landing the fighter walked to the tree where she sat to look up at the night sky. The zatz began to reflect and pray about her lost ones. The guardian closed her eyes and thought of each of her family members one at a time. The 19 year old found herself crying. Zea still had guilt eating at her insides even as her computer did her best to calm her lifelong friend.

"Why are you crying?" a voice cut the air. The guardian jumped up and faced the tree in a fighting position. "Clam down little one I am not going to hurt you," the voice said calmly. Quickly wiping the water from her eyes the female called to the air, "I am not a little one," Looking up in the treetop trying to see who was with her. "Who are you?" the black one asked. "I am not here to harm you. I just want to ask you if you are okay?" the other questioned. Zea finally spotted two golden eyes. "Why do you ask?" the zatz inquired. "Someone as beautiful as you should not be crying," the gold eyes spoke. "Why would you care, we do not even know each other's names," the guardian explained. "Well, let me introduce myself..." the other stated while jumping down from the tree.

"My name is Talon," he smiled. Zea now stood face to face with a black male. He had the same coat of her father. As she looked at his face their eyes locked. "My name is Zeaytera KatOynera," the fighter whispered. "That is a tongue twister," Talon laughed. "My friends call me Zea," the female spoke softly still grazing into the golden eyes. "So what are you doing here?" the male asked. "Because I wish to be and you?" the guardian replied. "Like you, I am guessing, this is my reflection spot," the black male told her. "Do you want to sit with me?" Talon continued as he walked back to the tree.

The fighter shook her head and voiced, "I do not think that is the best idea. I do not know you. What clan are you from?" "Do clans matter? Would you stop talking to me if I was from a certain clan?" the male questioned. "No, I guess not. I was just asking," Zea stated. "You have many questions but not a lot of answers," Talon smiled. "I have many secrets. I am not like others," the guardian voiced while observing the area. She knew it was rare to find a Kat by him or herself.

"I think you are beautiful. I have never seen a coat or eyes like yours before in all my life," the male told her. "Thank you for the kind words but I think I should be going I have to get to my clan soon," Zea stated while bringing her attention back to the male. "You are going to go back to the EnyoRhea's camp?" the male asked. "Yeah," the fighter smiled. "Can I see you again?" Talon inquired. "You want to see me again?" Zea questioned with surprise. "Yes, I still need to find out why you were crying and why you really came to his tree," the male explained. The guardian laughed. "Sure, I will meet you again and here because this spot relaxes me and I feel safe here looking over the land. I enjoy watching the sunset and rise. I also love the night sky," the female agreed. "When?" Talon asked with excitement. "I do not know?" the fighter replied.

"Well, I will come find you unless that is a problem for you," Talon suggested. "I guess you could," the zatz voiced. "I will be careful and no one will know," the male comforted. "Should I not talk about you?" Zea questioned. "For now because we do not know each other that well we might want to keep our meeting a secret," Talon smiled. "Well, it was nice meeting you Talon. Have a good night," Zea told her new friend who replied, "Till we meet again," the male called. The guardian flexed her back and let her wings come out of hiding. Talon's eyes widened as he watched the female's wings come out and watched her take off in the night air.

Once in the air Zea spoke to her computer, "We need to work on that." –On what? – the life lone friend asked. "From now on when my emotions are running strong will you put my scanner on full power so no one sneaks up on me again?" the guardian asked. –Yea, I think that is a great idea, – the computer laughed. "I am glad you are happy," the female voiced. The fighter flew back to her home with a smile on her face. When she was back safe in camp she checked in with Sunflower and last went to her hut to sleep.

The next morning Zea woke up with the male on her mind. At the first meal of the day some of the others noticed the fighter was daydreaming. During one of her breaks with Sarah they started to talk. "What is wrong with you?" Sarah questioned. "Sorry, there is just a lot on my mind right now," the zatz explained. "Like what?" the pink one asked. "My past, my future," the guardian stated. "If you need to talk you know I am here for you," the warrior voiced. "Thank you and I know. I now know what it is like to have sisters and I love it," Zea smiled. The two laughed and talked till a new group came in for training.

Later that night when Liz was sitting with her black friend in front of the fire they began to talk. "What is up with you today?" Liz asked with a laugh. "I do not know," the black one smiled. "You have been acting up all day," the warrior explained. "If I tell you it will be out little secret. Right?" the zatz told her friend. "I give you my word," the dark furred female stated very seriously. "Well, the other night I left to reflect. I flew to a spot I found about a year ago and there I met a male. We started talking and I think I like him," Zea spoke very softly but with a large smile. "Really?!" Liz exclaimed. The zatz only laughed. "I guess I am now not the only with a secret crush," the golden eyed one cry out with joy. "I cannot talk about him yet but when I can I give you my word you will be the first to know," the guardian promised. The two talked for a while then went to sleep.

In the morning Sunflower told the new member it was time for her to make a hut of her own. That day she would not work but build a home. The leader told her to build her new home where ever she pleased but a few spots where she pointed out to the black one. Zea walked into the woods to find good wood for her new hut. The fighter knew for the most part she was safe because of the watchers, which roamed the area.

After looking for a while she found a good-sized tree. The guardian did a pulse and made sure no one in the area. When the coast was clear she brought out her red ray gun and cut down the tree. Bringing gun in the fighter carried the tree into the camp. The zatz got an ax and a few different kinds of blades and began to cut the tree. By mid-day the all the black one had to do was make a roof. Heading back into the trees the female went back to the stump. Using an ax the fighter the stump down to the ground then on the way back to the camp she gathered plants she would need to make her roof.

Once back to her new home the zatz wove her roof with the plants and a small table out of the stump. Next the black one went to the blacksmith, Antoinette; she was a very light blue with matching eyes. Her name's meaning was irreplaceable and for the camp she was. Antoinette made all the weapons and other metal objects for the camp. She liked to hang out with Liz and Sarah. The fighter asked Antoinette to make her a few hooks. The blue one smiled and told her to come back in an hour or so.

With a smile the black went to another friend who was in charge of making cloths for the camp. Her name was Jagg and there Zea asked her for some extra cloth or strong rope. Jagg was happy to help the new member and gave the fighter what she could. When the guardian got back to her build site she began to weave the cloth and rope. When she finished the black one went back to Antoinette who had the hooks ready for her.

After a hug two went back to their work. Zea went inside her new home and hung her bed. Last the black one made her way to the carpenter who already had a table, chairs and a dresser for her. By nightfall Zea's new home was complete and Liz came to see. "Wow, you are fast. I am glad are huts are not far a part from each other. You even have a hammock to sleep in at night. I like your new home. I know it will be odd not having you in my home. We can still have a light night talks if you want," Liz stated. "That would be great," Zea voiced. Then the time had come to go to the last meal of the day. After a great meal the guardian went back to her new hut where she went to bed early. She was tried from a long days work.

Zea was awoken from her sleep by pebbles flying through the wind and hitting her. Slowly sitting up the guardian caught the next pebble and threw it back out the window. Next someone jumped into the dark room. "You did not have to hit me," Talon whispered as he rubbed his head. "I did not mean too," Zea giggled. "What are you doing right now?" the male asked. "What do you think I was doing, I was sleeping," the female stated with a smile. "Do you want to fly with me?" Talon questioned. "Sure," the zatz agreed. They both crawled out the back window then went onto the roof. Zea flexed her back muscles and took to the air. Then she put her hand down for the male to grab. He looked at her hand then her face then back at the hand. After some thought he took her hand and the guardian threw him into the night air.

As Talon gilded towards the cliff as Zea did aerial moves around him. He was amazed with her ability to move so gracefully in the sky.

Landing at their reflecting spot the two started to talk. "How did you get to my hut unseen?" the guardian asked. "My job is to move without being seen," Talon explained.

"Just you or your clan?"

"I do not talk about my clan a lot. How long have you been with the EnyoRheas?"

"A little over a year. Did you grow up in your clan?"

"I was not born into my clan I had to join. What about you?"

"I was not born here in this land. I had to leave my home and I traveled to this great land."

"What happen when you came here?"

"I was sleeping by a tree and I was awoken by two Shadow Kats. After trying to talk them we realized that we spoke different language. More Shadow Kat showed up and we began to fight. Soon I was taken in by and clan. Pyro met me and was taken by me. I escaped ran into Bear who helped me and took me to his clan. I stayed with Dark Star's Clan for a while. I had some ups and down and now I am the newest member of the EnyoRheas. What about you? What was your old clan?"

"I was born in the Black Stone Clan where I was raised. I have a mother, Oriyn I never really knew my father until a few years ago. Now I am in my new clan and I have never been happier. Soo, if I may ask why were you crying the other night."

"Well, I lost my family at a young age and I was thinking about them and I got a little emotional."

"I am sorry to hear about that how young were you?"

"I think I was two years of age when I lost my father, Domatu. Then two years later I lost my mother, Sunyro, and four years after that I lost my older brother, Gyro. I think those are the right ages, it was a long time ago. I do not like talking about my past it is very painful for me."

"Well thank you for sharing with me that much. I wanted to tell you I think you are very beautiful and you are amazing. I like your wings."

Zea smiled, "Thank you."

The two talked for a while longer till the guardian realized dawn was on its way and told Talon she was having a great time but had to get back to camp before the sun rose. They took to the air and Talon flew Zea home. They said their goodbye and Talon flew home while Zea crept to her bed.

The next few weeks Zea continued to see Talon and they were soon taken with each other. He always came at night and they never really talked about what he did all day. Both shared happy times and the male talked more about his childhood more than Zea. Talon looked like a strong fighter and was very good with words. As the zatz got to know him she wondered what clan he was from and why there were so many secrets but if she kept secrets from him she felt all was fair.

Liz became very curious about the mystery male. The dark furred female asked as many questions as she could to find out who Zea was seeing. Finally one night Liz sat down with her friend. "I think I know who you are seeing. If I say his name will you tell me if that is his name?" Liz questioned. "Sure," Zea smiled. "I think his name is Talon and I also think that he belongs to the same clan that my mecko, Jester belongs too," the dark furred female explained. "Is that a bad thing?" the zatz asked. "Well, I am not sure. I should not talk a lot about the clan. I bet he is good but just be very careful. To be honest I bet Bear would not want you to get involved with him," the good friend voiced. There was a small pause of silence. "I think next time you two get together you should talk about everything and get all the secrets out into the air," Liz continued. The two talked for a while longer and then went to sleep for the night.

A few nights later when Talon came to see Zea they took to the air like all the nights before and flew to their reflection spot. Once they were there they sat down by the tree and began to talk. "I was wondering if we could have a serious talk tonight?" Zea questioned. "Sure," Talon smiled. "I am hoping this evening we can talk about all of our secrets. You tell me your clan and I tell you about my childhood, what really happen," the guardian purposed. "I do not know," the male voiced. "I want our relationship to grow and I really want to tell you about me but I cannot give my all to you if you do not do the same for me," the black one explained. There was a long silent pause.

"If you would like I will tell you but with that information comes consequences," Talon warned. "I will start," the zatz stated. The guardian then proceeded to tell Talon about Jabo, being a slave, her scars, her escape and all the deaths of her loved ones and enemies. During her talk she showed her friend the artwork on her back. When she finished silence crept into the scene and soon all than could be heard was the night song of the crickets.

Finally Talon spoke, "I had no idea. I do not what to say or think but I am sorry and if there is anything I can do please tell me. I do not think at your young age you could have prevented the death of your family. I think no matter what Jabo would have found a way to kill your family." "The choice was mine and I made the wrong one it is as simple as that," the zatz told him. "But you were so young how could your choose your slave owner over your father?" the male questioned. "That dose not matter, now it's your turn," the zatz voiced strongly.

"Well, okay but with your permission, I want to talk about your childhood later," the male stated. Then he proceeded to tell Zea about his clan. "I am a guardian. My clan is made up of about twelve males and we are the most wanted group in the land. Many of the clans have bounty on our heads. The Shadow Clan has the largest and we pride ourselves raising the price. We have symbols and when we do an act we leave the mark of the guardian and our own. If the clans found out who we were together then they might use you to get to me and I cannot betray my clan. One can only join my clan if they are chosen by us and pass all of our tests. I am one of the most wanted because I am second in command," Talon explained.

Zea's eyes grew with every word. Now she fully understood why Bear did not want her to say that she was a guardian out loud. "Your clan sounds amazing but what kind of acts do you do?" the zatz asked. "We fight against the Shadow Clan and all of their allies but we do not really ever have a side. We do what we please and every young male wants to join some females and us but we have never had a female in the clan. We are the best fighters in all the land," Talon told her. "Really, the best in the land?" the female asked. "Yup," the male nodded.

"And are you the best or the second best in the land because you are second in your clan?" the zatz inquired. "I am the greatest," the black male exclaimed. "I bet I could take you," the fighter joked. "I do not think so," Talon laughed. The two joked and had fun for the rest of the night. At the end of the evening before Talon left Zea for the night Zea voiced to Talon, "I do not care what clan you are from and how dangerous it is I still want to be with you and I do not care who knows." "Are you sure?" the male whispered. "Without a doubt," the zatz whispered strongly. "Here I want you to have this," Talon stated softly as he handed Zea his neck chain. "You can wear it where ever on your body but it tells everyone who sees it you are with me and that can be a good and bad thing just be careful," he stated. "Always," Zea smiled as she slipped the chain twice over her hand and onto her wrist.

They locked eyes and slowly Talon came closer to Zea and kissed her lightly. They said their goodbyes and Talon left to small hut. The fighter was over come with emotion and glided to Liz's hut. Once she was there the zatz told her sister everything and showed her the neck chain. The two females were up all night laughing and talking.

The next day both fighters were tired. The word spread around camp quick of Zea's new jewelry. Many looked at her and others asked her if what she was wearing was real. As Zea was practicing her fighting she realized that Dark Star's clan was coming to the camp in a few days for the yearly meeting. Her heart raced thinking of her male friends would see the neck chain. The day went by very fast and that night at dinner the leader of the camp began to speak of the meeting of the two clans. She went over the rules and then told the group to have a good night.

When the day finally came all the females spent the whole day getting ready Zea had no idea they put so much time and effort into the event but the same excitement was in the air. When the sun was setting the female sat round camp like they had done nothing all day and soon the males started to walk into camp.

Josh, Roberd and Robby were the first males to see Zea. They hugged and were overjoyed to see her. When they sat down to talk the male noticed the fighter's chain. Roberd was the first to notice and then began to whisper to his friends. Right when they were going to ask the zatz saw her father and jumped to her feet. After excusing herself from the group the black one ran to her father. As she ran she knew the group would be talking about her.

Reaching Bear they embraced each other. Bear walked over to Sunflower and gave her a greeting and a sign of respect. Next he went to a small fire with his daughter where they could talk. "How have you been Bear?" the female started. "I have been doing well. Everything back at camp is the same but I have heard you have been busy. When word spread that you were a true member of the EnyoRheas our clan feasted in your honor. I was very happy to hear you were doing well," the kat spoke while looking at his daughter.

As he finished he noticed the black one's new jewelry. "What is that?" Bear questioned while pointing at the chain. "It is a gift from a very good friend. I met him a while ago and we have been seeing each other. A few nights back he gave me his neck chain," Zea explained. "Which one and do you know what that means?" Bear asked. "His name is Talon and yes I now know that this symbol means we are seeing each other," the zatz stated calmly. Bear did not look pleased but did not look mad. The fighter was not sure what she should do.

Finally she asked, "Are you mad? Do you approve?" "I do not think it matters if I approve it seems you two are taken with each other and nothing I say or do will change that fact. I do not fully approve because of who he is but you have my best wishes because you are a strong warrior and I bet you could take him," he answered and they both laughed. "I am not mad at you, Zea; I just did not want my daughter to be going out with an outlaw of the land. The guardians are over a good group but many clans hunt them and at times they came be trouble to us. I trust your judgment. Not much is known about the clan. I just wish you be careful," the father said softly. "I am always cautious," Zea comforted.

The fighter talked about joining the EnyoRheas and how she met Talon. As his daughter told her life story, the father observed the female. She had grown. Many Kats stop developing when they are 18 years of age. Zea was now taller and her body was not only gaining muscle mass but also she was becoming full figured. The male wondered if she would still growing because now she was about average height for a female Kat, maybe a little on the taller side.

When there was a good break in the conversation Bear asked Zea about her adolescent advancement. The EnyoRhea had a quick private conversation with her computer then told her father that she would most likely stop growing at the age of 21. Soon Bear was asked to join the main Kats in a meeting. "I will come see you before I leave tonight," Bear told Zea as he stood and made his way to the leader's circle. The black stood up and joined her friends in the fun and games.

When morning was on its way, Bear said, "Goodbye," to his daughter and left camp with Dark Star and the remaining males who were not sleeping in the EnyoRheas camp. The next day the females picked up camp and rested from the night's actions. Then life was back to normal.

Snatched

Zea loved her new way of life and living in an all female clan. She was a now great friend with everyone in the group. Liz knew almost all of her secrets. They did not know about Zea's computer. The young female also had a few meeting with the leader of camp after she joined. The zatz felt that she must be honest with her leader and Sunflower knew everything about Zea except for her computer and mental power.

Sunflower liked that Zea was very loyal and respectful for her leader. She realized that the black zatz was very serious about pleasing and keeping a good relationship with her. The black one loved playing all day and teaching the little ones of the camp combat skills. Zea also did a lesson for the older members of the clan for those who wanted and many were delighted to lean the new one's techniques. Life was good and everyone was blissful.

Zea continued to see Talon they were falling in love with each other and soon Zea felt safe to share some of her secrets with him. First she showed him the eyelids, then the gills, next and last was her ability to change from a two-legged to a four-legged zatx. He was very impressed and still loved her for who she was.

One night she asked Talon if he shared her difference with his clan. He told her that he did not say how she was diverse but that she was. Then Talon asked Zea if she had any more secrets. The young one looked down and shook her head yes but then spoke very soft, "There are two left. One I have only told my father and the other no one knows. I just do not think I am ready to share it with anyone." There was silence. Then Talon whispered, "It is okay. I trust that if it was truly important you would tell me. You take your time and when you feel prepared tell me and I will understand." He hugged her tight.

But after that night the male was acting different he did not come see her as much and when he did he was always looking around, jumpy and made to visits short. When asked about his behavior he said it was nothing and everything was all right. Then he headed home. Zea was worried but trusted him to tell her if anything was wrong and did her best to clam him while they were together.

One night four outsides flew and sneaked into the EnyoRhea's camp. While three encircled Zea's hut one crept inside. The fighter was having a nightmare and was moving a little in her hammock, which made the outside tense. Carefully the intruder laced rope over the opening of the hammock then gave a signal to the others that everything was ready.

Zea suddenly awoke from her rest but not from the nightmare but her bed being pulled together. She was now in a net trapped. Bring her claws out the fighter began to break free. The two others came into the hut quickly while the forth stay and watched for the EnyoRheas. The three attackers placed the female into another bag and tied many ropes around her body. Zea continued to fight and with the little movement she had. She continued to try to break though the net. When the three outsiders were done placing ropes and bags over their target they placed a trinket where the female's bed use to be and raced out of the camp.

The fighter remained calm and continued to brake free as she was carried far from her home. Then the black one felt her body move up and she knew that the group was now flying. A few minutes later the group arrived at their home and walked underground to a group of cells. Next the attackers threw the female into one of the cells and locked the door. Then they left the underground.

As the stillness took over the dark hall Zea continued to break free from her netted trap. As she used her claws she realized there was someone in the cell with her and was trying to help her out of the ropes. Finally the fighter got a breath of fresh air as she climbed out of the net. "You are a female!" the other called in a loud voiced with confusion.

As the zatz stood she could here other voices all male. Looking around the black one could see she was in a cell with a white and black striped male. The cell had two beds and was very small. There were no lockups across from hers but there were many compartments in a row. The female walked to the bars and started to look for a weak spot. "What are you doing?" the male asked. "I am looking for a way out of the cell what are you doing?" she responded. "Why would you want to escape?" the striped one questioned. "I do not like being in a cage and I do not why I am in this chamber.

One minute I am in my bed and the next I am here with you," Zea explained. "You must be clueless," he laughed as he laid down on one of the beds. "I am sorry to be rude but who are you?" the zatz inquired. "I thought you would never ask. I am Sport and I am from the Moon Clan," the striped voiced as he stood to greet Zea. "I am Zea and I am an EnyoRhea," the female introduced herself. "If you do not mind me asking what is going on?" the fighter continued. "Well, I guess I well help you. I mean you are a female. The Guardians have chosen us. They are looking for another member to join and for the next few days they will be testing us to see who they want to join them. I think every day they take at least one of us out of the running. If you are the last one they are bring in then there are about fifteen of us in the running.

There has never been a female in the Guardian Clan so good luck," Sport stated. "I heard they are always watching us and everything is a test," the striped one continued. "Well, I do not like being in a cage and I will not just let someone cage me unless they have talked and convinced me to stay. The fighter walked over to the bars and began to look for weak spots again.

An hour later Zea broke one of the bars and continued to make an opening for her to escape. "What are you doing?" Sport questioned. "I am leaving are you coming?" the female replied as she slipped thought the bars. "No, are you crazy?" Sport yelled. Zea shook her head with a big smile as she made her way down the dark hallway. There were two males in every cell. The zatz asked anyone if they wanted to be let out but no one wanted to leave so the black one slowly left the underground.

Waiting outside was all the Guardians. They were standing in a half circle and were all wearing masks so there faces were unseen. The zatz looked at every member waiting for a response. One of them walked forward and spoke in a loud and clear voice, "Welcome, Zea. You are the first one in years to break out of the cells. Is there a reason?" "I do not like cages. Never have and never will. If what Sport said inside was true and you would like me to stay in a cell I will respect your decision and go back into a lockup but courteously I would rather not be in a barred chamber," the black one answered.

The male smiled and laughed. "I never liked cages myself," the guardian voiced. "Show her to the real rooms," he called to the air. A black male stepped forward and walked with Zea into the woods. As they walked he whispered, "Zea, do not try to act too friendly with any of the guardians. If you recognize any one of them pretend like you do not know them especially me." "I will do what you ask of me, Talon," the zatz also whispered.

Finally they reach a building where the Guardian opened the door and lead Zea to a room where there were two beds. "Stay here till you are told to leave by a clan member you will have a roommate shortly, I hope," Talon ordered and then left shutting the door behind him. Zea did not know what was going to be happening over the next few days so she picked a bed and did her best to rest for the trails, which lay ahead of her.

Later the door opened and a Guardian walked in and placed a tray on the floor and left the room. "Thank you," Zea voiced as the door shut. Almost a 24 hours later the door opened and another Guardian asked the female to join him. They walked outside where everyone was waiting. "All have you have been chosen and now the tests will begin. If you want out at anytime tell one of the Guardians and you will be taken back to your home. If anyone is caught cheating, trying to leave or hurt another then that one will leave. Are there any questions?" the male spoke. There was only silence.

The next day the zatz was woken up as the sun rising. Soon the group strolled to a meadow with a small platform in the middle. "Here is your first game one at a time you will stand on the platform and close your eyes and the rest of the group will spread out and the goal is for the spotter to find all the other members. If you are on the ground your goal is to touch the platform without being spotted by anyone. The last twist is the one on the platform will throw rocks and try to hit anyone in the grass that is spotted. If you are tossing the rocks you do not want to hurt anyone. Lets begin," one of the Guardians explained.

Zea reached the stage every time and no spotter could find her. Soon everyone wanted to see the female on the stand and when her time came many smiles grew. Standing on the wooden platform the fighter closed her eyes and focused. –Do you want me to do a pules?- her computer chimed in. –Lets see how I do, if I need too I will ask, thank you for offering – The female answered. When she heard the sound to begin the black one picked up a few rocks and scanned the area using not just her eyes but her ears as well.

At one point she closed her eyes and focused on just using her hearing. Within five minutes the fighter pegged all the Kats in the grass but one. The zatz continued to hunt for him and a few minutes later heard the grass move and quickly turned around and through the rock in one graceful move and then game was over. The group was lead back to their rooms.

This time Zea's roommate was a light tan color with green eyes. He was from the Mask Clan and his name was Andyi. For the rest of the day they talked about the challenge, which just took place. Andyi was amazed on how well the female did. Zea told him she had been trained for a good part of her life and they game they played was nothing compared to her training. Then they talked about the clan they were from. Andyi was very kind to Zea.

The days that followed were the same. There would be one main challenge a day and the rest of time Zea would be in a room with another roommate. With every test Zea could see there was only one real challenger in the group and his name was Mist. He was Black furred male with gray patches. His eyes were a bluish green. Mist did not talk much but was very strong and smart.

Zea tried to talk to her roommates and be friendly. The males enjoyed talking about the challenges. Some of the tests that Zea passed were, making a new weapon where she made a bow and arrow, a day in the water where she had to hold her breath and play water games, teamwork, escaping, finding and tracking and much more. Zea felt like she was traveling and being tested again by her computer. The tests were all hard but not as difficult as the ones her life long gave her. Every time there was a new test everyone looked around to see who was missing. Zea had not lost one test and was always the first one everyone went after. The fighter loved the challenge.

The day came where there were only two in the group left. Mist and Zea had to room together the last night. He did not talk even after the zatz tried to start a conversation. "You are a great warrior. What ever happens tomorrow good luck," she voiced. "I know and I do not need your luck," he stated. "I guessing you do not want to talk," the female said. Mist did not respond but lay down on his bed. The fighter decided to lie down as well. As silence took over the room Zea began to think about all the guardians. She knew who Talon and two others seemed very familiar. The fighter differed off to sleep.

That night Zea had another nightmare and awoke with Mist leaning over her asking if she was okay. "I am fine, thank you. I get bad nightmares from time to time," the female whispered. "I guess," Mist stated as he lay down in his bed. The black one did her best to clear her mind and go back to sleep. "What were you dreaming about?" the male's voice cut the air. "My past," Zea answered. "What do you mean?" Mist inquired. "I did not have a normal childhood and I do not like talking about it. I do not mean to be rude or cold to you but I have a hard time trusting others because of my past," the zatz did her best to explain.

"I am guessing you were hurt," the male voiced. "In more ways than one," the female spoke softly. "Do you have any brothers or sisters?" the female continued. "I have two little sisters, Hazel and Hope. Do you?" Mist smiled. "I had an older brother, Gyro," Zea whispered. "Where is he?" the male questioned. "He pasted away," the fighter voice was weak. "I am sorry, Mist, but I really do not want to talk about this. I think I am just going to try to go back to sleep," the female stated as she turned so she faced the wall. Zea made sure that when she turned her wings were in tight. The black one closed her eyes and did her best to fall asleep as she voiced, "Good night and thank you again," to Mist.

Morning came too fast for the fighter. The door opened and the masked male woke both Mist and Zea up for the day. They walked to a green grass field where the Guardians were spread out in the field to make a large circle. Mist and Zea were placed in the middle and told that this was the last test and their assessment was to fight. One of the Guardians told them all the rules which were they could use what ever was around them, they could use what was on them, they had to stay in the circle and the fight was to a knock out not to the death. Last the Guardian asked if there were any questions and there were none. He walked to join his clan mates as the two fighters looked at each other.

"Good luck and I hope you have as much fun as I am going to have," the female smiled. "I told you at the beginning I do not need your luck and I have been waiting for this moment for a long time," Mist voiced. They shook hands and the fight began.

Zea backed off and got in her classic defense position as the male laughed at her. Mist then came at the EnyoRhea with kicks and punches. In one graceful move the black one ducked to the ground and tripped the male and as he fell to the ground the zatz flipped to her feet and then took to the air. Mist knew that he could not beat Zea in the air so he waited for her to come down and fight.

Seeing he was not going to join her in the air the warrior landed. They started to fight again hand to hand. The day went by and there was no break for the two challengers. Soon Mist grew tried and Zea was just breaking a sweat. The fighter decided to just end the battle quickly and wanted to stop playing. Getting in the right position Zea flipped herself and was now behind Mist. Next she pushed on his shoulder using a pressure point and a drop of venom. Mist fell to the ground out cold. Zea made sure he was okay as the Guardians walked up to the two fighters.

Two Guardians carried Mist back to the house and Zea walked with the others there was only silence. Once back at the dwelling Zea was asked to stay in a room and wait as the group made their choice.

A few hours dragged by. Finally the door opened and one of the Guardians asked the female to join him. They left the structure and took to the air flying to a cliff. There the rest of the clan waited and there was a fire going. The sun was just setting and there was only the sound of the great fire in the air. When they landed the Guardian joined the others and Zea looked around wondering what was going to happen next.

One of the males came forward and began to talk, "Zea you have passed all of the tests and we would like you to join our clan. As you might have heard we do what we want and many want us dead. We wear the mark of our clan where the outside world cannot see easily. Once you are a member you stay a colleague to the death. If you choose to go we ask that you share nothing of what you saw or did. If you decide to have a child the little one cannot grow up in the clan. We keep no secrets from each other and you must be prepared to share with the group. You are the first female to join the clan and so there might be knew challenges but we are willing to face them if you are."

"I would be honored to join your clan and become a Guardian but what about my promise to the EnyoRheas. Can I just leave my old clan without a thought?" Zea stated. "I have talked to Sunflower and we have been doing this for years. Sunflower and the EnyoRheas would be overjoyed to hear that a female has joined the Guardians and even more excited to know the female was from their clan and a friend," he explained. "Then I would be honored to be a Guardian," Zea smiled.

"Then let the ceremony begin," the same male called out to the group who cheered. The main male who had been talking carefully took off Zea's EnyoRhea necklace and told she could keep it but could not wear it. Then asked where she would like to wear the mark of the Clan. Zea decided to have them place the symbol on her lower back right above her tail. Her cloth and belt would cover the symbol.

As two Guardians came up to hold the female's arms another lowered her belt to clear a spot for the mark, a fourth offered to place a small wooden branch covered in leather in the female's mouth, who accepted and last another male stepped forward with a hot iron and proceed to brand the Guardian mark on the female who did not cry out. She did let a few tears fall from her eyes from the pain.

The same male who first spoke came forward again and began to talk once more, "There is one more thing you must do before you can join. Each member who joins for safety reasons changes their name and makes a symbol for their new name." After much thought and suggestions the group came up with a new name, Darayca, and a symbol for her new name. "Let it be known, Darayca is now a member of our clan and a Guardian," the main male yelled. All the males again cheered. Then the group flew to main home.

The Guardians

The group sat around a fire in the woods. One at a time they took off their masks and introduced themselves to the new member. The first one was a Kat who looked like a tiger and has greenish yellow eyes his name was Blade and he was the leader. Second was Talon who smiled and welcomed the female to the clan again. Third was a spotted furred Kat who looked like a jaguar and his eyes were a light green. His name was Chance. Forth was Dargyo and now Darayca knew who he was. Her eyes widened when she fully saw him. He smiled and looked down at the dirt floor. He was the same Kat who was the first male to take her down from the Shadow Clan.

"Let me give you are quick explanation because you recognize me. I was under cover to spy and work against the Shadow Clan. That is why Bear talked to me and I fight differently," Dargyo explained to the new Guardian. Luke was number five. He had firry golden eyes. With black fur and red streaks like patches with a hint of sliver fur around his head and back. The sixth had sliver fur with black stripes and spots. His name was Sean and he had dark green eyes. Seventh was Scorpiyo and he is a clay red color with dark marking on his face and back with coppered colored eyes. Eighth Kat to remove his mask was Jester and he was the second Kat Zea remembered.

Jester was Liz's male. Jester also smiled because he knew that Zea recognized him. Lighting was ninth to introduce himself and he was dark blue with three yellow and jagged streaks starting from the top of his head and traveling down his back stopping just before his ringed tail. Next was Ice who was a white and had a light blue and sliver underside. Ice had sliver and black eyes. The eleventh was Swift who had brown eyes. He was orange with a white chin and underside. Then Shadow removed his mask and he was a dark gray with green eyes. Last was Venom. Venom's fur was made up of different shades of green and his eyes were very dark brown. After everyone was introduced they sat down to a good meal.

Sean explained to the female they had several clan sites but one main one. The group was moving around the land so much they wanted a safe place to stay. Once the fire was out the group walked quietly into the woods. Soon the sound of the waterfall over powered the symphony of crickets. Darayca was surprised to not go to the waterfall. The band went to a large tree where they climbed on to a thick branch. Moving a hidden door in the bark the group made their way inside the tree.

After climbing down the tree trunk there was a under ground cavern. Next the female found herself in another open area with a table, chairs, two fire pits, and mats for sitting or lying. While a few of the males lit the torches on the wall others put their packs down and started to get settled.

Chance gave the zatz a quick tour. As they walked the female did a pules and realized they were in the mountainside. "We can fly out through the waterfall?" she asked out loud. "Yeah, how did you know?" the male laughed. The hair on the back of the female's neck stood on end. "I can hear one of the tunnels the crashing water is a lot louder," she quickly responded. "I do not know how to can determine that but you will have to teach me some of your skills," Chance voiced while looking at the nervous one. "Do not worry. You have amazing abilities; never feel bad about being able to use them. We choose you for a reason," the male continued and comforted.

Darayca learned in each campsite each member had his or her own room. Because this was the home closest to her fathers and sister's clan and the reflection tree she wanted this to be her main room. The female put all of her possessions in the room on the shelves. The warrior was happy not to carry all of her belongings in her back. She knew once she found each of her rooms the female would put specific treasures in the different rooms.

Now that the Guardian was alone she had a conversation with her computer. The two discussed their excitement for being in the new clan. As the two talked Darayca brought out her red ray gun and very carefully cut off the EnyoRhea's armband. The metal hit the ground and the sound echoed off the walls. He also asked Zea about her new name. --I have had so many names in the past I know that I now have one with a fresh start. Darayca will not bring back any memories of lost ones or pain. I welcome the change-- She explained. –I agree with you and no matter what your name is you will not forget who you are and where you come from,--- the computer voiced. –Do you want me to call you Darayca?—he continued. –Yeah, I guess so, I would like to go by one name at a time or I might get confused. I have also never met anyone with any of my names so I will not be mad it you…-- The female started "What are you up too?" Talon unknowingly interrupted.

When the new guardian did not answer he continued, "Were you mediating?" "Something like that," the female finally spoke.

"What was the click noise?"

"I took off my arm band so my new actions will not be tracked back to the EnyoRhea's"

Looking at the cut metal Talon asked, "How did you do this?" "I will show you later, I promise. I am very tired right now it has been a long and exciting night," the female answered. "I understand," he smiled. The two talked for short while longer and gave kisses goodnight and parted.

When the sun's light kissed the land Darayca's computer woke her up and they recalled all that happen the night prior. A small pain came from her lower back. The new scar was healing well. Blade walked into her room and asked if she was doing well. Darayca thanked him and told him she was great. "Today you can go back to your old clan and say your goodbyes also you can go to Dark Star's Clan and tell them that you cannot be found at your old tribe. All I ask is you take someone with you and be back here before dusk," the leader stated. "Thank you, I will be back before the sun sets," the zatz promised as she stood.

Blade smiled and walked away. Darayca prepared for the day and made her way to the main chamber. Looking around and saw that Talon was gone but she spotted Jester who was delighted to join her. They ran through the falls and took to the air. For the first time Darayca got a good idea where she was. They were coming out of the forest, which was across the meadow from her reflection spot. The two Guardians took to the air and flew to the EnyoRheas.

Darayca loved to fly and land in the middle camp. After landing many of the EnyoRheas came to greet her. Jester stayed high in the clouds so no one could see him and waited for his clan member to tell him to come down and join her. "Zea, you are back from the testing! How are you and how were the tests?" Sunflower asked with great excitement. "I am sorry Sunflower," the black one started. "You have mistaken me for someone else for my name is not Zea but Darayca. I have come here to thank the EnyoRheas for everything and talk to you and Liz, if you will allow me to stay here for a few hours," the zatz stated. "Sure," the leader voiced with great joy.

The Guardian made a whistle call and Jester came and landed beside her. "Will you find Liz I wish to speak to her later?" the female asked Jester who smiled and answered, "I would be delighted." He found Liz who was in her hut where he could watcher her and be alone as Darayca and the leader went into the leader's hut.

Once inside the young female relaxed and spoke to her friend. "Sunflower, it was amazing! I had so much fun and last night they made me a member. I am now a true Guardian. I would have never made it this far without you and for that I thank you with all my heart. I asked my new leader about you before I joined if you would be hurt about me leaving your clan. He told me you would be joyful for me to leave and be a Guardian. Is this true because you are my first leader and I must hear your approval or I will carry much guilt," Darayca told her Sunflower.

"I am overjoyed that there is finally a female Guardian and I am even more elated it is you. There is no one I can think of that could handle the stress of being a Guardian but you. You are welcome here anytime even if there is a war because no matter what happens you will always be a sister EnyoReah to us. We can give you safe hiding. I am glad you had fun during the testing and if you ever see Zea tell her she will be missed and we will drink in her honor tonight. Never carry guilt from leaving our camp because you will never leave our sisterhood. I give you more than my approval but my blessing as well," the leader answered. The two talked for a while longer on the tests and how the camp was doing while the black one was gone. Then Darayca gave Sunflower her last sign of respect from member to leader. From now on her signs of respect were going to be different and more equal than leader.

Next Darayca left the hut and walked across camp to Liz's hut. On the way old friends came and greeted her. Avis, Sarah, Antoinette and many others stopped to talk to their friend and the black one had to tell them that Zea was gone and she was Darayca.

Finally after many little talks the Guardian walked into Liz's hut. Jester and Liz quickly pulled away from each other and looked down while smiling. "Jester was there any problems?" "Nope," he replied as he stood. Then he walked outside to stood guard as the two females talked. "How are you Liz?" the black one began. "I am doing well. Thank you for letting me see Jester, you a great friend," Liz thanked her.

"I wanted to thank you for all your kindness and for trusting me. I would have never been able to get this far without you. Letting you see Jester is the least I could do to thank you."

"I will miss you but I know you will be having fun and you will still come see me. Thank you for also being a great friend and trusting me. I would have never been this close to Jester if you had not helped me. You know you are always welcome to crash with me. Come see me when ever you wish."

"I will hold you up to that. Stay strong and watch out for any danger."

"I will, you too,"

The two talked for a little about the testing and about Jester. Then the Guardian stood and left the hut with Liz by her side. Darayca said her goodbyes to the EnyoRheas and then took to the air. After helping Jester into the air the two flew towards Dark Star's Clan.

Darayca landed in the same way as in her old home and again Jester staying in the clouds. Many of the males came running up to her. "Zea, how are you?" many asked. When she spotted Dark Star and Bear the female spoke, "Thank you for your welcomes but I am sorry to inform you but you have mistaken me for my name is not Zea but Darayca and I am not an EnyoRhea but a Guardian. I come here to speak to your leader, the one named Bear and a few others." Many of their eyes widened on hearing the female's words.

"Can I stay in your camp for a few hours?" the zatz asked. "Sure," the leader replied. Like the time before Darayca made the same call to the sky and Jester landed by her side. Dark Star, Jester and Darayca walked to the leader's hut where Jester waited outside and talked with some of the clan member as the other two went in the hut to talk.

"Hi, Dark Star how are you?" the female began. "I am doing well and it looks like you have been very busy," the leader stated. "Yes, I am no longer an EnyoRhea. I just wanted to come here and thank you for all you have done for me. I cannot find the words to express my feeling," the black one voiced. "I am overjoyed to know you are a Guardian and I am sad that I will not be seeing Zea but tell her she will be missed and we will drink in her honor tonight," Dark Star smiled. "I will miss you and the clan. With your approval I will come visit you when I can," the zatz spoke. "You know you are always welcome here no matter what happens we can give you safe hiding and protect you. You are a daughter of this clan and that will never change," the leader explained. The two were happy to see each other and talked about what was new with both fighters. Soon time had come for Darayca to move on they shook arms and said their goodbyes. The Guardian left the hut and walked to Krist's hut.

On the way Darayca ran into Josh who was cheerful to see her. "I see you have a male's neck chain," he stated. "Yeah, I am seeing a male at this time," the female smiled. "Well, if he hurts you, you know I will teach him a lesson if you need," the pinked furred one voiced strongly. Darayca laughed and thanked him for all his kindness and friendship and then moved on to meet with Krist.

Reaching his hut he came to greet his old friend. They talked about everything that they had been up too and made sure their friendship was still strong. They were so delighted to see with each and know that both were still strong in every way. They said their goodbyes and the Guardian made her way to Bear's hut. One the way she ran into Robby and Roberd. They also talked for a short while and both said the same thing Josh did when they noticed the neck chain around her arm. Darayca thanked them for everything and gave them her best wishes and finally walked up to her father's home.

While Jester waited outside the female walked into the dark room slowly. Bear was sitting at the table with a small meal for her and a smile. "I have missed you little one," he stated. Darayca's ears pricked no one had called her little one in a long time. She ran into her father's arms and began to tell him more about Talon and joining the Guardians. He was pleased to know that his daughter was happy and over all safe even though she was with a group he wished she had never met.

They sat, ate and talked. Bear asked her how her nightmares were and sharing herself. The black one answered him and asked how his scar was healing. They had a long talk and were glad to see each other again but the sun was low in the sky. Darayca hugged her father goodbye and told him she would come visit him soon and told him not to worry about her. The Guardian started to walk out of her old home and glance one last time at Bear before she flew off with her new clan mate.

The two Guardians landed back in camp just as the sun was kissing the horizon. They were greeted by the clan and sat down to the last meal of the day. Darayca sat by Talon who was happy to see her. Blade stood before the clan and told them that every night one clan member would stand before the clan and talk about themselves and their past. The clan keeps no secrets from each other to show trust and friendship in the group. That night he would start. Then he proceeded to talk about his childhood. The zatz was surprised to learn that Talon was Blade's son. When the leader finished speaking they all played games and then rested for the night.

Then next day Ice and Shadow taught Darayca all the calls and ways the clan talked to each other. And Talon talked about himself at night. On second day Swift and Lighting showed the new member the land all the good clans, all the bad clans and all the hiding places. Venom talked to the group that night. Then next day Darayca taught the whole group a new game called flags and soon everyone loved it. Also Sean and Darayca played a lot of Musmag or what they called cards. That night Scorpiyo talked to the group.

As the days went by the new member started to get use to the way the clan worked. Everyone took turns doing chores and working for the clan. Every night they had a meeting where anything could be said and it would never leave the group. The first few days each clan members were sharing themselves to the clan for the new member and soon she would have to go, which made her nervous.

Darayca loved being a Guardian. They would help each other with fighting skills and many of them wanted to learn about pressure points and the fighter told them that she would teach them but they would not be able to knock others out. The zatz was taught how to act in front of other kats and clans and shadowed many trips to clans before she could lead them. Many of the clans did not believe her or listen to her until her clan mates landed behind her and then she was never questioned again.

Then the night came where the female stood in front of the group. She took a deep breath and began. Darayca started with her birth and talked about her family and Yaottyro. Next were the Qothos and Jabo. As she talked about her time with Jabo and the loss of her family member she showed the clan her scars. The escape was next and the fighter did her best to describe the weapons she used but did not say she had a computer, which held them. Hutto and Zutiyro were the following topic and how they were friends, heroes, teachers and how they were lost.

When the female talked she also braked to show the clan her eyes, gills and her way of changing. Darayca talked about her traveling and training and last about coming to the new land. From her first run in with the Shadow Kats to finding her father, her betrayal, joining of EnyoRhea and now being a Guardian. The zatz also discussed about her difference in time. The group could not believe all that the female had done and been through and all her differences. They asked her a few questioned and thanked her for sharing. After the meeting Darayca walked up to her leader and asked to speak to him. He was happy to help.

They walked away from the group and climbed a tree. Then the zatz began to speak, "There is still two more difference that I did have not talked about I have not even told my father. I ask that I can wait a little more before sharing these secrets for I am trying to think of the best way to tell and share the group. I am sorry I am not strong enough the show you now and if you truly wish I will do my best to show you now but it would be very hard for me to do."

There was a long silence pause and then Blade spoke, "I will allow to keep your secrets but I ask you tell the group as soon as possible for we do our best to keep no secrets from each other but I also know you come from an usual past. You are also being honest with me now so I will allow this." "Thank you Blade, I will tell the group soon I promise," the zatz stated. They walked back to the group who was laughing and telling stories. Everyone still welcomed Darayca and wanted to be friends. A few nights later Darayca found herself sitting in her reflection spot and sun was setting.

Epilog: Now

So that is my story up until now. Blade told me that when a new leader takes over the Shadow Clan there is a clam time and then the new leader strikes. I will have to keep my eye out for Pyro because I know he is up to something. Talon and I are now meka and meko. Both of us priced our left ears to show our bond for each other and I am thinking if everything goes will we will be maskas some day. I am planning to share my computer with my new clan and my father within the week and I ask my lost love ones for strength and guidance. I am nervous but I am sure I can do it. I am so happy that I am now a true Guardian and I am apart of a clan that makes a difference. I know I will do great things with this family and the fun and adventure will never end. As I sit here in the darkness and reflect on my life I am pleased that I now have my place in this new world. I am Darayca and I am a true Guardian. Standing and stretching I take a deep breath and disappear into the night sky.

www.ingramcontent.com/pod-product-compliance
Lightning Source LLC
Chambersburg PA
CBHW082033170626
46817CB00010B/3140